AUTOGRAPHS

I0535436

"Reloaded version 2013"

Time To Know-RELOADED
TIME WILL REVEAL PART 4
by
Black Coffee

TIME TO KNOW-RELOADED-Time Will Reveal- part 4

Published by True's Relate Publishing
Time to Know-RELOADED (Time will reveal: Part 4)
Library of Congress Control Number: TXu 1-772-774
Copyright ©2003, 2008, 2011, 2013 True's Relate publishing/LTBROWN
All rights reserved

REGISTERED TRADEMARK-MARCA REGISTRADA
ISBN:978-0-9844701-4-3 & 978-0-9892092-4-3

Printed in the United States of America
Set by: True's Relate publishing
Cover design by : Gregory Spencer of Misvision Graphics info@misvisiongraphics.com
Logo design: JayRocOne [@ age 9] JayRocOne Designs], Jalen Williams
Photography by B.R.T.L "Born Ready To Live photography by Jamal Q.
Cover Models: Che'la Johnson and Thomas Fredrick
[Find all of the above on Facebook]
Requests for information on ordering, scheduling the author for signings and
appearances should be addressed to:
Black Coffee's websites
http://www.blackdollone.com
http://www.truesrelatepublishing.com
http://twitter.com/AuthorBlkCoffee
Group:
The Time Will Reveal-RELOADED series Crew Nation #Crew4Life

Manuscript Preparation: Black Coffee
blackdollone@att.net
True's Relate/ThugRelated publishing company
P.O. Box 2911
Gulfport, Ms. 39505

PUBLISHER'S NOTES

iii

Time To Know- RELOADED-Time Will Reveal 4   Black Coffee

TIME TO KNOW-RELOADED-Time Will Reveal- part 4

[QUOTES/DEDICATIONS/UP NEXT]
"Respect your wife and the females of this family, to the utmost. Raise them to be strong, loyal and wise. They're our ribs, our lovers and our child bearers. Our rocks and our partners for life."
-The male crew motto-TIME TO KNOW-Time Will Reveal part 4
[Dedicated to:]
Bone Thugs N Harmony
&
The entire Mo Thugs Family for the host city inspiration!
"My Eternal Love and Support for you"

THE TIME WILL REVEAL SHORT STORIES
#1 MORE THAN 4 ADMIRERS-RELOADED
"The Threat to a Legacy."
#2 MR. WRONG AND THE RATS-RELOADED
"Sweet Ray, Sonya, Shuntay & Tina"
#3 CREWS 1ST PRIORITY>THE FEMALE CREW-RELOADED [TBA]
"Goodbye deviled Angel"

ORDER THE FULL SERIES AT:
www.blackdollone.com
www.truesrelatepublishing.com

The Time Will Reveal-Novel series
Time To Learn-RELOADED-part 1
Time To Grow-RELOADED-part 2
Time To Love-RELOADED-part 3
Time To Know-RELOADED-part 4
Time To Feel-RELOADED-part 5
The Making of AJAY-Every Man-A Time Will Reveal novel-RELOADED
Time To Show-RELOADED-part 6
Ajay and Ebony 1-Time Will Reveal-Time To Give 7[TBA]
Ajay and Ebony 2-Time Will Reveal-Time To Live 8 [TBA]

CHAPTER 36

BLIND FAITH

Time To Know-RELOADED-Time Will Reveal part 4

Ebony is at the airport to pick up her NBA All-Star husband, Ajay. His flight has just landed and is taxiing the runway, as it heads toward the terminal. He has arrived in Cleveland from New York. He and his *Miami Heat* team played and failed to win game 5 in *Madison Square Gardens,* just hours ago. She already knows he isn't going to be in the best mood. She doesn't expect him to be, after any lose. But surely not 1 which ended the season. With a team fight in game 4, then losing game 5 and the season. He isn't going to be in the mood for any type of nonsense or dumb shit, *whatsoever.* She's going to get on her job and change his spirits, that's for sure. What he'll need is some very sensuous loving, coupled with all of her attention. She's going to give him some champion head and fulfill his every desire. She's determined he won't go to bed tensed. Not for the *entire* off season, if necessary. Or at least until he can refocus. She's more than willing and she's excited to have him home. She needs to feel his embrace, so badly. And she longs to hear his sweet whispers of comfort, coupled with his tender kisses.

But there was a violation which occurred in their home. She wasn't able to hide it over the phone. Shielding it in person isn't even an option. She can never hide anything from him anyway. So she doesn't even try too anymore. The first thing she's going to do when she gets him home, is tell him about her *complex* experience. The *entire* ordeal. Starting with her unscheduled visit to Dr. Weston. Then she'll tell him about his 1st cousin disrespecting her and their home. Rich was poised to hit her and she knows it. It was in his stance and his eyes. She'd seen that look before he went off and hit her 1st cousin, T-baby.
The nerve!

She's happy her big mama was there. Because she believes he would've hit her or maybe a lot worse, had she not been there. Truth is. Rich is probably much more happy than she is, that he *didn't.*

Richie Rich had an encounter with *"the Ajay"* back in the day. If he

had hit her today. Then surely shit would change *drastically* in their plush Jackson Heights community, *this* evening. And who knows. Shit still may change.
If he would've hit me. This would be a different kind of homecoming. Surely if Anthony was to come home and see me battered and bruised. He would end the life of the perpetrator. And I don't believe it would matter that the perp was his first cousin either.

Bronson drove Ajay's *Jeep Cherokee*. With Officer McDaniel in the front seat, they chauffeured Ebony to the airport so she wouldn't have to go out alone. They have come inside to wait at the gate with her also. Ajay always insist that security come 4 deep. Which they have. Two came in while the other 2 stayed with the Jeep and the security vehicle which trailed them. Crew still doesn't travel alone. At the same time, Ajay is a celebrity now. They knew there would be anxious fans gathered at the airport. They were correct. Fans are lined up in front of the airport and some are even inside, at the gate. Bronson and McDaniel help airport security keep them at bay. And though security drove Ebony there, They'll ride back in their security car and escort the *still* newlyweds, back to Jackson Heights. This way, Ajay and Ebony can have privacy and time to catch up on their discussion. While knowing security is just a car away, if the need arises.

Ajay has many fans lined up with signs, letting him know they still support him. Even though his team didn't advance. They also let him know how much they want him to play for the *Cavaliers*. He feels the same way and that's already in his plans, once his initial contract ends. The fans do recognize Ebony, as they wave and yell her name while declaring their love and support for her husband. She smiles and thanks them while major butterflies swirl in her stomach. It's chilly this early May morning. She waits outside of the gate in her *Snow Star Golden Verigated section Mink bomber jacket* with the Fox collar, for her 1 and only love to glide through.

Ajay is seated in 1st class. But he opts to wait for all of the other passengers, some who ended up getting autographs as well, to get off of the plane first. That's so they won't be held onboard while he attends to his fans in the gate lobby.

Finally he makes his way into the terminal. His 6 foot 8 frame commands attention as his eyes search and then find his woman. He smiles big when their eyes meet. She's giddy as she smiles back. No matter how stressed she was, waiting on his arrival. Seeing his face and smile, fixes that automatically. He goes to her immediately.

"Hey baby," he says, "How are you feeling?"

6

TIME TO KNOW-RELOADED-Time Will Reveal- part 4

He gives her a big hug and a long kiss. She smiles very big and bright as she holds onto his hand.

"I'm fine," she says.

"True that," he says as they smile again.

It takes him another 45 minutes to an hour to take care of all the fans autographs, then answer hometown media questions.

Afterwards they head out to the Jeep. Security had already retrieved his bags from baggage claim. Ajay hops into the drivers seat, after securing Ebony on the passenger side. He trails their security car to Jackson Heights while they listen to their *Outkast Aquemini* CD.

"I like *Liberation* with *Goodie Mob* and *Erykah Badu* on it," she says as she smiles, "It's so good. That's *real* Hip Hop, baby."

"I like *Badu*," he says, "Her album has a jazzy feel to it. It's good."

"You use to play *On and On,* a lot. But you hardly played *Next Lifetime*. I love that one too."

"You know the lyrics in that song, right?" he asks.

"Yes," she says as she giggles because she realizes where he's headed with that remark.

"Enough said. It's *this lifetime* for us," he says as he laughs.

She giggles some more at his sensitivity to words. Even in a song that *suggest* they might have other partners.

He doesn't talk about the call from Nina during their drive home. But he does make a few comments about her antsy behavior.

"Baby what's on your mind?" he asks.

"I'm just tired of studying, I guess," she tries.

"Okay," he says, "I guess you wanna just wait and tell me when I get you home. Is that it?"

"Okay. I do need to talk to you about some things," she admits.

"You wanna talk about it when we get to the crib?" he asks.

"Yes. Yes I do," she answers.

"Okay, that's cool," he says.

"So how is Jarvis and Gwen?" she asks.

Ajay's college teammate and good friend Jarvis Rhodes had been drafted to the New York Knicks. He had graduated with Tank, June and Rich's class and went to the Knicks in the 2nd round.

"Jarvis wants me to hook him up with Jb," he says, "He's ready to get out of New York. He says his agent is bullshittin'. He only had a two year contract. He don't wanna extend it. His agent is moving *too* slow."

"They're due any day now," she says, speaking of his expecting fiancée Gwen.

7

"Yea," he says, "And Jarvis said he really wants to talk to me about something *real* important."

"You have any idea what it is?" she asks.

"Not really," he says, "But I know it's not money. He handles his, just like I do. But I can tell it's something that means a lot to him. Because he wants us to sit down and discuss it."

"Yes you have too," she says, "That's your wingman. He looks up to you. I know whatever it is. It's something he's passionate about. He's become like a younger brother to you."

"True that," he says, "We'll talk as soon as his season's over. Since I couldn't end it earlier."

They stop to get coffee for Jacobson and Officer Joiner, who are on duty at Jackson Heights. Less than a minute later, they drive up to the entrance booth. Jacobson was waiting for his 4 security guys to make it back. He's being relieved by Bronson, who'll man the booth until 9am. Ajay stops to speak. Jacobson is happy to see Ebony smiling.

"Hey misses Ebony," Jacobson says as he chuckles, "You look like you're feeling better, this morning."

"Yes I am" she says, "It's all good now."

She smiles as she looks at her man. She has 2 large cups of coffee for Jacobson and Joiner. Then she says, "My girls and I are gonna stock the refrigerators, later today. So be sure and leave a list to let me know if there's *anything* in particular you want us to get. That goes for all of you."

"Anything you ladies put up in here, is good for us," Jacobson says as Bronson and the rest agree. "Y'all set us up nice, out here. Thank you."

"You are all very welcome," she says.

"Again I have to thank you all for taking such *great* care of my most prized possession," Ajay says as he smiles at Ebony.

Then they say goodnight. Ajay drives down CrewLand drive pass the other 3 homes and on around the curve to their estate.

"Everybody must be at the clubs, ha?" he asks.

"Yes they are," she says, "Nina called and asks if I was coming out. But I wanted to wait for you."

"Do you wanna go?" he asks.

"No. I wanna go home and chill with you," she answers and smiles.

"That works for me, baby," he says, "I need some quiet time tonight."

He pulls into their driveway and on into the garage, then lets their automatic door down. He parks, hops out and opens her door. She gets out and helps him get his bags into the house.

"I'll start us a bath," she says, "Your dinner is in the microwave." She sets the timer to warm his plate while he sits down at the island bar. She goes into the master suite to prepare a bubble bath for 2. He tosses some treats to Ike and Tina, who are happy to see daddy come home too. They're putting on a show for him. They're running back and forth between the kitchen and the master bathroom, where Ebony is. He loves that they're happy in their new home. More important, Ebony is happy having pets in her life again. She rejoins him in the kitchen and sits at the island next to him, while they wait for his plate to finish warming. Ike and Tina are trying to get up the stool legs, to get to her lap.

"No guys," she says, "Daddy's about to eat. You know you can't get on any counters or tables, where we eat. Go get up on your own table." Her and Ajay laugh as the dogs run and jump up on the little counter he'd had installed for them. It's the same height as the island counter, so they can still see them at eye level.

"They love you, baby girl," he says, "But I can understand why. I've been telling you for years, that you're irresistible." The dogs have really taken to Ebony *and* they're very intelligent puppies.

"So are you, daddy," she says as she gives him a kiss. Then she sits his warm plate in front of him, pours some ice tea in his glass and says, "You know what? It wasn't hard to train them at all. Tank will tell you that too. They're naturally smart. *Oh* and I found them a great vet and a neat groomer too. Both of them are in *Cleveland Heights*."

"Tina got ribbons in her hair," he says as he chuckles, "Is that nail polish?"

"Yes," she answers and giggles, "She's a girl. She should be *glammed* up." They laugh as he inhales his smothered turkey breast with celery gravy, steamed rice, mixed vegetables and buttered potato rolls. Then he scuffs down a piece of Chocolate cake. She clears his dishes away and cleans them.

Then they go into the master suite where their Jacuzzi tub is just about filled up for their bath. He gets out of his clothes. She takes them to the hamper where she undresses and leaves hers. Then she meets him in their master bathroom. He's just getting into the tub.

"This water's just right," he says as he slides into the Jacuzzi. He reaches for her hand and helps her in. Once she's in the tub, she faces and straddles him. Then she starts massaging his neck. He's massaging her shoulders while planting tender kisses on her neck.

He smiles and says, "Dinner was good, baby. Now before I start fuckin and making babies. I need to know what's got you so tensed?"

9

"I went to the doctor today," she says in 1 breath.

"*Weston*?"

"Yes," she says, "I wasn't trying to be sneaky or anything. I just wanna have your baby. I was just trying to convince her to come on over to my side."

She smiles. He smiles briefly before he speaks again.

He says, "Baby you're gonna get pregnant. I'll be here for four months. Drilling this sweet pussy with everything I got." His smile brightens as he slips his fingers between her legs. Then he says, "I asked you to be patient."

"I know but I *can't*," she says, "This is taking *way* too long. I really am scared, I won't be able to get pregnant."

"You *can* wait," he says, "You can get pregnant and like I just said before. I'm home for the off season and we'll have more time to work on it. We've only seen each other three times, for a total of 10 days, since the wedding. You have to be *ovulating*. Can you say that word?"

He laughs. She can't help but laugh too. She cracks up laughing at him and says, "I know. I know. Okay." She giggles before saying, "You know *way* too much about women's bodies."

"I grew up with five females in the house," he says as he smiles, "And I'm gonna know everything it is to know, about *this* body."

He's wrapping his arms around her, pulling her to him and squeezing her tight.

"True that," she says with a big smile. "I'm sorry for going behind your back. I promise I was gonna tell you, first thing."

"I know," he says, "I'm not *sweatin* that. I know how anxious you are to have my baby. How can I be mad at that?"

She smiles bigger. She's relieved he isn't upset.

Then he says, "But I know *that* can't be the reason why you're not talking to your girls."

"No it's not."

"Then what's that about?"

"I saw Rich and June cheating," she says in 1 breath.

"*What*?"

"Rich was kissing on some woman in the backseat of June's car," she says, "While June was in the front with his arm around another woman. They know I saw them because they saw me."

"Is that's why you was speeding?"

"How do you know-"

"-Don't worry about *how* I know," he says, "Is that why you was upset behind the wheel of your car?" he asks, more sternly.

"Yes."

"That's unacceptable. Baby that officer told Jacobson that you pulled out into oncoming traffic and almost wiped out," he says very concerned.

"I did."

"That's not gonna work for me," he says, "Don't let nobody get to you, like that. Or cause you to risk your life, get hurt or maybe even killed because of something *they* did. I need you alive. There's nothing about any other person that's so important, that you get upset and risk *your* life. Do you *understand* me?"

"Yes Anthony."

"Oh what?" he asks as he smiles, "I can't be daddy, no more?"

"I thought that was just for our sex moments," she says smiling.

"That's until you help me to become a daddy," he says, still smiling, "Then you don't ever have to say it again."

"I'm trying to make you a daddy," she says as she pouts her lips.

"Good," he says, "I'll get at them about that bullshit, later on. I don't want you sweatin it. You got me?"

"Okay. But that's not all, daddy," she says with puppy eyes.

"What else is it?" he asks.

"Rich came here while big mama and I were discussing it," she says, "He was saying some *mean* things to me."

His smiling face and sexy eyes changed instantly. He stares at her as she continues, "He called me out of my name, over and over. *Bad* names too. He was acting like he wanted to hit me. I told him to get out but he wouldn't. He didn't know big mama was here. She came in and told him to leave and that's when he finally got out. I'm so glad she *was* here. He just kept getting closer and closer up in my face. I felt afraid of him, for the last few minutes. Daddy, he had that look in his eyes that I've seen before."

Ajay is quiet. She knows to leave him be when he's like this. He face grows so cold. She can see the anger in his eyes. His grip around her waist starts to tighten. He's still quiet and she can see that he's in deep thought.

How could he be that damn stupid to chastise my wife? Everybody knows I don't play that shit! I'm Ebony's man and the man of my damn house! And this nigga done violated both! Yea. That's nigga shit, right there. He wouldn't have ever tried that shit, if I was here! Fuck!

She sits in silence while he works things out in his mind. Finally, he speaks.

"I'm gonna get at his ass about that," he says, "He won't be coming back up in *here* wit no more bullshit. Believe that. I'll take his ass back to

11

elementary school, if I have too. *Now* I know we have time to make up for, baby girl. So I'm not gonna bell on you at this moment. But just so you know. I wanna find him before his bitch ass runs off somewhere."

His eye jumps and his lip starts to quiver, as he stares past her. He's angry. But she can tell he's trying not to allow it to ruin his homecoming. He wants to make love and this bullshit is threatening to interfere. He needs to hear her say that she's okay. He loosens his grip now, realizing he was squeezing her a bit. He asks, "Are you okay, *really*? Did he touch you in *anyway*?"

"No baby," she says, "He didn't. I would've called you, right then and there. And not waited, if he had. I knew you had a big game and this could wait. It just really bothered me to see them messing over Rebbie and T-baby, like that," she says, "I don't know how to face my girls."

"Let me handle it," he says, "You don't have to tell them not *one* thing. If anybody's gonna confess. It's gonna be them. If Rich even have a *fuckin* tongue left."

She can see that he wants to leave and deal with his 1st cousin, for having the gall to disrespect his home. But she wants to have their private time too. She has to take his mind away from violence. Before he leaves her to go and beat the fuck out of Richie Rich.

"I just can't fake with my girls," she says, trying to take his focus back to the cheating. "If I know something like this. I can't hide it. How do I smile at them, knowing this?"

"You're not gonna have too," he says, "Just let me handle it."

"Okay daddy," she says Then she completely switches her gears and says, "Now I need for you to focus on me. I need your mind and body to be here and on me."

"Is that everything?" he asks, struggling to get the idea of violence off of his mind.

She can see that downward frown above his brow. It's in his eyes. He wants to thwart Rich's escape, to wherever he would run to avoid him. But she can also see that he's looking at her bare breast. Then from there to her full lips, then to her eyes. He's horny and she knows he can be persuaded to deal with his cousin later. It's up to her to change his mood, as only she can. She can take his mind where she needs it to be. She *has* too. It's her job to keep him stress free. She goes for broke when she answers him with, "Yes that's everything. *Well*, not quite."

He looks into her eyes and his eyes are impatient. He thinks it's going to be something more on the disrespecting of her or their home side of things. But she pulls a fast one when she grabs his penis and strokes him underneath the bubbling water.

12

TIME TO KNOW-RELOADED-Time Will Reveal- part 4

She says, "I need for you to bring my dick from under here. I'd love to get up close and personal with it."
She moves her body up against his and starts kissing on his neck and chest. Then nibbling on his ear, she whispers and asks, "Daddy can I taste you?" He moans and closes his eyes. That move worked and she knows it! He's all in as he starts to massage her breast. He knows exactly what she's doing and he wants it to work, just as much as she does. He tries to smile and make himself relax.

Suddenly he lifts his body up and out of the Jacuzzi. He sits on the edge. He looks down at her and gives her a sideways smile. She begins to massage his dick as she looks up into his eyes. Confirmation is all she needs from him. Just let her know that he's ready to allow her to bring him home *properly*.

"Okay I'm good," he says, "I'm focused, baby. Can a man get his welcome home *loving* up in this joint?" he asks as he chuckles slightly. Then he says, "You're good, baby. I swear. I'm lovin this whole vibe."
He's playing with her hair and her ears as he lets his fingers trace the outline of her lips. He smiles. His eyes are super intense. She knows he's ready. He wants *head* as *Prince* would say, *'Til you get enough.'*
That's my man. He's not gonna miss out on his welcome home loving for nothing. I love you, Anthony!

"Yes you definitely can, daddy" she says, "I love you, Anthony." She starts to kiss his dick while massaging it. He moans, then releases a long sigh. She takes him into her mouth as she moans too. He plays with her hair while she sucks on the head of his dick as if it's releasing some of the sweetest juices she's ever tasted. He's loving it and tells her so.

"Oh that's so damn *good* baby," he says, throwing his head back and closing his eyes. Still rubbing in her hair, he says, "I love you, Ebony. I'm not gonna let nobody fuck with you, baby girl. Do you hear me?"

"Mmmm huh," she moans as she takes his dick to the back of her throat.

"I'm gonna make sweet love to my wife," he whispers as he pulls her head up and pushes it down on his dick. "I'll handle his ass tomorrow. Gimme them lips, baby. Oh *shit*."
She does just that as she goes to work on him. She tries to measure exactly how much of him she can take to her throat. She figures about 8 inches. Anymore and she feels like she'll gag. But that doesn't mean she isn't going to figure out how to take it all in, *in time*. She plans too. She sucks on his balls and he shivers.

13

Oh that shit felt nice to him!

She continues from his balls to his dick and back again. Then to her throat and back up. She's sucking on him like he's shaved ice. He's squeezing her breast so hard, it feels as if they'll pop. He can't wait another minute for her sweet black pussy. He puts his hands under each of her arm pits as he slides back away from her and lifts her out of the water.

"Come here baby," he whispers.

He lays her on the carpet, right next to the Jacuzzi. He doesn't want to lose any of the steam she has. She's dripping wet. He reaches up to the nearest towel bar and grabs the 2 towels that hang there. He spreads 1 out, then moves her over on it. He puts the other 1 over her but leaves her pussy uncovered. That's where his mouth is going.

He parts her legs quickly. Placing 1 over each shoulder, he sticks his tongue as far into her pussy as he can get it. She lifts her ass up off of the carpet. That sensation was just *breathtaking*. He licks her and pulls on her clitoris with a master's stroke. He's gotten quite good at his new craft. Its obvious that he loves to do it to her too. He's sucking and pulling on her clitoris and she's moaning loudly. The sounds she's releasing are driving their puppies nuts. They can hear her and they howl in response. She can't help but think they might be a bit confused.

But mama's getting hers right now, babies. I promise you daddy ain't hurting me none.

She *cums* hard and in an instant.

"Ooooooooooo baby," she purrs, "Oh Anthoneeeeeee! Daddy! Oh yes! Yes, babeeee! Ohhhhh!"

"Gimme this sweet juice, baby," he demands, "Mmmm huh."

He laps up every drop of her honey, before coming up on his knees. He pulls her ass up toward him and shoves his solid hard 14 inches of raw man into her pussy. *No announcement. No warning.* His face is intense. His breathing, shallow. *His mission? Complete and absolute satisfaction!* She must be horny as *fuck*, with the way she asked for *her* dick. He's on his job and looking to do overtime, if that's what her body needs. His abs are already glistening with sweat. She can see it roll down his chest and over his abs, as it disappears somewhere between them. She can feel the sweat from his face, dropping into her pubic hairs. Every so often a drop of sweat lands directly onto her clitoris for a refreshing sensation. Every now and then, he strokes her clit with his fingertip as he looks into her eyes. He's fucking her with everything he has. Suddenly he pulls her heels over each of his shoulders.

14

TIME TO KNOW-RELOADED-Time Will Reveal- part 4

He holds onto her bottom and pushes for the max. She yelps.
"Oh daddy!" she cries out, "Oh baby! Oooo!"
"Uh huh, baby girl." He whispers, "My dick is hard as a brick. You're gonna get this off me. You made this, baby. Handle your shit."
He's fucking her harder and harder still. The pain had long arrived. But this damn good loving man, still manages to pull a *2nd* orgasm out of her.
"Ohhhhh yeaaaaaa! Ssssssssssss."
She can't even form words. He's churning into her and looking from her face to his work and back again.
"You lovin this shit?" he asks as he bites down on his bottom lip. "Is this dick good to you, baby?"
"Yesssss, daddy! Yes! Oh my Goddddd!"
She's out there and he's on his way to join her. She's sent out so many yes's and she holds the S's a long time. That shit only turns him on *more*. He starts pumping his dick into her and talking plenty of shit.
"You're gonna keep this shit wet for me, baby," he instructs, "This muthafucka will not be dry as long as I'm at home. You hear me, girl?"
"Yes baby! Oh!"
He's about ready to cum. That means the very bottom of her tunnel is going to take a beating. He's already frustrated behind losing to New York to his wingman and ending his season. But then he comes home to find out that his less than stellar 1st cousin, has brought his dumb ass into his home and threatened and disrespected his wife. He was already going to pour out his heart to her about not getting to the championship. And how much hurt that caused. He really didn't need Rich in his *fucking* business. He's worked up this nut and it's massive. Ebony is getting her ass whipped thoroughly. *Right now*. She expected it on the game lose *alone*. This extra isn't directed at her. But who else is going to get this off of her man? He looks directly into her eyes. She can see the veins in his neck and in his face too. The grimace on his face tells her he's about to cum. She's so ready for this man to dump this load and end this pussy beating. And oh God, here he cums!!!!
"Oh baby girl," he says in a whisper which fades to a whimper before his eyes squeeze closed and his lips poke out.
He looks as if he's going to cry. His face is so intense and torn up. Then his head goes back as he fights to look at her. But the pussy is going to win this battle. He can't stare at it and cum in it, at the same time. Not this time. He'll have to try that later. For now, he lets his load go.
"Ah shit! Shit! Baby. Ooooo baby. Yea! Yea! Ahhhh!"
Afterwards, he collapses on top of her as she holds him close. They're both breathing heavily. He's crying. So is she. She's crying because he's beat the
15

fuck out of her pussy and yes, it hurts. He's crying because he couldn't get past the 1st round of the playoffs and because once again, someone has put his love in harms way. This is *his* anger. He knows he's going to see Rich eventually. And when he does. He's going to have to pay *the man*. For now, he has to comfort his girl.

"Are you good?" he asks.

She wipes his tears and says, "Yes. I'm good daddy."

"No shit," he says as he tries to chuckle. "You're good all the damn time. I think about my pussy everyday. Whether I'm at home or not."

She can remember when seeing tears in his eyes shocked her. But now, she knows why they're there. She knew and expected them. They've been here before. He was a last game winner, every year since he started playing the sport of basketball. So his lack of championships at Cincinnati had brought this out. She became familiar then. She wipes his tears. He wipes hers too.

"I love you, Ebony. I got you. You know that, right?"

"Yes. I know that without a doubt," she answers, "But you'll have to handle Rich after we sleep. Okay? You're not leaving me *this* morning. And when you do go to confront him. Make sure you make it back home without any chance of someone coming here to get you. Okay?"

"Am I suppose to *promise* that?" he asks as he looks into her eyes.

"Yes," she says as she plants kisses on his face and lips too.

"My intent is to come-"

"-*Promise* me," she interrupts.

"I promise baby," he says.

They kiss for the next few minutes until he's caught his breath. He raises up and stands to his feet. Then helps her up. He lifts her into his arms, cradle style and carries her to bed.

"You ready to sleep?" he asks, planting kisses on her face, lips and neck.

"I am so ready for some sleep. Yes," she says as he lays her down on their extra long California King sized bed.

"You want something to drink?" he asks.

"Whatever you're having," she answers.

He grabs a 2 liter bottle of Gatorade from their mini-fridge and joins her in bed. He gives her the 1st drink. She takes down 3 ounces easy. He drains another 10 ounces before giving her another drink. She takes another 4.

"I'm good," she says, signaling to him that he can finish the rest and he does.

They snuggle up close to each other, under their bedding. Their bedroom stays cold. He likes it like that because he knows she'll stay close to him all night. She yawns hard.

"Goodnight baby girl," he says as he lays behind her and pulls her ass cheeks right up close to his penis.

Then he kisses her goodnight.

"Goodnight Anthony. My big daddy," she says as she giggles.

They started their lovemaking session in the tub and ended up on the carpet. By the time they make it to the bedroom. All they have the energy to do, is kiss and spoon, then turn in for some sleep.

Once the room is quiet, Ike and Tina jump through their doggy door and back into the bedroom. They've come to curl up on the floor at the foot of their bed, since daddy's home. Otherwise, they'd be at the foot still. But they would be up on the bed, like some twin Pekinese guard dogs. 1 at each corner.

****

Angel must have seen the news of Ajay arriving at the airport. Just like clockwork, the stupid bitch has been calling the club all morning. The word had gotten to Ebony's girls by 3am. They volunteer to sit in Renee's office for the next ring. Sure enough, at 3:10am the phone rings again. And Nina, T-baby and Rebbie are sitting there waiting to put Angel's ass on the speakerphone.

"The Chill Spot," Nina answers in her best receptionist voice.

"*Is Ajay Jackson at the club tonight?*" Angel asks.

T-baby takes the lead on this call. She's been waiting to finish this one.

"Hello bitch. It's me again," T-baby spits, "Your *unfriendly* phone fanatic. The one that clocked your ass at the *you [U Apartments*]. Remember you tried to run from us when you claimed you loved Ajay *so much,* that you killed my cousin's baby? What the *fuck* do *you* want?"

"*Bitch I'm not about to argue wit you,*" Angel says, "*I wanna speak to Ajay please. It's important.*"

"People in hell want ice water, ho," Rebbie says, "All you're getting is a beat down as soon as I get my hands on your ass. Shall we pencil you in for,... let's see,..... two thousand *seven?*"

"*I don't have time for this bullshit,*" Angel starts, "*I need-*"

"All you got is time, *bitch,*" T-baby laughs. "What are you doing? Fuckin the guards? How is your bitch ass on the phone at this hour, slut?"

"*I'll put my foot in your ass, tramp,*" Angel spits.

"You ain't gone bust a grape in a fruit fight, bitch," Nina tells her. "You got nuts since you went to prison? Who made this call Angel? I see the number on the caller ID, you stupid whore! All you bitches can get it!"

17

"No joke. You dumb bitches!" Rebbie adds as the line goes dead. The 3 girls crack up laughing as they turn the speaker off.

"I'll bet that's those bitches, Alana and Farah hooking up these calls," Nina says.

"We're gonna trace this fuckin number," T-baby offers.

"No joke," Rebbie says, "Let's get Kilo on that, right now."

They head back to VIP and send a message to Kilo. He radio's back. He'll get on that for them, *"pronto."*

They continue their morning at the club until it's time to close and go home. They're still wondering why Ebony hasn't called either of them.

"We're gonna wake her butt up, first thing in the morning," Rebbie says, "I can't take this, not hearing from one of my sisters. She has to know we have her back. No matter what's going on. Right?"

"She will today," T-baby says.

"True that," Nina adds as they head home.

****

Later that morning at Ajay's, before they can even roll over, the house phone is ringing. Without even looking at the caller ID, he already knows it's Ebony's girls. He grabs the house phone.

"I guess we wasn't answering the cell phones fast enough ha?" he asks sarcastically. "You know some people like to go to bed *and* wake up to each other *first*. Did you know that? Did that ever cross your mind?"

He chuckles. He can feel the desperation in Nina's call because she hadn't cut him off with a *smart ass* comment. He can also tell his sister hasn't slept much since he talked to her in mid flight.

"Ajay stop being a jerk," Nina says, "What's up?"

"Hey girl," he says, "We're still sleeping, round here. Why are y'all up so early?"

"I'm checking on baby girl," she says, "Jeremy wanted me to check on her too."

"Her daddy's got that handled now, big headed girl," he jokes.

"Stop playing with me, ole egg headed boy," she says and bursts out laughing. "Tell me what's up with my sister."

He laughs and says, "She's still sleep, punk. Where's Tank at? Let me see if he can't dole out some banana, around that curve. And keep yo ass off the phone long enough for your neighbors to wake up and get theirs."

She continues to laugh as she says, *"Anyway.* He's watching cartoons with Jerica. You want him?"

18

TIME TO KNOW-RELOADED-Time Will Reveal- part 4

"Yea. Put him on and let me see if I can't get him on his job, around there," he says as he chuckles more, just to play his sister off.

But Ajay is nowhere near jovial. He eases out of bed and into the 1st floor library. He wants to talk to Tank about what's really on his mind, without disturbing his slumbering wife. Tank takes the phone from Nina and asks, "What's up partner?" with a chuckle, as Ajay gets right to it.

Tank's chuckle will soon fade when Ajay tells him about the new situation. He explains it, detail by detail. Just as Ebony had told it to him. But when he gets to the part about Rich coming to his house. He leaves no doubt in Tank's mind that he wants blood.

"Get muthafuckin Rich on the line and bring his ass to me," Ajay orders, "Don't tell him I'm gonna be there. Just act like this is something you're doing. Tank that nigga rolled around to my fuckin house and cursed my *wife*. Called her out of her name too. He was acting like he wanted to hit her, man. Now crew, you know it ain't gonna be no circle shit for him. Not this time. I'm getting in his ass, brother. By my *damn* self."

"What the *fuck*?" is all Tank can ask at the moment.

"Exactly," Ajay says, "Get him over there, man. And June too. Let's get this shit over with, all at the same time."

"I'm calling Chill, man," Tank says.

"Not for me, Tank," Ajay tells him. "Not to stop me. I don't wanna be calm. I'm not even trying to be. He know what the fuck he did and he knows what the fuck it cost. He didn't give a damn. He did some bitch ass shit. My whole crew, our parents and even muafuckahz who know me from fifth grade. Know this type of shit ain't getting no pass. Rich is crew. So you already knowing he knew what the repercussions would be. Ain't nobody gonna fuck with baby girl and he did. *Knowing* some of the shit she's had to deal with."

Ajay is becoming emotional. He doesn't want to wake Ebony and have her worried about what he's going to do. So he tries his best to calm himself down.

He says, "I'm telling you Tank. He did that shit to fuck with me. And he got his wish. Bring that nigga, crew."

"Ajay I'll get them together," Tank says, "You know I'm not feeling him fuckin with twin. But I got to get Chill and junior involved too. I can't let you loose. Not without somebody else to make sure you don't go all out."

"Well you better bring a squad," Ajay suggests.

Tank is angry too. Right away he suggest they get June and Rich in a meeting with *all* the men folks and get it all resolved immediately.

19

TIME TO KNOW-RELOADED-Time Will Reveal- part 4

"If it was *just* the cheating," Tank says, "I would do this without the elders. But since Rich violated your home, wife, my twin and all that shit too. I'm not even sure if I can keep June or my damn self for socking his ass, a few times. I'm calling the monarchs. I'm not negotiating that. They'll make the call. And Ajay, they'll give you room to be the man. You're gonna have to accept whatever they allow. We all know that. They're not gonna overlook what he did. Are you wit me bro?"
Ajay is quiet. Tank can hear him breathing and he knows he's worked up. "Are you wit me?" he asks again.

"We need to meet at your house," Ajay says, "Because you know that muthafucka is not about to step back up in here."

"So you're down to let him live, right man?" Tank asks for clarity.

"Whatever," Ajay answers impatiently.

"Promise me, bro," Tank says.

"*What the hell is it* with you and Ebony and all this promise shit?" he asks growing more agitated.

"Because we know you're a man of your word," Tank says and tries to chuckle. "So let me hear it Ajay. I can't allow you to lose."

"I promise I'll leave him breathing," Ajay says, "That's the best I can give you."
Tank tells him he'll call Rich and June after he gets a few others to sit in. Then they'll all get together at his house.

"Send Nina and Rebbie over to T-baby's until we finish," Ajay says, "I don't want them to know what either of them did yet."

"Nina's on her way round to your house, man," Tank says.

"I'll catch her at the door," he says.
He and Tank hang up. He calms himself down, puts on his silk pajamas and matching robe.

He runs to his weight room and grabs a couple of his 50lb weights. He'll act like he was throwing them around, if Nina inquires as to why he's so worked up this early.

When he answers the door, not only is Nina there. But both T-baby and Rebbie are standing there with her. They're demanding to see Ebony.
"Y'all come on in a minute," Ajay says, "Let me explain something to y'all. I'll be right back. Have a seat and entertain Nee Nee's twins," he says while chuckling, as he refers to their twin puppies.
The ladies laugh as he heads across the kitchen and disappears behind the family room wall. Nina is already thinking of a come back for when he returns from the master suite. The 3 ladies sit down at the island counter in the kitchen. Ike and Tina entertain them while Ajay goes into his bedroom.

20

TIME TO KNOW-RELOADED-Time Will Reveal- part 4

His bride is still sleeping. He sits on the edge of the bed. Ebony opens her eyes immediately and looks at him like she knows something's brewing.

"Your girls are here," he says.

"Oh no," Ebony says, "I dreamed about this."

"Is that why you was so uncomfortable a few hours ago?" he asks, "Because you was all over the bed this morning."

She's laying at the foot of the bed now. She had tossed and turned a lot throughout the morning.

"Probably so," she says, "I'm sorry for elbowing you."

"No problem," he says, "I told you I play in the paint a lot."

He chuckles, then he says, "Look here. I'm gonna tell 'em you and me had a disagreement on our cell phones, yesterday after you got home. And I told you to come home, stay here and you couldn't talk to nobody until we got thing's straightened out. In the meantime, I'll handle this crazy shit with June and definitely with Rich too. I'm gonna send the girls to T-baby's house until we finish. I'll handle the girls, for now. It'll be alright."

"Will Chill be there when you see Rich?" she asks and he's slow to answer.

"Will he be there? Did you tell Tank what all happened?"

"I told Tank what you told me," he says.

"Good," she says, "I know Tank will make sure you get back home. Thank you, daddy."

"No problem," he says, "I remember when you asked me to fix things with my boys, not so long ago. That's when it was all three of them. Your girls was broke up wit 'em and wanted us to be broke up too. I can see the worry in your eyes. It's Like you think *this* will put a strain on our marriage. It won't."

"No that isn't gonna happen," she says and smiles.

"Damn right," he says, "So just relax. I'll be back."

She gets up and goes into the bathroom as he heads back to the kitchen where her girls are waiting and enjoying Ike and Tina.

"They are so cute and smart," Rebbie says.

"Like babies," Nina says, "Ike do favor you a little bit, Ajay."

He laughs at her and says, "Yea but he's got your legs."

They all burst out laughing again. Then he asks, "Ladies y'all know Ebony has to do what I tell her to do, right?"

"Yes we know," Rebbie says and smiles.

"But why can't she talk to us?" T-baby asks.

"Because I told her to come home and stay off the phone until we

21

talked," he says, "We had a disagreement when she got here. She didn't wanna talk to me right, while we was on the phone. I had my game last night. So I told her to stay home and wait for me. She still has to do that until I tell her otherwise."

"Can't she come talk to us while you're standing here?" Nina asks.

"Nina," he says giving her an impatient look, "She has to do what I say. When I'm satisfied, you'll know. Because she'll be calling. Go to Tee's house, for now. Me and Tank need to discuss some things with my fellows while I cool off. We're gonna be at Nina's house. I'll get back to y'all, okay? Ebony can't see nobody until I'm done at Tank's and we can finish our talk. I'm giving her time to cool off too. She'll tell y'all, I'm sure. Whenever I say it's cool."

"What does Rich have to do with it?" T-baby asks.

"Whatever I tell him," he says, almost losing his patience.

Then he says, "We're gonna talk about what guys talk about. But it's all good with Ebony. Just give us time to talk first. Then she'll call."

"Ajay tell me what's up," Nina tries.

"Nina you know you're not gonna get into my business," he says, "Go on and wait until we call."

They leave reluctantly, heading to T-baby's house to wait. Still they try to figure out what's happened. Neither of them try to call Ebony because they already know she isn't going to answer. But now they think it's because of some problem her and Ajay are having. That's fine with Ajay for them to think the problem is him. So long as they don't put his wife in an uncomfortable position.

Ajay goes back to their bedroom where Ebony's laying across the bed on her back.

"They're gone," he says as he stretches out on top of her. "They tried to pick me for information. But I wasn't having it. I gave them the story I told you."

"Do you think they believed it?" she asks.

"Yea," he says.

"They think *we* had an argument," she says smiling, "I *argued* with you. *Really*? Why would they believe I wouldn't call them after we had a disagreement?"

She's smiling because she knows her control freak husband is loving that her girls believe she isn't going to go against what he tells her to do. But she has to hear him admit it.

"Because they know if I tell you *not* to do something," he says, "Then you're not gonna do it. I told them you're on punishment. And later,

22

TIME TO KNOW-RELOADED-Time Will Reveal- part 4

I'll tell them it was because you went to the doctor without me. I said you couldn't talk to nobody or see nobody. Until you get off punishment."

"Wow. That's amazing," she says, looking up into his face. She adds, "I guess I'm well trained."

He gives her a wink and a kiss. Then he says, "Hell yea, you are. And you know it."

"Uh huh," she concedes with a shy smile. She's looking unsure as she asks, "But am I *on* punishment, though?"

He cracks up laughing. Then with a smile, he says, "You might be. At least until I get caught up on my pussy fix."

They laugh hard. Then he gives her another sweet kiss. He raises up off of her and sits at the edge of the bed. She had hung an outfit on the outside of his closet room door and placed a fresh pair of Jordan's on his wardrobe chest.

"That's what I'm wearing to kick Rich's ass?" he asks with a smile.

"You're gonna *talk* things out and get an *understanding*," she offers.

"Nah," he says, "I'm gonna kick his ass. I'd rather wear my timbo's, some jeans and a white tee."

He gets up and grabs a crisp t-shirt off the hanger. He wears the Reebok tracksuit she'd picked for him. But he opts to sport a brand new pair of Timberland suede boots, instead of the latest Jordan's.

"If he bleeds on these," he says to her with a sideways smile, "I'm killing him. Cause my baby just got these for me."

She rolls her eyes and says, "Give me a kiss and get back here. *Without* any warrants or police presence *all* up in my community. Okay daddy?"

"Baby," he says as he stands and prepares to leave, "that depends on him."

Before she can say anything else, he leans over her from the opposite angle and kisses her. Then he leaves his guard dog Pekinese's in charge of their mother. He grabs the keys to her Camry and heads to the garage.

Ebony's girls sit at T-baby's house trying to figure out what could be wrong with her and Ajay. They cast a few guesses out but neither think it's anything bad. They know there's no way Ajay has broken her heart or anything that serious. And surely not already.

"It's probably some kind of sex game, knowing those two," Nina say as she smiles.

"You're probably right," T-baby adds, "And they don't want us to know because they're a couple of perverts and we'll tell them they are."

23

They laugh as they click on the TV over the kitchen counter and wait patiently for Ajay to call them.

Meanwhile, Ajay arrives at Tanks house to a driveway full of cars and trucks.

"Damn Tank," he says to himself as he observes the many vehicles. "He got my pops, poppa, papa Charles, papa Brown, Chill and junior over here. *Fuck*! I'm still hitting his ass. They can get ready."

He hops out and heads toward Tank's house. Big Al, Chill and Jr meets him at the door.

"No," Ajay says before they can say a word.

"It's all good, cousin," Jr says.

"No it ain't," Ajay says as he heads inside.

Once inside, Tank ushers him to the family room where the other men are waiting, along with June and Rich. Ajay heads straight for Rich, who tries to stand and move quickly but Ajay is a little more determined to grab him, then Rich is at moving out of his reach.

"Come here, nigga," Ajay says as he grabs his shirt and punches him in the jaw.

Rich falls to the floor but scrambles to get back to his feet and move. Big Al, Chill and Jr grab Ajay as Tank and June jumps between them and Rich.

"Hang on, Ajay," poppa says, "What the devil is going on here?"

Tank hadn't had a chance to fully brief all the men on the extent of the story. He had only gotten as far as the cheating.

"Poppa Jones, big mama didn't tell you what he did?" Ajay asks, "Oh Tank, how you *playing*? You didn't tell them what he did *after* his cheating ass got back out here?"

"Tell us what?" Big Al asks as Chill and Jr prepare to tell them. Chill says, "It's what I was about to get too. *Before* you pulled up, Ajay."

"Well get to it, bro," Ajay says impatiently.

"Ebony witnessed these two on their little caper yesterday," Chill says, "And they saw her. But instead of Rich going on home and fixing it with his wife. He went to Ajay's house."

"And threaten my wife," Ajay adds as he finishes Chill's sentence.

"What?!" June yells after hearing this new revelation.

"Why would you do that?" papa Brown asks Rich.

"I was drunk and wasn't thinking," Rich tries.

"Well I'm gonna knock some sense into yo ass today," Ajay adds, "You called my wife a bitch and a slut. Rich, I'm gonna kick yo ass. I don't care if it takes me a year. Ain't nobody gonna stop me from defending my

24

home. You crazy if you think you're safe in here. You damn fool!"

"Hang on Ajay," Big Al says, "Let us get the discussion out of the way. Then we'll deal with whatever needs to be done."

"*Shit!*" Ajay says in a very disgusted tone.

He's made up his mind that no matter what they decide is the fair call. He's going to fight Richard Jr today.

"Ajay just chill out for a few minutes, man," Tank says, "Bro, I know you ain't gonna break up all of Nina's furniture and shit."

"I can replace whatever gets broken," Ajay says.

He's still staring at Rich and inviting him to come from behind the others.

Finally Tank gets everyone seated in his family room. Rich and June are nervous. They know this talk is about what they'd done at the Medical complex. They don't know if the men are going to demand that they tell their wives or not. Ajay didn't know his niece was still in the house. Not until she peeks around the corner to see what the commotion is. When she sees her grandpa Al and uncle Ajay, she comes running in there. She goes straight to where they are. Al is damn near sitting on Ajay with Jr on 1 side and Chill in front of him. Tank stands behind Ajay.

After Jerica hugs everyone, Tanks says, "Jerica baby. Go over to your cousin Tee Tee's house with your mom, so the men can talk. Okay?"

"Yes sir, daddy," she says as she grabs her favorite doll and heads for the kitchen door.

Tank watches her until she's safely inside of Rich and T-baby's home. Then he comes back into his family room to rejoin the 8 men and they get to it.

"Now what the hell is up with y'all?" Tank asks immediately.

"It wasn't that serious, cou-," June tries.

"Dude you're fuckin over Ree Ree," Ajay interrupts, "That shit *is* serious."

June says nothing else as papa Charles, *Rebbie and Rich's grandfather,* looks on. He hasn't said anything yet. He's just observing.

"What's up with you, Rich," Jr asks, "Cousin how you gonna be all out in public wit a bitch? You know that's crew rule number one."

Rich is quiet. His nervousness is showing. His grandpa Charles finally speaks.

He says, "If shit like this gets out. That's gonna be heat on every man in this family and y'all know it. From the top to the bottom."

"He's right about that," poppa says, "That's gonna get our wives stirred up. The women in the crew will hold meetings on our ass, if y'all go out there and start some infidelity shit."

"Who the fuck was y'all with?" Chill asks.

25

"Regina and Diana," June answers, "But y'all knew that."

"Y'all still fucking with them ho's? Even *after* the bachelor party?" Tank asks, sounding as calm as John Sr would, back when he'd had to discipline him. "Are y'all just happy that ho's offered to give y'all some pussy? Cause those ain't even no top notch asses to have on the side."

"Cousin y'all in the NFL," Jr adds, "Those are just some regular ho's. Y'all out in public, cheating on crew ladies with some regular run of the mill ho's?"

"Crew this shit is stupid," Al says.

"And this shit *will* cease," papa Brown finally says.

"Let me knock some sense into Rich," Ajay says, "I'm telling y'all. He'll get right after I split his damn head open."

He's sounding like Al. Very calm and cool. But inside he's fuming. He's been staring at Rich the entire time. But Rich is yet to make eye contact with him.

"So what will it take for y'all to straighten this up?" Tank asks.

"What it's gonna take is for them to just stop seeing them," papa Charles says.

Ajay says, "Y'all got my wife around there, scared to even talk to her girls because she don't want to hurt them wit *this* shit. *Y'all* bullshit. Shit y'all muafuckaz did. And y'all know I don't want Ebony Jackson uncomfortable, for shit. Certainly not no bullshit. *Feel me?*"

Rich and June both squirm in their seats. Ajay can't hold this any longer. "And Rich, how are you gonna run up in Ebony's face, in *my fuckin'* house, like you're gonna fuck *wit her*? How muthafucka? Ha? What?!"

He stands up. Chill, Al, Tank and Jr spring into action by blocking any path he has to Rich.

Ajay continues, "What *Rich*? You can't hear nigga? Why did you fuck with Ebony? Because she *saw* you fuckin' up?"

He's giving Rich an evil stare. Rich finally makes eye contact with Ajay.

"I was wrong for that, Ajay," he finally says, "I was guilty and caught up in my shit. I just didn't want her to call Trisha."

"Who cares what you didn't want," Ajay goes on as he points his finger at Rich. "You *know* me! You did that shit to fuck with me!"

"I promise I wasn't, Ajay," Rich pleads, "I would never *wanna* go after you, Ebony or nobody else in my family. I was just wasted and I fucked up."

"We already know that's a damn lie," Ajay says, "You've been going after T-baby for years."

That comment cuts Rich deep. He has no come back. No answer for it. All he can do is shake his bowed head as he starts to cry. He's playing for sympathy now.

"Ajay," Chill says, "He knows he fucked up, bro. Let him make it."

"Come on, Ajay," Tank adds, "He's feeling you man."

Al and the older men don't say anything. They just look from Ajay to Rich. Ajay isn't nearly done. He doesn't want to let Rich off with just 1 lick. He wants to make him feel lower than an ant hill.

"Rich don't you ever do no shit *even close* to that again," Ajay oozes, "Or you will deal with me. *Point blank*. Do you understand that?"

"Yea crew," Rich concedes, "My bad, cousin."

"I mean that," Ajay continues, "I don't give a fuck what Ebony do or what you *think* she did. Or *is* doing. You don't check her. That's my business right there. That's *my* woman and *my* wife."

"Cool man," Rich says.

"Yea whatever," Ajay continues as he's on a roll now. "It's not gone be no muafuckaz chastising my wife *but* me. Ask her brothers. Her father and her grandfathers or Chill and June. They're related to her by blood. They know if there's a problem with her. They bring it to me."

"True that," June adds.

"For the last twelve years," Tank says in agreement.

Rich is silent because he doesn't want any further confrontations with Ajay. He still remembers the worst fight they've had. It was when they were 10 years old. He'd stolen Ajay's special edition *Dr J* rookie basketball card and claimed it as his own. Ajay had asks him for it back, only once. Rich had refused to return it. Ajay blooded his nose and nearly broke his wrist before Al and Rich Sr could get to him and break them up. They *all* know Ajay's temper very well. He fights to win. And if he doesn't win. Then the next fight, he fights to kill. *Period*. There's only been a very few things in his life that he's truly cared about. That card collection is 1 of them. He still has it, in mint condition. It's in he and Ebony's 2-story library, shelved and cataloged. His other care is Ebony. Everybody in his crew and even those outside of it, knows that too. No one in this room wants him to get upset to the point of fighting. Sure, all 9 of them together can handle Ajay. But he isn't mad as hell at all 9 of them. Just at Rich. Even if the 9 of them did stop him today. He wouldn't quit until he avenged them all, in some way. Thank God it won't come to that. Ajay shows signs of calming down. Rich knows Tank isn't going to stop Ajay if he was to come at him for real. June and Chill, being 2 of the people who always spoiled Ebony. Most likely won't try to stop Ajay either and Al definitely wouldn't.

"Cousin I'll apologize to Ebony," Rich says to Ajay, "I would

27

never hurt her, man. I was just fucked up and got caught. That's all."

"Oh I know that shit," Ajay says to him. "Because if you fuck with my woman. You *know* you're gonna have to see me. That's real talk."

"So what are y'all gonna do about them ho's?" Tank asks, trying to switch gears and pull Ajay back from anger.

"We're gonna end the shit," June says as Rich shakes his head in agreement.

"Cool," Tank says, "Now what can we tell T-baby, Rebbie and my wife because they're on the prowl right now."

Ajay wants the cheating talk to end too. Because he knows how much Ebony is stressed over not hurting her girls. For that reason, he decides to go that route with his conversation. Only because he wants a solution for his girl. Something they can tell Nina, T-baby and Rebbie to cool them down on why Ebony can't speak to them.

"Look here," Ajay says, "First we need to agree that y'all gonna stop wit all the bullshit."

June and Rich agree, they'll stop instantly.

Ajay continues, "Okay then we're gonna keep this shit on the hush for now. This is the story we're gonna go with. We'll tell the girls, y'all saw Ebony coming out of the clinic parking lot. Y'all found out she was seeing Weston and she was there without *me* knowing. Then y'all accused her of going behind my back and called me about it. After that, I called her and put her on lock down until I could get here. She got upset with y'all about making me fuss at her. She wasn't talking to none of y'all because I found out and told her to stay home and stay off the phone. I told y'all wives that part, this morning."

"That shit might work right there," Tank says with a chuckle. "But we have to say y'all had a big argument at the complex, first. And she left the complex hauling ass and almost wrecked her car too."

"Alright?" Ajay asks.

"Cool man," Rich says, "Whatever it takes."

"So are we straight on everything?" Tank asks.

"Yea," the others agree.

Rich finally walks over to Ajay to give him a pound and apologize again. Ajay punches him in his other jaw, knocking him to the floor again.

Then he says, "You need to be apologizing to my wife. If she's good. Then I'm good. But I'm not shaking your hand. Fuck you."

With that, he walks out the door. The other men follow him. They all head to T-baby's house. Ajay calls Ebony and tells her, he's on the way to pick her up so they can meet the others at T-baby and Rich's house.

28

She says, "Okay but you haven't had any breakfast. It's almost lunch time."

"We'll grab something at the restaurant baby," he says, "I was to worked up to eat."

He's pulling into their driveway. She meets him at the door. He gets out of the car, walks up to her and gives her a kiss.

"Did you behave yourself?" she asks, "I don't hear any sirens."

"I was good baby," he says, "I was Ajay."

"Oh God," she says with a smile.

"Are you ready?" he asks.

"I suppose," she says, "But I have one question."

"What's that baby?" he asks.

She asks, "Why do we have to start lying *after* we get grown?"

They laugh as they get into her Camry and he drives them back around to T-baby's house.

The guys tell the girls the story they'd come up with, at Tank's house. The story Ajay and Tank see as the only way to save the crew's good relationship spirits. T-baby, Rebbie and Nina believe them. They could see Ebony being upset earlier. They know how she is when it comes to Ajay's perception of her or when he's upset with her. She does whatever he tells her to do. She's always been that way, for the most part. They believe the story. Rich and June apologize to Ebony. She accepts, though she feels eerily uncomfortable around them now. And especially around Rich.

CHAPTER   37

THE SOUTH IS ON

As Mother's day comes and passes, it becomes easier for Ebony to put the cheating out of her mind and be civil to Rich and June. Still Ajay constantly reminds her that his concerns are only about *their* relationship. And if she feels uncomfortable around anyone. She doesn't have to be in their midst. He also tells her, his only demand is that she keep in mind that their priority and concern is on *their* marriage being solid. And even though they want the entire crew to stay together. No one else's problems will be allowed to interfere with them or their peace and harmony. She tells him that's something she can focus on and certainly live up too.

Ebony tells Ajay, "Big mama told me that the same day it happened. She said the same things that you're saying now. So don't worry. I won't ever let anything or anybody ruin what we have."

"That's all I wanted to hear you say and with conviction" he says, "I know how tight this crew is. And you and your girls are like *one*. But our marriage will stay, just as it is. No matter what happens in theirs. You hear me?"

"I hear you and I agree," she says and gives him a kiss.

She loves her crew and wants all of their marriages to last, just like those in the crew's before them. But she's on her points and quota's when it comes her and Ajay. She'll never allow anything to come between them. Nor will she allow herself to become upset over someone else's problems again. The only thing troubling her *this* mother's day is that she *isn't* a mother.

****

}*Cincinnati*{

It's graduation time for the foursome. They're all in Cincinnati and the ladies are raring to go. The entire crew attend. While they're all there for the ceremony, the guys are having surprises done for their wives, back at home. Either a surprise gift of jewels for Nina and Rebbie, a fur coat for T-baby and for Ebony, Ajay has salon equipment installed in the *hers* side of their master bathroom. The reasoning he'll give to her will be, to prevent her from wearing a scarf to bed. She said she does it so her hair can look nice the next day. And he always pulls it off and gets into her hair, every night. He decided they needed a comparable fix. And further, he has given Nina advance pay to come over and do Ebony's hair whenever she feels she needs it done. It's also for when she *does* get pregnant and has to be on bed rest. Which they already anticipate. She won't have to go out to have it done. She has her own shampoo bowl, chair, dryer with a chair and mirrors on the walls to check her do. There's already a couple of large TV's in there. 1 on each end. Both are visible from the Jacuzzi too. Ajay loves to spoil his wife and especially when it benefits his needs too.

The family heads back to Cleveland for the celebration. The party is already rocking when Rob, who's home from Atlanta to deejay the event, breaks a new record from an artist Ajay had turned him onto last year.

Trick Daddy, the rapper from Miami, has a new album out titled; *Thug.com.* On the album there's a break out hit single titled; *Nann Nigga.* It features a newcomer. A female rapper who goes by the name of *Trina.* She's from Miami as well. The county of Dade. She's taking the world by storm on her 1st outing.

"That's a foul mouth girl. *Damn!*" Justine says as she laughs, "But that verse is *bangin.* I love it!"

"No joke," Kilo adds, "She's gonna blow the fuck up from that *one* verse."

"Yea I know," Justine says, "Because she's saying things that most guys wanna hear. Like *you don't know Nann bitch, who suck dick like me.* And things like *Do bout five or six best friends.* That right there will get her in the door with most men."
She laughs as the other ladies agree.

"Sad but true," Ebony says, "I wonder if she's fucked and sucked my man?" she asks as she laughs.
Ajay hasn't admitted to it and he would, if he had. Besides, from Trina's raps, she sounds like she is the *going after a man's pocket* type. Ajay has a lock on his pockets with his wife holding the only spare key.

"She just sold a million dollars worth of pussy on that verse alone" Nina says as she laughs.

"Do she need an accountant?" T-baby giggles.

"Pussy is still lucrative," Rebbie adds and laughs too.

"We just never had that type of role model, you guys," Ebony says, "She may have learned that growing up. Don't look down on her."
Ebony is an old soul to the heart. She believes every person has something good to offer and that's what she looks for first. Ajay was dead on with his assessment of her. She knows how to find the good in people.
"So let's not look down on her," she says again.

"We're not looking down on her," Kim says, "Whomever she's sucking is."

31

TIME TO KNOW-RELOADED-Time Will Reveal- part 4

Kim continues the joke. They all laugh and enjoy the 1st official *kick-off-the-summer* celebration. This is the same night when Ebony finds out that Angel has been calling the club *frequently*.

It happens when she goes into Renee's office to send an email to Lynn about the grand opening of the southern businesses. While she's using Renee's desk computer, she sees an email sent to Renee and Chill from Kilo. He'd reported back on the number which was being used to connect Angel's calls from prison. It was a land line registered to Farah Benson's family business. The note from Kilo reads:

To Chill and Renee,
I was able to get a trace on the land line that Angel's many
calls to the club had come from. The line is registered to
Benson Companies, Inc. Farah Benson's family brand. I
suspect her and Alana are linking the calls. Both from
Pittsburgh and from here in Cleveland. In addition, I've
been informed that she has also been seeking out someone to
make physical contact with Ajay and to harm Ebony. I'm on
it and I'll have more info soon.

Kilo

Immediately she goes back to her table to get Ajay. She brings him back into the office to see the email. He reads it thoroughly.

"Angel has been calling the *club*," she says in surprise.
But looking at his expression, she can tell he isn't as startled as she is. His look is 1 of disgust but familiarity. She can see it in his eyes. He isn't caught off guard by her discovery.
She asks, "You knew about this?"

"I knew she had called. Yea," he says, "And I asked Chill to have her knocked off. I don't know what he's waiting for. I didn't know she was trying to send somebody after me and you. But that shit don't shock me. It's the same shit she was doing when she was out here. That's why she needs to die."

"Why am I *always* the last person to know things like this?" she asks, "I never know anything until I just stumble upon it. Why is that?"

"I just try to protect you from bullshit, baby girl," he says, "It's not like we was trying to hide it-"

"*We?*" she interrupts, "Let me guess. Everybody knows about it except me."

"No," he says quickly, "I don't believe everybody knows and they don't care to know either. Angel is a piece of shit psycho ass bitch, Ebony.

32

TIME TO KNOW-RELOADED-Time Will Reveal- part 4

This is a public place and I'm a public figure. My guess is she's keeping up with news on me. When she sees me on it, in Cleveland. Or she thinks that I'll be here. She calls here. Chill has some folks on her, in prison. That's how Kilo got this info. So there's no threat to you or me. I would know if it was and so would you. Because I wouldn't keep something like that from you. I just don't want you stressing over that bitch no more than necessary. But if she was anywhere near getting to us. You would know. You would have to know because she would die *that same* fuckin day I found out she'd found somebody to harm you. That somebody would die too."

"Do you promise?" she asks, "Is this all? All that *you* know?"

"I promise you," he says without hesitation. "But I need Chill up here, right now. I need to know what else is going on. And why I didn't know about this new shit."

"I agree," she says.

He calls Chill from his cell phone and ask him to meet them in Renee's office. Within minutes, Chill is there wondering what's happened and why the urgency.

"What's going on?" he asks.

"I saw this email, Chill," Ebony says, "I had no idea this *murderer* was calling the club. *Our* club. Y'all have to stop protecting me to the point of leaving me ignorant to things like this."

Chill and Ajay are quiet for a minute. Ajay knows he isn't going to change his formula. Chill can't change his if Ajay doesn't give him the word. Suddenly Nina, T-baby and Rebbie come in wondering what's keeping Ebony.

"What's up with y'all," T-baby asks.

"Angel has been calling the club, cousin," Ebony says.

"She called again?" Rebbie asks.

"Wait," Ebony starts, "You know too?"

"She called here that night when you wasn't allowed to speak to us, Ebony," Nina says, "And when we got word of it. We came in here to sit by the phone. That's how we found out she was calling. We put Kilo on her, the same night. I would've told you but you wasn't talking. *Remember*? And by the time you was. I hadn't thought of her ass no more. It was more important to me and I'm sure to Tee and Ree Ree too. To know what was wrong with you. But we let her know that ain't nothing changed for her."

"Yes we sure did," Rebbie says, "We waited for her to call back and she did. That's how we got the word to Kilo to trace the number on the caller ID. Cause we wasn't gonna just let it go with *just* cursing her out."

"We're not underestimating her bitch ass, no more," T-baby adds.

33

"Y'all know now and still didn't tell me?" Ebony asks in surprise.

"We didn't wanna worry you with it," T-baby says, "I only thought about it once in the two weeks *since* that night. I've been listening to Richard crying and feeling sorry for himself, over the meeting they had." Ebony doesn't want to bring up Rich or June. She knows she has a secret that she hasn't shared with them. But hers is about their husbands cheating. Now she wonders just how many secrets do they really have between them.

"Is there anything else I *don't* know?" Ebony asks.

"I wanted to asked that same thing," T-baby says.

"You wanna know if it's anything else *I* don't know too?" Ebony asks T-baby.

"No," T-baby answers, "Not you. I wanted to know what else it is that *I* don't know."

"What do you mean?" Ebony asks, treading lightly.

"Like why did Ajay hit Richard?" T-baby asks, stunning them all. Ebony knows why her husband had hit *his 1*st cousin. But telling *her 1st cousin* could lead to her having to tell the secret that she has been keeping from them this entire 2 weeks. So she knows she has to lie. And quickly.

"What?!" Ebony asks, trying to sound *very* surprised. Then she says, "Ah no," as she looks at Ajay. She adds, "I didn't know he did."

"Yes I did, baby," Ajay says, covering for his wife. "I didn't like him raising his voice at you. T-baby knows about that. We told them the same day it happened. I clocked his ass at the meeting. *Twice.* And I'll do it again if he *ever* tries to chastise my wife. I handle my own business and my personal. Nobody is gonna do that *but* me."

"So wasn't Brian apart of that too Ajay?" Rebbie asks, "He didn't look like he had been hit and he never said he'd been hit. But Rich was red and swollen. I guess his light skin shows his bruises better."

"I didn't hit June because he didn't call my wife out of her name, when they saw her down there," Ajay says, continuing to cover. "Rich did. He was screaming on Ebony like he had a right too. Which he *don't*. Y'all know I don't play that shit. So let's get back to the matter of tonight. *Can* we? That's old shit there and it ain't gone change tonight."

Again he wants the pressure off of his wife, at all cost.

Chill notices, jumps in and says, "We're gonna step up the shit on Angel. Get her ass whooped good and send her to the infirmary. That way we can keep her off the phone for awhile. And in the meantime, I'll see about putting something in place to get rid of her for good. But I have to be mindful that it could bring negative press for you Ajay. I'm not gonna do shit that'll lead back to you, baby girl or this crew, in anyway." Then he

34

turns his attention to Ebony and says, *"I've* been keeping the calls from Angel, on the low. Basically because I'm doing what I've always done and so is Ajay. From the time he knew about it. He wanted me to just send a hit at her and get rid of her. But that's gonna bring press to *your* doorstep. Just on her history alone. The shit she did to you and Ajay is the reason she *went* to jail. The media is gonna dig that up. I know you're not ready to relive that bullshit, are you?"

"No," she says, "But I'm trying to get pregnant again and I'm not trying to relive what happened to our last baby again *either."*

With that, she grabs Ajay's hand and walks out of the office bringing him with her. That's the only way she can escape that scene without giving away more than she wants to, about what really happened at the complex. It was just the way her 1st cousin looked at her. Something tells her that T-baby knows more than what she's admitting to about why her husband got *knocked the fuck out.*

They eventually get back to the party and put the Angel talk to the side, for now. Ebony and Ajay are satisfied knowing Chill is going to fast forward his surveillance of Angel. Perhaps he'll employ some of the trustees and correctional officers, who are on his payroll, to rough her up. Anything to put her down long enough for him to come up with a more permanent plan.

For the remainder of May, things are going smoothly. Nothing else has been said about the cheating. Nor has Angel called again. The foursome are still unbreakable. They shop for their homes and families, at least once a week. Everything is going smoothly with their husbands too. Rich and June have chilled with their infidelity, as of late. As a matter of fact, Rebbie and T-baby seem happier than ever.

The foursome have decided they're going to take those graduate classes they'd discussed during their last semester at Natty. But they're going to enroll at CSU for the fall. Rebbie has already been selected and invited to the performing arts program where she can do her student teaching classes. She can also work with professionals in the art, who will fly in monthly. Jerica will attend those special classes as well. This was all made possible by Mrs. Briar. She's the UC Alum who had approached them at the beginning of the year. The foursome's graduation was just the start of what will be a hot summer of action and big moves for the crew.

By Rich, T-baby, June and Rebbie's 2nd anniversary, things in T-baby and Rich's household are becoming a little tense again. But for the

35

most part, they're doing okay. Rich hasn't stayed out all night lately. And though he has had some very late nights. He makes sure to be ready to tend to his wife's every need when he *does* get home. That keeps T-baby pacified. She doesn't grill him as much about what the real reason was that Ajay had hit him twice. But something tells her there was another reason why Rich felt he had to go at Ebony. Something other than him just taking up for Ajay. The man whom Rich has always played second too. She's felt like he's been cheating for a long time. But since he's making it home before she falls asleep. She doesn't question him. Rich even stops complaining about Ajay jumping on him. He doesn't say anymore about it because he wants T-baby to stop mentioning it. He has been careful not to lose his temper on her and end up admitting more than he wants too, as well.

Reaper graduates on the 5th of June as the lone crew member from high school, this year. He's going to attend college at *Clark-Atlanta University* where he'll be closer to Rob and his music. He's leaving next Monday with most of the crew. They're flying to Atlanta to help with the openings.

****

ʃAtlantaʃ

The southern businesses are opening this week. Jb has lined up the hottest artist in the south. *Juvenile* from *Cash Money records,* out of New Orleans, will have his listening party at *The Dirty South Chill Spot* for the grand opening. Many of the crew are flying down to lend a hand. Juvenile's CD, *400 Degreez* is hot. He's certainly expected to put the south all the way on the map with his hits; *Ha, Follow Me* and *Back Dat Ass Up!* The entire *Cash Money records* family are in attendance for the grand opening. Also *Juvenile* has a few guys whom he's planning to promote. He has a label he's calling *UTP* or *Uptown Rec*ords. His label consist of *Skip, Wacko, Young Buck* and *Red Eyes,* just to name a few. *Juvenile* has hopes of signing them and his own label to *Cash Money* in the near future.

The crew are loving the Cash Money energy. The *southern* energy, for that matter. They can see that Atlanta is a city on the rise for Hip-Hop, Fashion or just business, in general. At grand opening weekend, *CMR* guys ball like no one they've ever seen. They spend major money on opening night. These guys are flashy with their gold teeth, shiny jewelry and beautiful cars. They move like royalty. One look at them and it's evident, this label will make changes in the Hip Hop game forever.

36

TIME TO KNOW-RELOADED-Time Will Reveal- part 4

While in Atlanta, Ajay gets a call from Jarvis Rhodes. His fiancée Gwen is by his side. She's very close to giving birth to their first baby. It's a boy. Jarvis wants to have that talk with Ajay before she goes into labor.

"What's up wingman?" Ajay asks, "This ain't face to face."

"You know I admire your upbringing and the way your crew gets down, Ajay," Jarvis says, "I've been around your family since meeting you in ninety two. My senior year of high school. I wanted to do this face to face before my son came. But our schedules may not allow that."

"True that," Ajay says with a chuckle, "I told you I'm gonna put you down. You and Terrell. I've been talking to Chill about it but what's up with you today? What's on your mind wingman?"

"Cool," Jarvis says, "But that's not the only thing I'm calling for."

"Tell me what's up."

"You know my son is coming any day now," Jarvis says.

"Yep," Ajay says, "Are you *bragging*?"

They both laugh, then Jarvis says, "I want you and Ebony to Christian him, for *one* thing. Well that's two."

"I don't see her having a problem with that," Ajay says, "But I'll run it by her and we'll get back to y'all after our extended honeymoon. How's that?"

"That's cool," Jarvis says, "My junior will be here by then."

They both chuckle and Jarvis continues, "Gwen and me, we really enjoy the crew and loved being apart of the crew family at Natty. So we've been talking about this a lot. We would really like it if, when you and Ebony do have a daughter. If you two would consider us raising our children to be together."

Ajay is quiet. He smiles to himself but he doesn't respond. He's touched by Jarvis' request. He loves him like a little brother. They will definitely be apart of each others lives forever. So why not considerate it?

"*Wow* wingman," Ajay says, "You must really look up to me, *for real*, man?"

"I do, Ajay," he says, "And I really want to raise my kids with the same loyalty and upbringing you had. I admire that shit so much, bro and that's on everything."

"I will *definitely* talk to Ebony about *all* of this," Ajay says, "You know I'll have to bring you to a meeting soon. Which would have to be set up, to get you *in* the crew. So now we'll just have three things to meet about. I'm gonna really think about it wingman. Cause at this point, I don't even have a daughter. But I don't know another guy on the non-blood relative side, that I would give that kind of a blessing to, *besides* you. So it's

37

TIME TO KNOW-RELOADED-Time Will Reveal- part 4

definitely possible. But I have to have Ebony in on that and our elders too. Let's try to set that meeting up for the fall, when you join the Cavaliers. Because I know Jb is gonna get that deal for you. We'll get together soon, alright?"

"Alright Ajay," Jarvis says, "Thanks man. I appreciate it."

"No problem, bro," Ajay says with a chuckle. "We'll talk soon."

Ajay smiles to himself. He's going to run this news by Ebony when they take their extended honeymoon in 2 weeks.

}Cleveland{

It's July. Ebony and Ajay are preparing to go on their summer honeymoon. Before they can go, they have a follow up visit at the medical complex. They go in to visit Dr. Weston together. They find out Ebony still isn't pregnant. She's a little more patient then she was in May. Even Dr. Weston notices that.

"It seems like you've realized that these things take time, misses Jackson, " Weston says with a smile.

"I have," Ebony answers with a shy smile, "Anthony is gonna be home for awhile. And we're going on a *longer* honeymoon. Hopefully we'll have some luck *then*."

"I remember you all saying that," Weston says, "I'm sure you're planning to work on getting pregnant while you're away too."

"We're gonna work on that before we leave too," Ajay says as all 3 of them laugh.

"Just keep your calendar updated and don't think about it so much. Like you were before," Weston says, "Oh and make sure all of your future trips to see me, include your husband."

"She will," he says with a chuckle, "She told me."

"I will," Ebony adds as she giggles.

They leave the complex and head home to pack their last minute items. Ajay goes out to do the necessary procedures to secure their home for when they'll be away. Ebony prepares the inside of the mansion and finishes all the packing. She's excited about their upcoming extended honeymoon to Jamaica and the Virgin Islands. She packs every piece of sexy gear she can find. She wants her man in overdrive so they can make this baby.

They leave for Jamaica on the 13th with a vow that they'll work on getting pregnant every single day and night, while on their on this extended getaway.

One day while in Jamaica, they find themselves talking about the

38

letter she'd sent to him back in 1990. The 1 where she'd claimed to be open to dating other boys since he was living with Darlene.

"I knew that letter was fake," he says, "I knew it from the time I read it. When we was sitting in Darlene's car. And I knew the reason you wrote it was because I was staying at her apartment. It had nothing to do with anything *you* was doing or was gonna do."

"That's the only time I can remember you being that angry with me," she says, "I was so scared that night at Chill's house. I was trying my best to make you understand. I only wrote it to get your attention."

"I knew that already," he says, "What made me mad was you was playing games with me. You felt like you could lie to me and get a positive response. I knew I had to nip that shit in the bud from jump. *Right away.* That's what I set out to do. I started it *that* night."

"I was only trying to get your attention," she repeats, "I could never let another man hold me. I didn't know you knew that, at *that* time."

"I knew you wasn't given up my pussy, baby girl," he says with a smile. "Cause you don't know *Nann Nigga* that slang dick like me."

They both laugh hard. Then he says, "You always had my attention. I was just going through growing pains. You know, sowing my wild oats. Or as my pops would say it, *maturing.*"

"Well you had many acres of oats, daddy," she says with a smile.

"But I got that shit out of my system before we got married though," he says, "I see a lot of players fuckin over their wives. And in Miami, the women lay that ass out there. But it's a trap. The NBA mystique is a trap. *Period.* Ho's will do whatever to get to us. But that shit is trouble. It'll end your success and could end your life, if you're not smart. It's just like the dope game."

"I feel like you're really good to me," she says, "You may have had your moments, growing up. But these days you're more open about things like that. I know now that you would do anything to keep me safe and to keep a smile on my face. I know that has a lot to do with who you've come to be, as a man. *My man.* And who you were all along. I'm just blessed."

"You know the extent of my fuckin and that's in my lifetime," he says, "I just got to the point where I realized that everything that turns me on, you already have. I don't have to tell you what to do or how to do it. It's like you're already there. I've fucked some ho's, in my lifetime," he chuckles. "Enough to know that everything *either one of them* had that was any good. I already had it at home, in you. The only reason they got some time back then. Is because you wasn't available. That's a *fact.* But anytime I could be with you, baby girl. I was. We got our shit tight over these years."

39

We molded it and made it perfect. But baby girl, that *side* shit. That was then. I can say that I'm through with *all* of that. I have every woman in the world, rolled into one. In you. And you are *all* mine too." He gives her a sweet kiss and adds, "I molded you to be all that I needed and all that I want. I'll be *damned* if you didn't get it down *perfect* too. I can't think of one thing you could do to make me feign for you, more than I do now."

"Same with you," she says as she blushes. "I learned to yearn for you, Anthony. Early in my life. I knew it was something special about your touch. Way before we ever did it."

"Did what?" he asks as he chuckles.

She giggles and adds, "Before we had sex. That night at the motel, oh my *God*! I'll never forget that night. And not because of our mothers coming either. I remember it because of *me* coming."

She laughs hard and he laughs too. He has to kiss her after that comment. Then he asks, "So you've liked sex since then?"

"Yes," she says, "Loved it and I've looked forward to it."

"That's what I'm talking about," he says with a smile.

She smiles, gives him a kiss and says, "You're the man, daddy. *My man*."

"I've dedicated my life to protecting your virtue and keeping you happy. I want you to give me daughters, who are *just* like you."

"Ah I love you," she says and they kiss again.

Then he says, "I'm gonna keep you smiling. Not crying or worrying."

"Rich and June can't say that," she says, "Because they've both been unfaithful. All out in the open too."

"Yea but that's over with," he says.

"Good because they're gonna rub off on you and Tank-"

"-No the fuck they're not," he says quickly, "Tank and I have been holding it down with you and Nina, baby girl. Nobody can make anyone do anything that's not in their hearts. Don't even try that."

"You're right and I always knew there was something special about you," she says.

He smiles. She says, "And back when I first started coming outside to play with y'all. It wasn't that I didn't like you. I was *scared* of the way I liked you. That feeling I had and still have. It was new to me. The way you looked at me. I just didn't understand that look, back then. But it's the same one you have now. You had experience with sex at a young age. You seemed like a grown man to me, I guess. Baby you didn't do regular boy stuff. Like Tank and June. You acted the same way as Chill, Stoney and Rob. You use to talk to me and I wouldn't say anything back. So you thought I hated you. I didn't. I was taken back by you. Anthony you was so mysterious to me.

Your eyes are *so* deep. I still can't stare back at you. You lived right next door to me. But when I started paying attention to you. I realized I didn't know anything about you. Remember when our parents took us to see *Beverly Hills Cop* with *Eddie Murphy?* That was in nineteen eighty four. I was eight and you had already made ten. You shared your popcorn and drink with me and you asked to kiss me. I wanted too. But I didn't know how and I didn't know how to tell you, I had a crush on you."

He smiles. She continues, "It wasn't until fourth of July in eighty six, when big mama was talking to granny. I was listening while I helped them crinkle the pie crust. Big mama said, *'Jo and Al's son likes our granddaughter here. But he said she looks at him like she's afraid of him. And all he wants to do is take up for her.'* I acted like I wasn't listening but I was. I know *now* that they knew I was. That's when I made up my mind, that the next time you asked me to kiss you. I would try it. Then I was just gonna smile so you would know I did like you. Afterwards I was just gonna wait for you to tell me what to do next. That first *real* kiss came on that same day too."

"*Wow.* I'm the luckiest man in the world," he says as he smiles.

"I had granny, papa, poppa, big mama, Chill, big John *and* my pops. All of them working with me to get the woman of my dreams. No matter what my crew or anyone else do. They can't make me do *anything* that's gonna hurt you. I never wanna do that again, okay? I just wanna shower you with love and affection. Then watch how you respond to it. That's my biggest thrill. It makes my dick hard as a brick, baby girl. No lie and that's how I know it's right and you're the one. No woman or girl ever made me feel that way and I've had lots of 'em. Nobody can make me do shit, I don't wanna do. You know that because that's how you are too. And that's what attracted me to you. Because that's what I like and I always did."

She agrees with him. She remembers when her girls were contemplating going out with Tim's crew. She knew she wasn't going to date Tim. Even though T-baby and Nina had accepted dates with Craig and Roger.

"You're right," she says, "Nobody can make you hurt the one you love."

"Hell no," he says. Then he changes the subject. He says, "My wingman is coming to Cleveland."

"Jarvis?"

"Yes."

"Okay," she says, "So long as y'all are past all of those test you use to have him run on me. He got with Jb?"

"Yea he did and yes the test are done," he says with a chuckle. "He's got a *Cav's* tryout. He'll make it and move to *see* town."

41

"And you're gonna wanna be home even more, ha?"

"Yep."

"Will he be in Cleveland before you have to report to camp?"

"Yea," he says with excitement. "He'll probably be there when we get back."

"I know you wanna be there twice as bad. Did y'all have the talk?" He smiles and she knows there's something crucial on his mind. She wonders what it could be, so she asks, "What is it?"

"Three things he wants," he says.

"And they are?" she asks with anticipation in her voice.

"He wants to be in the crew," he says.

"I always knew that," she says, "Since Natty, I knew that. I knew it when I got there."

"And they want us to Christian the son they had a few days ago," he says, "One day after my birthday."

"I'm okay with that," she says, "We'll have two God kids. That's two. What else?"

"He knows about our crew and how tight we are and all," he says with a smile. "He knows about our upbringing and how you and me was born to be together. You know I schooled him on all of that and.."

"Daddy you've got my attention. What in the world is it? *Please* tell me."

"Him and Gwen just had there son, you know,..-"

"Oh God! Please stop torturing me," she says as she lay in his arms.

"Okay," he says, "They want us to Christian him plus they're getting married in February. They want us to be in it. They went to the jay pee, last week. Their anniversary is the same day as Chill, Renee, Tonya and Jr."

"Okay, we can do both," she says, "I don't have a problem with any of that. But the wedding date's not it either. Now tell me what it is?"

"He wants his kids and my kids to be….., groomed like we were."

"Oh I see. Wow!" she says, "And you're *open* to this?"

"Only if you are," he says, "I know Jarvis is good people. I know he has my back. He's morally straight, got good genes and he's been my best friend in basketball since ninety two. We talked about this while we was at Natty. He knows he'll have to meet with the grandparents and parents, to discuss it. That's *my* rule. Even if it wasn't a crew rule. But he knows how I am and he knows what his daughter would have to be. And he knows his son will have to be one hundred times more than that."

"I think Gwen is very sweet and perfect for him," she says, "And I

42

know their kids will be beautiful too. He's brave to even try to match a son with *any* daughter you'll have. And even braver to wanna match his daughter with my son. But that shows the respect he has for you and the loyalty he has *to* you. He knows you, what you expect *and* your ways."

"Most of all, he knows the crew and the family," he says, "And he knows what this would be about. He's always wanted to be crew. It's an honor to me, baby. I don't know how I'll feel when my kids arrive. But for now. I couldn't think of anyone else I would want my kids to date besides crew. But they'll all be related, so we'll have to have outside blood."

"Yes daddy we will," she says, "So yes baby. I'm open to it. I'm happy to see you're talking about it already. I really didn't think that *any* daughter of yours would ever be able to date."

They laugh hard before he says, "They won't. Not unless I pick him. I'm going with the crew formula, all the way. So let's see where it goes."

They enjoy the rest of their honeymoon. They go snorkeling, diving and parasailing too before heading back home to see what new situations unfolded while they were away.

}Cleveland{

Ajay and Ebony return from their extended honeymoon. There are many things going on.

First, the NBA is going into a lockout for the beginning of the 98-99 season. Ajay will be home for a little while longer to work on that baby. Second, Jarvis is in Cleveland for the tryouts and he's likely to make the team. Third, Chill has set up the meeting for Jarvis with the males while Renee has Jason Carr helping him to find temporary housing for his family. But during the tryouts, Ajay insists they stay with him and Ebony.

"Y'all can stay in the garage apartment," he says, "Or on the third floor, if you want two rooms."

Jarvis accepts his hospitality and tells him, he'll let Gwen decide on which they'll choose. As Ajay and Ebony sit with Chill and Renee to discuss Jarvis. Ajay adds another option to the future meeting. He recommends if Jarvis receives approval from the crew. Then he'd like for him and Gwen to be allowed to build in Jackson Heights. Ebony, Renee and Chill agree and vote with him. Ajay and Ebony go home after the discussion. They're excited Jarvis might get to be apart of their crew. So are June, Rich and the rest of the crew who've known him since Cincinnati. Tank is mildly pessimistic about him and Gwen actually *staying* together. Rebbie seems shocked that they're *still* together. Ajay is just happy Jarvis is here. But

43

what has his attention the most is the lockout. He'll still receive a portion of his salary and payments from endorsements, regardless. He's happy him and Ebony will have a lot more time together to work on getting pregnant.

"So you don't have to go to Miami next week?" Ebony asks him.

"No. We're in a lockout until the commissioner and the union can come to an agreement," he says.

"Uh good," she says, "I'll have my husband at home indefinitely!" She jumps into his arms and plants a huge kiss on him.

"Not indefinitely. But it might take a while," he says carrying her into their bedroom. "The honeymoon don't have to end though."

He undresses her and lays her on the bed as Ike and Tina leave the room.

"Uh huh," she moans as he enters her with force.

"Ebony I'm gonna work on this baby until I do have to leave," he whispers, "Now put this good pussy on me, baby."

"I'm so blessed to have a man that can make me cum every time we have sex," she whispers in his ear.

"I'm taking my time in this pussy, baby girl. We ain't got to rush a *damn* thing."

They turn in early this evening, listening to *The Score* by *The Fugees*. At the start of this session, they're still having a conversation. She wants to make sure he knows the next music she wants while allowing him to have the pleasure of her.

"Daddy do you know *Lauryn Hill* has her solo CD coming out next month?" she whispers and moans at the same time.

"Yes. *The Miseducation of Lauryn Hill*," he whispers back while slowing his stroke. "It's hot too. Rob got some advanced tracks from it. I'll get him to send us some until the album drops."

"I want her album, daddy," she purrs.

"And you'll get it baby," he says, "Bet that. Now *fuck* me."

They turn in and turn each other on for the remainder of the evening. Ajay had turned 24 just before they honeymooned in Jamaica. With the NBA in a lockout, he won't have to report to camp this 1st week of August. He's excited because now he can be home to support his wife's new business venture too.

Ebony and T-baby are opening *Jackson and Williams Accounting and Real Estate,* this month. They hire their ex-MLK teammate to be their office manager. Her name is Claudia Jordan.

The news of the lockout is big. Ebony was expecting Angel would've called the club or that she *has* been calling. However, Chill let's them know he'd exercised his power and gotten her ass whooped good

44

while they were on their excursion. She's in the prison infirmary and has been for 2 weeks. Ebony asked Ajay if he'd heard anymore than that.
His response, "No. And I'm not trying too either. I hope that bitch die. That's what I asked for. But Chill got somebody to beat her ass. Hell, she's probably immune to ass whippings by now."

"It just doesn't seem like she's ever gonna go away," Ebony says, "It's eerie to still have her hounding us. Especially when we're trying to get pregnant again."

"She's not a factor," Ajay says, "Chill and I *both* are gonna see to that. Baby lets enjoy ourselves and our time together. Fuck that ho."

Chill had taken the same attitude. He's business as usual. Him and the crew have formed a good relationship with a lot of southern artist, thanks to Jb's work down in Atlanta. Several of the artist from *Cash Money Records* have hired *Crew Details* to *floss out their whips*. They spare no expense when it comes to what they put in and on their cars. While Brian Sr and Rich Sr take in jobs for the detail shop, Chill gets busy booking their artist for the clubs. He books the next major artist from their label. He goes by the name; *BG*. He's going to do a listening party at *The Chill Spot*. Chill loves this dudes style. His voice is unique and it's obvious he's seasoned in the street game. Same as Chill. His singles, *Cash Money is a Army* and *Bling Bling* are an instant and explosive impact on Hip Hop and the music industry as a whole. Never before has artist worn so much iced out jewelry. Not only on their bodies but in their mouths. *Slick Rick the Ruler* and *Run DMC* had worn big chains but not like this. These cats have diamonds and white gold in their teeth. They have the colors of the rainbow in diamonds, which Ebony loves. The size of the tires on their cars must be twenty inch rims or they're just not *grown*. Not keeping up with the game. The crew are loving the new era and it's very profitable for them and their enterprise. They know the upcoming party is going to pay big.

True enough the listening party profits for the weekend of BG's opening set a record for *The Chill Spot*. It brings in upwards of more than $80K. Cash Money Records premiered music from their next release as well. The multitalented group; *The Hot Boys* which include *Juvenile, BG, Young Turk* and *Lil Wayne*. Their single, *I Need A Hot Girl* is on fire and *We On Fire* will be the groups 1st official single. If tonight's premiere of it is any indication of how it will spin. Then the album will sell millions. It got a record number of request for replay, all night.

"We need to get Lauryn Hill in here too," Ebony shouts to Jr, over

the music. "Her CD is a classic. Watch what I tell you."
The Miseducation of Lauryn Hill spun many hits. Some of Ebony's favorites are; *The Do Wop Song, Looking back, Lost One* and *The Ex-Factor.* Chill says he'll try to book her very soon too.

"Maybe I can get her for Christmas and your birthday," he says.

"That works for me," Ebony tells him as she smiles.

By early September, Chill and Jr's homes in Jackson Heights are complete. They move in during the 1st week of the month. Arthur and Michelle remain in the old house in Shaker Heights, while Kilo and Justine take over the house that Jr and Tonya vacated. Stoney's old house. Kilo and Justine have been dating for over a year now and are talking about settling down. Kilo has a son who lives back in New Orleans with his mother. Justine wants Kilo to be more active in his life. She's assisting him in making that a reality.

Al and his sister Jessica are on much better terms these days. He decides to share the part of their father's inheritance he'd saved for her, with her. She's grateful. Al had truly wanted to keep a close relationship with her and Terrell. Only Al, Jessica and Jo know the amount he gives her. She invested some of it right back into the crew's businesses, which was the only stipulation Al gave to her. Ebony handled the transactions. Jessica will receive shares from the profits which she put in Terrell's name. It yields a large commission for Ebony as well. She's happy all the way around and so are the crew. They want Jessica and Terrell to be a part of whatever it is they do. Whether Dr. Layton comes onboard or not. Terrell is happy to have shares in the southern businesses where he works.

****

Chill is usually low key when it comes to spending excessively. But this month him and Jr decide to enjoy some fruits of their labor. They purchase twin black 1999 Mercedes Benz 500's for their wives upcoming birthday's. Renee will be 29 this November. Tonya will turn 27 on the last day of this month, when Rich III makes 3. Chill and Jr buy matching Ninja Bikes for themselves. Crew Details is in charge of all the accessories for the 4 vehicles. Things are looking up for the crew. But as always in this family, when things are good. Some shit has to be thrown into the game.

2 weeks before Rich III turns 3, his father stays out all night. Rich's Jets team didn't have a game this weekend, so he had flown home to see his crew. Friday night after leaving the club, he didn't go home. T-baby was

46

very pissed. Finally by late Saturday afternoon, he makes it to Jackson Heights with very little patience for a discussion. Still T-baby tore into him like never before. He has no viable excuse for being out all night. She's suspicious of him again and this time, she's sure he's having an affair. He argues that he's not but she shuts him down.

"I don't wanna hear it, Richard!" she yells, "You think I'm a damn fool but I'm not! I know you're fucking somebody and you won't be fucking me! That's for *damn* sure!"

She moves into 1 of their guest bedrooms until he leaves on Sunday night, heading back to his team. She doesn't even drive him to the airport which makes Jr and Chill suspicious. Chill asks her if there's anything she needs. She tells him no. Still to him, it's obvious she's internally torn over something. But until she's ready to talk. All Chill or her crew can do is let her know they're there and available to help.

T-baby tossed and turned all night. She's still pissed the next day as she hooks up with her girls at *CrewLand*.

"Here I am trying to plan a birthday party for our son and this asshole is staying out all night," she says to her girls as they eat lunch at their restaurant the following Monday. "I know he's fucking around. It's been too many signs. He has a different smell even. Then he thinks he's gonna come home and lay up with me? He must think I'm stupid."
Rebbie and Nina offer words of encouragement to T-baby while Ebony says nothing. She knows it's very possible he's messing around. She's *seen* him doing it. She keeps in mind that her girls are still in the dark about the real deal at the medical complex. She had given Anthony her word that she wouldn't tell her cousin what she knows. She's keeping her promise to her husband. Though it's killing her inside to have this secret. Apart of her wishes T-baby would try to pull it out of her. She would probably give it all up. Or call Ajay and demand he tell her what brought on the socks to each of Rich's jaws. But for now, she holds it in. They finish lunch and head back to work.

Rich left for New York last night, without even making up with his wife. Ebony can tell by T-baby's demeanor around their office, that this has left her very sad and heartbroken. But she puts on that tough girl front like she's known to do. They get through today.

****

Reaper calls Rebbie to tell her, he's finally releasing his 1st full length CD. Rob has release parties scheduled for both of the clubs in

47

Cleveland as well the Atlanta spots. Brittany J is featured on the CD. Reaper has built quite a name for himself, down in Atlanta. He's opening for the Cash Money tour right now. And he performs regularly at college shows. He tells Rebbie he's considering dropping out of college to do his music fulltime.

"You'd better be sure about this," Rebbie tells him. "Because mama and daddy will not wanna hear that. You need to have your degree. I know we have CrewLand Enterprises. But still you have to have something else to fall back on."

His mind isn't made up completely but he confesses to her that his grades are suffering because he has to be on the road a lot. The degree might be farther out of reach than she's thinking. He tells her, he doesn't want to risk his GPA dropping below 2.5.

"You can withdraw for now. Just while you have to be on the road," Rebbie suggest. "But pick it back up later. You don't wanna put all of your eggs in one basket."

"You sound more and more like mama, every day," he says to her and they laugh. But he does take her advice. He says, "I promise I'll go back and get my degree. And tell Ally I'll be there whenever she have that baby too. I got her back. *Still*."

"She's going in soon," Rebbie says, "She's so petite and that baby is wearing on her, *big* time."

They talk for over an hour before they hang up.

****

Today Al drives out to Ajay's mansion to hang out. He loves the sports room or boys club, as he calls it. It's just outside the door to the basement party room. Ajay has a full bar, arcade, foosball game and a billiards table. He even has a ping pong and black jack table in there too. Ebony says that room and the basement is his male bonding sanctuary. It's where Ajay, Jarvis and his Cleveland team have spent a lot of this lockout season. But Jarvis has taken Gwen and Jarvis Jr home to visit family this weekend. Ajay and Al sit in 2 of the 9 large recliners, drinking beers and watching college football on a lazy Saturday while their wives shop with the rest of the ladies. All of the fathers are kicking back at their son's homes. Chill and Lil Kenny practice football out in the newly built *CrewLand Park* located in the center of Jackson Heights.

"So son, how's married life treating you?" Al asks with a chuckle.

"*Damn* good," Ajay answers, "I don't have *any* complaints."

48

TIME TO KNOW-RELOADED-Time Will Reveal- part 4

"You shouldn't," Al says, "You've got everything laid out just like you need it to be. Now when are y'all gonna get some children to fill this big ass place?"

"We're working on it pops," he says with a chuckle. "With this lockout, we've got a lot more time. So it's coming."

"I like that Jarvis wants to go *John and me,* with you," Al says as he laughs. "John and I feel honored to know that you talked to him about that. And even more honored that he wants to repeat it. Especially since it's our grandbabies he wants to match up with. Papa and my father loved it too. It's sad that Jarvis doesn't know his father very well. But we're gonna try to help him with that."

"He appreciates all the love and support the family is showing him," Ajay says, "It'll still be awhile before he gets to be apart of any delicate history though."

"Exactly right," Al says, "That's not something we're use to doing. Bringing somebody into the fray. But we already know he ain't a Jake. So we'll make it work however. Once he passes all the crew test."

"That's my wingman," Ajay says, "He made me better at Natty."

"I agree and you're doing great," Al says, "I'm proud of you. I'm glad you know your boundaries. And for damn sho, I'm glad you cut lose those dumb ass broads who was just stupid with their affection. Like this Angel bitch."

"You know that ho still calls the club?" Ajay asks.

"Chill told me and John about it," Al says, "We put some inmates on her. She don't know how deep this crew shit goes."

"I want her done, daddy," he says, "On everything. I know that ho is gonna be a spoiler. All this I've worked and built up will be done for, if she comes back around here."

"She still got nine years to go before-"

"I don't want her to make it to parole," Ajay admits, "Can't you holla at papa and the matrons about getting their contacts to silence her? I hate her fuckin ass with a passion. Out of all the ho's I fucked wit. I could strangle the life out of her, looking right into her fuckin eyes. Let's get her gone, pops."

"I suggested that but big Joshua and Charles don't wanna do it. They said that'll rain all over you. The media will make it a story. And some nosey ass, looking to blow up with a scoop *reporter* might fish out the connection. They feel it's too risky. They called looking for a story when she got beat up. None of us are gonna risk any of you. Know this."

"Shit."

49

TIME TO KNOW-RELOADED-Time Will Reveal- part 4

"I even asked them about trying it after she's about half way through," Al says, "Poppa Jones said they've got the guards working on someone to possibly set her up when her parole comes up. Or maybe even to kill her, after she gets out. So that it's not a scar on the prison. But they'll want us to pay them for it."

"I'll pay it," Ajay says, "I just feel like she might get lucky. I have nightmares about her doing something to Ebony. I just wish I'd never met that bitch, for *real*. I didn't even like her pussy, pops. I was fuckin her out of sympathy. She use to beg me to let her be wit me. And still I would tell her, *fuck you. You can give me some head but I don't wanna fuck. I'm tired.* When really, I was just feigning for Ebony."

"Son we all made our mistakes *and* had fatal ho's like her," he says. "Just be happy it wasn't something left out here that would link you to her. Like a kid."

"Ah man I would've killed her if that had happened," Ajay says, "Because I ain't never even get head without a condom. From none of them ho's. *Too date*. So if she would've been pregnant for me. It would've been on some sleazy shit she did. Like stealing the condom or something."

"I'm watching and looking at all the angles," Al tells him, "You enjoy your NBA career and just focus on your home life. She won't even get close. You've got my word. We're all watching. Rather you know it or not. And we're watching Alana *and* this white girl she brought back here too. You was raised up knowing how we always had to watch out for danger. So you know we can watch her too."

Ajay says okay but he's not letting go of his desire to have Angel's blood on his hands. He can't live down the fact that she took away his 1st child. Especially not at this time in his life when him and Ebony are trying so hard to make another baby and just haven't had any luck yet. He knows Angel is plotting daily to take Ebony's life. He's talked to Ebony's girls since they learned of the calls. He told them to stay close to Ebony. And this time, he has them watching for the unexpected. He doesn't want her bothered at all. Not even with anymore thoughts of that foul bitch.

Tomorrow is Rich's birthday. But today is his son's 3rd birthday and party. T-baby's girls are helping out. At the party's close, Rebbie is called to the bathroom to check on Ally. She's gone into active labor and is rushed to East General.

It's 7pm when she arrives the night before Rich turns 23. Steven is excited to see his child born. But he doesn't want it to have his brother-in-law's birthday. He still hasn't forgiven Rich for his domestic violence days. However he knows he doesn't get to pick which hour or day, the baby

50

TIME TO KNOW-RELOADED-Time Will Reveal- part 4

comes. He decides to bury that hatchet for now and just be supportive for his girlfriend.

Ally stays in labor all night with Steven right there with her. Subsequently she gives birth to a girl whom they name Ashanti Diavonni Brown, on the early afternoon of October 1st.

Name: Ashanti Diavonni Brown
Born: October 1, 1998
Weight: 5lbs, 6ozs
Height:18inches

Steven is excited about becoming a father. He cuts the umbilical cord, then he weighs his daughter. It's an overwhelming feeling for him. He promises his mother Sandy and his father Greg Sr, he'll graduate high school and college. He wants the best for his daughter.

Ajay and Ebony are there and they're still going to Christian her. They've already gotten the clothes and set the date with Pastor Tucker. Ebony plans to keep her every chance she gets too.

Welcome to the world......................Ashanti Diavonni Brown!

The talk around Cleveland is about the Browns football team returning for the 1999-2000 season. The crew are huge fans and this is great news to them. They have already signed on for season tickets and to host events at their businesses. June and Rich have even asked Jb to try and work out a deal for them to play at home. Jb agrees he will and reminds them, they'll have to play out their original contracts first.

Rich has made a conscious effort to make up with his wife. He was home for his son's birthday party. He tried to be fully attentive to T-baby and her needs while he was at home too. But she still wasn't willing to share a room with him. While their crew congratulates them for making up. They have no idea T-baby still has insecurities and they aren't going away *anytime* soon. Slowly she goes back into that shell she was in at the start of the year. She doesn't tell her girls she's unhappy because she's also still feeling like there are some secrets being kept from her.

****

Ajay and Ebony Christian Ashanti on the last Sunday of October.

51

TIME TO KNOW-RELOADED-Time Will Reveal- part 4

She's 3 weeks old. Ebony and Ajay have and will continue to be hands on with her. They've bought her so many things and they pay for her health insurance. They also go with Ally and Steven to get her immunization shots.

"As soon as she makes six weeks old. I want her to spend the night with us," Ebony says, "We've decorated a room for her."
Ally and Steven say that will be fine. Having Ashanti around will give Ebony a little relief from not having her own baby but not much. She loves Ashanti but still, she wants her own child.

Her real estate firm is doing very well. She has to thank her and Ajay's wealthiest supporter, Mr. Parkwood for all of his links. He's helped her to acquire some very upscale property in and around the Cleveland and Cincinnati areas. Having her real estate office open plus helping with Ashanti, keeps her really busy. Still she longs to be a mother.

November marks the upcoming listening party for Reaper. The crew are planning for it and the Thanksgiving holiday. The family will gather at Ajay and Ebony's house this Thanksgiving. Ebony is looking forward to her 1st dinner party in her own home.

The day before Reaper's listening party, June and Rich pull a Jr and Chill move. They buy matching 1999 *Navigators* for Rebbie and T-baby. The girls love their SUV's. Ebony can't help but wonder if these are guilt gifts while her and Ajay are riding to Reaper's premiere party with T-baby and Rich in T-baby's Navigator. Tank and Nina ride with June and Rebbie in Rebbie's new SUV.

The listening party goes well and opens up lots more work for Reaper. His decision to forgo this fall semester seems to have been a great move. He's doing well. His 1st single is on 400 stations across the country. The crew are proud of him for bringing music back for the family. They pledge their support and they're going to promote him too.

It's a week before Thanksgiving and time to shop for the food. T-baby drives Ebony and big mama to the grocery stores. They're meeting the other ladies so they can shop for the family's Thanksgiving meal.

"T-baby we can get everything up in this whopper," Ebony says, "I *love* this truck."
The crew ladies get all the foods and items for Thanksgiving dinner. They'll meet at Ebony's home, Sunday after church for early food preparation. She's so excited to be the hostess for a holiday get together. She remembers all of the holidays they celebrated between her parents and Ajay's parents homes. Now they're the host and hostess. This is truly an honor for her.

52

She has her family room set aside for her mother's crew to play cards in. But she's going to learn during the preparation party about 1 tradition she wasn't aware of. Or she'd never paid attention to it, at least. But today she'll learn that no women's card game will happen at her home on Thanksgiving. After the women have shopped for the foods, liquors and wines, they return with all the groceries and put them away at Ebony and Ajay's estate. Then Ajay takes Ebony out to dinner at Crew's House.

Tameka is working tonight and they sit in her station. Right away, they notice her reluctance to wait on them. Ajay calls her over to their table. He has a feeling there's something going on with Tameka and his gut tells him, Rich is involved. Tameka comes to the table but she offers no real information as to why she's hesitant about approaching them.

"Is everything working out alright for you here?" Ajay asks her.

"Yes it's great," she says, "Your grandparents are *so* nice to me."

"That's good," Ebony adds, "We want you to be comfortable."

"I am," she says, "I really love working for y'all."

"All good then," Ajay says, "You seem uncomfortable. That's why I asked. You do know you can tell our grandparents anything. Even if it's about one of us bothering you, the wrong way. Just tell them, okay?"

Tameka makes eye contact with him. Her expression says to Ebony that Ajay had hit the nail on the head. Yet Tameka still says she's fine. She takes their order and turns it in to the kitchen.

"Something's going on with her," Ebony says, "I can sense it."

"Yea me too," Ajay says, "I think it's my cousin fuckin wit her."

"Oh *come* on," Ebony says in disbelief, "*Her too?*"

"Yea. I don't think she's wit it though," he says, "That dude has been acting real strange again. I've been checking him out every since that complex shit happened. This lockout is giving me more time to really pay close attention to him and his actions. Even though his season is on. There's still some shit in the game. First I thought he was just being weird because I hit him. But it's more than that. I noticed it when we rode with them to the listening party. I don't think Tameka feels comfortable telling us what's *really* going on. She knows how loyal we are. That's all outside folks see, most of the time. But I believe he probably threatened her, baby girl. That's the kind of punk shit he'll do when he knows he can intimidate somebody. Knowing he ain't gone bust a grape."

They don't know it right now. But Ajay is dead on with his assumption. It's even worse than that. Rich has been forcing himself on Tameka, at least 1 night a week when he's in Cleveland and not off with his team. He rarely hangs with his crew and when he does, it's June or his mom and dad.

"She's gonna have to talk about it and admit it before anything can be done about it, daddy," Ebony says. "Just keep reminding her."

"I agree," he says, "I will. I hope she does. And soon."

"So do I," Ebony says. Then she changes the subject. She says, "I enjoy Jarvis and Gwen."

"Me too," Ajay says, "I'm gonna miss having them around the house."

Jarvis is in the process of building a home in the cul-de-sac. Just across from Ebony and Ajay. His family is gone home for Thanksgiving. They'll be moving into their home in the next few weeks.

}Jackson Heights{

It's the Sunday before Thanksgiving and all the ladies gather at Ebony's to prep food for the Thanksgiving celebration. They have wines to sip. Plus cheese, meat and veggie trays to munch on while they cut up foods, make pie crust, marinate meats and arrange tarts.

"Give me some more wine while you in there, Bren," Pearl says.

"Somebody's trying to get loaded," Brenda says and laughs while filling her and Pearl's glasses with more *White Zinfandel*.

"That's right," Pearl says, "I wanna be right when I get home to John tonight. So I can set it out, just right."

"Mama *please*," Ebony says, "*Too* much information."

"Baby girl you don't think you and Ajay invented getting your freak on, do you?" Pearl ask as the ladies giggle and laugh. "You married a man who's just like your daddy. So if you didn't know. John and I are still very active in the sex department. How do you think you got here?"

All the females laugh. Ebony frowns at her mother and shakes her head as if to be disgusted with the thought of her parents still having sex. But she can't help but smile. She knew they wasn't going to bed early for nothing.

"Auntie Pearl," Brittany starts, "You and uncle big John still getting busy?"

"Girl *yes*," Pearl answers, "Y'all act like we're old or something. Shoot we're only forty three and forty four and still vibrant."

"You can be vibrant *way* past forty something too, you know?" grandma Sally adds with a chuckle.

"I know that's right," big mama adds and giggles too.

"Big mama, you and poppa still, you know?" Brittany asks.

"Brittany?!" Brenda yells.

"Brenda she wants to know," big mama says, halting her youngest daughter from chastising her youngest granddaughter. "My granddaughter

54

TIME TO KNOW-RELOADED-Time Will Reveal- part 4

wants to know if her body will still yearn for a man at sixty years old. I'm here to tell her. Yes it will. Same as it does today. It's in your blood, baby."

Renee asks, "Big mama, you and poppa still getting y'all freak on ha?"

"Honey hush," big mama smiles, "After that man looks at a few of those playboy magazines. He's an animal." They all laugh.

"I love this family so much!" Tonya yells as she giggles.

Then Pearl asks, "What is daddy doing looking at girly magazines?"

"How do you think *you* got here?" big mama asks Pearl with a smirk. "You're asking baby girl. But you and John didn't invent it *either*."

"Uh huh mama," Ebony says as she laughs. "But I don't want Anthony looking at no naked women though, big mama."

"And why not?" grandma Annabelle interjects.

"He's not being unfaithful by looking," grandma Sally adds.

"But isn't he fantasizing about another woman?" Ebony asks.

"Maybe so. But who knows if they aren't already doing that?" grandma Annabelle asks.

"I buy Percy a magazine every time I see a nice one in the store," big mama says with a chuckle.

"Anthony needs to be thinking about me. Not some naked tramp in a magazine," Ebony says, "So we can go on and make this baby happen. I'm not buying him any magazines."

"Baby girl just because he looks at magazines doesn't mean he'll have desires for the women he's seeing in there," big mama says, "That's just something to get his juices flowing." They all laugh again.

"Juices or whatever," Ebony says, "We need something though."

"Everything y'all need to get pregnant you already have," grandma Sally offers, "Especially with Ajay. He's just like Al and John. He ain't never had a problem getting ready for the sack."

They all laugh hard as Ebony blushes. Then she says, "I have to agree with you there. But we've been having sex. We only got pregnant once from all of that activity. That means we need to get some help."

"Help staying in that bedroom all day, is all," Annabelle offers.

"And that's it," Sally adds.

"I'm telling them if they start messing around with that fertility drug mess," big mama says, "Like Percy told her, she's gonna end up with a litter."

They laugh very loud. Their female bonding party is very enjoyable.

"Ebony you know twins run in our bloodline, don't you?" Brenda asks. "Brina and Brandon come from our side. You know I'm a twin too."

Brenda had a twin brother. He'd drowned in a swimming pool when they

55

were 7 years old. They were on a vacation bible school trip when his death occurred.

"And we never went on another trip after that happened," Pearl adds, "We miss our baby brother. He was the youngest."

"What was his name?" Roo asks.

"His name was Brendan Lonell and I'm Brenda Lanett. I was two minutes older than him," Brenda says. Then she agrees with her sister. "He was the youngest but he was the protector of both of us, as brothers are."

"He sure was," Pearl agrees, "Jb and June remind me of him."

"It's devastating when you loose a child," Jackie adds.

"I know that feeling," Ebony says.

T-baby says, "So do I. Even though they hadn't been born. You still feel it." They're having a great evening. Drinking wines, snacking and talking about life. Old and new times. Ebony learns about a family tradition she'd never paid much attention too. She never had a reason too. Until it involved her own husband. She has an *instant* problem with it.

"I'll bet you didn't know Anthony has the men's party planned for the basement this Thursday, after dinner?" grandma Annabelle asks, "The wife is the hostess for the dinner. The husband host the after party."

"That's right. The husband is the host of the all male party, the night afterwards," grandma Sally adds, "This is your party today."

"No I didn't know this," Ebony says, "He hasn't said anything to me about it."

"See. Maybe if you would let him look at a few magazines every now and then," big mama says as she giggles. "He would be a lot more open to telling you about his male parties and such."

"I know he's not bringing no strippers up in here," Ebony says.

The 3 oldest women chuckle. They know there will be a few *fan dancers* included.

"How did y'all find out about it?" T-baby asks.

"We have an understanding with our husbands," Annabelle says, "We don't try to stop them from doing guy things. And they don't try to hide it from us when they *do* guy things."

"I have to talk to daddy about this," Ebony says suddenly.

"Ebony let Ajay be the man," big mama says, "That's the only way you can be assured that he is *your* man. It doesn't matter if he looks at other women. As long as he doesn't act on it. And Ajay won't act on it."

"Sandy and Debbie's crew are the one's who made the men go into hiding," Sally says with a chuckle, "They started with all of that being bossy and telling the men what they could and couldn't do."

56

TIME TO KNOW-RELOADED-Time Will Reveal- part 4

"And the men started keeping the party locations a secret after that," Annabelle says, "Until they'd had enough and just sent them to a different house and had their party, *right* on."

"They sure did," big mama says, "They kept right on having them. And their generation was the one's who started that, having Bachelor parties in secret too."

"Because we wasn't gonna be okay with them having sex with anybody other than us," Debbie says.

"And in one of our homes, at that," Anna says.

"Not and live through it," Jo offers as everybody laughs.

"So the reason *our* crew is catching hell trying to get in our *own* man's parties…..," Nina starts.

"…..Is because mama and her girls ran up in the parties, fighting and carrying on," T-baby finishes as they laugh again.

"Whatever it took," Sandy offers with a smirk.

"So that's where we got it from," Rebbie says with more laughter.

"See the foursome didn't know why it was so easy to sneak off to Chill's house to see Tank, Ajay, Rich and June," Jo starts.

"But we was out trying to find y'all daddy's and see what they was up too," Sandy adds.

"While y'all asses was starting a whole new set of problems," Debbie says as they all laugh loudly.

"But all in all," Belinda says, "Things like this is what keeps this crew rolling and revolving. Because they settled their butts *down*."

"Yes," Rena says, "And keeping our foot on their damn necks when necessary, helped too."

"And keeping them sexually satisfied always," Pearl says, "So we could cut down on the amount of dick the ho's could get."

"Oh my Lord!" Rebbie screams.

"My father ain't never messed with no whores!" Ebony shouts as they all laugh and finish up the prep work so the ladies can head home.

The men are hanging out at CrewLand at *Stoney's Sports bar and grill*. Ebony lets Ajay know the ladies are leaving and she needs to talk to him. He tells her, he's on his way home.

"I'll be there in a few minutes," he says.

He comes home as soon as he can get there. But Ebony waits until after they've had dinner and are preparing for bed before she inquires about the party. She asks him if he's having an all male party in their

57

basement. He gives her the details. She's still against it. He thinks he's convincing her by saying it's a tradition and a necessity.

"You know every Thanksgiving week, the guys do something like this, right?" Ajay asks her.

"No I didn't know that," she answers.

"That's because I've never been the host," he says, "But now I have my own place and well now, you know. I'm the host so it's my obligation," he says with a chuckle.

She isn't really happy about it but she accepts that the party is going to take place. Rather she likes it or not. Immediately she starts thinking of a way to foil it. They retire to bed. Ajay is ready for loving and so is she. *Sort of.*

"You feel real tense, baby girl," he says, "I hope I can work these kinks out with ease. Or is it gonna take all night?"

"I don't know," she whispers and he can tell she's pouting.

He turns her around to face him. Then he slides 2 fingers into her pussy. She exhales just before he sticks his tongue into her mouth. She receives it. They tongue kiss with heated passion while his shooting hand wraps around *Penny* and squeezes her tight. Ebony grinds her hips and fucks his fingers. He knows she's ready.

"You need me?" he asks arrogantly.

"I could use you. Yea," she answers in kind.

They chuckle and he orders her to, "Put me where you want me, ole sweet ass girl."

She goes down on him. Surprising him and taking his air at the same time. She's sucking him for *her* say in this Thanksgiving day matter. She wants to be the only woman, mouth or pussy that's on his mind as he parades whore after whore down her basement steps.

"Oh shit," he whispers and moans as she sucks hard on him.

Perhaps there's just a little aggression in her jaws too. He's only minutes from spraying but she's in it for the long haul. He pushes against her but she won't release. He forces her away from his dick and she protests. He spins her around so he can taste her too.

"I need something to do too, baby," he whispers and dives in.

They're orally fixated on each other for ten scrumptious minutes. Then they fuck like ravish beast for the next twenty five. The only thing left in either of them when their done, is very little breath. As they lay in each others arms after another night of great sex, she's consumed with how she can get his attention away from his all male party. He knows that already.

"Forget about it baby girl," he says, "I'm not cancelling the party and you're gonna be at whichever house the females gather at, until it's time for

for all of us to hook up again. But if you're still mad at me. You can fuck my brains out again, if you like. I deserve that shit. For *real.*"
He chuckles. She doesn't.
"Okay daddy," she concedes as she cuddles up close to him.
He knows she doesn't really mean that. She's not willing to allow no fucking strippers to have her man's time. And definitely not in the home he's paid for, for him and her to raise their babies in.
I found his bachelor party when no other girl in my crew found their soon-to-be husband's party. Even though we didn't get in it. I still found it. I have to figure out a way to get into this party. This is my man and my house. I'm not okay with no strippers coming up in here. Tradition or not! Fuck that!

}Thanksgiving Day{

June's team has an early game against the Bengals. All of the crew attend except for the grandmothers. Big mama, Annabelle and Sally stay at Ebony's house and cook. They invite Ida Mae Graves and Mrs. Green to come over and help. They invited Ida Mae for another reason too. Though it's against John Sr and Greg Sr's wishes, the grandmothers want her to be papa Brown's dinner companion. This is surely going to cause more tension during dinner then there already is with the male bonding party.
The crew have a great time at the game which the Ravens win. They hurry back to Cleveland with June and some of his team in tow. They go to Ebony and Ajay's immediately and dinner is served.

The grandmothers had offered the servers from the restaurant, the opportunity to serve them dinner, eat with them and make a full days pay for their work. All of the employees and their families are present. Tameka is 1 of the servers. She still acts uncomfortable. Even more so with all of the crew around. Ajay and Ebony speak to each other about her demeanor again today. Ajay inquires again and Tameka offers no real explanation. He has no doubt that she's afraid. He checks out Rich and the arrogant look he displays, every time he goes near her.
Look at his dumb ass. You'd think he'd be on his best behavior. Considering I allowed his ass to be up in here today. I need to hit his ass again. On G. P.

He knows his cousin is harassing Tameka and he's going to find a way to make it stop. Tonight after dinner, he's going to tell their fathers. He feels it's time to let them know what Rich has really been up too. And see if they can talk some sense into him before he gets himself into something *way*

59

worse than a real ass whooping from him. He has to crack a wise joke before everybody heads to the dinner tables which are set up in the banquet room.

"If any of my wife's shit come up missing," he says, "I'm gonna kill me somebody. So everybody act like you got some home training so I can stay in the NBA."

Everybody laughs. They enjoy the large home and game rooms. Until time to have dinner.

Jarvis and Gwen are still living with Ajay and Ebony. Their home across the Cul-de-sac is nearly complete. Ajay and Jarvis both wanted them to build there. The request he'd proposed to Ajay has been discussed a lot more since him and Gwen are staying at the estate. Ebony and Ajay spend lots of time with Jarvis Jr. They keep him and Ashanti often. Pearl and Jo have met both Jarvis and Gwen's mothers. While Al and John had meetings with both fathers. Al and John invited their extended families to Cleveland for Christmas and they've all accepted. Though both Jarvis and Gwen's parents thought Jarvis' plan was crazy initially. They did warm up to the idea. Only after meeting the extended crew. Jarvis' father who's name is Freddie Rhodes, has even committed to taking a more active role in their lives and his new grandson's life as well. But Jarvis believes it's only because of the NBA prefix in front of his name. Valerie Smith formally Rhodes, who is Jarvis' mother, agrees with him. Pearl, Jo, their crew nor the senior crew are in favor of the *divorced* status of Jarvis' parents. But they do promise to try and help them work through their differences. Just for the sake of their son and grandson. Valerie and Freddie's inability to get along would need to be fixed before any arrangements for a future with a crew child can be made. The crew desire newcomers to possess the type of stability they have. They demand it from any child seeking to be apart of any crew child's future. They have to start with a solid foundation all the way around, in order to build a strong relationship and expect to maintain it.

"We didn't put in all of this work on this family tree, just to have it crumble three limbs down," papa Jackson Brown had said at their very 1st meeting.

"There is a certain order that has to be maintained," poppa Percy Jones added, "They're gonna have to start there before I'll even entertain it. And that is final."

TIME TO KNOW-RELOADED-Time Will Reveal- part 4

CHAPTER 38

MIMOSA, ALIZE & CALI BUD

After all of the crew, their guest and staff are served including Jacobson's crew and Shantel, it's time for all of the females to leave.
"You ain't gotta go home-!" Jb starts.
"-But you got to get the hell *outta* here," Rob, Ced and Jr finish while laughing as the women file out of Ajay and Ebony's home.
Ebony is still against leaving. She starts her protest immediately.
"Daddy can I stay. *Please*?" she asks Ajay.
Big John starts to answer before he realizes she isn't talking to him.
"Baby girl if everybody else has to-" big John starts.
Ajay answers her with, "Baby we've already discussed this."
"*Damn*," John says with a chuckle. "I didn't know when I gave you her hand. She wouldn't be calling me *daddy* anymore."
Tank laughs and says, "Daddy they doing some *strange* stuff up in here."
"Well what do you call me *now*, baby girl?" John asks her.
She looks embarrassed so Ajay takes the liberty of answering his father-in-law by saying, "She still calls you *daddy*. It's just that mine is different. Maybe she can call you big Daddy?" They all laugh.
"No Ajay," Jb says, "Juvenile says '*call me big daddy when you back that ass up.*' So she needs to call *you* big daddy. Not just daddy."
John laughs and shakes his head as they escort the ladies out to the cars.
"Please daddy let me stay?" Ebony continues to plead with Ajay.
"Baby you're going with the women," he tries while kissing on her.
He opens the passenger door of Renee's Benz so Ebony can get in. She gets into the front seat reluctantly.
She says, "I don't like this. I don't, daddy."
"You can come back tonight if you want too," he jokes as he kisses her again and closes the door.
"Oh you better know I'm coming back," she says, "I live here."
"Then I'll have something to look forward too," he says.
"You'd *better* be happy I *trust* you," she says.
"I am," he answers quickly and kisses her again.
Renee starts the car with a chuckle and pulls away as Ebony still protest.

The females are converging on the other 5 homes in Jackson Heights until the men are done with their private party.
Big Mama, Annabelle, Sally, Mrs. Green and Ida Mae go to Jr and

TIME TO KNOW-RELOADED-Time Will Reveal- part 4

Tonya's house. They take Ashanti, Orian, John III, Rich III, Jerica, CJ, Destiny and Brad III with them.

Pearl, Jo, Brenda and Debbie along with Belinda, Rena, Anna, Sandy and Jackie go with Jessica, Roberta and Sedina to Chill and Renee's house. Roberta and Sedina are Rob and Cedric mothers. Al's sister Jessica had come with Terrell and this time, Dr. Jonathan Layton came too. He's at the all male party. The mothers are going to have a card party.

Renee and Kim's crew ladies are taking over Nina, T-baby and Rebbie's homes until their men are partied out. Tonya, Lynn, Jan and Bre plus Ebony, Brit and Erica, Roo, Pam and Chaundra. Along with Ally, Brina and Claudia, who was Terrell's date for dinner. Michelle, Shantel, Tameka and Justine are all there for their chronic, Alize and mimosa party. This leaves only the males at Ajay and Ebony's house to have their *shindig*. All of the couples will hook back up at midnight to go to the clubs or home.

Ajay gets the men together to talk before the entertainment arrives. He wants to get the Monarchs onboard and aware of the help Rich still needs to stay on the right path. Since they already had 1 talk the day he'd locked his jaws up. They needed to be made aware that he still hasn't stopped his infertile ways. While in the back of his mind he can't shake the feeling he has about the conversations between him and Ebony, this entire week. He's going to honor the family tradition and at the same time, make certain she knows she's on his mind all night. He'll get to that discussion with the fathers after he sets up the talk with his 1st cousin.

"Uncle Rich, I need you and the fathers to talk with Rich about his indiscretions," Ajay says, "Before he ends up getting us all in *deep* do-do." They all chuckle before Rich Sr, grandpa Charles and Joshua, Archie Sr and Tank pull Richie Rich to the side for a powwow.

In the meantime, Ajay pulls his father Al, big John, poppa and papa to his office to discuss the uneasy feelings Ebony has with the all male party tradition. He asks them for suggestions on how to handle it.

"I'm really surprised she's not here," Al says as him and the rest of them laugh hard. Then he adds, "I wish the ladies wouldn't have told her. She's got my son wrapped around her fingers. He's gonna sell out."

"It's not her fingers," Ajay says as he covers his eyes and they continue laughing. Before he adds, "I'm sprung though. I'll admit that."

"Keep our traditions Ajay," John says with a chuckle. "I know you was raised right. And I know you're your daddy's son and you run your household. And I know Al told you *not* to lose the few traditions we still have left."

62

"Yea he did," Ajay answers as he continues to laugh. "But it's not easy to tell her *no*. I think I got her convinced that she can't stop it. But-"

"She's my baby. My *only* girl," John says as his *Courvoisier* starts to kick in. "She's just like her mama. Don't let her spin you up in that web." Ajay laughs as he sips his Hennessy. Jb joins them and tells them the entertainment has arrived.

"I do tell her no, when it's something like this," Ajay says, "But for some reason it don't seem like it works as well as it did before we got married."

"My grandbaby knows that she's done something well enough to get a mansion. Plus *2* houses in the backyard," papa says and they burst out laughing again.

"Yea your shit is done, Ajay," poppa says, "Thanks a lot kid."
They all howl with laughter. Ajay can only laugh too. Jb has to have his say.

"Ebony done tore my partner down, man," Jb says, "He use to be the one *everybody* said would never be broken. But look at him now."

"You was suppose to be our savior son," papa says, "We knew Ebony was use to having her way since birth. But so were you."

"You just make sure you get the last word," poppa says, "You've done well so far. Don't loosen the reins. Eloise and my crew ladies, they're talking to her. They know her power. They know how you bend the world for her. So just be mindful of that. Now let's join this damn party."
They all laugh as they head back towards Ajay's male sanctuary.

"She had a point though," Ajay says as he, papa, poppa, Al, John and Jb rejoin the rest of the guys. He continues, "When she asked me would I be okay with her bringing male strippers in here."

"You're the man of *this* house," poppa says, "No way in hell is she gonna have naked men in here. That's all it is to it. This is a long standing tradition and she's gonna have to except it and get over it."

"We take care of our families," papa adds, "Every woman in this family before her, has had to get use to it. She will too. It's a crew thing."

"It's a crew thing," Ajay repeats and they go into the basement.
The music is loud. There must be more than 100 skimpy clad ladies moving about. Squirming, squatting, some dancing on the stage where there are 2 poles. They know how to work them too. The younger males are already enticing them to remove everything as they place money in their g-string underwear. They're yelling for them to, "Take it off baby!"
The ladies are obliging them quickly. The party's at a fevered pitch early and the males are loving it. Ajay feels more like a chaperone as he reminds them not do anything they can't live down, with or can be killed for.

Ebony's crew of sisters settle in T-baby's house so they can view her house from the back patio windows.

"Damn they're having a blast around there," Nina says of the party at Ebony's house. "You can hear their asses all the way up here."

"We have to get in that fuckin party," Bre says.

"For real though," Lynn adds.

"How?" Kim asks.

"Yea because they're gonna turn us around as soon as they see us," Renee says, "Trust me. Tonya, Jan, Bre, Lynn and I have tried before."

"I'll bet you baby girl can get up in that shit," T-baby says, "Cousin you can get us in."

"I've been trying to think of something but I haven't figured out what to do yet," Ebony says.

"This is some *good* ass weed," Jan says.

"That's that Cali bud, crew," Bre says.

"Watch that shit, Jan," Lynn warns, "It'll have you horny as *hell*."

"Hell yea! That's how Lynn and Jb got little Jb," Bre laughs.

"Fosho," Lynn says, "We went out there to visit after the Olympic games. Bre and Cedric had us on this shit. *Hard*."

"Next thing I know she was calling me, talking about she was pregnant," Bre adds with a giggle.

"Well pass it to me," Ebony says, "I need all the help I can get."

"I need some help too, Ebony," Jan says with a laugh before passing her the blunt.

"Y'all still shooting blanks," Rebbie says as they giggle, "It's time for y'all two to have a kid."

"It's not like we're not trying" Ebony says as she hits the blunt, "We're the only wives that don't have any kids, Jan."

"I know, baby girl," Jan says, "This shit is crazy because I know we're getting ours. Ajay and Rob use to talk about this shit when we had the apartment at the U. And neither one of us still ain't got a baby yet."

"We all know Ajay and Ebony getting theirs too," Tonya says as they all laugh. "The World! The *world* knows they fuck like jack rabbits, lions and tigers and shit."

"This shit kicks in quick," Ebony says as she cracks up laughing, "I'm already buzzing off of just two hits."

"That's that one hitter quitter," Michelle says and they laugh.

"Oh Fosho," Justine adds.

"What I tell you?" Lynn asks, "That shit's like raw oysters, *main*."

"I hope daddy got some of this," Ebony adds.

TIME TO KNOW-RELOADED-Time Will Reveal- part 4

"Oh he does," Bre says, "Cedric got some around there."

"Good because if he's horny. I know what to do to get in that party," Ebony says with a sly grin.

"He's horny," Lynn says and they laugh.

"What's up Ebony?" Rebbie asks.

"I'm gonna *show* it to him," Ebony answers Rebbie.

"What are you gonna do?" Ally asks Ebony, for clarity.

"I'm gonna go around there. Watch me," Ebony says, grinning as her voice and look is more determined and fueled by the weed and *Alize*.

"What's your plan, girl?" Nina asks and she's grinning too.

Ebony tells them what she's come up with and they all agree it will work.

"Daddy can't resist this when he's straight," she says, pointing to herself. "So if he's on this weed like *I know* he is. He's gonna be ready for some *baby girl*. He already knows I don't want that party in my house. He's expecting me to run interference anyway. I can't disappoint my man."

She giggles. Her plan is to go to the front door wearing nothing but her London Fog, her 4 inch stiletto's which have been at Nina's house since the night they went out in ho gear and her bright smile. Nothing *underneath*.

"You're gonna freeze your ass off going around there in nothing, girl," Tonya says.

"Not if Renee drives me," Ebony says.

"Alright, alright," Renee says as she's feeling the plan now. "I can drop you off at the front door. Then move my car out of sight until you're inside," she adds with a laugh.

"Ajay won't dare send you back around here," Lynn says, "Not once he sees you're not wearing any clothes. *Shit*. My brother is *way* too possessive and stingy wit baby girl to do that shit!"

"But what if he makes her put on some more clothes?" Erica asks, "And send her back?"

"He won't," Lynn says, "You're about to learn yo big brother."

"Once he see she's naked under that coat," Nina says, "He's gonna be ready to fuck, for sure. He's not gonna tell Ebony to leave."

"Hell no he's not," Lynn agrees, "That's a Jackson man! *Dammit!*" They all burst out in laughter. Some of them jump up and down, stomping and all because they know this plan is going to work.

"Baby girl you done did it again!" Jan screams, "I know it's gonna work! She always gets shit done!"

"That's because my cousin is the horniest muthafucka on the planet," Bre says.

They laugh as T-baby, Nina and Rebbie mix up more drinks for the road.

65

"That shit's gonna work crew," Kim adds, "Let's do it."
They get another Mimosa or *Alize*, then get down to the business of setting their plan *Operation Cali Bud* in motion.

Meanwhile at the all male party, the strippers are still entertaining and the men are enjoying them. Most of the men are having breast rubbed in their faces while receiving lap dances. The dancers are naked by now. Some are engaging in sex acts with crew men. Ajay isn't 1 of those crew men. The none married ones are and of course, the *usual* suspects. There are a few fathers and a grand pop or 2, feeling up strippers too. Ajay hasn't witnessed any sexual activity. Nor has he tried too. So long as they keep their activity out of his sight and in the basement apartment area. That's where the 10th and 11th bedrooms are. Ebony knows about them but they weren't included in the blue prints. Ajay had them added by request, while the building of their home was in progress. Ebony knows they're there but she'll never have to clean them. He's already instructed the cleaning staff that his wife is to never clean anything in the basement. Therefore when his teammates stay over and leave evidence. She won't be burdened with it. But that just makes her even more determined that she will check those rooms, from time to time.

As for tonight, the men who *are* in there know to clean up their evidence and yes, they all have to share that communal space. No sexual activity is allowed in any other area of the mansion. Ajay isn't watching the basement activity with eagle eyes. Simply because he really doesn't want to witness any of it. He's just making certain *he* isn't engaging. It seems like every time he thinks about fucking over Ebony. He remembers that phone call he had with David Jacobson and her laying at the bottom of Cliff View with his dead baby in her belly. That memory alone is enough to insure that he keeps his dick in his pants. All and all, the men are having a blast. They have no idea of what the girls are planning.

Jesse and Greg Jr are playing *play station* in the downstairs family room when they hear the door bell ring. Jesse runs to answer it and finds his only sister standing there.

"Hey Jesse," Ebony says, acting distracted. She asks, "Can you ask Anthony to come here for a minute please?"

"Are you alright sis?" Jesse asks.

"Yes. I just need to get in my closet to get something for Pam and Brina to wear," she says, "Ask him to come up here so he don't think I'm trying to crash his *little* party."

She steps into her foyer while Jesse goes to the basement to get Ajay.

66

TIME TO KNOW-RELOADED-Time Will Reveal- part 4

When Ajay comes up, Tank follows him. Tank heard Ebony was here and he already smells a rat. He protest the second he lays eyes on her. "You're not slick, twin!" he yells, "We got two more hours to go!"

"Stop hating, *twin*," Ebony says, "I just need to get in my closet." Ajay is just smiling seductively.

He's horny alright. That's my big daddy.

Meanwhile Tank continues trying to make his case, as he says, "Yea right, you do."

Ajay does what comes natural to him. Which is being attentive to his bride.

"What are you doing home baby?" he asks with a smile and a sexy sparkle in his eyes, as he senses that she's up to ending his part of his party.

"I need to talk to you alone for a minute," she says, peaking over his shoulder to see if Tank is still there while Ajay is already hugging and kissing on her.

"You can't go anywhere other than out with *us*," Ajay tells her. Thinking Lynn and Erica are using her to get them all out to a party somewhere else. "So if that's what you're gonna ask. The answer is no."

"She's up to something man," Tank says, "I'm telling you, bro. She's trying that bachelor party move again."

"I got this man," Ajay says to Tank, "Go ahead. I got it."

With that, Tank heads back to the basement, leaving Ajay and Ebony alone in the foyer. Right where Ebony wants him and where Ajay wants to be.

"So what's so important baby?" he asks, still kissing on her neck while knowing she has an agenda which involves him *personally*.

"I wanted to give you something," she says.

"Oh yea?" he asks, "What you got for me?"

"Just this," she says as she puts her palm on his chest and nudges him back from her.

"What are you doing?" he questions, not liking to be pushed away.

"I need you to have this *now*," she says as she opens her coat and exposes her naked body to him. "I'm horny as *fuck*, daddy," she purrs.

"Uh huh," he says and his expression changes to 1 of *definite and passionate* interest as he moves in for the kill.

He starts rubbing on her breasts and between her legs, right there in their foyer. But then realizing they're still out in the open. He wraps her up in her coat, puts her over his shoulder and carries her down the hall to their master suite.

After 15 minutes, Renee calls Tonya and the other ladies from her cell phone. She's giddy with excitement as Tonya picks up the phone.

TIME TO KNOW-RELOADED-Time Will Reveal- part 4

"Ebony is in, y'all," she says, "Come on down. It's crash time."
The ladies drive around to meet Renee. They all crash the basement party
just as the strippers are preparing to leave. Their guys don't object because
they're all high and horny by now. Or they know they'd damn well better
act like it. The fathers and grandfathers leave heading to the homes where
their crew of women are. Chill and Bruce crew's continue to party along
with their ladies. Ebony and Ajay are noticeably absent as always. They're
still in their bedroom. *Captured.*

Ajay rolls over onto his back, struggling to catch up to his breath.
They've just finished a session of lovemaking. He's quite winded but not
Ebony though. She's in rare form tonight. At least that's how it starts.
"Are you tired daddy?" she purrs as she climbs on top of him.
She's aggressively kissing his neck, ears and chest. She's breathing heavily
and acting *very* impatient.
"Give me a minute," he says, still breathing hard.
But Ebony is so wired up she can't wait for him. She takes her tongue
downward to his belly button and eventually, to his dick. She takes it into
her mouth like a pro.
"You're gonna get this dick hard again for your baby girl. Right,
daddy?" she asks in a commanding voice as she teases his dick with the tip
of her tongue. She says, "This is my dick, daddy. And I want mine."
He can't even lift his head at the moment. He's winded as he moans in
anticipation. Knowing she's about to suck him very well. She still doesn't
quit. She doesn't know what's building.
"I need some more of my dick," she taunts arrogantly.
She's *too* happy she'd succeeded in pulling him away from his party.
She asks, "Can you accommodate me daddy?"
She takes his dick to the back of her throat. That makes him gasp.
"Oh baby," he manages.
"Uh huh. Get it hard for me, daddy," she oozes, "Right *now*."
That mixture of Alize and California weed has her in rare form and digging
a hole she's about to get buried in.
"You're off the chain wit it tonight, baby girl," he whispers as he
watches her work.
"Uh huh. I want my daddy," she says from her southern position.
"I need to feel you inside me again. I *need* you."
She can feel him become hard in her mouth. This turns her on, even more.
"Oh yes daddy. That's it," she says.
She's proud of her work. She knows if he's fucking her. He's not at that

68

TIME TO KNOW-RELOADED-Time Will Reveal- part 4

party. And now that he's hard. She moves up and straddles him.
"Can I ride it, daddy?" she whispers in his ear while kissing him wildly from his neck to his lips.
"Hell yea baby," he says, "Get on up here."
He can see that she's ready and impatient. He doesn't like being the 1 *not* ready for sex. He definitely feels like he has to save face. He has to win. They both moan as she takes him into her already wet pussy. She's riding him wildly, within seconds.
"*Damn*! You're hot baby," he says, "Fuck me then. Get *all* you want."
She obliges him. For the moment, she's in control. She's rocking and riding him like she hasn't had sex in months. He watches her. He lays on his back, pushing up into her. He caresses her breasts, shoulders and her hips. He's thoroughly enjoying the assertive actions of his wife. The more of her, she gives. The more he wants now. She's giving him pillow talk drowned in tender passionate kisses.
"You taught me well, daddy," she whispers in his ear. She continues, "You taught me what you liked and how you wanted me to be. When I'm not near you, all I can do is think about your hands on me. I'm addicted to you too. I need you *so* much."
Bingo!

He comes to life in an instant. Like a metamorphosis, he regains his composure. He flips her over onto her back and dives in for the kill.
"Is this what you want woman?" he whispers as he drives his dick deep into her.
"Oh! Oh *yes*," she purrs, "Make love to me, daddy."
She pulls on him for him to come closer to her. As if they're not already as tight as they can get. They grind against each other. She's handling him better than usual and he likes that. He likes that a lot.
"Work this pussy for daddy," he whispers, "I like this shit."
He sounds so sexy to her. At the same time, her hip action has caused him to become fully aroused. She can feel the difference. All 14 inches of him is on duty. Reporting and ready to bid on her pleasure. He's back in effect.
"Let's get this pussy good and wet, baby," he whispers as he takes the nipple he calls *henny*, into his mouth and suckles it.
Pennies got next. All the while his dick is stirring slowly inside of her. She moans in anticipatory pleasure. She knows ecstasy is on deck. He positions himself so that his pelvic area can rub and massage her clit on every stroke. So it can brush up against it with every push from him. He knows her body so well. This is an action she likes a lot. He knows what to do to make her

69

Time To Know- RELOADED-Time Will Reveal 4   Black Coffee

cum. She likes her clitoris to have *plenty* of attention which Ajay *always* gives it.

"What's got you so hot tonight?" he asks in a whisper. "Ha girl?"

"I just need you daddy," she purrs. "It's all I could think about during dinner."

That's all he wanted to hear. It serves as extra motivation or *ammunition*.

"You need daddy to season this pussy for you," he says. "Don't you, baby girl? You need me to beat this shit *good* for you?"

"Mmmm yes," she says as her mind starts going out there.

She feels that familiar tingling in her upper thighs and in the pit of her stomach. Ecstasy is near.

"Oh daddy yes! *Please*! I wanna feel it," she moans, "Do it! *Do it!*"

"You ready for another one baby?" he whispers.

"Yes please daddy! Please! Oh!" she manages before erupting.

"That's what I do," he whispers arrogantly into her ear. "Pleasing you is what I do. That's my main job."

She's in ecstasy as she screams, "Oh daddy! I'm *cumin* daddy!"

"Uh huh. Get this shit wet baby," he demands, "Get it wet for *yo* daddy. Come here! Ooo shit. You hot as fuck. Yea! I like it baby!"

She's grinding out of control. But he keeps up with her. He's holding her hips in his hands as she gyrates wildly.

"Mmm yea, baby," he whispers, "This is good, Ebony."

"Oh yes! It's *so* good!" she yells.

She's still out of control with this orgasm. It lasts longer than usual and grows more intense. Rather then tapering off as he grinds and whispers.

"Uh! It's so good and wet," he whispers as he drives his dick into her like a piston. Over and over again. He whispers, "Let daddy work it out. I need to make my baby tonight while I got you wide open like this."

Now she starts to feel pain mixed with pleasure, as she tries to regroup. In Ajay's words, *"Running."*

"Uh uh. Don't run from me," he orders, "Take this dick. It's yours right?"

"Yes!"

"Then take this shit," he orders with a growl, "And stop running."

She's doing the best she can but he has always been too much for her to handle when he's giving her, all he has. She tries to move around on the bed. He follows her for awhile until he becomes impatient.

"Turn over," he instructs.

He doesn't wait for her. He flips her over and pulls her up on her knees.

"Give me some of this doggy style," he orders as he slams his dick back inside of her. "Ah! I love my pussy, baby. It don't take shit for me to get in

70

it. Not a *damn* thang! I'm always thinking about fuckin you. You know?"
"Oh! Ouch!"
"Uh uh baby girl," he whispers, "Don't cheat me. You brought my pussy home, hot as a muafuckah. You said you needed me to put this fire out. Didn't you?"
She doesn't answer. Not out of defiance but because she's bracing herself for the brunt of his girth. But he wants an answer so he takes it as defiance.
"Didn't you?" he asks again as he slams his dick, the length of her walls.
"Yes!" she screams, "Oh God! Daddy wait," she whispers, trying to calm her voice.
"Why should I wait?" he asks, being coy. *"You* couldn't. Remember? You need this dick right now. Ain't that what you said? We can fuck all night. In any position you like," he says, nibbling on her ears.
She knows he's into her so much right now and he's going for it all. He isn't going to stop until he's done. He's going to do her, *his* way. In the positions, *he* likes. He's fucking her like she's being punished. Which she *most* likely is. Not only for breaking up his party but for not doing what he told her to do. Because horny or not. She still came home 2 hours early and disobeyed his instructions. He knows when she's in the mood. But more importantly. He knows when she's trying to challenge him. It's true she was in the mood to fuck when she came in. But not anymore than she was when they woke up this morning. Or when she left after dinner. And no more than she would've been after the party was over.
"Open this pussy up baby girl," he oozes, "Let daddy make this baby tonight. You focus on taking this dick and we can get it done."
"Daddy! Ouch! Oh!" she yells.
"Take me baby," he orders, "You're gonna take it all. Every inch of it. Because it's yours."
She can't do anything now but yelp each and every time he strokes her. She has nothing left. But he's wound up again.
"Come on woman," he says, "You came home for it, didn't you? You tried to be slick? You think I don't know you're the one who can break up our parties? And I know your girls know you can too."
He grimaces and drives his penis harder and says, "Hell yea I do. So baby. Is *that* what this is?"
She can't answer but he doesn't need her too. He chuckles as he fucks her.
"I know I'm right," he says, "Who don't know I love to fuck my girl? You know I love to fuck you. Don't you Ebony? Huh? Don't you?"
"Yes," she says and her voice is hoarse and faded.
"Yea," he says, "You can get this dick anytime you want it. You

71

know that. I'll wet this sweet muthafucka any time you need me too."
He's pounding into her flesh with maximum force. He seems to know, *no end*. He's arrogantly taunting her with his questions. Knowing she doesn't have any energy left.
"Was this your plan? Huh?" he asks as he continues to work her.
She can't say anything. He slows his rhythm and pulls her up by her hair. He asks her, "Do you hear me talking to you baby?"
"*Yes*," she says breathless now with no energy at all.
"Was it *your* plan?"
"*Yes*," she admits.
"Good," he says as he goes back to work. He whispers, "Because *you're* the one who's gonna pay me for it. And I *love* your money Ebony."
She's at his mercy now. He has a mission to fulfill. His wife had come home love starved. But even worse than that. She was being conniving. He's damn well going to feed her. Plus he's going to break her from thinking she can be sly at the same time.
"Baby girl, you was straight up gangster when you came home," he says with a chuckle. "All naked and shit with this body all out for me," he whispers, "Where you at now? Huh?"
"Oh daddy," she manages.
"This is my type of action right here, baby," he says, "And I'm gonna fuck the shit outta you because that's what you need. A good fuckin will bring my baby on. You know that. *Don't you*? A good fuckin will get you opened up so my seeds can swim."
He's smiling. She can't speak. He pauses for a few seconds to kiss her on the back of her neck and shoulders. He's sweating profusely as he holds her up by her hair and arrogantly asks. "You're done?"
"Daddy I don't have anything left," she tries.
"Your con game got recognized," he says and he isn't smiling this time. "Just so you know. I knew you was coming home."
He lets go of her hair and she flops down on the bed. *Limp*. He lays down on her and continues to grind. He's kissing her shoulders, nibbling on her ears, sucking passion marks on her neck and watching her expressions.
"You know better than to come at me like that, baby!" he says in a louder tone than before. "You was all naked and shit! You can't just quit now!"
He's almost laughing as he works her. She's defeated and she knows it. He loves for her to initiate. But he always acts as if he has something to prove when she does. He's fucking her well and all she can do is scream on impact.
"I'm sore!" she tries but he isn't stopping until he's done.
"Oh yea? Sore?" he whispers, "That's it? I'm not stopping until I

I swell this muthafucka shut. Then it can hold my baby inside of here."
He's smiling. She's sliding off the bed. He pulls her right back up.
"Stop running baby girl! *Shit!*" he orders impatiently.
He becomes a little frustrated. "Take your dick, baby! It's yours! You
acting like you don't want it! You don't want it?! You don't want me?!"
She's speechless. He flips her over onto her back and reenters her for some
missionary action. He wants to see her fuck faces and witness his work too.
"I'm the muthafuckin man, girl!" he yells, "You're fuckin with the ace,
baby! That con shit?! That's still lying, Ebony. You know I hate lies."
He's going for gusto and she's done. All she can do is take the brunt of him.
"This pussy damn sho got some heat in it," he says, "You got fever, girl?
Are you running a temp or something?" he chuckles.
He's so damn full of himself right now. He knows he's the victor and he's
enjoying his spoils. His breathing is rapid as he feels his climax coming.
"Come on baby girl," he says, "Give daddy this nut! I need to make this a
good one since you was *feigning* so bad."
He pulls her hips to him. Slamming his dick into her as he works her good.
"Give me my muthafuckin pussy! Give it here! Give it to me!"
His voice grows loud. More and more impatient. He continues until finally
his 2nd climax makes an appearance. It isn't a minute to soon as far as
Ebony is concerned.
"Oh! Oooo shit yea! Ah!!!!!" he yells as he throws his head back and cums
inside of her.
His grimace is the most intense it's ever been. She screams for the mercy
that hasn't come during this *entire* session. And will only show its face once
his climax is complete.
"Take this nut, girl! Daddy doing you *good*? *Ha*? I'm giving you what you
need right? Yea that's right!"
He moans and pants as he loads her up. His body is so tense and tight, that
when he cums, he almost growls. Then he all but falls down on her. His
back rising and falling. Sweat pours from him and her too. Their bed feels
saturated. His body feels twice as heavy now as he squeezes for every drop
to be released. This session has taken a lot out of him too. He feels dizzy as
his climax peaks, then starts to smooth out. He feels lightheaded and
somewhat nauseated before it's done. Ebony has been clutching her pillow
over her face to drown out her screams. He moves the pillow so he can kiss
her lips and her face. She's spent and he knows it. He is to, as he flattens his
body out on top of her.
"*Damn.* That shit was so good," he manages.
He looks at her. She has tears streaming down the side of her face and into

73

her ears. He musters up enough strength to wipe them away.

He asks, "Are you alright?"

"Uh huh," she moans slightly with a voice that's barely there. She doesn't have the strength to talk. She's nearly asleep already.

"Damn! I'm too tired to move," he says as he lays there, still inside of her. He says, "I'm gonna lay here and marinate."

He's still dizzy and nauseous. A feeling he now realizes is familiar. In a instant he knows he's scored the ultimate shot, this Thanksgiving night. He tries to tell her.

He whispers, "Baby girl I just sent one. My baby is in there."

She doesn't hear him because she's asleep. He kisses her lips and stares at her through his nearly closed lids. He wraps her up tightly in his arms, smiles and says, "Daddy gave you his seed tonight, sweetheart. You sleep good, okay? You made it happen with your hardhead."

He smiles. He's still inside of her as he lays on top of her and falls asleep.

2 hours later and the basement party has ground to a halt. Most of the crew couples have taken the opportunity to go home for a quick sex session themselves. Plus they had to get dressed for the club. After doing so, they return to Ajay and Ebony's house to hook back up with them. But Ajay and Ebony are still missing in action.

"Do you mean to tell me those sex slaves haven't come out of there *yet*?" Chill asks as he laughs.

"Hell no," Nina says, "They probably done *fucked* each other to death."

They all laugh as Tank heads through the house and to the master suite area. Nina is with him. Tank is still making his case from earlier.

"I told my partner to watch out for twin!" he yells, "I knew she was being slick when I saw her at the door! She probably got my dog chained up, back here!"

The rest of the crew laugh as they hang out in the up and down stairs family rooms. Some make themselves drinks while Tank and Nina attempt to wake up the host and hostess.

"Hey Ajay! Twin! Are y'all feigns alive in there!?" Tank yells through the door.

"Get your ass up, Ajay!" Nina adds as she joins her husband at the bedroom door, in an effort to revive their best friends. *"Let my girl live! She can't help it if she can't be without you for a second!"*

Her and Tank snicker outside of the door.

"Ajay! Are y'all going to the club wit us!?" Tank yells again.

TIME TO KNOW-RELOADED-Time Will Reveal- part 4

Ajay wakes up groggy and realizes they've been asleep for more than 2 hours. He clears his throat and tries to speak, *"What up man?"*

"Apparently not you!" Nina yells as her and Tank laugh.

"Are y'all going man?" Tank yells through the door at Ajay.

"Yea. We have to get dressed. Hold on."

"We know that part," Nina yells back and rolls her eyes. *"Get up and come on now!"* She laughs. *"Let my girl out o' there right now!"*

"We're coming," Ajay yells back, *"I have to get baby girl up."*

"We're not waiting all night!" Nina yells.

"Get away from the door!" Ajay yells at her as he tries to laugh.

Nina laughs and says, *"I'm giving you twenty minutes and I'm coming in."* Her and Tank go back to the family room to wait with the rest of the crew.

Inside the room, Ajay is still laying on top of Ebony. He's worn out and feels as though he doesn't even have the strength to lift his own body. Eventually he raises himself up to look down at her face. She's sleeping soundly. He nudges her, trying to get her to wake up. She starts breathing hard and her face holds an angry frown. He keeps nudging her. Her reaction to his actions aren't good. She doesn't want to move.

"Baby girl we have to get up," he says and as he gets up off of her and out of bed. Then he shakes her.

"Huh? I'm tired," she says, "I don't feel good."

"They're waiting for us to go to the spot, baby," he says, "We're hosting all day. Come on and get in the shower with me."

She manages to get up and sit on the edge of the bed.

"I think I drank too much Alize," she says, feeling queasy.

"I feel sluggish too," he says, "Let's take a shower. That should help. I'm tired too."

He pulls her up off the bed and onto her feet. Then he leads her to their bathroom. She goes immediately to her toilet and starts vomiting.

"Baby are you okay?" he asks in a very concerned tone.

She doesn't answer. She only waves her hand as she vomits for more than 2 minutes. Then she says, "I don't know about going out."

"Do you wanna stay in?" he asks.

"Let me wash my face and brush my teeth," she says.

He joins her at their matching sinks. He watches her with concern, the entire time.

He says, "We don't have to go if you don't feel like it, baby girl."

"But we're the host. And crew always hangs out on Thanksgiving night," she says, "I'll be alright after a shower. But I'm not drinking no more alcohol."

75

"Sure not," he says with a smile, "You can have juice or milk."

"What are you talking about?" she asks as she starts the shower.

He grins and says, "I'm not saying, right now. I'm just gonna watch you."

They shower and get dressed. She pulls her hair up into a ponytail. She's going to wear some big hoop earrings.

"I'm so pale looking," she says, "I need to wear some foundation. Just so I don't look dead tonight."

"Okay," he says, "Don't put on too much."

"I won't," she says, "I just wanna look like the living."

They both smile.

Once they finish dressing, they join the rest of the crew in the family room.

"It's about time, *shit*," June says, "Y'all maniacs look like y'all still down for the count."

Everybody laughs as Rebbie asks, "Ebony are you alright?"

"I drank too much *Alize*," she says, "But I'll be alright."

"Alize? Yea right," Nina says looking doubtful, "Y'all done fucked each others brains out. That's all."

"Yea but she got us up in the party though!" Renee laughs.

"True that!" The females yell.

"Yea but at what cost?" Ebony mumbles.

Ajay hears her and chuckles as he helps her into her fur coat. They all load up in their cars and head to the club.

Their fathers handled the opening. The crew arrive at midnight. Once Chill and his crew arrive, they handle the adult club while they're fathers run The Spot II. Ajay and Ebony stay in VIP the entire time. She isn't feeling like hosting so her girls and their husbands do the honors.

"We're gonna head home soon," Ajay tells her, "You don't look like you're gonna make it much longer."

"I'm never gonna demand sex again if this is what I'm gonna feel like afterwards," she says as she tries to smile.

"It's not the sex that's got you feeling like this," he says and smiles.

"No," she says, "It's *your* type of sex that has me feeling like I've been in a train wreck."

"Not exactly," he says as he continues to smile, "Let's go baby."

They inform their crew, they're going home so Ebony can go back to bed. Lynn can't resist 1 last shot.

"Baby girl, we got the party crashed already," she says and laughs, "You can chill out now. We're good."

"Y'all gonna stop using my baby to do the things y'all can't," Ajay says, "Because she has to deal with me, long after that shit's over."

Ajay and Ebony get an escort back to Jackson Heights. He gets her back home and tucked into bed.

"I feel like crap, daddy," she says, "I'm sorry I ruined your party. But me coming home without my clothes, wasn't your sisters idea. It was mine. I came up with the plan. That's probably why I'm still paying for it."

"You're forgiven," he says as he cuddles up next her.

He pulls her hair back from over her eye, with his fingers as she stares at him. Then he says, "But you're gonna have to stop letting Lynn and Nina use you. You can get your dick anytime you want it. Who don't know that? But don't use that to disobey me or to break our agreements. You feel me?"

"Yes."

"They got the benefit of you doing that. Then I have to hear about it from the guys," he says, "And there's nobody *but* you who can pay me for it. *My* pussy you're carrying, is *way* to tight to pay that kind o' debt."

"I think you made that point all to clear, earlier," she says.

"You know me, baby girl," he says, "Just like I know you."

They both smile as she says, "You shook that Alize right up out of me too."

"That's not Alize, baby girl," he says, "If you hadn't had nothing to drink at all. You would still feel sick right now. *I smacked it up, flipped it and rubbed it down* up in this muthafucka," he chuckles. "But that's what it took to get your mind right. And I left you *one* heavy."

"You did smack it and flip it," she says, "But what's one heavy?"

"You're pregnant baby," he says, "You're carrying my seed."

****

The 1st week of December, Ajay gets a call from Jb. He tells him the *NBA* lockout has ended. The season will start the 1st week in January and he'll need to report to Miami for practice immediately. He's happy the season will resume. But he isn't happy with leaving Ebony at this time. She hasn't been doing well since Thanksgiving. She's pregnant and he knows it. He wants it verified before he has to leave. So today they're going to visit Dr. Weston. Ebony has been feeling bad. But she isn't overly confident that she's pregnant. She just feels like Ajay wants to give her hope. When she was pregnant before. She wasn't sick from day 1. And even though for the past week, big mama and the elder women have told her that every pregnancy is different. She's not going to say it until Dr. Weston does. Ajay didn't want to use home test at all. He wants the real thing. So that there's no more room for doubts.

They hold hands as they sit in the lobby of Dr. Gladys Weston's

TIME TO KNOW-RELOADED-Time Will Reveal- part 4

Obstetrics office. Ajay can't stop smiling. He's making Ebony blush a lot. After kissing the back of her hand, he says, "What do you wanna bet me that I'm right?"

"If you're right. I'll love you for life," she says as she giggles.

"I got that already," he says with a smile.

"What do you want?" she asks, "And don't say sex all the time. Because you're already getting that."

"Hmm, okay." Still smiling, he says, "When the test comes back positive. You have to do *everything* I request you to do to make sure my baby is born alive and healthy. Including staying off of your feet. Deal?"

"Deal," she says with a smile.

"Promise me," he says, mimicking her as he chuckles.

"I promise," she says with a smile as she gives him a sweet kiss. Nurse Tenischa calls them to come to the back. She smiles at them and says, "Today is gonna be different, lovebirds. Y'all even look different."

They all laugh and as they head to the examination room, Ebony says, "We're always going in here for a test. Only to find out it's negative."

"I don't think it'll be negative today, baby," Ajay says still smiling. Dr. Weston joins them and Tenischa in the examination room. She has Ebony to go pee in a cup for the urine test. Once done, Ebony is asked to sit up on the exam table.

"How are my favorite newlyweds?" Weston asks.

"I'm not doing as well as I would like to be," Ebony says.

"I've got to get her better before I can be all good," Ajay answers.

"Well all three of you *appear* very healthy today," Dr. Weston says with a bright smile.

"All *three* of us?" Ebony ask as she's tempted to smile.

"All *three* of you," Dr. Weston repeats.

"You, me and the baby makes three," Ajay says as he laughs and says, "I told you baby. Thanksgiving night. We pulled out all the stops."

Ebony starts to cry. Ajay puts his arms around her and hugs her tight.

"It happened. *Finally*," she says as she cries while giggling at the same time.

"I told you two, today was the day," Nurse Tenischa says, "I've been knowing y'all a long time. And I could *see* the difference. I was rooting for y'all."

They all giggle. It's true Dr. Weston's entire staff has a special relationship with the crew. But more so with Ajay and Ebony since the incident with Angel. Also Dr. Weston had made them all aware that Ajay was the 1st child she'd delivered since she started her residency.

78

TIME TO KNOW-RELOADED-Time Will Reveal- part 4

Ebony is crying happy tears while Ajay holds her tight and plants sweet kisses all over her face. His eyes are welling up too.

"I told you there was nothing physically wrong with either of you," Weston says as she tears up too and pats them both on the shoulder.

"I had to get it marinated just right," Ajay says as he leans over Ebony, who's still lying back on the examining table.

He wants a real kiss. She obliges and kisses him with so much passion. That Dr. Weston and Tenischa considers leaving the room.

Weston even asks, "Should I come back later?"

They all laugh as Dr. Weston congratulates them and Tenischa leaves the room momentarily.

"I love you Anthony," Ebony says, "I love you, so much. God knows you were *so* patient with me. I'm so happy baby."

"I love you too, baby," he says, "And I'm always gonna do what I have to do to make sure whatever it is you want, *within reason*, happens. I finally got another seed in there. My wife is pregnant!"

He yells it loud enough to be heard up the hallway.

Marshel, the receptionist, comes back to the examination room along with Tenischa, who's returning to the room.

"Well congratulations!" Marshel squeaks with excitement. "We had an office pool going. We had a bet that y'all would be pregnant before Christmas!"

"Especially after we heard about the lockout," Nurse Tenischa adds and they all laugh hard.

Marshel stays in the room with Weston and Tenischa. She wants to know all the details too. Ebony is finally pregnant and she's already experiencing morning sickness.

"*Yay*! I'm so glad the test was positive, you guys," Dr. Weston says with a lot of excitement and still a very bright smile. "I'm so happy for you two."

"It's about time," Ebony says.

"And without drugs too," Ajay offers, "*You got that*? I told you baby. I wasn't shooting no blanks."

The celebration is shorten, just for the moment when Dr. Weston reveals that there will be complications.

"Can she do this?" Ajay asks, "That's what I need to know first."

Ebony clings to him as she feels the urge to cry tears of sadness. She's expecting and bracing for bad news. Ajay smiles at her and winks his eye. He doesn't want her to get uptight.

"Oh *yes* she can do it," Weston says, "But you're going to have to

79

get plenty of rest in your first trimester, is all. We already know you're a high risk with the anemia. Plus you've gained ten pounds since I saw you in July. That's very unusual for you. So I want to watch things carefully until we can get a good ultrasound. We all want this pregnancy to be successful. So you must follow my instructions precisely. Okay?"

"I will. I promise I will," Ebony says, "I want the baby to be okay. Will the baby be okay if I follow your instructions?"

"Yes. Of course it will," Weston says, "You'll just have to be off your feet much more then you'll be on them. And this baby will be fine and healthy."

"She'll stay in bed the whole nine months, if that's what it takes," Ajay volunteers, "There won't be any chances taken. I don't even have to guess."

"I'm counting on you to make sure she gets plenty of bed rest for the next few months," Weston says to Ajay.

"You know I can make sure she stays in bed," he says and smiles.

"I want her to get rest too," Weston says as they all laugh. "Your bedroom activity isn't in question for anyone who's known you for as long as I have. I just want you to know what an honor this is for me. Ajay, you was the first baby I delivered. Now I get to deliver your first baby."

Ajay and Ebony hug Dr. Weston and promise her they will follow her orders. Their due date is August 21, 1999. They can't wait to call everyone with their good news.

They head down the elevator and to the lobby. They wait in the lobby while security brings the vehicles to the curb. Ajay hasn't stopped smiling since the announcement.

"Remember our bet?" he reminds her.

"I do and I'm *honored* to honor it," she says with a smile.

They get into his Grand Cherokee and they all pull away. He has instant instructions as they head home.

"Everybody is gonna have to come to the house to see you and say their congratulations and all," he says, "Okay?"

"Okay."

Ajay calls CrewLand with the news. He tells them to come by the house to see them both. He has to leave first thing in the morning for Miami. He isn't happy about that part. But Ebony has given her word and he knows she isn't going to take any risk when it comes to following the instructions she was given. Not after waiting over 4 years to be pregnant again.

Ebony calls April and Yolanda on a conference call to tell them they're going to be Godmothers.

"Oh God yes!" April yells, "I get to be a Godmother! I am so happy for y'all, Ebony!"

"Yes! Yes and me too!" Yolanda says, "We're coming up there to visit. Tell Ajay not to worry. We're gonna make sure you're not getting up and moving around. The first break Jb gives us, we're coming!"

"We're gonna tell him that's why we need it!" April says.

"We'll get it for sure, then," Yolanda says as they laugh.

Ebony tells them they can give the news to the Atlanta crew. That's their first job as Godmothers. They're excited as they tell her, they will. Then they hang up so the girls can get on their job of spreading the baby news.

Later that evening the crew comes by Ajay and Ebony's house to celebrate and wish Ajay a safe trip back to Miami. Jarvis and Gwen are back with young Jarvis too. They're home is complete, just in time for the season. They're waiting for the furnishings to arrive.

During this visit, Ajay restricts Ebony to the sectional on the 1st floor of the family room and he isn't hearing any excuses. He had told that to Chill on the call to CrewLand. Chill orchestrated this crew visit and made sure they knew Ebony would have to keep her feet up at all times.

This evening John and Al move big mama's things to Ajay and Ebony's house for the next morning. During the crew's visit, they organize and get her things set up while they visit Ebony and Ajay.

"Oh yes kid!.," Rebbie screams, "We've got another foursome baby coming!"

"Now it's complete," T-baby adds, "And it's about time!"

"You need to have a boy," Nina says, "So we'll have two of each."

Everybody laughs.

Then Ebony says, "It doesn't matter to us. So long as it's alive and healthy. None of our kids can date each other anyway."

Ebony's statement is a fact. In their parents crew, the only blood relatives are siblings. Unlike in Chill's crew where there are siblings and cousins. And all of the babies from Chill's crew are blood related. Except his, Arthur, Kilo and Wayne's. Even Stoney's daughter CJ, who's mother is Bre, is related to both Nina and Rebbie.

"The crew will have a lot of blood lines in another thirty years," Chill predicts, "We've got my man Jarvis and his wife Gwen, vying for that job already. These babies here are already set for life. Because our crew stepped the game up."

They all spend the early part of the evening laughing and reminiscing. Then it's time for the guest to leave. Ajay wants his last night in town, alone with his expecting wife. Everyone leaves. Jarvis and Gwen head to the garage apartment for their last night before they move into their new home.

Ajay and Ebony are finally alone. He gets up, then pulls her to her feet. Only long enough to pick her up cradle style and carry her into their bedroom. He lays her on their bed.

"Are you ready for a hot bath?" he asks.

"Am I," she says with a bright smile, "That sounds perfect."

He starts the water in the Jacuzzi and adds their scented oils and bubbles. Then he returns to the side of the bed. Ebony watches every move he makes and she can't help but smile.

"What's up?" he asks, smiling back at her.

"I believe in you," she says as they both continue to smile.

She repeats it, "I really believe in you."

"Good," he says, "I need you too. I'm so happy to know I've got a kid on the way again. I really need this change."

"Me too," she says.

"I need you to be careful and take security with you," he says, "No matter where it is. And your graduate classes are still online so that won't be affected. But your safety is my biggest concern. Just like always but even more now. Your security detail. I want them on all sides of you. If you're outside of here, take them with you. Or if you feel uneasy in here. Call them. Okay?"

"I will," she says, "I want you to have security too, baby."

"I know," he says, "I got them. But I got my gat too. I just need to know you're covered at all times. Then I can focus and play my best. So you keep that in mind and we're gonna talk everyday and night. Just like we always do. I want you to keep me informed of every change. No matter how small you think it is."

"Okay," she says.

"If you feel anything new," he says, "Call me."

"I will," she says, "I promise I'll keep you up on every change."

"Okay," he says, then he gives her a sweet kiss. He says, "I think the water's ready. Are you ready?"

"Yes."

He helps her up and carries her to their bathroom. He undresses her and helps her to get in. Then he goes and gets a Hennessey on the rocks for himself and pours her a tall glass of milk. He joins her in the tub.

"No more alcohol for me for a long time," she says with a smile, "And it's worth it."

"Are you happy now?" he asks, returning a smile.

TIME TO KNOW-RELOADED-Time Will Reveal- part 4

"Yes daddy," she says as she wraps her legs around him. "I'm *completely* happy. I'm the happiest woman alive. But I've been happy for a long time. I'm ecstatic now."

"Good," he says, "Because I'm still happy too. Soon I'll have a kid to call me daddy and you'll be off the hook."

They both laugh before he says, "Come here."

He pulls her chin to his as they get closer and cozy in the Jacuzzi. He's still got something on his mind.

"I was wondering," he says, "Should I release the pregnancy news?"

"I want you too," she says quickly. "We vowed to live and love and we aren't gonna shield our accomplishments and happy moments on account of some idiot fatal attraction. We'll just have to get her television privileges revoked or something similar."

"I want you to be comfortable with it," he says.

"I am and I'm gonna be off my feet and inside of this community," she says, "When I do have to leave. I'll have security drive me. But I meant it when I said I want you to take the same precautions too."

"I will," he says, "So I guess this'll be a news conference."

"If you want, we can do it from here," she says, "But we'll take the time and plan it."

"Okay," he says, "That sounds good."

He smiles, gives her a kiss and says, "I knew we made a baby, Thanksgiving night. I knew it. I knew just by how drained I was."

"You said it too," she says, "But you should've been. You was doing me like you was trying to fit me for a neck brace or something."

"Spanking that ass for being hardheaded," he says with a chuckle. "You already know how your man is. Don't try me. I don't care what kind of prize you're bringing me. If you disobeying me. I'm punishing it."

They both smile and she says, "I was so focused on breaking up your party. I didn't even *think* about getting pregnant. I'm scared a little bit, though."

"Nothing's gonna happen to my kid, baby" he says, "I give you my word."

She starts to kiss and caress him as she says, "My hormones are changing, daddy. Even when I feel nauseated. I'm still horny. All the time."

"You know I'm gonna help with that," he says as he starts giving her kisses. Then he says, "You know that, *right?*"

They make passionate love in the Jacuzzi. She's so into it. He loves her vibe. Afterwards he bathes her while she bathes him back. Then he carries her to bed where they have an even more passionate session. Afterwards, they share a nice late night of conversation.

83

TIME TO KNOW-RELOADED-Time Will Reveal- part 4

"Mmm," he says, "I like this pregnancy thing already. You stay in the mood."

"I do," she agrees, "I really do."

"I got big mama staying with you while I'm gone," he says, "She's going to let herself in and she'll be cooking breakfast before my shuttle comes."

"You take the best care of me, daddy," she says as she smiles.

"That's my job, baby girl," he says smiling back at her, then wrapping her up in his arms.

She snuggles up next to him and they get some sleep.

Big mama wakes them at 6am and they have breakfast together. Ajay's shuttle comes at 830am. Him and Ebony say their goodbyes and he leaves for the airport at nine. Ebony cries for the next hour as big mama comforts her.

"You're going to have a baby," big mama says, "I don't want you to cry too much and make the baby sad or mean."

Big mama chuckles and makes Ebony laugh.

"I just can't stand not having him around," she says, "I feel empty when he's not near me. Is that weird?"

"No baby," big mama says, "That's not weird. That's *real* love."

Ajay calls before his flight departs so they can talk awhile longer.

****

Tonya finishes up Cleveland State Universities graduate school of business, the next weekend. Her and Jr are able to work on their addition to the family now. Jb, who is home to do the paperwork for his future sport's agency office at CrewLand, teases them about trying to make a baby.

"Junior, you and Tonya been talking about another kid," Jb says, "She's out of school and y'all can't make excuses no more."

"We're getting to it," Jr says as they laugh and he looks at Tonya.

"Yes we are," she says, "It's time to give Brad the third, a sister or brother. You and Lynn ought to be about ready to go again too."

"Tell her that," Jb says as he laughs again.

The other reason Jb came home was to buy Lynn a Benz identical to the ones Renee and Tonya have. He takes the 96 Lexus Coupe he'd bought for her after the Olympics, as his car. He sends her Benz to crew details. It's going to be her Christmas gift. June is with him when he gets the Benz. He buys a 99 Tahoe and leaves it with Crew Details too. But the Tahoe is a

84

TIME TO KNOW-RELOADED-Time Will Reveal- part 4

gift to himself. He'd just gotten Rebbie a Lincoln Navigator, last month. The crew celebrate Tonya's graduation at the club, later that night. June has to leave for Baltimore before the party. But Rich's team has a bye, so he's at home this weekend. He's at the club tonight. So is T-baby and Tameka.

Tameka is there in an employee capacity. She works at *The Spot* after the restaurant closes each night. She wants to earn some extra Christmas cash. But tonight, she refuses to work the VIP section. This sends up a red flag to Chill and Renee.

"She always works VIP so she can get the best tips," Renee says.

"Rich is harassing her," Chill offers, "Ajay told me to watch him when we had the all male party on Thanksgiving."
Chill and Ajay have talked on this already. They're both convinced that Tameka's problem is Rich. Although they don't have any actual proof. They feel he's harassing her and possibly threatening to take her job if she doesn't comply. They don't have any idea that he's been sexually assaulting her for almost a year Because she's afraid to tell anyone.

Rich has kept a bead on Tameka's movements, all evening. Later when she goes on her break, she takes the crosswalk to Stoney's to get some food. She gets to the crosswalk, only to look back and see Rich following her. She had managed to avoid him for the last 2 months by staying at a motel, rather than her apartment. She would ask 1 of the grandparents for a ride home to avoid standing at the bus stop where he'd forced her to ride with him, several times. Tonight she's determined to avoid any contact with him. That was her main reason for passing on the opportunity to make upwards of $500 in the VIP. For less than $150 on the regular floors. Still Rich has watched and waited for a chance to catch her alone. Just like it's been for the past year. She makes it across the crosswalk, down the steps and to the door of the grill before Rich catches up to her. He demands to see her after the club closes. Tonight she says no. Rich threatens to tell the crew that she needs to be fired. She considers telling him to go to hell but she doesn't risk that.

"Rich why do you keep bothering me? I don't want any trouble with your crew or with your wife," she says, "I'm just trying to do my job here. That's all."

"Ho you work for me!" he spits, "Don't get it twisted! I'm coming to get some pussy when we close up and that's that! And you'd better go home!"
She knows she won't open the door for him if she was going to go home. Her thoughts now are if only she can just get away from him. She'd feel
85

safe. He can see that she's still not interested but still he stalks and harasses her. She tries to walk away. But before she can open the door to the grill, he grabs her arm.

"I'm gonna have sex with you tonight, bitch," he snarls, "Bring your ass through here!"

He's trying to force her into the breezeway which separates *Stoney's Bar N Grill* from *The Spot II*. But tonight she resists and makes a fuss. Big John and Al finally notice her. They see Rich pulling on her and they come outside to check on them. They notice Tameka trying to pull away from Rich. She's crying and begging him to leave her alone. The fathers tell Rich to leave her be and go on about his business. He does but he has a sour attitude about it. He goes back up the stairs to the crosswalk and back to the club. Tameka thanks John and Al for rescuing her. They bring her inside the bar-n-grill and sit her down so they can talk to her.

"Young lady you don't have to feel pressured by him," John says, "Not at all. If he's bothering you. Tell us or someone in this crew."

"We don't tolerate cheating, harassment, abuse or any of that type of shit in this family," Al adds, "Do you understand? We have daughters too."

She says she understands. Then suddenly she breaks.

"He's been doing this for a long time," she admits, "Longer than a year. That's why I always ask one of my bosses to drive me home."

"We'll check his ass," John says, "Even if we have to watch your place until he shows up."

"I've been having to spend my rent and bill money to stay at a motel," she says, "I don't want him to find me. My parole just ended and I don't want no more trouble. I don't want his wife to think I want him because I don't."

"We'll handle her," Al says.

She tells them about the past year of assaults and harassment. And that she doesn't want to lose her job. She asks them if they'll make sure she doesn't get fired.

"Your job is solid, honey," John says, "Don't worry about that."

"He doesn't have any pull here to fire you, no way," Al adds.

She's relieved and as she orders her food, she cries from the weight that's been lifted off of her shoulders. When she's calm. She eats and gets ready to go back to work. Al had called Renee and told her to give Tameka as long as she needed for her break. Then him and John watch as she walks back. They notice Rich and T-baby waiting just to the other side of the crosswalk. Before Tameka can get back into the club, they confront her.

TIME TO KNOW-RELOADED-Time Will Reveal- part 4

Rich has told T-baby, he had words with Tameka. He made it seem as though Tameka wants him and was hitting on him. He doesn't know that Tameka has finally told someone about his indiscretions toward her. T-baby is ready to fight Tameka. But Al, who had walked up behind Tameka as she was going back to the club. Tells T-baby not to bother her.

"Tameka did *nothing* wrong," he says, "And you're not gonna bother her. We saw her, the whole time."

He's looking directly at Rich who now fears big Al will tell T-baby what he witnessed and what *really* happened. Rich decides to calm his wife down and get her away from there.

"It's cool Trisha," Rich says, "Let's get out of here and go home so we can handle our business, baby."

He's playing her for a fool and they leave without T-baby knowing the real truth.

The next day Jarvis and Gwen finally move into their 3300 square foot home. It's a week before Christmas and it's just in time for both their parents to visit. Mr. and Mrs. Lance and Edith Russell, Gwen's parents, have come out to help them get settled in. They're planning to stay through the Christmas holiday. Jarvis' mother arrives today as well. His father will be in tomorrow. Jarvis and Gwen have 6 bedrooms. There's 1 in their double garage apartment, similar to Ajay and Ebony's.

Mr. Freddie Rhodes arrives the next morning. To Jarvis' surprise, everyone opts to stay at his house. He thought surely his father would want to stay as far away from his mother as possible but that's not the case. The crew must be affecting some change on him. Either that or Jarvis' 3 million dollar per year salary is the reason. Everyone gets along fine on the 1st day.

Jarvis and Gwen have dated since high school so their families are *very* familiar with each other. They're from Anderson Indiana. Gwen's sister Nickeia comes up to visit along with their parents. She's going to help Gwen and their mother complete the wedding arrangements for Gwen and Jarvis' public nuptials. Nickeia still has that serious crush on Ajay. She's had it since she was in 8th grade. Back when Jarvis signed his letter of intent with Cincinnati in Fall 1992. She's 18 years old now and hopes Ajay will see her as a real woman. Not the little girl she was when him and Jarvis first met. Gwen has no idea her sister is after Ajay. She knew of the crush but she thought that was long over. Her and Jarvis have decided to keep their wedding date in February. Because now that Ebony is pregnant, she would be too far along to participate in a June wedding. They still have to run the new date by Ajay because he hasn't said he's going to be okay with Ebony

87

being on her feet, even in February. But he's off with his team and won't be home until Christmas week.

The Jackson Heights beautification and decoration crew come out and decorate all of the homes and the community for Christmas. It's very beautiful when they're done.

At Ebony and Ajay's mansion, they go all out. Ebony loves their 30 foot tree which is in the family room. It extends the full 2 stories. Ajay has already said he's going to use the window cleaning crew to help him put the star on the top of it. He's looking forward to having to use a lift to reach the top of his holiday tree. That's something he's dreamed about for years. Ebony is just excited that he'll be home for their 1st Christmas and their 1st anniversary.

TIME TO KNOW-RELOADED-Time Will Reveal- part 4

CHAPTER   39

NOT ALL ABOUT SEX

Ebony and Nina turn 23 and the crew have a wonderful Christmas 1998. Ajay comes home for he and Ebony's 1st Christmas as husband and wife. He has practices to report for, during the week. Then he'll return for their 1st anniversary. Ebony spends a lot more time in bed, these days. Ajay isn't unhappy about that part in any way. But Ebony *has* noticed a difference in their love making sessions. He treats her more timid now, then he did before. And he doesn't seem to want her to give him head anymore. She hasn't sucked his dick since the morning before they visited Dr. Weston and got the positive pregnancy test report. He's been home 3 times and he hasn't requested it. But he's still eating her pussy during every session. And afterwards, it's like he rushes his dick inside of her before she can grab hold of his dick. During penetration, he's not as commanding as he use to be either. He isn't giving their sex sessions nowhere *near* the force he'd used on the night they made the baby. But he's still *very* attentive to her. It's evident that her comfort and what she consumes is Ajay's biggest concern. He's just not the Anthony who dominates the bedroom. She's going to find out why. Maybe not on this anniversary trip but very soon.

The crew comes by to visit them before going to the club, for the New Year's Eve party. Once they leave, Ajay and Ebony bring in the New Year at their home with Ike and Tina. Ebony is past her 1st month and doing well. But she's still having lots of morning sickness and discomfort.

"You keep getting your rest baby," Ajay says, "We worked *too* hard to make this baby. We're not taking any chances. Okay?"

"Okay," she says, "You don't have to worry. I'm gonna stay in the bed. Or here on this sofa. I'm tired *a lot* now anyway."

She assures him she's going to follow his and Dr. Weston's orders. He won't have to worry so much while he's away. Though he still will.

Keeping with the traditional anniversary gift which is paper for the 1st year. He gives her the deed to their home and the 50 acres it sits on. He has it framed in a authentic gold case with crystal glass.

"This house and the land it sits on, is yours," he says, "And I really appreciate you letting me live with you."

She giggles and says, "This is *our* house, daddy. You're always giving me *way* too much. This is ours *together*. It was fine with both our names on it."

"This is for you and my kids, Ebony," he says in a serious tone. "And just so you know. My stipulation for myself is that I have to be on my *best*. So if I wanna live with you. Then I'm gonna have to do right by you."

"I wouldn't put you out," she says with a sly look on her face. "No way would I send all of that away from here. You'd have to sleep on the third floor until I'm in the mood."

They laugh hard. He looks into her eyes as he pulls her hair back away from her face.

"That would be hell," he says, "You would have a problem outta me. I'd be breaking into the master suite *twice* a day. I'd come in there on my knees. Ready to lick and stick my way back into bed with you."

"And it would work too," she says as she continues to giggle. "I could never tell you no. I want you to know that. You started out putting so much time into making sure that I was satisfied. You wanted me to like what you was doing. Well I've grown to love it. Don't change it and I won't ever, *not* want you to make love to me. I'm always gonna be willing to give you, *your* juicy. Like *Biggie* said *'so if you don't know. Now you know.'*

They laugh again. Then he says, "Now you know how I feel."

She looks into his eyes. All of the passion she'd seen before is still there. All of the concern for her happiness and her comfort is still there. Maybe he was just distracted about the end of the lockout, the last time they had sex. He could be worried about whether his team can get it together well enough, in this half season to make the playoffs and he just hasn't felt like talking about it yet. He seems fine right now. He reaches into a small velvet bag. He has another gift for her. A full carat pair of diamond earrings.

"Oh Anthony!" she says, "We agreed we wasn't gonna buy any gifts. We was gonna be each others gifts for our first year."

"I said *that*?" he asks, looking goofy.

She laughs and says, "Yes and I'm so glad I didn't fall for it."

She opens the drawer of the end table which sits next the large sectional.

"I got you some paper too," she says as she smiles.

"Oh wow," he says as he waits, not so patiently, for her to pull the papers from the leather envelope.

He asks, "What in God's name did you get where the paperwork comes in a leather envelope? You can just give me the envelope."

They laugh as she unfolds the papers. She hands him 1 sheet at a time.

"What's this?" he asks as he reads aloud. "A cancelled check from mister Bert Parkwood's company for how much? Whoa!"

"It's been cashed already," she says, "That was the commission I earned for two property sales. I can make money from home. It's great."

"Uh huh. *And*?" he's smiling as she unfolds the next sheet.

She says, "This is what big Brian and big Rich helped me to spend it on."

"What?" he asks, looking at the next sheet. "This is a car title for," he looks at her, then he says, "A *Jaguar*, baby? You bought me a *Jag*?"

"I leased it. Yes," she says and smiles.

"A Jaguar," he says again. "Baby you must want me to pull ho's?" They crack up laughing. He examines the title and she hands him a picture of the car.

"*Damn*! A convertible Jag. *Oooo Weee!*" he yells as Ike and Tina's ears stand up and they look at him.

They're prepared to run after something or someone. He rubs their heads to calm them down, as he says, "Carolina blue convertible Jag. Two seats."

"Yes," she says, "And I know if this is a boy. I won't have a seat." They laugh again before he says, "I'll have to teach him how to drive. Then put you in my lap. That's how my pops did when he had that *Saab*." They continue to laugh and she asks, "So you like it?"

"*Hell* yea," he says, "I love it, baby. Come here and give me some of that sweet sugar."

He lays a passionate kiss on her and she hands him the keys.

"It's here?!" he asks.

She says, "Yes. It's in the boat garage. Since we don't have a boat. I had them to hide it in there so you wouldn't see it before I could surprise you."

"I'm starting to like surprises," he says as they laugh hard again and he says, "I love my gift baby. And I love you."

"I love you and my gifts too," she says, "Now take me for a ride in the whore magnet before the groupie slob gets all over it."

They laugh and he adds, "That's a date. Let me pull it up to the main door. I'll be back in to get you. You get door service *and cradled* for this one."

She smiles as she watches him head toward the back portion of the house.

"I'd settle for you fuckin my brains out," she says to herself.

He doesn't hear that part. He goes out to the boat garage where his 1999 convertible, baby blue *Jaguar XK8* sits. He loves his car. He hops in, starts it up and pulls around to the front of the mansion.

"My woman done got me a sports car," he says to himself, "She trust *the hell outta* me."

He smiles as he heads back inside to get her. He takes her and their twin Pekinese for a joy ride up the Shoreway expressway and back down again.

After the ride, they head back to the mansion. He wants to spend time holding his wife before he has to fly back to his team. She's all for that and she can't wait. She still hasn't mentioned his change in sexual behavior. She won't do that tonight either. She's decided she'd rather wait and bring that up to him when he first gets in town. That way, they have time to talk,

91

disagree and agree. Or agree to disagree. All in all, she just wants to know why he's fucking her differently but still holding her the same.

}*The Chill spot{*

No Ebony and Ajay milestone could be complete without some outside interference from the usual suspects. Darlene, Farah, Alana and their group are clubbing. All the while, Darlene is watching the access to VIP while looking overhead at the glass wall. She's so sure Ajay and Ebony are going to be here.
Of course they're gonna hang out with their family. It's their anniversary.

Wrong. Darlene never knew Ajay. Not the real 1, anyway. Not the Ajay who loves hard and looks forward to spending every free minute he has with the love of his life. She was never his woman nor his love. So she *couldn't* know. She only knew the Ajay that stayed in the streets, sold drugs, hustled and fucked ho's while she waited and hoped he'd fuck her.

Another Ajay milestone crasher is Angel Taylor. *Prison Angel.* She decided to make her presence known in the club tonight too. Not only does she want her *Ajay fix.* But at the same time, she's set out to show Alana and Farah that she doesn't fully trust the 2 of them to handle her agenda. Tonight she sends her cousin, James "The Bulldog" Taylor to make contact with Ajay. It's obvious her and Darlene knew Ajay, about the same. Angel's cousin James is a body builder who strips at some local spots in Ohio. He dances and lifts weights. Basically, that's it. Angel has convinced him that Ajay led her on, fucked over her and then dumped her for his debutante, Ebony. James already thinks he's a bad ass. But he didn't grow up in Cleveland. He wouldn't know about the crew. He has no idea about their lethal force or reputation. The crew are so made, at this point, they don't even have to do their own dirt if they don't desire. There's always someone auditioning to knock a nigga off, just to prove that they'll be loyal to Chill and his crew. So that tight ass that James has been shaking for dollars. And the pretty boy mug he can't keep out of *"any"* mirror USA. Could be rearranged for something as small as free admission to *The Chill Spot.* And if Chill was to throw in free drinks, the job seekers would give him a bonus by uploading James' demise on *Youtube. The Bulldog* and his arched eyebrows are barking up an unshakeable tree which his fatal attraction ass cousin didn't bother to hip him to. Or the world he was sashaying into. That bitch Angel is loyal to no one but Angel. All she wants is what *she* wants. And she doesn't give a damn about the cost. She hasn't rehabilitated any. She never considered or cared that she was sending her cousin *and his nuts* into a full force and irreversible *meat grinder*. The Bulldog brought his girlfriend Julie Von Reese along with him tonight, to check things out. He plans to get the lay of the place before making his move.

Keep in mind this crew already has the inside track on Angel. Every time she gets a visit. The crew get a name. Every time she has a call. The crew are informed of any particulars which involve them. So when this rump shaker showed up. He was already recognized as a visitor on Angel's visitors list. The crew had the low on Mr. stripper man before he'd even talcum powdered his balls for the club tonight. So when he started asking *21 Questions* before he had even gotten partially processed through the door. That put Wayne on high alert. 1 question he asked while being signed up for his frequent *clubgoers* card was, "Is Ajay and his wife in the club tonight?"

From that, Wayne hit Chill up. Just that 1 question alone caused Chill to have Arthur to run a background check on The Bulldog. Thinking he might've been connected with big Jake Johnson's clique and could've possibly sought out Angel after knowing she'd had a run in with the crew. From the time James waltzed in thinking he was inconspicuous and could play himself off as an overzealous fan. He was being monitored. Oh sure, Ajay *is* a celebrity and in most eyes, so is Ebony. And 90% of the folks who frequent CrewLand Enterprises are hoping for a spotting or a chance to met Ajay Jackson. But fans of Ajay Jackson don't come up asking for Ajay *and* his wife. Just like the crew, Ajay's fans know he's a possessive ass man who doesn't want any man inquiring about his woman. Even without that. The crew are going to be extra cautious. Because of their decade old beefs. And also after knowing Angel has been trying to find someone to fuck with Ajay's misses, for many months. So when it was time to put the double oh seven to work. Who did the crew look too? None other than Arthur *"The money shot"* Owens.

Arthur is a crew treasure. He's technology savvy and a genius with the lens too. Arthur had The Bulldog's info, right down to his social security number in a matter of 1 hour and 27 minutes. The amount of time "The Bulldog" had been in the club. By 3 hours in, the crew put the word on the streets of his relation to the same bitch who's death certificate they want stamped. Even if the crew didn't have insider information. The Bulldog wasn't ready for them. He was on some bullying shit. Like Ajay was going to run or bow to him. Without the crew, that wouldn't happen. The Bulldog is a rookie who doesn't realize the size nuts he'd need to have for the g-string he's looking to sport. And if he decides to piss on the wrong grassy knoll. His toe tag request form will be ordered. If it wasn't for Ajay being in town to visit. Chill would've had him killed tonight. Just to send a strong message to Angel Taylor or whomever really sent this clown, that the crew hasn't lost *shit*. Nevertheless, *The Bulldog* has been discovered and plugged. He's no longer anonymous to *any* member of the crew. Last step for tonight was when Chill sent Ajay a text message before closing up. *There goes the element of surprise Bulldog!*

}*Jackson Heights*{

It's morning in Mr. Anthony Jackson's neighborhood. Chill had sent Ajay a text message to hit him up before he got out of town. Ajay responded by inviting Chill and big Al to breakfast. Big Al brought big mama with him. She makes breakfast while Ebony sits in the recliner, Ajay had moved into the kitchen for her. The 3 men meet in the parlor by the sanctuary. While the ladies bond in the kitchen.

"I had to let you know. Angel sent some pussy ass negro to the spot to look up you and baby girl," Chill says, "And I've checked him out. It's all about Angel and not that Johnson bullshit."

Ajay looks at his father impatiently. Al holds his hands out, signaling for Ajay to just hear Chill out.

Chill continues, "This nigga is green, Ajay. He's on some *Bruce Leroy* type of shit and his ass is *Vanity*."

Ajay can't help but laugh at that reference to the film, *The Last Dragon*.

Chill continues, "He's a male dancer. *A stripper*. He's actually been asking around to see where Ebony likes to go. The streets got back to us before quitting time. We got this shit, *lil* brother. I would've done him last night. But I didn't want no type of shit to shake out that links to that rat bitch, Angel. Not with you in town, that is. I got that little bit right there, straight from our father here. He told me not to do anything that could be construed into a retaliation from you. He said that, before last night even happened. So I was on mine."

"I almost thought this guy was smart and came out on a club night when he knew you was in Cleveland, to keep *from* being killed," Al says, "Like he knew we'd err on the side of caution and not do a deed when you didn't have an alibi. But I'm hearing it was nothing like that. He wasn't tactical nor intelligent."

"This guy. James Taylor is his name but he goes by *The Bulldog*," Chill says, "He acts like this is about a fight at the playground, Ajay. He ain't no killer. He's got a white girl with him. Julie Von Reese. But she's loyal to crew. She was on the track team with Lynn. She overheard him selling wolf tickets at an after party in Lorain. She latched onto him. Just to

94

peel him back and see what his plans were for Lynn's crew. Then she let us know. I put *money shot* on it. Julie got right at Renee and told her, she felt like he was gonna try and start a fight with you. She told Renee, she remembered her as a good friend of Lynn's. It seems Lynn beat a bitch off of her, back in high school or something. Lynn said she's been loyal since then. And she's gonna hold us down because Lynn took up for her."

"I know who you're talking about," Ajay says, "Lynn beat Addie Johnson's ass for trying to bully her. Addie is ole dead ass lil Jake's cousin. They put Addie off the team to settle the fighting and Lynn stayed on. That's because Lynn was miss Ohio, in Track. Okay yea. I remember Julie. She ran cross country. She almost made the Olympics too."

"She gave Renee *her* number for Lynn," Al says, "She gave her The Bulldog's number, for us too. Chill already got Kilo and Arthur linking up to it so we'll be able to track all of his conversations."

"I had Renee to put a grand on his phone bill," Chill says, "That way, he'll be sure and keep the shit on until we can do away wit him."

"In the meantime," Al starts again, "Julie is going to be our ears. Whenever The Bulldog mentions you or Ebony. She's gonna report it and she's asking him to get her on the visitors list for his cousin. So she can be there on those visits too."

"So y'all think that's all valid?" Ajay asks, "Because I can't have no *maybe* type of shit. My baby's pregnant. We all know how vital it is that she be okay. And we all know how much that bitch would like to change that. *Again.*"

"Yes we do and Ebony will be safe," Al says, "If I have to put a bullet in his head in the middle of Richmond Town's food court."

"And he won't be alone on that hit," Chill says, before getting back to the point. "Ebony won't leave Jackson Heights unless she has the Presidential security. And only at a time when you can be on the phone with her. Is that gonna be enough?"

"I'll call Lynn," he says, "She's gonna hook me up on three way with Julie. I wanna hear her voice. I wanna hear if she's sincere. Then I might relax a little."

"Done," Al says while dialing Lynn from his cell phone.
They set up the call for Lynn, Julie and Ajay. Then adjourn the meeting just in time, as Ebony yells, "Breakfast is ready daddy, daddy and Chill!" They all chuckle as they head to the breakfast nook.

They have breakfast, then Ajay has to leave. Al and security take him to the airport while big mama stays with Ebony. Chill heads home to work up a plan for James "The Bulldog" Taylor's demise.

Ajay's team plays and wins their 1st game on the 5th of January. While he's away, he and Ebony talk every morning, afternoon and before they slumber, each night. Every break he gets. He calls her. Today he calls just to show that he's always thinking of songs he'd like to dedicate to her.

"I'll be home soon," he says, "And when I come. I've got a song I wanna play for you."

She smiles and says, "Okay. I can't wait."

"Yea but I know you will though," he says and they laugh. Then he says, "I miss you a lot. The scenery has really gotten boring down here."

"I know baby," she says, "Jb's working on that option, so you and Jarvis can play together again. But if you early out. You have to pay them. And as your financial advisor. I'm not advising that."

They laugh again and he vows to take her advice.

"You have never steered me wrong, baby," he says, "Our home is a huge tax write off and every car we get, we'll lease them. Instead of buying, from now on. You was dead right with that one too. It's a lot better that way. We'll only buy the ones we wanna keep and restore."

"Got it," she says. Then she switches her gears and says, "Jb also told me to tell you that he's setting up the press conference for the next time you're home. The media is lurking outside of Jackson Heights, daddy."

"I know they are," he says, "They're hounding me too. They smell a baby. That plus the streets are talking about how Angel killed the first one. That's what's making it a media event."

"And the word got out that her relative has beef with you and I," she says, "I hear whoever he is, he's been going to our club asking for us." She's talking to him over the phone about *The Bulldog,* as if neither of them know anything about him. He plays along too.

"I heard that too," he says, "It's got mister Parkwood bothered."

"He called me too," she says, "He said he would be up to visit, the next time you're home. He wants to be here for the press conference."

"I can't wait," he says, "I know he's got a solution."

"Big mama said he's the Jeb Baker of our crew," she says and he giggles.

"Based on all the stories we've been told," Ajay says, "Rebbie's great-grandfather was a hell of man."

"He sounds a lot like *my* man," she says.

"Saying things like that, will get you anything you want," he says. They laugh together. He has to hang up and head to practice. She settles in for another nap. She's thinking about nothing but him and their future, as she smiles and drifts off to sleep.

TIME TO KNOW-RELOADED-Time Will Reveal- part 4

With Ajay being a professional athlete and a damn good one. Plus a celebrity to fellow Clevelanders. Any and everything he does is news. So the fact that he's about to become a father is big news too. With this new news, the drama about their 1st attempt is back in the headlines as well. Unfortunately, so is Angel Taylor. There's even talk of a reporter trying to schedule an interview with her from prison. Thus she finds out about Ebony expecting another baby. As soon as she gets word of it. She doubles up her call time and her persistence in calling the club. Chill has put her on alert for the last time. Still he's bidding his time with her. She calls the club just before opening. Chill answers and gets right to the point.

"This isn't a wise thing for you to keep doing," he tells her, just as he had on several occasions. He says, "My crew has no patience for you. I would advise you to move on. This is the last time I'm going to advise you." She would only skip a day and call again on the 3rd day.

Ajay decided to do the press conference while he was on the road. The media had gotten so persistent that it was cutting into his ability to focus on his game. The owner and coaching staff had asked him to *please* give them a statement. Plus Ebony told him, not only were they still camped out outside of Jackson Heights. But they had found out 1 of their house phone numbers and was calling nonstop. He does the press conference and fields the questions about Angel's crime, very well. Ebony smiles with pride as she watches him on their bedroom TV. He calls her as soon as he leaves the podium.

"So how was I?" he asks.

"Perfect," she says, "You did wonderful and the phone stopped ringing too. Except mister Parkwood. He's still gonna meet you here. His wife Barbara is coming too. He's already called Wheeler. Their gonna set up the meeting and bring his wife Trina Yvette. Do you remember her?"

He laughs. Then he asks, "Should I?"

"You know you do. You and Tank was checking her out and telling everybody how fine she was. And *so much* younger than him," Ebony giggles and adds, "She *is* a lot younger than him though. She was watching you hard too. That was at your appreciation dinner. The one at the Downtown Marriot."

"Oh yea," he says and laughs, "Yes I remember her."

"Oh I know you do. And she told me if I ever needed some time off from *taking care* of you, to let her know," Ebony says as she still giggles. Ajay laughs and says, "*Shit*. And have Wheeler sending my ass to the gas chamber. He got him a young fine ass wife and she'll cheat, baby girl."

97

"I know she will," Ebony says, "Especially when she told me, she wants to be my back up."

They both laugh and she adds, "She's an investment attorney and she represents Parkwood Enterprises. But she wants to open up a branch in my office."

"*Really*?" Ajay asks in a serious tone. He isn't liking where this is going. He says, "You know she wants to hit me."

"Uh huh, I know," she says, "I'm not insecure and she knows I'll get rid of a bitch for trying to get in my space."

They laugh hard and he says, "I'll let you make that call, Ebony. Just be careful. Okay?"

"Okay."

"And she can't come to the house *without* Wheeler," he says with a chuckle.

"Okay," she says and giggles, "Well she'll be here for the meeting. Parkwood said him and Wheeler are setting it up. They're gonna talk to you about how to get murderess Angel out of our lives."

"Good," he says, "It'll be well worth having Trina Yvette there, undressing me with her eyes all day, then."

"Uh huh. I'll undress you in the rest of the ways," she says very seductively. "And take care of those needs, she'll be fantasizing about."

"My dick's getting hard and it's people out here," he says, not trying to stop her from talking sexy.

She stops herself because she knows her man. He'll have this conversation with her while the camera's roll, if she keeps at it.

"We'll finish this when you get to your room," she purrs.

"I'll call you as soon as I get there," he says.

He has to finish his press assignments and have a meal with his teammates. Then he'll get on to his hotel room.

He says, "I'll see you soon."

"Okay," she says, "I love you, daddy."

"I love you too," he says, "In a minute, baby girl."

"I'll see ya," she says and they hang up.

}*CrewLand Mall*{

Later in the month of January, while working in his office in the middle of the afternoon, Chill's club line starts to ring. This is usually the time when Angel would call and she only has the main number for the club. But when he looks at his caller idea expecting to see a strange cell phone number, which is how Angel usually calls for free. He discovers it's not

Angel, this time. The call is from Captain Wesley Jermaine Stewart. His wife's youngest brother. He grabs the receiver quickly.

"Hello?" Chill answers.

"What's up, big Chill?" Wesley asks.

"Nothing much, man! What's going on?!" Chill replies jubilantly.

"I need to ask you a favor," Wesley says.

"I know it's not money because you handles yours, very well," Chill says as he chuckles. "But you can get it though. So what's happening and how's that baby girl?"

"I'm looking into moving there and building a home for me and Jada Renee," he says, "I want my daughter to be closer to her namesake and auntie. Jada is great, man. She's looking forward to seeing her first cousins too. I wanted to know if you could help me out with finding some property near you."

"Oh for sho, brother-in-law," Chill says, "I'll get you in touch with Ebony. Ajay's wife. She can hook you up, right out there on our street."

"Ajay's doing his thing down in Miami. I see him and Ebony are still hanging in there," Wesley says with a smile. "When we was younger. He was a mean ass dude who could play some basketball. He didn't want nobody to look at Ebony then. I saw some footage of their wedding too."

"He hasn't changed," Chill says as they laugh. "He just got richer, that's all. They're expecting a baby in August."

"*Wow*," Wes says, "I wish them the best. I heard what happened with the first one. Ebony is beautiful. All those ladies are nice looking. So my big sister fits right in."

They laugh and Wesley continues, "I remember Ebony's cousin too. I liked her style. I was checking her out when I came for the wedding. She smiled at me a few times. I've thought about her every since the first time I saw her. Even after Paula got pregnant and we got married. Otherwise, I would've *been* said something. I see where she married that knucklehead who plays with New York. I'm still keeping up with her. But keep that between us," he adds and laughs.

"No problem," Chill says, "For now."

They laugh. Then he takes down all of Wesley's information for Ebony.

"So my nephew is going to the NFL too?"

"Hell yes," Chill answers and laughs. "He's got it, brother-in-law."

"I can't wait to live there. You know I'm a sports nut," Wes says, "I appreciate you looking into this for me too."

"It's as good as done," Chill assures him, "It's damn good to hear from you."

"Same here. I want the move to be a surprise for Renee," Wes says, "Her and I were always the closest of my siblings. I wanna be close to her when I retire."

Chill says, "That'll be wonderful for Renee too. It's gonna lift her spirits to have one of her blood relatives close to her," he adds.

They talk for several more minutes. Then Wesley tells him he's going to call Renee. They hang up and he dials his sister immediately.

"Hi Wes!" Renee says, looking at the caller ID, "How are you?"

"I'm doing pretty good," he answers, "I'm coming out of the Army and putting my degree to use."

"I'm glad to hear that," she says, "How's Paula?"

"We're getting a divorce," Wes reveals.

"Oh Wes. I'm sorry," she says.

"I'm not," he says, "She's been having an affair for the last three of the five years, we've been married. She moved out over a year ago."

Renee expresses her sympathy and disappointment in her sister-in-law.

"How's my little namesake?" she asks.

"Jada Renee is doing great, sis," he says, "She's five now and as smart as a whip. How's my nephew Kenny and my niece Destiny?"

"My babies are doing great," she says, "They have their own spot to hang out in now. And Kenny is *so* protective of his sister. Just like you."

"I can't wait to see him," Wes says, "He's fifteen and a superstar. Jada loves to talk to them. She wants to see them, other than in pictures. We're going to fix that, real soon. Jada wants too. She knows she's got a girl cousin and she wants to grow up with her. She's a little lady."

"She takes after her auntie and namesake," Renee says as they giggle. "Wes, you was always on the honor roll and winning science fairs, spelling bee's, you name it. She has no other choice but to be smart. Her father was high honors, all through high school and college. I'm so proud of you. Even though you made a baby at seventeen. You still went in the military and got your degree too."

"Just like my big sister," he says, "You had Kenny early. But look at you now. You're a college grad and a multi-business owner."

Wes' daughter was born on Renee's birthday, November 21 of 1993. Wes and his wife Paula named her Jada Renee Stewart. The middle name after her aunt Renee. The 1st name after their favorite actress, *Jada Pinkett Smith*. They picked their daughter's name on the same day they found out they were having a girl. Her being born on Renee's *actual* birthday was the icing on the cake.

"When are you coming to visit?" Renee asks.

"Jada and I will probably be coming later this year," he says, "If everything works out."

"That's great. I can't wait to see y'all," she says. They talk for over an hour before they hang up. Renee goes about her day, singing and humming *Tre's* parts of *Family Scriptures* title track from the album with the same name. From Cleveland's own, *Mo Thugs Family*.

Chill gets that call from Angel. He was in a great mood after talking to Wes and wasn't willing to allow her to change that. He didn't even give her a chance to get her full greeting out. He hung up on her and called big Greg and big Sam on a conference call.

"What's up brothers?" he asks and they both say they're well. He tells them about the new construction coming soon with Wesley's house. They had just completed Jarvis and Gwen's home. Greg Sr and Sam Sr are the carpenters in the family. They've had a hand in every building project in the crew family, thus far. With much more to come. With all of the work in Jackson heights. They've been able to hire their own crew and buy the work tools, machines and equipment they need. They sub-contracted for bigger jobs, like Ajay's mansion and CrewLand Mall. They'll be opening an office at CrewLand in the future. For now, they sublet out of T-baby's office and she handles the finances. Big Archie does the drafting and blueprinting with Jr assisting. The crew are almost totally self contained. Greg Sr was always great with his hands, as is his older brother John. The men had all been taught a skill by their fathers, which pays off each and everyday of their lives. 1 way or the other. Greg's youngest son Steven and Sam's son Sam Jr are already planning to work with them after college.

"What you got for us Chill?" big Sam asks.

"Mo money, mo money," big Greg says and laughs.

"Yes sir. That's what it is and it's mo family too," Chill tells them as he laughs and says, "Renee's baby brother is coming here to live. I wanna put him in Jackson Heights, of course."

"Will do," big Sam says, "We'll get it done."

"Soon as Ebony gives us the go ahead," big Greg says, "We'll break ground."

"I'm about to call her," Chill says.

"It feels good to know we're all making money together," big Sam says, "That's our parents *and* grandparents dream come true."

"Chill I'm so proud of your crew," big Greg adds, "Y'all have brought in the kind of financing and degrees that made this a lot easier to do. We're all proud of y'all. Man, you're just like your father and your

101

grandfather. Either one of them could make a dollar out of fifteen cents."

"Thanks man," Chill says and chuckles. He adds, "We told y'all we wasn't gonna try to sell dope for a career. We just had to fund the early projects and keep the mall taxes paid. The guidance y'all gave to us was on point. We couldn't lose. No way we could lose."

"Y'all helped pay the taxes and sometimes, more than that," Sam Sr says as they all laugh.

"We're ready to get to work on whatever comes up next," big Greg says, "Shoot it to us. Trisha called me last night and said, *'Daddy you cleared some ducks on the Jackson Heights jobs.'* And I told her, she didn't have my permission to be looking at my paycheck." They laugh hard and he adds, "Her and Ebony got the money jobs. They can see what comes in and what goes out. Again, we're proud of all of your crew. We're self contained and getting stronger." They all agree and soon hang up.

Then Chill calls Ebony with Wesley's information. He gives her the details she'll need to get his property purchased. She tells him, she'll start the paperwork to acquire the building permit right away. She'll give him a great price on the land in Jackson heights.

"Put him on Payne's Lane, alright?" Chill requests.

"I'm way ahead of you, Chill," Ebony says as she giggles.

"So how are you doing today?" he asks, "Renee told me you're still dealing with morning sickness."

"Still running back and forth to the bathroom," she says and laughs. "But other than that. I'm doing fine."

"It's worth it though, right?"

"I wouldn't trade it for anything in this world," she says.

He's happy to hear good news and tells her so.

She says, "I'll have Claudia to bring me the tools out here. And I'll get started on the paperwork, *this* afternoon."

They hang up after a brief talk. Ajay is calling on the other line. He has that song for her to hear and it won't wait until he gets home.

"Hey baby," he says with that longing in his voice that makes her want to jump a flight and go to him. He says, "You sound good. Are you feeling better?"

"It gets a little more bearable everyday," she says, "Of course, hearing your voice helps too."

"I'm gonna put my phone on speaker so you can hear this new *Pock* song," he says, referring to *Tupac Shakur.* "It's a song for you, for mama and for my brothers too."

"Oh wow. Let me hear it," she says.

He plays *Unconditional Love* and tells her it just came out today. It's the 26th day of January. 1 day after Tank's 24th birthday. Ajay has sent the song to the club too. He requested they play it for his crew, from him. And let them know how much he wishes he could be there. Ebony hooks him up with Nina on 3-way. He makes her promise to play it for mama Jo. She tells him, she's going to do that before Tank's birthday party starts tonight.

"I promise I will," Nina says, "I'll go get a copy of it now. Then go by *Big Mama's House* and play it for her, in about an hour."

They hang up with Nina so him and Ebony can continue their talk. Ebony loves the song so much, she's singing background by the 3rd rotation.

"I'm gonna play it for you when I'm home, next week," he says.

"I'm looking forward to it," she says.

"We go back to Weston, right?" he asks.

"Yes. I'm excited."

"I am too," he says, "There's no All Star break. So I can spend that time with you."

"I'm smiling bigger," she says as they both laugh.

They have to hang up so he can make it to practice.

}*Ohio State Penitentiary*{

It's February. Angel is calling Alana for their *crew* talk. She knows about Ebony's new pregnancy and she calls Alana to find out if there's been a lot of talk and celebrating over it.

"It's true," Alana says, "I heard him on TV and I heard it from Nicole and Angie too. But Ebony don't come to the club no more. I guess he's got her on lock down."

"She *is* pregnant," Angel says sadly and changes the subject. "My baby would've made the all star team again if it wasn't for the lockout. They're not even having one this year. But they interviewed him about being an expecting father. He said his wife is pregnant and he's excited that they have the chance to become parents again. Then the media talked shit about me and the other baby. They made me sound like a monster."

"He did *too* Angel," Alana reminds. She says, "He looked mad as fuck when he talked about you. His look changed from happiness to mad as hell when they brought up your name."

"I'll make him understand it was because I love him so much," she says, "I think I've gone crazier just knowing that bitch has let herself get pregnant again. She's determined to keep him from being with me."

"You know he thinks about you every time he thinks about that first baby," Alana says, as if that's a compliment.

"I know he does," she says, "I wish he knew how sorry I was about that. I just wanted him so bad. I still do."

"Bad enough to kill his woman," Alana says, "That's gangster."

"Yea it is but being in here ain't though. I wish I would've done it differently. I wish he wouldn't have told me it was over. I lost my damn mind that night. I wanted to start over but he told me to get the fuck on."

"Do you think he would've *ever* loved you?" Alana asks.

"Do you think Tank would've ever loved *you*?" Angel asks.

"Michelle got her man," Alana says, "And she was ready to whoop my ass for Nina, the last time I tried to talk to her ass. And Tameka fuckin Rich again. I heard he be taking that shit if she act stank about it too."

"I read about all that in your letter and was like, *damn!*" Angel says, "They both kicked us to the curb. Like we was never shit to them."

"They're in with the crew and we would fuck that up for them," Alana says, "But once we get our men. They're gonna come crawling back."

"You can't be helping your aunt get to Ajay," Angel says, "Don't be taking her to the club. She's too old to be fuckin my man *anyway*."

"She loves the same dick you do," Alana says, "But girl don't worry about Dee. She's not gonna take the chances you take to get to the crew. That's why Ajay don't pay her ass *no* attention. She didn't even get to suck his dick at his bachelor party." Alana burst out laughing.
Angel doesn't. She asks, "So who did? Do you know?"

"I hear he went in the back room with some Puerto Rican chick," Alana says, "That chick is from Natty. She's the bitch he probably kept on the side when he cut your shit short. Angie said she's that nigga Tim's, baby mama."

"She *fucked* my man?" Angel says, "She's gonna get it too then."

"Angie and Nicole said they heard her tell her girls, that all she did was suck his dick," Alana tells her.

"He loves himself some head," Angel says, "I use to love to suck his dick too. Even though he *did* make me do it with the condom on. He was a safety dude, for sho."
They laugh. Then Alana tells her about the argument between Rich, T-baby and Tameka, at the club.

"He still wants to fuck her and she won't even fuck wit him?" Angel asks, "That stupid bitch."

"I heard he's *been* getting that shit since she was locked up and whenever he wants it," Alana says, "She's scared to stop him because she works for them. It's all over the Cleveland state campus. I don't know how his wife ain't heard it. But that bitch don't know shit because I heard she was accusing Tameka of trying to get with Rich. And saying he don't want her. That's a dumb ass bitch."

"All them bitches slow," Angel says, "They got the biggest dogs in Cleveland."

"All them niggaz fuck around," Alana says.

"Don't call them nigga though," Angel says, "My baby said there ain't no niggaz in his crew."

"*Anyway,*" Alana sings. Then she says, "Rich fuckin that ho. She's just trying to keep it on the low because she don't want his wife to fuck up her game. The C-S-U campus got all the dirt on that Ni-. *Brother.*"

"You still got your dudes over there?" Angel asks.

"Yes. My fan club is in tact," Alana says with a giggle. "I know what I'm gonna do. I'm gonna audition to dance at their stripe club, one of these days. I just have to get my nerve up. Maybe I can fuck my boss too."

"Oh shit yea, Ay," Angel says, "That might be what brought it on. Knowing that *stick wit my clique* ass family. Maybe the only way to get with the men and get some respect is to work for them."

"I plan to find out," Alana says, "I ain't done wit that Tank dick, by a long shot. You *heard* me?"

"If you get hired," Angel says, "Then you know I'm coming up there for a job too. As soon as I get out of here."

"You already know it," Alana says, "I know I'll get the job. Because I can work this ass and these hips. That's what that Nina bitch is so fucked up about."

Angel doesn't tell her about *The Bulldog* because he's sent there to watch her aunt Darlene's ass too. They talk for 30 minutes. Back to back calls. Angel hasn't gotten over her obsession with Ajay. Not even after being in prison for 3 years. She still has it in her mind, that he will fuck her *if* she accepts that he's going to put Ebony first. Alana is under a similar impression with Tank. These 2 will prove to be hard to get rid of for the crew but the crew plays to win. Which is something these stigmatic females know nothing about. But if they come wrong, they'll surely learn.

}*Jackson Heights*{

With no All-Star break, Ajay is still in Miami. It's business as usual. Ebony is at home with big mama. Resting as she promised to do. After she has a long talk with Ajay, her and big mama keep each other company while discussing some family history.

"Ebony are you feeling well enough to eat something, sweetheart?" big mama asks.

TIME TO KNOW-RELOADED-Time Will Reveal- part 4

Ebony is exiting the bathroom for the 4th time, this late morning.

"I can try and see if I can keep it down, this time," she answers as she crawls back into bed.

Big mama goes into the kitchen and makes Chicken and rice soup for the 2 of them. She serves it to Ebony in bed, along with some saltine crackers and apple juice. Then she sits down in 1 of 2 huge overstuffed chairs, next to the bed. She has some of her own soup while Ebony hits her with more pregnancy questions.

"How will I know if everything is okay? How much longer will I be throwing up? And how do I keep Anthony from worrying that he'll hurt me during sex?" she asks.

}*The Chill Spot*{

Chill calls Ajay. They talk on how he feels about not having an All-Star break. Ajay tells him any other time he would be upset. But with Ebony having a hard time with the pregnancy, he wasn't focused on it anyway. He would rather be home, taking care of her. The NBA is only going to have 50 games this season. And since there's no break, Ajay has to be in Miami for practice and games. He's not very happy about that either.

"I wished it was a break and we could go home for it," he says, "But I know big mama is there. She'll call me if *anything* goes wrong."

"I know you're worried about her, man," Chill says, "But she's good, bro. We all got her until you get here and even after that. Okay?"

"Okay," he says, "And you *do* know how much I appreciate that."

"Already."

}*Jackson Heights*{

After finishing her light brunch, Ebony feels a little better. Ajay calls right back after hanging up with Chill, to check on her before he goes to practice. He hangs up after talking with her and big mama. Then heads to *American Airlines Arena*. Big Mama and Ebony get back to their talk.

"You look a little perkier today, baby girl," big mama says after they hang up with Ajay.

Ebony says, "I feel better and a lot stronger. Anthony's voice is medicine."

"You're ten weeks now," big mama says, "This morning sickness should subside in a few weeks. He's really worried about you."

"I know. He always worries, so it'll be better on him too when I'm not sick all day," she says propping herself up on her back rest and grabbing her laptop. She adds, "Because I'm sick of that part already and I don't want him to worry so much."

"He'll never stop worrying about you, baby girl," big mama says as she smiles. "He always has. I'm so happy you all was able to get pregnant *naturally*. That's a blessing."

Ebony smiles in agreement and says, "I must admit. I am too."

"I knew you and Ajay would make it, honey," big mama adds, "As a couple, I mean."

"I know you always *told* me that. Even when I wasn't sure myself," she says, "You and Anthony have always been close, big mama."

"He was always calling me to talk about how he felt about you," big mama reveals, "He was doing that before you came to stay with me. But he called me three times a week, *after* you came to stay. I can remember you would be fussing and crying to me. Saying he wouldn't write to you or he didn't care enough to check on you. But he was. He didn't want to hear you arguing at him. So he would talk to me and ask me to talk to you. You didn't know that part."

"No I didn't. I knew he was talking to you but I didn't know exactly what y'all talked about. Nor how often."

"Baby girl, you and Ajay are the real reason I decided to go on and have the surgery," big mama admits.

"*Really*? How's that?" she asks.

"I knew if I didn't have it. I would keep feeling bad and getting worse," big mama says, "And Pearlie was gonna keep sending you down there to stay. That was driving Ajay, me and Percy *crazy*."

"Big mama that's the ultimate sacrifice," she says, "I feel so bad because I didn't wanna leave him, to come to Houston. I was worried about you too. But I didn't wanna leave him."

"You only find true love once in a lifetime," she says, "I wanted to make sure yours and Ajay's had every chance. I didn't want my being sick, to be the *only* reason you was around me. I wanted to be well so we could enjoy the times we spent together. Like now."

Ebony hugs her grandmother real tight and says, "Thank you, big mama. From the bottom of my heart, I thank you for everything. I was so scared when you got sick. Isn't breast cancer hereditary?"

"Yes it tends to run in blood lines, baby. Why?"

"Well then there's a chance I can get it too, right?" she asks.

"It's possible but the trait comes from my real father's genes. Not my mother's," big mama reveals.

"I know your real daddy is a white man, right?" she asks.

This subject is one, only touched on briefly if it's even discussed at all.

"Yes, mister Edward Prescott," big mama answers.

TIME TO KNOW-RELOADED-Time Will Reveal- part 4

"He assaulted grandma Alice, didn't he?" she asks.

"Yes he did. She was working for him and his wife, misses Clara Prescott," big mama says, "Misses Clara knew he was a womanizer and she tried to protect my mama as best she could. But one day he was just *not* gonna accept no for an answer and he raped her. He would do that over and over. Until mama couldn't take it anymore and she told misses Clara."

"Did misses Prescott believe her?"

"Oh yes indeed," big mama says, "She knew he was always abusing the staff like that. It's a rumor that I have other siblings by other staff members. But I never met any of them. Misses Prescott knew the man she married. She knew he was an abusive man. *Period*. He abused her too."

"So what did she do?" Ebony asks.

"She found a way to protect mama, in the end," big mama says.

"Didn't she kill him?" Ebony asks.

"That's what the sheriff says," big mama answers, before changing the subject, "Are you done with your soup?"

"Yes ma'am. Thank you," she says, "It was really good."

"That's because I know my *stuff*," big mama laughs as she clears the dishes and takes them into the kitchen to wash them up.

The kitchen doorbell rings while big mama is finishing up the dishes. She answers it to see Gwen, from across the street.

"Hi sweetheart," big mama says, "How are you and this handsome young man?"

"We're great," Gwen answers, "How are you, big mama?"

Big mama tells her she's fine. She's about to start dinner prep. She tells her Ebony is in her bedroom relaxing and has her laptop in bed with her. Gwen has come over to visit and see how Ebony's getting along. She has Jarvis Jr with her. Big mama escorts them to the master suite and into the bedroom with Ebony. Then she kisses Jarvis Jr's cheek. Ebony puts her laptop on the nightstand. Her Godson is giggling and reaching for her to take him. Gwen brings him to her and she takes him into bed.

"You know you're the only man who can get in bed with me and not upset *The Godfather*, don't you?" she asks with a giggle as her Godson bounces up and down on her legs.

"You've got a God sibling coming. Did you know that? Yea you know that. Don't you, little man?"

She loves playing with him and he loves to see her. He always laughs and coos for her and Ajay. He's 9 months old and already the height and size of a toddler twice his age.

"Jarvis says he's gonna play ball," Gwen says as she smiles.

108

"He'd better or his daddy, Godfather and every man in the crew who loves him and loves watching his daddy play, are gonna disown him. Same as they will with a son of me and Anthony."
They crack up laughing. Then Gwen has some important news to tell her about the small wedding they were going to have this month.

"I'm gonna wait on the wedding," she says suddenly, "I guess you figured out I wasn't gonna do it. Since I didn't have crew gear doing any dresses yet. I just wanna wait and do it on my actual wedding date and maybe not even *this* year. Does that sound unreasonable?"

"No it doesn't," Ebony says, "I'll be as big as a house by then. You know Anthony isn't gonna want me standing for a wedding, that late in the pregnancy. If he didn't want me to do it, *this* month."

"That's another reason I suggested to Jarvis that we wait and do it next year," she reveals, "After you've had the baby and can help me and Nickeia to plan it all. I want you to be one of my matrons. I want Shantel to be a maid. My best friend from Anderson, Mary Woodall will be another matron of honor. How's that sound to you? That won't upset the elders in your family, will it?"

"Of course it won't upset my elders, Gwen," she says, "You guys are already married. You don't have to do a wedding at all, if you're doing it just so others will know. My family knows you're married and so does yours. No one else matters. Besides you're the bride. It's your choice of when and how you want your wedding day. Or whether you want to have one at all. Don't let Jarvis put pressure on you about this whole arrangement thing with our kids. My family has it's good and bad moments too. We're not judgmental people. There's no need for you to beat yourself up over any decisions you make. We aren't perfect people and we don't expect you to be. But whether you have a wedding or not, won't disqualify this little prince from being my son-in-law one day. That's gonna be up to him and my future daughter. *Then* the rest of us. But only after they show interest in each other. Nothing else matters before that."
Gwen hugs her and thanks her for being so understanding. And for taking the time to explain it all to her.

"I'm gonna have big mama talk to you Gwen," Ebony says, "If she can't make you feel one hundred percent better about it. Nobody else can."
"I would love that, Ebony," she says, "I would love that so much."
They finish their visit in the family room and with lighter conversation.

Ajay calls after he's done with practice. He's coming home for their 3 month checkup. While they're on the phone, Jarvis shows up after his practice, looking for Gwen and his son. He speaks to big mama and

Ebony. He speaks with Ajay briefly, before him, Gwen and little Jarvis leave to go home. Big mama invites them to come back for dinner and they accept.

"We'll see you three this evening, then," big mama says.

She locks the door behind them as they head back across the cul-de-sac, over the icy street to their home.

Ebony asks big mama if her and poppa will have a talk with Gwen and Jarvis about crew rules and guidelines.

Big mama says, "No problem."

Ebony gets back to her conversation with Ajay while big mama goes back to the kitchen.

****

Mr. Parkwood and his wife Barbara are in Cleveland to visit with Ajay and Ebony. Bert Parkwood has asked for this meeting for 1 reason. He wants to offer guidance to them for their Angel Taylor problem.

"I know how much this woman gets under your skin," Parkwood says to Ajay, "I have a suggestion if you're willing to hear it."

"I sure am," Ajay says, "I'm always open to your suggestions, mister Bert. I've always looked up to your guidance too. I wanna hear it."

They all laugh. Then Mr. Parkwood and Ajay head to the sanctuary to talk, man to man. Parkwood asked him to invite Wheeler, big Al, big John and Chill along. He does. When they arrive, they have poppa, Jo, Pearl and Renee with them. Attorney Wheeler had brought along his wife Trina Yvette Sloan-Wheeler. The ladies join Ebony, big mama and Barbara Parkwood in the parlor while the men are in their private meeting.

In the parlor, Ebony gets right to the questions she's had for awhile. Keeping in mind, Mrs. Wheeler is sweet on her husband. Still Ebony doesn't have any ill feelings toward her and she finds that *really strange*. Yet she feels comfortable having this talk with her present.

"I know y'all may have never thought I would have a problem with my sex life," she says, looking embarrassed.

"I know you don't," Renee says as she giggles.

"We all know," Pearl adds, "What do you *think* is a problem?"

Trina Yvette looks on with a strange interest and wry kind of glee. Big mama and Barbara Parkwood notice her and give each other the eye. Ebony is about to answer her mother but before she can, Jo steps in, after big mama pulls on her arm and brings Trina's look to her attention.

Jo says, "Let me try to answer this one for you, daughter-in-law.

Because I'll bet you I already know what you're gonna say. Shall I try?" Ebony looks at her and smiles. Then yields the floor as big mama smiles. Jo asks, "Ajay has changed his mannerisms in the bedroom, right? He's less aggressive?"

"Oh mama Jo," Ebony says, "That's it *exactly*! Is this another thing that's passed down? When your wife is pregnant. You don't have sex the same way you use too?"

"Not in my house," Pearls says as she chuckles.

"Mine either," Renee says.

Big mama adds, "And definitely not mine."

"Mine either," Mrs. Parkwood adds, "That sounds like a case of the jitters to me."

Trina Yvette doesn't say anything. She was hoping Ebony would keep talking but Ebony isn't going to feed her hunger, just yet. She finds it more tantalizing to know that another successful rich and beautiful woman finds her husband desirable. Surprisingly to her, it's a turn on. Her and Ajay already know her score. So Ebony gives her a tease of conversation. She knows the older ladies have scooped it and their alerts are already on. Jo keeps the floor.

"Something like that," Jo says, "Allen was the same way. Each and every time I was pregnant, he changed the rules of our sex life. Then after I had the baby. He wanted to go back to sex as usual. Pearl, now I know you remember when I use to tell you about this."

"I do," Pearl says, "I sure do. I just thought it was an *Al* thing."

"Ant is his father *warmed* over," Jo says, "I've watched him with Ebony, for years. Or since we knew and *accepted* them as a couple, at least." They all chuckle and Jo continues, "I see a *lot* of Allen in our son. Allen is a dominator in the bedroom. And I've heard Ebony talking to Nina and the girls enough to know. Ant is the same way. He dominates but he's skilled, just like his daddy. After hearing her talk about him, when she didn't know I was listening, of course," Jo giggles as Ebony smiles. She adds, "Then I understood why she was bucking against you to be with him, Pearl. He was mesmerizing her."

They all laugh as Pearl adds, "She was bucking against me, for awhile. But I knew he had a lot of qualities. Like John, as well. Like his inability to tell her *no*. Or trying to give her every *little* thing she wanted. As long as it was good for her. But I never faulted him for their sex though. I tried to say it to slow *her* down. She could very well have gotten that from me."

She giggles as Ebony looks at her in surprise, before saying, "Oh *now* you admit it," she giggles.

"Ebony comes from hot women," Big mama says and chuckles. She adds, "We are virtuous and very choosy. But once we choose that someone special. And whether we feel he'll be able to feed our erotic needs, has a lot to do with that choice. Then we go all out for him. He's gonna do the same for us too. I need to add this too. No other woman has ever. Nor will one *ever* be able to take his attention away from his crew woman."

"That's because they mold us the way *they* want us to be," Jo adds as the ladies 2nd her. "And an outsider trying to harm or hurt one of us. Is considered to be the highest form of disrespect to our men."

"I agree with that," Renee says, "Kenny is that way. No matter what they do in the past. Once they're locked in. They're like lion's over a pride. They don't tolerate another female attempting to hurt us in any way."

"That sounds really romantic," Trina Yvette finally says, "If that makes any sense."

"It does," big mama says.

"That's what keeps us in love," Pearl says, "Because we see what they do for us and they don't hesitate to show us we're protected."

"Thank you mothers," Ebony says as her and Pearl laugh.

Ebony is clued in now. She knows why her elders are going in. They've already caught on that Mrs. Wheeler would like a sample of Mr. Anthony Jackson.

Ebony continues the talk with a smile, saying, "But he's holding back a lot. He acts like he's gonna break me."

"The only thing that'll make him *not* be aggressive," Jo says, "is pregnancy."

"Great," Ebony says, "He didn't warn me that the sex would have to be adjusted once I got pregnant."

"I'm still finding this hard to believe," Renee says, "I'm in shock."

They all crack up laughing.

"Renee," Jo says, "Kids are the only thing that comes before sex, with a Jackson man."

They all giggle then the ladies give Ebony some sound advice. They tell her to talk this over with Ajay before she goes any further with it, with them.

"Let him explain his feelings to you," Pearl says.

"Right," big mama says, "Because he adores you and he may be worried about harming the baby. Lots of men go through that. But to change his sex habits?"

"Not Ajay," Renee says, "Just talk to him about it."

"Let him know he can't harm the baby," Jo says, "Try that.

112

It helped me *some* of the time. Allen treated me like fine china during pregnancy sex."

"It'll help if you have Gladys Weston to back you up on it too," Pearl suggests.

"Everything they said," Mrs. Parkwood says and big mama agrees.

"Okay," Ebony says, "I will. Thank you mothers. Thank you."

Trina Yvette doesn't offer another comment. She just smiles throughout the remainder of the talk.

It's bedtime at Ajay's home. Ebony has been relatively quiet since their parents, their crew leaders, attorneys and the Parkwood's left. She sits on the edge of their bed in her nightshirt which is a replica of his game jersey. Ajay is happy to be home and he's looking forward to their appointment with Dr. Weston tomorrow. As he removes his shoes and socks, he notices his wife is still not talkative.

He asks, "Are you okay?"

She doesn't answer. She only looks at him and smiles. Ebony is horny. She's determined she's going to have sex with her man, the way they had it before whatever calm demon took over him. She wants to taste him tonight. Instead of answering him, she calls him over to her. He comes over immediately and asks, "What's going on?"

"Can I undress you?" she asks.

"Yes you can," he answers with a bright smile, "Hell yea."

She stands and unzips his warm-up jacket. He removes it quickly. Then she pulls his t-shirt over his head. He helps her. Then he tosses it along with the jacket, onto the oversized chair next to her side of the bed. She unties his bottoms as she looks up into his eyes. He's looking back into hers. He's smiling. Damn near chuckling. He likes her assertiveness but wonders just what she plans to do or change tonight. He pushes his warm-up bottoms to the floor and steps out of them. She sits back on the edge of the bed, right in front of his midsection and looks up at him. All the while he's looking down at her as he pulls her hair behind her ears. She's smiling as she slides his boxers down. He backs away suddenly. He removes them from his feet and tosses them on the chair with the rest of his attire.

"Lay back," he says placing his fingertips under her chin and giving her tender kisses on her lips and face.

"I wanna taste my dick first," she says boldly, figuring he'd like that.

Surprisingly he says, "Not right now. We'll get to that later. *Way* later."

That's not a good enough answer for her. Not tonight. That answer isn't going to cut it. Nor is it going to play well. Neither is she. She wants hers.

"What's the problem, Anthony?" she ask as her eyes well up.

She's thinking the worse. She knows he isn't getting it somewhere else, like before they were married. She would know that. But something has changed.

She pleads, "Please tell me. *Please*. Because I know there's something wrong. Our sex is different. Please tell me."

"There's nothing wrong," he says as he climbs into bed, "Come on and lay down. Let me wet my pussy."

"You're not gonna talk to me?" she asks.

He can see the tears welling up in her eyes. Coupled with the worried frown over her brows.

"Okay baby," he says with a sigh. He adds, "Asks me whatever it is you wanna know."

"Why is our sex *not* like it use to be?" she asks, "I mean, the way it was before I was pregnant and the night I *got* pregnant, even."

"How is it different?" he asks.

"You're not giving it to me like you was before," she says still being bold.

"Because you're pregnant," he says, "I'm not gonna be roughing you up while you carrying my seed. I'm not trying to do *no* damage like that, right now. I don't want my baby having *dick* nightmares."

She cracks up laughing. He laughs too. Only not as hard as she does. She tries to stop laughing but she can't. Finally he's had enough.

He says, "Alright. It ain't *that* funny, baby girl."

"Anthony you can't injure the baby," she says, still giggling.

"I don't know that," he says.

"I'm telling you. You can't," she says, still chuckling, "You can't. Not unless you kick me on the floor. Or push me down the stairs."

She howls with laughter. He isn't even smiling at her last comments. She gathers her composure and asks, "Is that what you're worried about?"

"Keep laughing," he says, "I can do more damage then you think."

"I know you can. But not from having sex" she says, "Anthony, I know you wanna make sure the baby is safe. We both do. But we don't have to alter our sex life."

"We'll talk to Weston about it," he says, "Until then. I'm not gonna beat this pussy up. That's all it is to it. You're gonna have to accept that."

"So why can't I taste you?" she asks.

"For the same reason you can't have alcohol," he says.

"It's intoxicating now?" she ask as she giggles.

114

He's perturbed by her asking him these things. She can tell he's mildly set off. So she does her best to make sure she doesn't laugh again. He says nothing. He doesn't even answer. He just stares at her.

She asks again, "Does giving you head, have the same effect as me drinking alcohol, daddy?"

"I don't want my baby consuming it," he says, "And whatever you consume, directly affects my child."

She's taken back by that. She never even considered he would say that. Let alone think it. She has to respond.

"So is this final?" she asks.

"Yes."

"For the *whole* pregnancy?" she asks.

"For as long as your intake is shared with my child," he says.

"So I need to find a boyfriend who will let me-"

"-You know I don't play like that," he says, cutting her off.

"I was trying to make you relax and laugh, daddy," she says.

"There ain't *shit* funny about my pregnant wife talking about having a boyfriend," he says, "Ebony come here and fuck me. And stop talking. You can't make me mad enough to punish you. Stop trying."

He's heated. His expression is serious. She can see his posture. He stares at her with conviction. He isn't going to compromise. Nor play *any* bullshit.

"Wow," is her response.

He really has turned into daddy. I'm a child up in this spot, tonight. Normally if I talked like that. He would whoop his pussy to sleep. Comatose!

He doesn't say anything else. He just moves over and straddles her. Then he captures both of her legs and pulls them over his shoulders. He dives in and starts to eat her pussy.

"Oh but you can taste me, ha?" she asks as waves of good feelings are going through her body. She's still trying him.

"Uh huh," he says, lifting his head up and making eye contact with her. He looks almost angry, as he says, "I'm gonna lick this sweet pussy and make you cum. Then I'm gonna enjoy my wet pussy and make you cum again. After that. We're gonna get some sleep."

He dives back in and she shuts up. Well, sort of.

Ajay wakes up this morning as Ebony is exiting the bathroom. She's more fatigued and still having morning sickness. It should be reason enough for her to understand why he isn't willing to be rough during sex. But what she sees differently about the night before. Ajay sees as precautions for what's to come or *who's* to come. This early March morning marks month 3 of the pregnancy. She's still putting on new weight. Even though she isn't keeping any food down. Ajay notices her ankles are swollen when she comes back into their bedroom.

"Baby I'm ready for this appointment today," he says, "You should be passed this sickness. Your ankles are swollen too. Do they hurt?"

"No," she says, "I'm fine."

Those are the 1st words she's said since, *'Oh but you can taste me, ha?'*, last night. He can tell she's uneasy. Even with the sickness. And even though she's upset with him. He's still going to look out for her best interest and the best interest of their baby.

He says, "Well I'm calling Doc Weston. I want her to know about this before we get there."

"Okay," is all she says.

He calls her doctor while he gets dressed. She's getting dressed too. Only slower. After he tells Weston the up-to-date circumstances. She's concerned too. She tells them to come on in for their early appointment. She wants to check everything out thoroughly. Ajay hangs up with her. He helps Ebony finish dressing. When their done and ready, they head to the kitchen. The staff is there and busy doing what they do. Big mama isn't sharing cooking duties with anyone though. That was established from day 1. She's made them a big breakfast. Ajay eats. Ebony has some orange and grapefruit slices and a slice of buttered wheat toast before they head to the medical complex.

Once they get there, Marshel escorts them back early. Weston is eager to see Ebony and run some test.

"You are gaining weight rapidly," Weston observes, "I want you to be aware of that Ebony."

"I'm not eating that much food," she says, "Because I still can't keep a lot of it down."

"You're eating for two, baby girl," Ajay says, "You *have* to eat."

"Yes but she doesn't need to eat *two meals,* daddy-to-be," Weston says with a smile.

"Please tell him, doctor Weston. Because he's trying to make me eat too much," she says with a pouting smile.

"She didn't really eat anything for breakfast," Ajay asserts.

"Only eat what you need," Weston says, "When you feel full. Then you don't have to eat anymore. Overeating will cause nausea as well."

"She's not overeating though," Ajay says, "She's barely getting one complete meal a day. Surely she needs to eat balanced meals, ha?"

"Again. She should eat when she's hungry and not stuff herself," Weston says, "The morning sickness should subside in a few days. Since you're into your second trimester. You're fourteen weeks along but I still need you to rest as much as possible. I'm going to do an ultrasound on the next visit. I have some intuitions that I need to satisfy."

"Oh she'll rest," Ajay assures their doctor, "She's gonna rest."

"What intuitions?" Ebony asks.

"It's nothing major," Weston says, "I want to see *just* how big this baby is. And if you'll be able to carry to full term."

"But everything else is okay?" Ajay asks.

"It's going perfectly, Ajay," Weston says with a smile.

"So what are the restrictions on our sex life while I'm pregnant?" Ebony asks as Ajay shakes his head and smiles.

Dr. Weston smiles and says, "Now that's one question I never thought I would get from you two."

"It's not from me," Ajay answers matter-of-factly.

He's a bit thrown off that she'd brought it up. But she was advised too by her matriarchs.

"You should have a healthy sex life, *still*," Weston says, "I wouldn't recommend hanging from any chandeliers. Or doing cartwheels or back flips," she chuckles, "But everything else within reason, is fine. Ajay are you getting out of hand?"

"I told you. It's not *me*," he says, looking at Ebony, "It's the one who asked you the question."

"Well I'm not placing any restrictions on you," Weston says, "Not this early, I won't. So if that's everything. Then I'll see you again in four weeks," Weston says as she finishes up the appointment and bids them farewell.

They head to CrewLand with minimal conversation. Only a brief discussion about lunch. Before going to get lunch, he drives her to her office so she can finalize the paperwork for Wesley's land in Jackson heights. She faxes it to him and to Parkwood's Office. Then she calls her uncle Greg and gives him the go ahead to start building on Payne's Lane.

Ajay visits Chill at his office while Ebony handles her business. When he walks in, Chill can tell something is on his mind.

"What's *poppin*, bro?" Chill asks, "I can see that *Vee* in your forehead. Tell me what's got you bothered."

"Chill, you know I don't usually discuss my wife's features and all, with *nobody*," he says.

"True that," Chill responds.

"But Ebony is fine as *hell*, right now," he says, "Her hips and her ass are sitting just right. Her skin is extra smooth and it smells like milk. And henny and *penny*? Oh my God!"

Chill laughs momentarily, before saying, "Oh yea bro. I know they get big as melons. I've been there. *Twice*."

"Her nipples look like them coasters, granny use to bring out for all the celebrations," he says and smiles.

"Then I know y'all getting it in," Chill assumes.

"That's just it," Ajay says, looking somber, "She stays in the mood. But I'm worried about *fuckin* something up."

"Ah bro," Chill says, "You're not the first one to come to me with this. And you won't be the last. I was the same way before lil Kenny. You can't do *no* damage to her, bro. Not unless you've got a sharp object."

They burst out laughing and Ajay says, "I swear. I be wanting to work it out. But then I don't want my child to be watching dick coming at him."

They crack up laughing again, before Chill says "Ajay that's not the case. I don't remember you being like this, before."

"Because she never poked out before," he says, "It seems like this baby went from just made. To making her stomach rise in the one month I was gone off to train. This is gonna be a big ass kid."

"Just try to relax, Ajay," he says, "I don't want you going at her, like you was in my old house that night. You know. After we relocated lil Jake and that other fool." They laugh and he adds, "But work your way up to what's comfortable for her. They can take a lot more when they're pregnant. It's like it just opens up. Getting ready for the baby to come through, I guess."

"*Man*," Ajay says, "It's so hot and soft. I *needs* to enjoy that."

"Then that's what you should do, bro," Chill says, "Just take your time and feel your way. Make sure she's comfy and get it in."

They chuckle again before Chill tells him, he has some irritating news for him. On this otherwise, jovial day.

"What is it, man?" Ajay asks, "Like I don't already know."

"Bro that bitch has still been calling here. Still trying to keep tabs on you," he says.

"I'm gonna hope for a different answer and ask who?"

"Angel is back to calling and now, it's every damn day."

"Because you're tolerating it," he says, "Man tell that bitch where the fuck to get off at. She's picking up all her info from the news. She knows I got another baby coming. She's plotting too. What are we waiting on to

TIME TO KNOW-RELOADED-Time Will Reveal- part 4

kill this ho and her stripper cousin too? For one of their asses to get *lucky*?"

"I don't accept the calls, bro and like I told you before," Chill says, "She must be off her damn rocker to even *think* she can call here and get a favorable answer. She's healed up from the beat down and still her cousin ain't got shit to report to her. But it's like I told you before. She's desperate. Those cellmates got pressure on her, to keep them connected to you and us. She still think *they're* the biggest threat she has to worry about in there. She thinks they had her whooped too."

"So what is she calling here for? *Protection*?" he asks, "I know you ain't about to tell me, you're gonna tolerate this shit here any longer?"

"None of that and she'll never get protection from the crew."

"She's thinking she will," Ajay says with a disgusted look on his face. "Or she thinks we're gonna go easy on her because she's doing time. But fuck no! We're *not*. It's time to off that stripper. Start there."

Chill tells him again that he would never accept a call from Angel. And as far as her knowing the number to the club. It's a public number. He also tells him she's going to be privy to whatever part of his personal life the media releases. And that's when she calls and why she's calling so much lately. Ajay says he don't give a fuck *who* told her the number or if she had it before she went to prison. He just doesn't want her trying to get a pass. He wants her life and that's all she can give to repay him for the life she took from him and Ebony. Chill has no comment but he can see the agony in Ajay's eyes. He promises him that before he would allow any of this to reach baby girl. He would put a hit on her and her cousin's head and end this. But he has to be sure that when it's done. There are no ties to lead back to him, Ebony nor any person in this entire family. Ajay calms down a bit and finally shakes his hand.

Ebony calls him and says she's done in her office and they can get some food. She grabs some work to take home and he meets her at her office door. They go to lunch at Crew's House of Soul Food. While there, they share the news of Ebony's weight gain and appetite. Poppa had picked big mama up from Jackson Heights so she could come to the restaurant and do the menus.

"You're gonna eat enough, baby," big mama says, "I'm gonna see to that. Me and Ajay both."

Ajay smiles in agreement. They have a filling lunch. Then they stop back into the spot so Ebony can see Chill, Tonya, Jr and Renee. Ajay knows Chill isn't going to share any of the conversation they'd had earlier. He sits in the office with Renee, Jr and Tonya while Ebony and Chill slip out onto the main floor to discuss the building permits for Wesley's house.

119

TIME TO KNOW-RELOADED-Time Will Reveal- part 4

"Uncle Greg and big Sam have the okay to clear and start building in one week," she whispers to him.

"Great news, baby girl," he says, "Renee is gonna be surprised when she finds out the house is for her brother. She thinks it's for big mama and poppa."

"Big Mama told me they're all playing along with it," she smiles. When her and Chill finishes talking, her and Ajay head home.

In the late afternoon, they take Ike and Tina for a stroll through Jackson Heights then return home. He prepares her bath and bathes her. She's thinking he'll want to have sex in the Jacuzzi but they don't. He gets out and orders their dinner, after putting her in the family room on their huge sofa sectional. He feeds their dogs and bathes them too. He does his own laundry and packing. All while she keeps her feet up in the family room. She knows he's trying to take care of her and she now knows he's afraid that he'll injure their baby. She also knows they're going to make love tonight. But she's just going to go with the flow. She doesn't want him to be stressed out about anything. Because she also know they're going to get through this. Just as they have with everything else. Tonight she's going to enjoy her man. He has to leave for Miami tomorrow and she doesn't want her to leave with stress. Big mama will be back to stay with her.

For Nina and Tank's 3rd anniversary, he ordered matching *Lincoln Navigator's* and had them detailed. Nina is totally surprised and she loves them.

"I think we should sell the Camry, baby," Nina says.

"I agree and I'm gonna get off of the Tracker too," Tank says, "But I'm keeping the truck. Hey instead of selling them. We can give them to Jesse and Erica."

She says, "I agree. They'll need transportation at college, next year."

Erica and Jesse are graduating high school with the *99 crew*, this May. Erica will be attending Oklahoma University on a dance scholarship. She'll be a member of their drill team. Jesse is attending Southern University in Baton Rouge Louisiana, on a football scholarship.

Tank calls John and Al about giving the vehicles to their younger siblings. John and Al both suggest Jesse and Erica need to work this summer and pay them *some* amount of money for them. They also agree that the 2 of them will need to have a vehicle for college.

"We'll help y'all get the paperwork done and we'll get them insured," Al says, "And we'll help them drive to college when it's time."

120

John agrees and adds, "It's cheaper than buying them new ones."

Tank and Nina alert their siblings that they'll be getting cars, this year.

As soon as they get the news, Erica and Jesse are thrilled. They agree to continue working at the businesses and add extra hours this summer, to pay Tank and Nina.

By the beginning of April, the titles have been changed over. Erica is now the owner of the 1995 Camry. Jesse owns the 1993 Tracker.

"This is an early graduation present, bro," Jesse says to Tank, "Thank you, man."

"Take care of my Jeep," Tank says with a smile, "That was my first vehicle. Keep it detailed and maintained and it should be okay until you go to the NFL. Then I want *Rolls Royce.*"

"I'll get it for you, big bro," he says as they laugh. "I get to drive to school, as a senior. You and Jb didn't get to do that. Only Ebony had a car in school."

"I drove hers though," Tanks says and they laugh, as Jesse thanks him again for the Jeep.

He drives it to Shaker Heights and parks it in Pearl's driveway. Which was the *Tracker's* first home.

CHAPTER 40

VISION OF LOVE

Ebony's still putting on weight. She's having an ultrasound today. Because frankly, everybody's concerned including Weston and she wants to see the condition of her and the baby so she can assure Ajay and the family that Ebony isn't retaining fluids. Or that there isn't *anything* wrong. Ebony's still experiencing morning sickness at 4½ months. She isn't stressing about sex, as of late because she really hasn't felt like it in weeks. Ajay is worried so much, he makes a special trip home on a game day. It makes the news and of course, dumb ass Angel calls the club. But that's not something Chill cares to share with Ajay today. He's only concerned about Ebony. She's already experiencing lots of movement from the baby at only 18 weeks. Ajay was being his usual protective self when he called Weston for an expedient appointment. He didn't want to wait until week 20. Weston wanted to give them some relief and she wanted to know as well.

"I need to know there's nothing wrong with my baby *and* my baby she's carrying," he says to Weston as they enter the examination room. "So please, just humor me."

"You have appropriate concerns Ajay," Weston says, "Because her morning sickness should've resided by now. Besides she's putting on almost twice the weight of a normal pregnancy. Are you feeding her steak *everyday*?"

They laugh as Weston squeezes ultrasound gel onto Ebony's protruding belly.

"She's bigger in the abdomen then normal too," Weston says, "I have a theory here, like I said before. But let's see what the ultrasound tells us."

"Please God, let everything be okay," Ebony says as Ajay holds her hand.

"It's okay, baby girl," he says, "We're just gonna make some big children."

"I usually wait and do the ultrasound after week twenty," Weston says, "But in your case, it's necessary."

"When the baby moves, I can't breathe well," Ebony tells her.

Ajay gives her a kiss on the forehead while he rubs her shoulders.

"I'm worried about her, doc," he says, "She just seems to be uncomfortable all the time."

"We're going to check her out and see *just* what we can see," Weston assures them as she starts the ultrasound and positions her paddle.

From the very onset, they can all see that her abdomen is very full and very crowded. Ajay and Ebony get a shocking surprise.

"There are *two* heads in there! Twins?!!" Ajay asks, "Oh my God, baby! You're giving me *two* babies!"

Ebony is so emotional, she can't even speak. All she can do is cry. From the ultrasound, they can see the sex of one of the babies.

"This one is a boy!" Ajay yells as he points to his genitalia. "Oh yes sir! That's *my* son right there! Look at his jewels! That's a Jackson man!"

Dr Weston laughs while Ebony hides her face in embarrassment. They're not able to see the other baby because for the most part, it stays behind the big boy.

"Twins," Ebony finally says while Ajay gives her another kiss. She adds, "We know we have a little Anthony. We're gonna break Jackson *and* Williams history if it's twin boys."

Weston says, "That explains the weight gain, the continued nausea and why you can feel movement so well, so *soon*. It also proves that my intuition was *correct*, newlyweds. Everything is perfect here."

"It took us long enough to get pregnant," Ebony says, "God is helping us make up for lost time. *Twins*. Oh thank you *God!*"

She still cries as Ajay holds her hands and kisses her repeatedly. Then he hugs her tight. He's overwhelmed with joy too.

"Baby girl, this is the bomb," he says, "I'm so proud of you."

"We still can't tell what the other one is," she says.

"I can try to make them switch around a little bit and try to see what the other one's gender is," Weston offers.

Ebony looks at Ajay and asks, "What do you think, daddy?"

"It's on you, baby," he says.

"No. I don't wanna know," she says, "We know we've got a son. I'd rather not know what the other one is."

"Okay we can wait until they're born to find out," he agrees, "But still leave the other nursery pink. They can share the blue one if it's two boys. Because I will have broken the Jackson mold!"

They all laugh. There has never been more than 1 male per family, on either side of Ajay's family. His grandfathers, father, uncle and cousins were and are, the *only* male child in their families. Ajay, like Ebony, wants the sex of the other baby to be a surprise. They can't wait to share this news with their family. Weston changes their appointments to every week and still instructs Ebony to get plenty of rest.

"You're going to need it for twins," Weston says and smiles. She adds, "Get all the rest you can *now*."

They finish up and go straight to CrewLand Mall. They want to share the news with their extended family, face to face.

Ajay arranges with Jo and Pearl to have decorators come and do both nurseries, just in case.

"We're going to have *twin* grandbaby's Pearl!" Jo screams with excitement and they're both ecstatic.

Next Ebony and Ajay head to Crew's House of Soul Food to tell all of their grandparents. Tameka is working today. She congratulates them and they thank her. Again they remind her that they're there for her if she needs them. Then they walk over to the club to see Chill and the others.

While at the club office, Chill asks Ebony to give him her opinion on the new colors for the VIP section.

"Ha?" she asks as she follows Chill to his office, "Are we changing the colors up here?"

"Not really," he says, once he's away from Renee. "I told Renee I was thinking about it, so she wouldn't know why the decorators was here yesterday," he admits, "They was here about Wesley's house. He wanted you to make sure they do the inside just like he ordered it. Do you think you'll be able to handle that?"

"I can get my girls to do the hands on stuff," she says.

"Good. Because I don't want you doing *anything* but having some healthy twins, baby girl," he says, "I'm so happy for y'all!"

"Daddy's not gonna let me over do anything anyway," she says as she giggles, "Trust me."

Suddenly there is a burst of noise, applause and laughter. There's shouting and congratulations coming from the crew in Renee's office.

"Alright! Yea! It's about *damn* time!" the loud cheers continue as Ebony and Chill go in to see what the commotion is all about.

Ajay, Jr, Tonya and Renee are on the phone with Jan and Rob down in Atlanta.

"What are y'all cheering about?" Ebony asks when her and Chill rejoin them.

"Jan and Rob are finally pregnant!" Renee yells and they have Jan on the phone.

"Alright!" Ebony and Chill yell.

"Hey Jan it was that Alize and Cali bud," Ebony laughs. "Tell Bre, thanks a lot. We got three out of that sack. One for you and two for us."

They all laugh. Then Jan tells them her due date is December twenty first.

"Another Christmas baby!" Chill yells.

They're all excited about the pregnancies.

124

TIME TO KNOW-RELOADED-Time Will Reveal- part 4

"All of our crew will be parents now," Ajay says suddenly.

"Things are gonna change forever," Jr says.

"Because we're gonna be on the parent side of the issue," Ajay says with a grin.

"Ajay you're gonna be the hardest father a girl can have," Renee says, "Like big Al was on Lynn. Jarvis is a brave dude."

"Because he knows there are gonna be little boys-" Tonya was saying.

"-We can cut that conversation now," Ajay says, "My daughter won't date unless I pick him out. Just like big John did with me. Jarvis knows and respects that. That's why he wants his son here from day one."

"The parent side is gonna be interesting," Ebony says, "Don't y'all think?"

"We've *been* on the parents side," Chill says as he laughs and adds, "And y'all still didn't wanna let us go."

"I know but that's because it wouldn't have been the same without y'all hanging with us and molding us," Ajay says laughing too.

"Man we're getting old, bro," Jr says with a laugh.

"Shit. I'm getting better," Chill says and the rest agree.

Jr and Tonya announce that she stopped taking her pills this month. They're going to work on a 2nd child.

"Y'all go right *on* ahead," Renee says as they all laugh.

****

The *99 crew* of Erica, Jesse, Brittany, Greg Jr and Sam Jr are all finishing up at MLK this May. The party has long been set and everyone's entire families will attend.

Also Ajay's team makes the playoffs again this year. And again, they lose to New York in the 1st round. Ajay is disappointed about not advancing but he's excited about being able to be back in Cleveland to await the arrival of his twins. Weston has told them that twins don't usually wait the entire gestation period and are often times born early.

At the celebration, it is announced that Greg Jr and Jesse will be attending Southern Baton Rouge on Football scholarships. Erica will attend the University of Oklahoma on a dance scholarship. Brittany is going to Clark-Atlanta University where she'll be able to work on her music with Reaper and Rob. Sam Jr will stay in Cleveland and attend CSU. He'll study construction and athletic representation. He's going to work with big Sam, in construction. He'll work out of Jb's Cleveland office as a sports agent.

125

This Crew are carrying on the traditions of the generations before them. They're getting their education so they can be successful in life. They're just going 1 step further by being *self employed*.

In June, Jarvis and Gwen have a small wedding. Chill, Jr and their wives celebrate 8 years of marriage while Jarvis and Gwen celebrate their 1st year. Jb and Lynn, Cedric and Bre plus Rob and Jan celebrate 4 years. June and Rebbie plus Rich and T-baby are on their 3rd year of marriage.

Ajay celebrates turning 25 at the mansion since Ebony has to stay in bed. She's having a harder time getting around due to the weight of the twins. She's in week 33 of the pregnancy and she's miserable. Big mama comes to stay with her and Ajay because *he'd* asked her too. She knows Ebony isn't going to carry the twins to the full 9 month term.
They're having a good time at the party but Ebony is having pain in her back and bottom. Before the party ends, she thinks she's in labor. Ajay is overjoyed at the possibility of his kids being born on his birthday.
"Let's get you to the hospital baby," he says as he and big mama leave for the emergency room.
Pearl is there already and Jo is meeting them there. Everyone loads up in their cars and goes to the hospital, only to be disappointed. It's false labor. Ebony is sent back home.

}*Parma Heights*{
Farah and Alana move to Parma Heights the following week. Darlene is going to live with them. Farah wants Darlene's sons to come too. But Darlene tells her she's keeping the lease on her apartment in Maple Heights, for her sons.
"I'm trying to help them get crewed up," Farah says, "So they can get us some weight with the crew."
"I wish I would've gotten pregnant for Ajay back in the day," Darlene admits.
"Damn auntie!" Alana yells, "Where did that come from?"
"I see how he is with his twins about to come," she says, "He stays on the news talking about his twins. I really think he's a different person now. I should've given him a son, *years* ago."
"And you would be getting some of that NBA salary right about now too," Alana says as they laugh.
"And living in that 11 bedroom estate, somewhere in Cleveland," Farah says, "Damn! I'm *gotta* find out where that *fine ass* Chill lives."
126

TIME TO KNOW-RELOADED-Time Will Reveal- part 4

"Salary, mansion and that fourteen inch dick," Darlene says, "I would've done anything to keep his sexy ass hitting *this* pussy."

"Have you tried to talk to him lately?" Farah asks.

"No," she says, "I don't really see him no more. Not since he got married. Not in person, that is. I didn't even know what to say when I *did* see him. He won't make eye contact with me. I feel like he thinks I'm trying to be trouble because of how things went with you and Angel," she tells Alana.

Alana says, "I'm sorry auntie. But try talking to him the next time you see him and see how he reacts."

Darlene says she will as they continue to unpack and organize the few things they have. The movers haven't arrived yet.

}2 weeks later{

Ajay and big mama make breakfast together while Ebony is in the bedroom trying to rest. It seems the closer she gets to the due date. The worse she feels. It's not only in the morning but most of the day now. Ajay is really worried. Big mama worries about them both.

"How's Ebony doing this morning?" big mama asks.

"She's really uncomfortable, big mama," Ajay says as he slices the fruit. "She barely slept last night."

"It's getting close to time for her to have those babies, son," she says with a pleasant smile. "That's normal pre-labor discomfort. Your twins will be here in the next twenty four to forty eight hours. In the next day or two. She's showing those signs."

"I hope so because I'm ready," he says with a smile. "I'm ready to have them here so she can feel better too."

"You are, aren't you?" big mama asks.

"Yes ma'am," he says, "It's killing me to see her *so* uncomfortable and knowing I can't do anything. But then, I'm the reason it started."

They both laugh as big mama says, "Don't feel guilty. That part is normal too, baby. But you're not nervous at all. Are you Ajay?"

"No ma'am," he says, "Not for me, I'm not. But for her. I am. I think I'll do okay but that depends on her. It takes a lot to get me rattled. You know that."

"Yes indeed. I know it," she says, "I know as long as my namesake is okay. You'll be okay too. That's a *very* admirable quality."

"Thank you," he says as they laugh, "And you're right again."

He heads back to his bedroom with a tray of food. He serves Ebony breakfast in bed and joins her there to have his. She's still uncomfortable.

127

But she also feels her *usual* sexy. She feels horny today. She's happy her man is home to take care of *this* need. Only she knows he'll be worried that he'll hurt her or the babies too. Still she wants him. At the beginning of the pregnancy she was horny, all the time. But the more she progressed and the twins grew, she became most uncomfortable and wasn't in the mood as much. But today she's in the mood.

While they're enjoying breakfast in bed, she looks at him and smiles. He smiles back. Knowing her actions as well as he does. He can tell she's in the mood and he is too. There's *still* that feeling in the back of his mind about her safety. Ebony is done with breakfast foods. She wants him.

"I feel *so horny* today," she says, all of a sudden.

He looks at her and smiles again. He can see it in her eyes. She's in that *Thanksgiving night* kind of mood. He knows he's in trouble if he say they can't have sex. Ebony's persistent, saying, "I wanna make love."

"Are you sure you're up to it?" he asks.

He's more than willing to oblige her. But he's very worried about her safety and the safety of their twins too.

"I *need* it," she says.

They've finished eating. He takes their dishes into the kitchen, then comes back and lays down next to her. He strokes her cheek.

"I hope you're in the mood," she says.

"I'm *always* in the mood and I know it's my job to give you what you need," he says while kissing her on her face and neck. He adds, "But I'm just wondering if it's safe."

"Uh huh I know," she whispers impatiently. She adds, "It's safe, daddy. I need it so these twins will come on down and *out*."

She wants him to fuck her like he did on the night they *made* these twins. She thinks a good strong session of sex will help her labor start. He rubs her stomach and gives her kisses, over and over. He kisses her stomach which he's done, each and every time he's near her.

"If we go *real* hard," she says, "It might help me to have the babies today."

"I don't know if I wanna make your labor start," he says with a chuckle. He adds, "How is *that* safe for my twins?"

"Daddy you can't affect them," she says, "Even though everybody has told you that. Including the men folks and me, about a hundred times. You still don't believe us."

He avoids her statement and changes the subject. "After the babies come. You don't have to call me daddy *anymore*. You remember that, right?"

"Oh," she says, looking disappointed. "You're just gonna change the subject on me? We already discussed that. I might still wanna call you

TIME TO KNOW-RELOADED-Time Will Reveal- part 4

daddy. It's sexy to me when I say it. It makes your eyes sparkle."
"Well okay," he says, "But only in private. I don't wanna confuse my kids."
They crack up laughing and he adds, "Plus that'll be more questions I'll have to try to answer for them. Our son or sons won't get it, at *all*. They'll be mad at me from day one."
"Is that why your son kicks a lot?" she asks, "I can tell it's his big butt. Feel here."
She puts his fingertips on her stomach. Then she says,
"You can feel 1 of his feet. The other one is under my ribcage. That's where it's been since you took the dishes in the kitchen."
"He must still be hungry," he says and they laugh.
He's able to feel the heel of his unborn child. He smiles big. He tries to convince the baby to move his foot so his mommy can breathe better and be comfortable. Ebony thinks it's funny but Ajay is actually successful. Either that or the baby was just ready to change positions.
"He moved," he says with a proud grin. "He did a three sixty. I can see him turning over. *Whoa.*"
"I guess he knows who *the man* is, ha?" she asks, looking seductive.
"He'd better," Ajay says. Then he starts to talk directly to her belly. He says, "Hey son. I need for you to chill out alright? Give your mama a break and your little sister too."
Ebony giggles and says, "You don't know that."
"It's got to be a girl," he says, "If it was two boys. You wouldn't be able to walk, talk or function. *Ever.* Because they'd be battling non stop."
"You always know how to make me feel better," she says, while still laughing.
"Making you feel good is my job," he says.
"I know it's harder to get in the mood now," she says, "Looking at how big-"
"-Don't go there baby," he says, "We haven't slacked off on having sex when you want it and you know that. I love how you look right now. And every time I've seen you. On *every* trip home. I even went against my own policy and discussed you with my brother. I *likes* this. Your face is so smooth. You look amazing to me. I think you're sexy as hell while you're carrying my kids. And on this parenting thing. You already got a head start. Every time I came home I noticed something new. I love the way you look *and* feel. Your skin is softer and smoother. Your hips are sitting out and this ass is plump. And my pussy is *softer, hotter, wetter*. And lord *knows* I love all of this weight *henny* and *penny* gained. Yes indeed," he says and

129

Time To Know- RELOADED-Time Will Reveal 4   Black Coffee

laughs, as he feels her up. He adds, "I ain't got *no* problems here."
She giggles as he heads south to her breast while he rubs on her round belly. He licks her large nipples. He isn't done with his sexy conversation either.
"I've been loving these big ass *titties* this whole pregnancy," he says as he suckles them. "I'm gonna miss these the most after the twins come. And this hot ass pussy too." He inserts 2 fingers into her moist tunnel.
He says, "I have to give up the nipples for my twins. That's gonna be the start of my sacrificing."
She giggles and moans. He goes further south. He sticks his tongue into her pussy and starts to lap up her juices. She moans as he licks her with speed and persistence. He wants her to cum and it's not taking her long to get there.

"Oh!" she yells.

"Uh huh," he grunts from her southern end as he gives her oral pleasure.
She still wants to serve him. She's about to try and make a case for it but he's still not hearing it. He hasn't allowed her to suck his dick since the test came back positive. Not even once since verifying that her intake goes directly to his babies. He's not even trying to risk his sperm going anywhere near his twins systems.
"That's still not up for compromise, baby," he says as he slides up onto his pillows and gingerly shifts her position.
He assumes his position behind her as she lays on her side. He enters her quickly. His strokes are gentle but effective. Still she wants the regular Ajay. She reaches her arm back and places it behind him. She grips his ass and pulls him into her.
"*Damn*! You want it raw dog right out the gate?" he asks, noticing that she wants him to pump her immediately.
He adds, "You're hot for real. Ha baby?"
He's pleased at her eagerness to have him go deeper inside of her. But he's still going to be cautious.

"Yes daddy," she purrs, "I feel *so* hot. I feel *so* ready. I just want you to fuck me, *Anthony*."

"I didn't give you enough last night?" he asks as his rhythms increase. "I'm sorry baby. Daddy's gonna make up for it."

"I'm addicted to you too, daddy," she says feeling unusually moist.

"Baby I know you didn't cum again. Did you?" he asks.

"No I don't think so," she answers.

"You're wet as a *muthafucka*, baby," he whispers as he continues,

130

"Mmm. You're wet and soft and hot. And you feel so damn good."
It isn't much longer before she feels her climax approaching. He's double timing it to insure that it comes. He's fucking her hard like she wants it.

"Oh daddy yes! Give it to me!" she yells, "It's so good daddy!"

"Get that shit, baby girl," he demands, "Get it!"

She gets her orgasm. Then all of sudden, she starts urinating. He pulls out and sits up quickly.

"You have to go the bathroom?" he asks as he laughs. He adds, "You could've told me first."

"I'm not trying to go," she says, "It's just coming by itself. I can't cut it off. This must be why big mama had them to add waterproof mattress covers. I'm so embarrassed. I'm so tired of embarrassing myself."

"Why are you embarrassed?" he asks, "We both know it's apart of carrying children, Ebony."

"I can't keep wetting myself," she says as she begins to cry.

"Hey. *Stop*," he says while kissing her and drying her tears. "You haven't been wetting the bed. This is the first time this has happened. You said I was gonna help the twins come, right?"

"Yes," she says, "But this ain't the first time. When I sneeze or I cough. I just pee on myself. And then you'll have to deal with that-"

"-I'll take you right to the bathroom and help you get cleaned up too. If that's what it takes," he says, "Just like now. So what of it? That's the only way I know the changes are here. Your body is on loan. It's not like you're doing it *intentionally*. This is the sacrifice you're making for me. I can handle whatever comes with it. Do you *hear* me? I'm here all the way. I don't know how many times you cleaned up my throw up after I got fucked up at UC. Or when I had the flu or a sour stomach. This is nothing. If this *is* pee. Then it's clear like water and it don't even have a scent. Unlike mine. I pee too. You remember it because we had to get a new mattress," he says as they both laugh. Then he adds, "Baby I don't have a problem with *any* of this. Don't cry. *Please*. This is for our babies. The ones we worked our asses off for. I'm good, baby girl."

He makes her feel better instantly. They laugh again as he helps her to her feet and leads her to the bathroom. Water streams down her legs as they walk. It's hilarious. They laugh hard but it's about to get a lot worse. They make it into the bathroom and he leads her to her throne. She sits on the toilet seat and he heads back toward their bedroom. While Ebony is seated, a big gush of water hits the toilet like she'd poured it out of a bucket.

"Daddy! Oh daddy!" she yells in pain, "It's got blood in it too! Oh my God! It's got blood and it looks like snot! Oh God! It's nasty looking! I

think my water just broke! Oh my God! Tell big mama. Please!"
He runs back into the bathroom to witness it.
He says, "Relax baby. Don't panic."
"Tell big mama it's time," she says with excitement.
He smiles and gives her a kiss.
Then he says, "I guess I did help to bring them on down, ha?"
"Oh yes. You sure did," she says as she gives him an appreciative smile.
He runs to the family room to tell big mama what just happened. She follows him back to the bathroom. She looks in the toilet after Ebony stands up.

"That's your mucus plug," big mama says, "Some call it *the bloody show*. Your water is broken. It won't be long before the babies are here. I told you. Nothing like a sleepless night to make a fetus wanna get out and rest on it's own."
They get Ebony back to bed and prepare her for the contractions which are starting to build up. Ajay can hardly contain himself. That is, until she screams out. He looks at big mama.

"That's a contraction," big mama tells him, "This is where your breathing exercises come in."

"Oh my God," he says, "I can't let her hurt like this."

"It's natural Ajay," big mama says, "It'll be a lot worse than this before it's over. So prepare yourself. And just know, this is the miracle of life. You're going to become parents very shortly. I want you to call the doctor."

"Okay," he says as he grabs the phone and calls Weston's office.
A minute later, he has head nurse Tenischa Dunning on the line. She's excited to hear *him* excited. She's hoping it's time for the twins to come.

"How are her contractions," nurse Tenischa asks.

"I don't know," he says. Then he asks Ebony, "How are your contractions?"

"She's in the middle of one right now," big mama says as she helps Ebony to stay relaxed.

"That was the second one, daddy," Ebony says as the pain eases up a bit, "And they hurt too. Oh my God! It's gonna hurt!"

"They're about eight minutes apart right now," big mama tells him and he relays that to the Tenischa.

"Okay," Tenischa says, "Meet us in labor and delivery when the contractions are down to five minutes apart. Okay?"

"Alright. We'll be there," Ajay says before hanging up the phone.

132

TIME TO KNOW-RELOADED-Time Will Reveal- part 4

He checks on his wife again and ask if he can do anything for her.

"Yes. You can have the babies for me," she says dryly.

Then she gives him a slight grin before they both giggle.

He says, "You got that part, baby girl. You've had it all this time. You may as well finish it. I'll pay the bills."

He helps her go back to the bathroom so she can get dressed. Big mama says she'll help her dress. She has something else for Ajay to do.

"Ajay. Son get the car ready so we can leave as soon as the contractions start coming sooner," big mama says calmly.

"Okay," he says.

Seeing how calm big mama is, helps him to stay calm too. He's slightly nervous now but more excited. He's about to be a father.

He prepares his home for their extended absence. Then he gets her bags and puts them in the Jeep Cherokee. He pulls right up to the door, then he heads back inside to check on his wife.

"We didn't even have my baby shower yet," Ebony whines as she comes out of the bathroom. "We was suppose to have it this Friday."

"Oh we can do that after the twins come, baby," big mama says as she helps her into a loose fitting maternity sundress.

She combs her hair up into a bushy ponytail before another big contraction hits.

"Oh! Oh! Oh! Oh!" Ebony yells.

Ajay runs into the bedroom to coach her breathing. While he's coaching her through a big contraction, big mama calls Jo and Pearl via 3-way and yells, "We're having the twins today!"

"Okay mama!" They say simultaneously, "We'll meet y'all there!"

They hang up. Pearl and Jo contact the rest of the family including the Parkwood's, Wheeler's, Jarvis and Gwen. Then they head to East General.

This family has made many trips to this *same* hospital over the years. It's been about life mostly. But a few times was about death. They'd come here and left without Al's parents, Jo's mother, Chill's grandparent's and parents. Stoney, granny Pearline and both the unborn children of T-baby and Ebony. The memory of her last trip here as a patient has been on Ebony's mind each time she witnessed the birth of her girls kids. But today she has hopes and dreams of seeing those two beautiful faces, attached to the lives which she has cultivated and felt come alive in her own body. This day, 1 which big mama and Pearl have tried to explain to her for years. Will forever change her life and priorities. For today will be the start of life long memories for her and Ajay's future. *Yes.* Today's trip will mammoth the past trips and sync them in a file for her suppression someday. For today

133

is all about true love and new life. Lives that her and Ajay created. Twin symbols of their love and dedication to and for, each other. Today is the day they will become parents and future role models. To 2 sets of eyes who will look at them and never see any wrong. Precious twin lives molded in their images. Twin lives from God and the only thing greater than God. At this moment, the only thing Ebony can think of is how blessed she is that her and Ajay are solid, have a great home to bring them too and that they are each others best friends and confidantes.

It's July 25, 1999. Ebony, Ajay and big mama are in East General's labor and delivery unit. Bert Parkwood has put his wife Barbara in charge of the private suite for Ajay and his new family. By the time the rest of the family and crew get there. Ebony and Ajay are already in their private labor room. And by late afternoon, Ebony is in hard labor.

"Come on baby girl. Let's do this," Ajay whispers in her ear.

"You're not doing this! I am!" she yells.

She's very tensed as labor heats up. But Ajay feels as though she's angry with him.

"Why are you being so mean, baby?" he asks with a smile.

"Don't you smile at me, Anthony! You did this to me!" she yells before she starts to cry.

"Baby girl calm down-"

"-No! Don't tell me to calm down!" she continues yelling, "This hurts me! It's your fault! Why don't you lay up here and see what this feels like?! I'll bet you wouldn't be saying that!"

She still cries. Pearl giggles and puts her hand on Ajay's shoulder as Jo laughs and teases him

Jo says, "Uh huh. You didn't know about this part of it. Did you, Ant?"

"No. *Man*. My baby clowning on me up in here," he says as he tries to smile. "Baby girl this ain't even necessary and you know it."

She continues to rant as nurse Tenischa comes in to check her progress. Tenischa smiles at him as she listens to Ebony rant and rave.

"She's dilated to eight centimeters in three hours," Tenischa says, "Two more centimeters and we can let her push. I know mister Ajay is happy about that part."

"That's wonderful," Pearl says, "Baby girl you won't have to bare this much longer, honey."

"I can't take this no more, mama!" she screams, "I want surgery!"

"Baby girl it's a blessing if you can push them out and not get cut on," big mama tries.

"I don't want a blessing!" she screams, "I want these babies out of

134

me! I want them out of me, big mama. I want them out right now!"
Pearl, Jo and big mama snicker to each other. Ajay is very nervous. He's
starting to sweat.

"Are you okay daddy?" Jo asks, "You're not done yet."
The mothers laugh again.

"Yea I guess I am," he says, "I don't know if I can handle all this
screaming. Is she really alright though? Do she know what she's doing?"

"Yes. She's just in labor, son," Jo answers as she wipes Ebony's
face with a cold towel.

"Anthony did this to me, mama Jo!" she says aloud, "He did this!
And now he's standing over me! Smiling at me! What is *so* funny?!"

"It's alright baby girl. I'll get him later," Jo says soothingly, "It'll
all be over with real soon, honey. Okay?"

"Oh God! Please make it stop!" Ebony continues to scream.
Ajay can't bare to see her in this pain. He feels helpless. Ebony has been in
active labor for 6 hours. Nurse Tenischa comes in to check her again after
another 30 minutes.

"Oh Tenischa! Please wait! I'm having one!" Ebony screams at her.

"Having one what?!" Ajay screams too.

"A contraction, Anthony!" she yells, "Don't you know?! I've been
having them all day!"
He looks around at his mother, mother-in-law and big mama and rolls his
eyes before getting back to his coaching duties. The women laugh.

"Breathe baby. Come on," he instructs her.

"Oh please! You breathe daddy!" she snaps, "I want these babies
out right now! Do you *hear* me?!" she cries, "Right now! Make them get
them out! *Now!*"
Everyone in the delivery room laughs. Immediately after the contraction
eases off, Tenischa checks her while Ebony begs for a caesarean section.
Finally Tenischa has some good news when she says, "Okay misses Jackson.
You're fully dilated. Let's get you in the stirrups and sitting up."
Dr. Weston comes back into the room to check out Ebony's chart. She loves
what she sees and says, "Now we're ready to have some babies. We're going
to break down your bed and get you in the stirrups for the delivery phase."
They work overtime and within minutes, Ebony is ready to push. Ajay is
more ready than Ebony is.

"Okay baby girl," he says, "Here we go. This is it."

"On the next contraction," Dr. Weston says, "Daddy I want you to
help her push, okay? We're going full circle today."

"Okay we're ready," he says, then looks at Ebony, "Right baby?"

TIME TO KNOW-RELOADED-Time Will Reveal- part 4

"Yes! Yes!" Ebony yells, "Please let me push!"

Nina and all of the crew are out in the lobby. They're packed in there like sardines and spilling all out into the hallways. Gwen and Jarvis are in attendance. The Wheeler's, the Jacobson, Shantel and Claudia are all here too.
"We know we've got a little Ajay coming," Nina says.
"I hope the other baby is a girl," Rebbie says.
"Oh yes," T-baby says, "Me too. Ebony needs a little girl."
"Yes indeed. They're gonna catch us on the first go round," Chill says as Renee laughs and agrees.
"I'm so happy for them, y'all," Tonya says, "Lord knows they was working for these babies."
"Yea and that's why they ended up with two," Jr laughs.
Jo comes out of the delivery room to tell everyone Ebony is getting ready to start pushing.
"Yes!" June yells.
"Shh," Brenda orders, "That's *too* loud."
They agree to lower their voices but they don't. Not by very much.

Meanwhile in the delivery room, Ebony has started to push while Ajay coaches her. She's doing her duty reluctantly. Dr. Weston announces that she can see the first head. Ajay can see it too. Ebony looks at Ajay. He looks like he's seen a ghost. He shakes his head. Then he looks at her in disbelief.
"Can you see it?" Ebony asks him.
"Oh yea baby," he answers, "I can see everything."
Big John wants this over with soon. Him and Al are standing against the far wall. They don't even want to witness the birth. They just want to see the babies once they are out of Ebony. They are there to be support for Ebony and definitely for Ajay too, who's legs are looking wobbly. John decides to say something to Ebony while Ajay regains his composure.
"Push hard Ebony!" big John yells as Ajay regains his legs.
"I can't daddy," she cries, looking for sympathy and hoping he'll make Dr. Weston move her to surgery and end her suffering but he doesn't.
"She's doing great," Dr. Weston says, "One more big push and we'll have the first head out."
"Oh my God," Ajay whispers while looking as if he'll pass out.
On the next contraction, she pushes with all her might and their son's head pops out. Ajay feels weak but he manages to keep it together. His emotions
136

take him over. His tears start to flow freely. He's feeling this moment for sure.

"I got a son. I got a son," he says, "That's my son's head."

Dr. Weston clears the baby's airwaves and pulls him out.

"*Waaaaaaah!*" Little Ajay cries loudly.

"He's got some lungs on him, don't he," Al says very proudly, "His voice is already deep too. That's a Jackson man."

"That's a Brown man," John tries as he and Al laugh loudly. John adds, "His voice is heavy and he's got some huge lungs."

Ajay has tears streaming down his face as he cuts the cord and says, "And that ain't all."

Proudly he looks at his sons jewels as he rubs his sons head and cries.

"That runs in the family, son," Al adds as Jo gives him the evil eye.

"Yes it does. *Twice.*" John adds as he and Al laugh again.

"I delivered your daddy, young man," Dr. Weston says to the screaming little Ajay.

After Ajay is able to tear himself away from his son, Weston passes him to the delivery team and turns her attention back to Ebony.

"Okay mama," Weston says, "We've got one more to go."

"Let's get the bonus baby," John says, very proudly.

Pearl and Jo are watching the staff weigh and clean lil Ajay Jackson while still looking at Ebony's progress.

"Okay mama," Weston says, "Next contraction. *Big* push."

Ebony is ready to push. The 2nd delivery is much quicker and easier.

"*Wiiiiih,*" comes a very light cry.

"It's a girl!" Ajay yells, "I got one of each! Thank you baby! Thank you God!" he kisses Ebony, right then and there.

"It's a baby girl!" Weston announces, "He's right!"

"Ah man this is......, it's unbelievable," Ajay says, "I already know I'll do anything to make sure they're comfortable, safe and happy. I love 'em."

"Well now you know how I feel about you," Al says, "You got a boy and a girl, son!" Al yells as he hugs Ajay and kisses Ebony on her forehead. "You did great, baby girl. You did a damn good job."

Ajay leans over to kiss his wife again. Then he cuts the cord from their daughter. Before going to view his kids, he turns his attention back to Ebony for a few more minutes.

"You did *so* good baby girl," he says with tears streaming down his face. "Thank you. Thank you baby. I'm proud of you. I'm so happy."

"Me too, Anthony," she says, very exhausted as she cries too.

Instantly the delivery team brings the twins over for her to hold. She takes them and holds them close to her chest and kisses them, over and over while letting them listen to her heartbeat. Her and Ajay's parents are smiling. They're *very* proud. But no one is more proud than Ajay. He's right next to Ebony as she cries and says, "I've been waiting so long for this moment. Daddy they're so beautiful."

"Yes they are and they're wrinkled too," Ajay says as he cuddles his new family. "Call me Anthony. *Remember?*"

"We must put the girl on a monitor for a bit," Dr. Weston says.

"Why?" Ebony asks with concern.

"She's a little under weight," Weston says, "She's two and a half pounds. I want her to be at about four pounds before I can release her go home."

Ebony becomes emotional. Ajay is right there to keep her calm. He asks Weston if she'll break it down for them so his wife will know that there's nothing to be upset about. Weston explains the situation to both of them.

"You guys know I'm going to take care of your babies," Weston says, "I want them completely healthy and ready to go home when you're ready to take them. That's all. Now little Ajay is almost as big as his dad was. He can go home in a day or so, with mommy. But little Ebony. I want her to be a bit bigger before releasing her. That's all, sweetheart."

"No please," Ebony says while looking at Ajay, "We're not separating them."

Ajay agrees, "He stays until she can come home. He can't leave his sister. He stays and so does Ebony."

They roll Ebony's bed over so her and Ajay can be right next to their daughter while they hook her up in her incubator. Ajay holds his son while they name them both.

"I know this is Anthony junior right here," Ajay says, "He's looking right into my eyes. Daddy ain't gonna lie to you, son. *Know that.*"

"Atlantis Shalon," Ebony says, "We named them years ago."

"She getting Nina's middle name, ha?" Ajay asks.

"Yes," Ebony says, "Just like Jerica has my middle name."

"Yea but my daughter's head will never get that big," Ajay says as they all laugh and then let the crew in. "Ant junior's legs are already bigger than Nina's too."

"Double crew!" Chill yells as he parades the rest of the crew into the delivery room.

Everybody is laughing and congratulating Ajay and Ebony. But Ebony is extremely tired. After all of the crew have seen the babies, Ajay is more concerned about his wife. He orders everyone out so she can be taken to her private room.

"She needs to rest," he says as everyone files out and the staff move Ebony from the delivery room.

"Bring our twins with us, Anthony," Ebony says.

"No doubt," he says.

Once she's in her private suite, she's more than ready to sleep. They have an hour or so of privacy before she falls asleep.

"Anthony we have some beautiful twins. You know what? This was the date of my next scheduled appointment before the car wreck and the same date I was released from the hospital, after the wreck."

"This date is important in our lives for worth *now*, baby," he says, "And even though we've got some real twins. Henny and penny are still my babies too."

She laughs and says, "Don't forget about Ike and Tina."

"I didn't," he says chuckling, "I got Tank going by there and taking them to their house until we get back home and settled in."

"The pediatric nurse said I can try feeding the twins," she says, "She said they're gonna have to tenderize my nipples so they can feed."

The look on Ajay's face makes her giggle. He feels left out of the loop when it comes to her breast because she's going to breastfeed. He's been on restriction from her breast because he was causing them to leak colostrums, the forerunner to breast milk. Ebony had the *hardest* time getting *him* adjusted.

He chuckles as he asks, "I didn't make 'em tender *enough*?"

"I would *think* you did as many times as I had to tell you, you was sucking on them too hard," she says and giggles. Then she says, "I thought you would've started the real milk flowing, the way you pulled on em."

They share a good laugh and she adds, "I wanna try them, baby. Just for a little while. See if they'll eat."

She's planning to breast feed them for the first 6 months or so. If they do well with it, she's going to continue. Her big mama and granny always told her, "*breast milk is the best milk.*"

"Okay but I want you to get some sleep too, baby," he says.

"The nurse said she can pump milk from me and put it in bottles," she says, "If they don't eat from me right now. I'll lay down and nap and let you try feeding them. I just have to see them eat before I can sleep."

Ajay agrees.

They prop her up in bed and she attempts to breast feed their twins. They don't take to her nipples right away. She remembers big mama telling her, newborns can sense their mother's moods.

She says, "I think they know I'm tired."

Then talking to her twins, she says, "Let's let daddy try with the bottles. After I'm rested, I'll try again for your next meal."

Ajay agrees with that too. First he helps her get comfy in her oversized bed. They're in their family suite which was provided by Parkwood. Once she's comfortable, he sits down in the recliner with his son on his right arm and his daughter on his left.

"I'm gonna feed y'all your first meal while mama gets some sleep, alright?" he says to them with a smile. "When she wakes up. You can get it straight from her. I love you, Ant and Lannie."

He smiles at Ebony. She smiles too as she yarns and whispers, "Anthony, I love you."

"Oh *now* you can say it?" he asks and laughs. Then he adds, "But in the labor and delivery room. You was treating me like an enemy."

He laughs.

"I'm so sorry I was mean to you, baby," she whispers, "But I was loosing my mind in there. It hurt a lot trying to make you a father."

"It's all good, baby girl," he says, "You did an amazing job in there today. I love you Ebony. I love my son, Anthony junior and I love my baby girl, Atlantis. Oh and you're gonna be losing your pet name too."

They both smile. They had picked out their 1st boy and girl names, years ago. She drifts off too sleep while he feeds his twins. Everyone else waited out in the lobby so they can have these 1st hours alone.

NAMES: Anthony DeVante' Jackson, Jr. & Atlantis Shalon Jackson
BORN: July 25, 1999
TIME: 5:57pm--------6:03pm
WEIGHT: 8 lbs 6 ounces-----2 lbs 9 ounces
LENGTH:24 inches----16 Inches

Ebony and Ajay spend every day and night at the hospital with their twins. All of their coaches and those who are important in their lives, show up and hang out. Plenty of their family and friends come to lend their support as well. The media has announced the arrival of the twins. They've been in to interview Ajay and Ebony who have received many gifts from fans and some of their gifts was from *hopefuls* too. Girls and guys, who either wanted Ajay or wanted Ebony. For the most part, all of the gifts were tasteful and things they could keep.

TIME TO KNOW-RELOADED-Time Will Reveal- part 4

By Rebbie's birthday, Atlantis has gained another pound. She's up to 3 pounds and 12 ounces. Both babies are breastfeeding well and doing great. Ebony and Ajay are staying in their suite until Atlantis is ready to be released. Then they'll all go home together.

During the week, Ajay had taken the Cherokee home and brought his Jaguar back for the time being since he was riding alone. Today Ebony is bonding with the twins while Ajay goes to check on the house, the dogs and the businesses. He leaves Jackson Heights and heads to the club to help Chill with the accounts while Renee visits the twins again. While Ajay is at the club, Chill receives another 1 of those annoying phone calls.

"It's Angel again, bro," he says, "She's on her *extra* shit since the twins came. They need to cut out her TV time. For *real.*"
Ajay decides he's going to try and put a stop to her nagging. He takes the call.

"What *bitch*?" is Ajay answers the call.
"I just wanted to say congratulations and to tell you how sorry I am for what I -" Angel starts.
"-Yea, thanks a lot," he says, not even wanting to hear her voice. He has some things he needs to convey to her.
He says, "If it wasn't for your dumb ass. These would be our second and third kids. And just so you know. I wanna kill you, you dumb ass bitch. I don't give a fuck what day it is. Nor how great of a mood I'm in right now. You're the muthafucka who killed my first child. *Still*! That's all you will *ever* be to me. So if you thinking there's a *possibility* I'll ever forgive you one day. You stupid ass bitch! There isn't. You killed a piece of me. All you'll ever be to me is a worthless ass, fatal attraction ass *bitch*. I could've known this joy five years ago. But you denied me that. And you tried to take my only love from me too. I couldn't be happy right now if that had happened. You wouldn't know shit about it though because you would be dead too. And if anything ever was to happen to Ebony or my kids. I would make sure you die a very slow and painful death. Do you understand me? I don't give a fuck about you, ho. I never have and I never will. Fuck with me again and I'll lose it *all*. I mean it. You die bitch."
He doesn't give her a chance to respond. He hangs up the phone.
"I don't believe that bitch, bro," he says, "She's got a lot of fucking nerves to even be *trying* to contact me. I meant every word I said to her ass too."

"I know you did," Chill says, "That time is fuckin with her ass, man. She's probably trying to get a reprieve too."

"She's not getting *no* help from me," Ajay says, "I know it ain't considered *gangsta*. But I *really* wanna turn her in to the penal system for

141

harassment. And get her some *more* time. I just might do it too."

"You know that's Alana, still in your business, bro" Chill says, "I'm sure you know that. She's in it for Darlene too though. Then again. You're a celebrity now. The birth of your twins is big news. They was all over the news man," Chill says as he smiles big, "They're gonna want y'all to do a reality show after while."

"Ebony ain't going for that publicity shit," Ajay says quickly. Then he gets back to his anguish. He says, "I don't give a fuck about neither one of them ho's, bro. The news either, for that matter. Or that Farah bitch. She's playing outstanding when she come through here. Like she's actually gonna move something."

"She is," Chill says, "We're gonna help her move some of that Steel Plant money." They laugh and he goes on. "She bought a crib out in Parma and left her man behind. Now that fool's been calling *here* for *her* ass. So see, you ain't the only one being harassed. But there's no telling what kind of lie she told back in Pittsburgh." The phone rings again.

"Let me answer this muafucka, bro," Ajay says as his face darns an impatient frown. He grabs it and without thinking, he yells, "Hello!?"

"Yes this is Wesley. Is Chill in?"

"Oh yea man. I'm sorry about that," Ajay says, "I thought you was somebody else."
He hands Chill the phone and tells him he's about to leave.

"Alright man. I'm gonna get back to the hospital," Ajay says.

"Go take care of that fine family, bro," Chill says, "I got this and that other shit too."

Alana is on her 2nd call with Angel. She had connected her with the club when Ajay hung up on her. Angel called her right back, crying. She has been crying the entire time since Ajay hung up.

"It's like he don't even understand that I *love* him," Angel cries, "I would do *anything* to make him happy. But he said he wants to *kill* me."

"Angel you killed his baby," Alana says, "He ain't the same guy he was when you was fucking him. Well he's still the killer side of that and then some, when it comes to you. I see him in a different way then I did then. He never did take no shit and now he's got major loot. So he can pay a muthafucka to off a nigga if he wanted too."

"He was in a good mood," Angel says, "And he still wanted to kill me."

"I told you he was gonna think about you every time he thinks about his baby that died," Alana says, "And he probably thinks about that

142

baby now that he's looking at them twins. He thinks about you everyday."

"But I think he's mad because he has to protect Ebony's feelings," Angel says, "If he didn't act angry with me. Then she would be mad at him. I think it's because of her."

"Angel I know you love him. But you have to be careful too," Alana says, "Let's pull back on calling the club for awhile. Because they know it's me hooking you up and you know I'm gonna try to get hired."

"We can hold off for awhile," Angel says.

Only because she knows she's got her cousin *The Bulldog*, who's back from his road trips to hook up the calls until Alana is ready again.

"In the meantime, you have to find a way to get his forgiveness," Alana tries, "And judging by how he sounded on the phone just now. It's gonna take a *fuckin* miracle. He was cold as *fuck*. I was scared *for* you."

"Just don't start calling for your auntie, home girl," Angel says, "Don't turn on me, Alana."

"I won't do that, Ay," she says, "I told you. My auntie don't go hard like you do. She'll never get in again."

They soon hang up.

****

By August 9th, Atlantis weighs 4 pounds and 1 ounce. She has reached the required weight to be able to go home. Ajay is overjoyed. He's looked forward to having his family in their mansion.

"Daddy can take his baby girl home," he says as he places Atlantis in her carrier and fastens her in. "It's ladies first. Your brother knows that already."

He gives her a kiss on her little lips. Then he straps in Ajay Jr and says, "Come on, pops Lil man. We're going home. I've got a big house for you to help me run." He kisses his son too.

Then he asks Lil Ajay, "Why are they trying to make your sister gain weight? God might've made her to be skinny. Her mama was skinny when she was a little girl and she got me."

Ebony cracks up laughing which makes Ajay laugh too.

"I'm so ready to take them home, daddy," Ebony says.

"Anthony," he says and chuckles.

"Ah man," she says, "I have to *unlearn* it."

Ebony was discharged on the 28th of July but she has spent every waking minute in her private suite with the twins. Ajay has been here *nearly* as much as she has. He's only left to check the house, switch vehicles, handle

143

business and practice his game. Security is ready to take them to Jackson Heights but not more ready than they are to go home.

}*Jackson Heights*{

Pearl, Jo, Ebony's girls and big mama are waiting at the house when Ajay and Ebony arrive home with the twins.

"Baby girl we've got your bed *already* changed and made up so you can get some sleep," Pearl says.

"I can't go to sleep with the twins up," Ebony tries.

"Girl we got these babies right now," T-baby says.

"You better take advantage of this free time while you can," big mama suggests as Jo and Pearl agree and they all laugh.

"Besides we're gonna have them covered for the next few days anyway," Jo says.

Jerica who's 4 years old now, 3 year old Rich III and Orian who's 2 years old are all here to meet their twin cousins.

"I like these babies, auntie Ebony," Jerica says, "They look pretty."

"Pretty," Rich III mimics her while Orian just smiles.

"Thank you Jay, Rye and Lil Richie," Ebony says with a smile.

Most of the family calls Jerica, Jay for short. She likes having a nickname.

"Jay you know all 3 of you will have to help me baby sit."

"Alright!" all 3 kids say in unison.

"Baby, maybe you should come lay down with me and take a nap. While we have all of this help," Ajay suggests.

"Naptime daddy?" Ebony asks with a smile. She adds, "We can't have naptime for another three weeks."

He smiles. Then he asks, "Are we still sleeping in the same bed?"

"Yes."

"Uh huh. That's all good then," he says.

"That ain't gonna work," Nina says as she laughs. She adds, "Y'all need to sleep in separate cities to make it to that six week mark."

Everyone laughs. Then Ebony says, "We have to put some bassinets in our room until they get use to the house."

"You want me to go pick some up?" Ajay asks.

"No we don't," Jo intervenes, she says, "We're doing the baby shower *this* Friday. The grandmothers have already taken care of that."

Ajay and Ebony thank them for the gifts, in advance. And also for staying to watch the twins so they can sleep a few hours. They retire to their suite, leaving the twins in the care of big mama, their mothers and Ebony's *Awesome Foursome* girls.

TIME TO KNOW-RELOADED-Time Will Reveal- part 4

In their bedroom, Ebony puts on her *Mariah* CD. The 1 with the songs that shaped their relationship. The very 1st CD which brought them to this moment. The soundtrack of their love. She plays, *Vision of Love*.
"May I have this dance?" she asks.
"Yes you can, baby," he says with a smile.
They slow dance in their room. Then they glance over at their twins 1st photos which are on the nightstands, on both sides of their bed.
"That's a vision of love," she says.
"True that. I love you, Ebony Brown Jackson," he says.
"I love you too, Anthony Devante Jackson senior."
"Has a nice ring to it," he says.
"Yes it does, *daddy*," she says and giggles.
He smiles at her. Then her gives her a very passionate kiss. They dance until the song ends. Then they shower together and take a much needed nap.
"I can still hold you, right?" he asks as they're laying in bed.
"Yes you can," she says, "I really need that. Now that you can get you arms around me again."
They laugh as they hold onto each other and fall fast asleep.

Welcome to the world, Anthony Devante Jackson, Jr & Atlantis Shalon Jackson

CHAPTER   41

TEACHING YOUR SEEDS

On Friday, Ebony's girls throw her a huge baby shower. Yolanda, April, Shantel, Bre, Lynn and Jan fly in from Atlanta with their men and kids. Gwen and the females from her and Jarvis' family are here minus Nickeia. And ex-teammates from UC with the exception of Katrina Dobbs. There are female employees and customers from CrewLand mall as well.

During the shower, Tonya gets a call on her cell phone. It's her sister Venitia Walker and she's in town. Her voice sounds troubled and Tonya has to leave. Venitia had gotten as far as CrewLand mall then she stopped to call Tonya.

"Vee, how are you baby?" Tonya asks as Renee drives her to meet up with her younger sister.

"I'm tired of mama, Tonya," Venitia says, "She don't want me to stay there no more. It's like I can't do anything right in her eyes."
Tonya remembers having these same feelings. Her mother would always put them down. While raising up Lonnie, who is her younger less productive man. If Lonnie accused them of something, then it was the law. Venitia is exactly like her older and only sister Tonya. She's independent. She's intelligent and she's choosy. Venitia and Tonya have the same father. He had died before Venitia was born and Tonya hadn't turned 8 years old yet. They have a brother who is Lonnie's son and has the same name. He's the only child their mother and Lonnie attend too. Lonnie Jr was born in 1983. He's 16 years old now and already has an extensive juvenile record. But still Tonya and Venitia aren't given any credit for being model women or model citizens. At 20 years old, Venitia is already a junior at Michigan State university. She has no children. She volunteers in their community and she works with the *Disabled Veterans of America*. She's a part-time Vee-Jay on the campus music video channel and she's always organizing and working on fundraisers of some sort.

"I've only seen her twice but I could tell she's a great girl, Tonya. Just like you are," Renee says as they drive to pick up Venitia. "I told you I feel like your mother blames you and her for your father leaving her for the wife he had at the time he died. She's jealous that you're the apple of your man's eye and she wasn't. She knows your father adored you and he was looking forward to Venitia being born. But he couldn't spend his life with her. I can tell he loved you from the way you described y'all times together. He adored you. Also the fact that both of you have stable heads plus you both know how to carry yourselves is a plus. That's something I feel your mama gets no credit for. You taught your sister how to carry herself before you felt that you had to get away from there. Now she's doing the same thing."

"She's gonna stay with me and Bradley junior until she can get her own place," Tonya says, "It's gonna be so nice to have her around. I've missed her. I'm gonna help her get transferred to Cleveland State and we'll go from there."

"And if she needs a job," Renee says, "You know we've got that covered too."

They laugh as they pull into their CrewLand mall priority parking lot, park and head into Crew's House. Venitia is ready when they arrive. She's going back to the baby shower with them and she already has gifts for the twins.

"I came prepared," Venitia says as they head back to Jackson Heights. "I saw it on the news. That's how I knew to come to CrewLand. Mama had cut off my phone. Even though I'm the one who pays the bill. She was starting to mess up my credit too. I *had* to go. I don't let nobody mess with my credit score."

They all laugh as they hop back into Renee's Benz and take that short ride back to Jackson Heights.

Tonya says, "You sound like Ebony and T-baby. They have businesses *dealing* with finances."

"We're gonna see where your best fit is, Vee," Renee tells her, "And we'll go from there. Welcome to the crew family."

"Thanks and thank you," Venitia says, "I've been planning to move. And now was definitely the right time."

They all laugh as they get out and head into Ebony's house for the remainder of the shower.

Ebony receives so many matching gifts for the twins that she has to store some in a spare bedroom.

"This is so much stuff y'all," she says with tears streaming down her face, "I'm gonna have to change their clothes, three times a day, for them to wear all of these gifts before they out grow them."

"They'll be three weeks on Sunday," grandma Sally says, "But they'll be grown before you know it."

"I know," she says, "Anthony stays up all night watching them sleep. He's so proud of them, just like I am."

"Yea but you take your butt to sleep when you get a chance too, don't you?" Lynn asks with a chuckle.

"Yes indeed. Because I know when he leaves in another month," she says with a sigh, "It's gonna be just me, up all night with them."

"I know he's having a hard time with that six weeks and no sex provision, right?" Nina asks as she chuckles, "I know the answer already."

"Oh my *God*," Ebony says, "Don't mention it. He might hear you."

"Everybody knows Ajay ain't gonna last," Tonya says.

"He was getting frisky in the hospital," Jo says, "I saw that."

"Venitia, as you can see. We know each other well," T-baby says.

"And you're in my age group," Kim says, "You're the same year as Reaper and me. He's in Atlanta doing his music, along with Brittany. That's me and Bruce's crew. So you'll be in our crew too. Erica and I will show you around and introduce you."

"That sounds great," Venitia says, "Thanks so much. It's already fun and I've only been here a few hours."

"We're cool people," Erica says.

"As long as you don't date our men," Pam says and they all laugh and agree.

"My sister already told me that part," Venitia says, "Don't worry. I'm not like that. I'm easy to get along with. I'm very independent too. I'm taking my time on the dating thing. Until I find the right guy. I'll be able to help baby-sit too. If anyone needs my help."

"I'm getting your number from Tonya, right now," Ebony says with a smile. "If they don't say it. *I will.* I'm not turning down *any* help after my husband leaves, of course. But I'll be calling you if I need you."

"Well I'm gonna be here too," big mama says, "Big mama's gonna be here to help you out."

"That's a blessing," Ebony says.

All the ladies enjoy their evening together while the guys are at Stoney's hanging out until club time.

****

The last week of August finds the crew preparing for yet another celebration. Bre's 25th birthday will be a big event because of the digital effect it will have this year. *9/9/99*. Anytime a crew member has a birthday with all digits matching. They celebrate it, *big time*. The last one was Chill's father, big Paul. His was *7/7/77*.

Ajay is at the club office where Chill, Renee and Jr are going over the final plans for the party.

"This is the first one of these parties since pops," Chill says.

148

"I remember that party," Ajay says.

"Cuz, you was like *almost* three," Jr laughs.

"I still remember that big ass banner that was hanging upstairs at Chill's house," he says, "It was right at the top of the stairs."

"Oh yea. We kept it hanging up for like two or three months," Chill says as he laughs.

"I remember it because mama brought me, Lynn and Nina over there while they hung it up," he says.

"Yea. You do remember then," Chill says, "Because y'all was in my room playing and meddling shit while they hung it over my door."

"Ajay," Jr says, "Your twins are a month old today."

"Yea man," Ajay says, "They was up early for their breakfast too. Way before I came up here."

"They're getting *big* too," Renee adds.

"They eat enough," he laughs, "But I can't take my eyes off of them y'all. They're amazing. They look at me with those eyes. Like they know I'm the one who has to protect them."

"That's how it is," Jr says, "Me and Tonya still working on having another one. But she was on the pill since Lil Brad was born."

"We'll we're not," Renee laughs.

"*You're* not," Chill says with a chuckle.

"We're getting up there, baby," Renee says, "We're thirty and twenty-nine. Do you know how old we'd be when the child went to college?"

"No. Not until it gets here," Chill says smugly.

"*If,* baby," Renee interjects, "*If,* it gets here."

"Renee you don't want any more kids?" Ajay asks.

"I don't know," she says, "I mean Kenny junior is turning sixteen this Christmas. Destiny just turned six. That's a big gap."

"It's almost ten years between them," Chill says, "But they get along great."

"Yes they do," Renee agrees, "Kenny is really protective of her."

"That's how it's suppose to be," Jr says, "Lil Brad needs a sister too. He'll be eight, a week from today."

"Y'all better get on it then," Ajay says and laughs, "I know I want some more kids and I'm not waiting ten years."

"What does Ebony say about it," Renee asks, "Does she want more kids? I know she always talked about having a big family."

"She said she wants two boys," he says.

"Oh shit," Jr says, "In a Jackson or Williams *family*?"

"They could break the mold though," Chill offers.

149

"I agree," Tonya says.

"Big Al and big John said they're gonna be the couple to have two boys," Chill says, "But it's gonna take a few girls first. About four."

"Mama Jo said she gave out after three girls in a row," Renee says, "Her and big Al was trying to get another boy. But after Nina, Erica then Pam. Mama Jo said that was a set up."

They all laugh. Then Tonya says, "But Ebony won't give up. She's gonna do it her way, for *her* Anthony."

Ajay blushes openly and says, "She's my soul mate, for real. I told her I want five, like my pops. But she said we're gonna have two boys before we stop. So hey. What can I say?"

"Y'all getting em two at a time," Chill says, "Five won't take long."

"Here is what I want to know cousin," Jr asks with a chuckle, "How are you handling the six weeks with no sex?"

"Really though," Chill adds as he laughs too, "Because everybody knows your drive ain't *no* joke."

They all laugh. Then Ajay says, "Man that shit there is for the birds, bro. We won't make it."

"Y'all better make it," Renee laughs, "Or that next baby is gonna be coming *way* sooner than later."

"I'm plan on breaking that down tonight," he says as he laughs and the others laugh and shake their heads.

"It's gonna be hard to get some private time with the twins there, Ajay," Renee says.

"I know but I got something working," he says with a chuckle.

"What are you up too, Ajay?" Tonya asks as they all laugh.

He simply smiles as he prepares to head home. Chill and Jr chuckle to themselves. They know Ajay is hell bent on breaking that 6 week rule which all the other crew men stuck too.

In Jackson Heights, Ebony is entertaining her 1 month old twins. They've had their baths and lunch. She took them for a stroll and walked Ike and Tina, along with them. After taking out items for tonight's dinner. She starts reading a book to them. She's still in the parlor reading when the house phone rings.

"Hello?" Ebony says, answering the phone with both eyes on the twins.

"Hi baby girl," Jo says.

"Hey mama Jo," she says, "How are you?"

"I'm doing just fine," she says, "I've got Pearl on the phone too."

TIME TO KNOW-RELOADED-Time Will Reveal- part 4

"Hey mama," Ebony says.

"Hey baby," Pearl says, "Ajay told us we can keep the twins for their one month birthday. Jo and I are *beside* ourselves to finally get them."

"He did?!" Ebony asks in shock.

"Yes he did," her mother says, "And they can stay overnight too."

"I don't believe that," Ebony says, "He didn't say *anything* to me about it. I know he would. Unless he's up to something."

"Maybe he has something planned for y'all to do this week," Jo adds, "Because he said we can keep them for a few days."

"Uh," Ebony grunts, "He hasn't said anything to me. But if he said it. Then I guess he does have something up his sleeve."
Suddenly she gets a call on the other line. It's Ajay. She says, "I have to answer this other call. It's his cell."

"Alright," They say, "We'll be on our way in a little while."
They hang up and she clicks over. She answers, "Hello daddy."

"Hey baby," he says, "Oooo. I'm daddy today, ha?"

"I *told* you. It's gonna take some practice to un *train* myself," she laughs, "The look you had in your eyes on that honeymoon was priceless, baby. I wasn't gonna disappoint you."

"Okay. See I like hearing that, baby," he says as he gives her a sexy chuckle. Then he asks, "So my twins got you strung out?"

"No," she says, "Actually they're sleeping right now. I was reading to them. You know we have some good babies," she giggles, "They had a bath and a lot of lunch. We took Ike and Tina for a walk. Then I read a book to them and they went to sleep. They drained henny and penny too."

"Ooo," is all he can say as they both laugh. Then he asks, "What took you so long to get to the phone?"
He knows he has an extension in every room.

"I was on the phone with our *mothers*," she says, "They told me you said they can keep the twins for a few days. Did you?"

"Yea. I told them that on the weekend," he reveals.

"You didn't even say anything to me, daddy," she says.

"I know, baby," he says, "I was trying to surprise you."

"Oh," she says, "The surprise master that *hates* surprises."

"Are you alright with it?" he asks.

"I don't know," she says, "Don't you think we'll miss them?"

"Of course we will," he says, "But we need some alone time, baby."

"We have two more weeks before-"

"I know that," he says, not wanting to hear about restrictions to his pussy. "We need some time to be alone. Like I said."

151

TIME TO KNOW-RELOADED-Time Will Reveal- part 4

"Alright daddy," she says with a doubtful sigh, "They're on the way. But I have to pump fresh milk for them, twice a day. And bring it to Shaker Heights."

"Okay baby," he says, "We're gonna do that. Whatever you need to do. You know you set the rules on that."

"Okay baby," she says.

"I'm on my way home right now," he says, "So I can kiss my twins before they leave. Do you need anything?"

She can hear him smiling. She says, "Just you. Home safe."

"Cool," he says.

"What are you up too?" she asks as she laughs.

"I'm trying to get reacquainted with my wife," he admits, "Is that alright?"

"Yes but *how* reacquainted?" she asks.

"We'll see," he says with a grin.

"I know you daddy," she says, "Without *any* distractions, I'm in trouble."

"For sho," he says as he laughs. "I'll see you after I stop at the restaurant and pick up some lunch, alright?"

"In a minute, daddy," she says.

"See ya baby," he says and they hang up.

****

The Bulldog and Julie Von Reese, the woman he thinks is his girlfriend, shows up at Crew's house and orders lunch.

"These people got all of these businesses and shit," The Bulldog says, "But they got my cousin locked up. Only because she wouldn't let their pro ball player use her and throw her away."

"Wait a second," Julie says, "She told me she was in prison for killing his infant and trying to kill the woman he's married too. Is that true?"

"Sort of."

"Okay so how are they throwing her away?" Julie asks, "I don't understand."

"See baby," he says, "They drove her to it. He was with my cousin and let her fall in love with him. Then he just replaced her when he wanted another model."

"James, I don't think Angel has told you as much as she's told me," she says, "She told me he was always with Ebony, his *wife* and life time

152

girlfriend. She said she met him at a party but him and Ebony was together, along time before she even met him. Make her tell you the truth first. I don't want to see you get hurt. You're trying to protect your family and I admire that. But she needs to tell you the *entire* story."

"That nigga used her," he insists, "He knew he was in a situation with someone so he should never have fucked with Angel, from day one. He knew what he was doing. And it wasn't an infant. She was *pregnant*. Angel was trying to stop her so she could beat her ass for taking her man. She wasn't trying to kill nobody. But now, they both needs to go."

"What do you mean *go*?" Julie asks.

"Die," The Bulldog answers, "I'm gonna catch them off theirs, one day. So I can get that bitch outta my cousins way. So Ajay Jackson don't feel trapped into being with her. *Then* he can do my cousin right and get her outta that hell hole she's rotting away in."

"How are you going to *get* her out of the way, James?" Julie asks.

"However I see fit," he says, "She's not untouchable, right?"

"Do you mean *kill her*?" Julie asks, "Because I can't take this here relationship to a personal point. Not if you're talking about murder. I just don't want to be in a relationship with a man who would kill someone. We're not going to make it to the next level, James. I can't even go there."

"So you're okay with people using other folks for their needs?" he asks, "Telling them they care about them and then just throwing them by the wayside like trash?"

We must be talking about two different people and situations. Because Angel hasn't said any of this. She's setting him up for the kill. Or he's just a damn nut.

****

Pearl and Jo arrive to pick up the twins about 30 minutes after Ajay and Ebony finish lunch. He had called them after hanging up with Ebony and told them to wait an hour before they come. They did. *Barely*.

"We've come for our babies," Jo says as she enters the mansion.

"Yes indeed," Pearl adds and she's right on Jo's heels.

They're full of smiles. They have Jerica and also John III, who's visiting from Atlanta until Jb and Lynn return to Cleveland for Bre's party.

"So you ladies gonna have *all* of your grandkids at once?" Ajay asks with a smile.

"Yes son," Jo says, "We're *finally* gonna have all four of them together."

153

"First time for that. Because it's the first time we're getting *these* cutie pies," Pearl says, kissing her twin grandbabies.

"Y'all saying that like we was suppose to have *been* sent our babies with y'all," Ajay says as he chuckles. "They just made a month old. Really they shouldn't go, for 2 more weeks."

"Neither should you," Jo says, "What's your point?"

They all laugh. His mother lets him know, her and Pearl and probably the world knows exactly why the twins are being allowed to go visit them at 4 weeks old. Ajay can't do anything but flash a guilty smile.

Pearl giggles at Ebony and says, "At least now you don't have to sneak around. You're grown and the consequences are yours and yours alone."

"I don't know if I'm okay with them staying *overnight* though," Ebony says as she finishes packing their bags.

"You'd better be okay with it," Pearl says, "Because the king of the castle has spoken and he said we can take them," she adds as her and Jo giggle.

"The *queen* of the castle has the last word when it comes to the prince and princess of the castle staying out *all* night," Ebony says without a smile.

"True that," Ajay says, "She does have the final word on where they spend the night. Because she's been putting them to bed since conception. We just got in on it on the twenty fifth of July," he chuckles, "She has the last word," he says again as he looks at Ebony.

"Oh baby girl. *Come on*," Pearl says, "Ajay has something planned. Why can't you just roll with it?"

"Baby girl do you think we're trying to get another grandbaby out of you?" Jo asks as they laugh.

"You know your son, mama Jo," she says with a smile as she looks at Ajay.

He smiles and plays with his twins. His look is guiltier than ever.

"Maybe y'all can try those condoms that you wasn't using back when you use to drive us crazy," Pearl says as they all laugh.

"Oh she's got jokes," Ebony says sarcastically. "Well how about if we just put the twins in bed *with* us? That's been *pretty good* birth control." She raises her eyebrow at her mother in playful defiance.

"Pearl they're not gonna use condoms," Jo says with a smile. "And baby girl we're not leaving here without our grand twins. Ant will have to try to convince you after we leave."

"I know," Ebony says, "He's up to something for sure. But the twins are gonna need fresh milk, twice a day. So either y'all can decide if

154

you're gonna come here to get it and bring them when you come. Or be prepared to see me several times a day. Because I'm gonna be in Shaker Heights."

"You'll probably come even right after we've just left here with them," Pearl says and laughs.

"Ant you'll have to keep her busy so we can have some time with our grand twins," Jo says, "We'll come and get the fresh milk and bring the babies when we come. No problem."

Ajay smiles while he helps Jo and Pearl load the 4 kids into the new van he'd just bought for his mother. Jb and Tank had gotten Pearl the same model, in a different color. Now they have plenty of room to ride all 4 of their grandkids at the same time. Ajay and Ebony kiss their twins, once more. They hug and kiss Jerica and John III as well.

"Y'all be careful with my babies," Ajay says.

"And you be careful with mine," Pearl says and they all laugh again.

Except Ebony. She looks as though she's going to cry. She hasn't let go of either of her twins car seats yet. Although they're strapped in already.

"Seriously ma," Ebony says, "Y'all be careful with them. And if they cry too much. Call us so we can come get them."

Ajay agrees.

Pearl chuckles and says, "We raised y'all and see *now*, you two can understand how *we* felt. Ebony I felt this way every time you was away from the house."

"We both did. And look at how you two turned out," Jo says as she chuckles too. "We can handle a few more kids. Trust me."

Ajay grabs Ebony around her waist. Eventually he manages to pull her away and close the door. Jo starts up her new luxury van and backs out. She doesn't give the new mother a chance to say anything else. Ebony's eyes well up with tears. She asks Ajay, "What am I suppose to do now?"

They watch as the van drives around the curve and disappears behind the trees of the undeveloped acres which line the street. They can see them as they pass T-baby's house and drive up the street toward the guard booth.

"What you're gonna do baby. Is relax for a change," he says as he puts his arm around her, "That's what you're suppose to do."

He walks her back through the kitchen entrance and brings her back into their mansion.

"I feel empty," she says.

"It's weird though," he says, "How if feels like they've been here all along. They've really changed my life, baby. Already."

155

"It sure does seem like they've been here forever," she says, "That's why I know I'm gonna miss them. What are they gonna do when they want mama?"

"Baby, if it's anyone in this world whom you feel comfortable with having our babies, when we're not there. Who would that be?"

"Our mothers and big mama," she says, "I know that. I just miss them already. They can't feel me."

"I can't either," he says with a smile. "I miss you a lot."

"*Anthony*," she tries.

"I do miss you, baby," he says, "And I wanted to let them get use to their grandparents and the family. We've been stingy with them. Our crew and everybody have made plans to go to Shaker heights to see them, *this* weekend. Even Jarvis and Gwen are going out there to see 'em and they live right across the street."

"Okay. I *better* have fun," she says as they are just inside the house. He locks the door and says, "It'll be fun. I promise."
He picks her up cradle style and adds, "Wow. I can lift you with ease now." They laugh as he puts her back on her feet.
She says, "I knew I was fat."

"You was carrying twins, baby girl," he says, "If you was fat. Then *how* are you as fine as hell now? It's looking like it did this time last year."
Ike and Tina are ready to play tag with Ajay. That's when he says, "We've still got these twins, baby. And I plan to get reacquainted with henny and penny. If you cooperate."
She smiles as she rolls her eyes and says, "I did get my shape back fast."

"Yes indeed you did," he says and drops a couple of steps behind her to admire her nice ass. "You sure did and your breast are still perky. How did you do that? Because I heard they go south after you have babies."
She laughs, then says, "*Breastfeeding*. It helps to shrink the uterus and helps your breast to stay firm too."

"Darlene and Anita should've breast fed," he says and they burst out laughing. Then he adds, "*Seriously* though. And them ho's from Houston too. I've seen henny and penny when you're feeding my twins. Ain't no stretch marks on them or nothing like that. They still look good and tasty but bigger. Which is better."

"You're so wrong for that," she says, "You're not suppose to be thinking about sexual things when you're watching me feed the twins."
She giggles and he starts to laugh before he says, "No baby. *They're* the ones who aren't suppose to think sexual things. I can think about whatever comes natural. And for me, when it comes to you, that's what I'm thinking

about. And it don't matter to me if you're naked or not. Hell, I'm thinking about it right *now*."

"You'd better behave," she says and smiles.

"Oh I will," he says.

He tells her all of her girls are also enjoying a day without their kids. All of the grandparents have their grandchildren for the weekend.

T-baby walks over to Nina's. Nina had called her over since they don't have their children.

"What's up, girl?" T-baby asks as she comes into the kitchen door.

"Not much right now," she answers, "Come on in."

"Where's Rebbie and Ebony?" T-baby asks.

"I still have to call them," Nina says, "We're all child free. We need to get in the wind."

"For real," T-baby agrees, "We need to do something."

Nina calls Rebbie and Ebony on the 3-way.

"*I'm wit it,*" Rebbie says.

"*Anthony has something planned for us,*" Ebony says.

"Oh yea. Like what?" Nina asks.

"*I don't know but I hear that y'all husbands planned to spend this time with y'all too,*" Ebony says, "*So we'd better not go too far.*"

"Who told you they planned something?" T-baby asks.

"*Anthony.*"

"Jeremy hasn't said anything," Nina says.

"*Anthony didn't tell me either,*" she says, "*He just arranged for mama and mama Jo to keep lil Ajay and Lannie.*"

"*Yes and so did Brian,*" Rebbie says, "*Mama and mama Brenda got Orian and Ashanti.*"

"Mama and Mama Anna got lil Rich and mama is helping with Ashanti too," T-baby says.

"*Ajay gonna be trying to get some,*" Rebbie says as she laughs.

"*I know and I'm horny too,*" Ebony admits, not knowing Ajay can hear her.

"Alright Ebony," Nina says, "Y'all gonna be pregnant again."

"*Oh God. That's what I'm scared of. But if we're here alone,*" she says, "*There's no way I'm not gonna give in and he knows that. I want it too and mama suggested we use the rubbers she gave us in college.*"

They all laugh. Just then, Tank comes into him and Nina's kitchen.

"What's up, baby?" he says to Nina and gives her a kiss. Then he says, "Hey T-baby. What's up?"

TIME TO KNOW-RELOADED-Time Will Reveal- part 4

"What's going on, cousin?" T-baby asks.

"Where's Rich at?" Tank asks.

"He's at the club with Chill right now," T-baby answers.

"Oh okay," Tank says before going to take a shower.

He had just left the spot and he knows Rich isn't there.

"Brian is here until tomorrow," Rebbie says, *"Him and Rich leave going back to football camp tomorrow afternoon."*

"Well let me head to the house and get in touch with Richard," T-baby says, "I wonder what he has planned for us to do."

Nina, Rebbie and Ebony hang up and T-baby heads home. Nina and Rebbie have to check with their husbands to find out what they have planned.

}*Parma*{

Farah and Alana have spent most of the day arranging pictures on the wall and decorating rooms. The moving van brought their things from Pittsburgh today. With help from their Cleveland clique, they have finally gotten moved into the house in Parma Heights. Two weeks before Farah starts her new job at MLK high school. But right now they have outfits laid out for the club. Darlene, Angie, Nicole, Anita and Samantha are all coming back over to have dinner and go out with them.

In the meantime, Marvin Huntley has been blowing up Farah's cell phone. She hasn't answered it. She left Pittsburgh with the clothes on her back and her most prized possessions. Which she had managed to sneak out of her and Marvin's condo, day by day. She had things stashed at the apartment of Alana's stepbrother. That's where the movers went to pack them up. That same apartment where Alana stashed the now incarcerated Angelise Taylor, better known as Angel. Farah began this move in mid-July. She left the furniture, kitchen appliances and linens at the condo with Marvin. She didn't want him to know when she was moving because she didn't want him to stalk or harass her. Her parents had let her stay at their home for a few days. Marvin had stormed out on her, back in May. The day he found out about the move to Cleveland that he wasn't invited on nor given *any* advanced knowledge of. Farah's parents are convinced that Marvin Huntley had turned violent with their daughter. So they no longer see him as the marrying kind. He has tried to tell them the truth but so far, they haven't believed him. They don't believe him or in him *anymore*. In fact, they had been the ones who sprung for the complete new house of furniture, Farah has here in Cleveland. They had bought her everything she needed to fill up the 5 bedroom home. Including patio and lawn furniture. Farah and Alana are set up nice. The best thing about it for Farah is,

158

Marvin has no clue of where she lives and her parents aren't about to tell him.

"Girlfriend I have to hand it to you," Alana says, "You're *good*."

"I told you I'd get rid of his ass before we moved, right?" Farah says as she giggles and slaps Alana a high five.

"But he's thinking you're hooking up with me," Alana says.

"No not really," she says, "He told my parents I was leaving him for a black guy. He was thinking that would get him back into their good graces. But I convinced them that he was only saying that thinking they would make me go back to him. They didn't believe him."

"So it's true that he's called the chill spot then, ha?" Alana asks.

"I guess so. Because the messages he's been leaving for the past 3 weeks have been straight up hateful," she says, "And there'll be a few more of them today. Most likely."

"But why would he call the spot?" she asks.

"Stupid! He found the autographs we had on the napkins. And those umbrellas we saved from the drinks we got on our frequent partygoer night," Farah says, "Because I haven't told him anything about Chill. Nor the club and you know it."

"So *damn*. He must've been dialing information like a mug?" Alana asks, "Or oh wait. The number is on the partygoer card."

"I don't know how deep he dug but I have no doubt that he did whatever it took to get a trace on me," Farah says, "Didn't Tameka say she heard that he'd called? And to tell you to relay the message to me that customers can't receive calls at the club?"

"That's a fact," she says, "I forgot about that."

"How many Marvin's do you know?" Farah starts, "That would call anywhere for me?"

"One."

They laugh as they prepare dinner for themselves and the other ladies who will arrive soon.

}*Jackson Heights*{

Tank and Nina, Rebbie and June, Ebony and Ajay all spend a quiet evening at home. T-baby spends the evening alone. Rich hasn't come nor has he bothered to call or answer his cell phone. T-baby drove to Mentor and didn't see his car at the mansion. She had even rode by Tameka's place. She had no luck there either. She returned home and stayed by herself. She was too embarrassed to tell her girls he hadn't shown up.

TIME TO KNOW-RELOADED-Time Will Reveal- part 4

But the scene at Ebony and Ajay's house is quite different. They have a romantic dinner for 2 and listen to their *Al Green, I'm Still in Love with you* CD in the family room. He has the movie theater set up to show romantic movies and all. She knows by his reaction to songs like, *What a wonderful thing Love is*, *Simply Beautiful* and *For the Good Times*, that she's in trouble. If she thinks he isn't going to want to cap the night off with some hot sex, then she's lying to herself. His eyes have that glare as he looks at her from across the table during dinner.

Later in the family room, he puts on a *Michel'le* CD. This CD has a song on it that's very special in their relationship. From when they went on his 17th birthday trip to Cincinnati. The same trip where he'd helped her put that Raymond attack behind her. *Something In My Heart* is the song that played that night. The night they'd gotten their sex life back on track and when he had told her what college he'd chosen and that he was going to kill Raymond for what he'd done to her. The love they made that night was tender, sweet and definitely true. So of course, he puts that song on first. Then he looks at her and smiles. Because he knows the song is going to help his cause, more than hinder it. The intro to the song begins,
'You take my love and I'm willing. There's no limit to the love I'm giving. The love I'm giv--ing--in--ing......, Oooo Oooo Ooo woo. Oh yea, yea!'

They look at pictures of them with their twins. He continues trying to caress her private spots. *Michel'le* sings on.
'There's no reason why, we should be apart. Hmm, oh baby. Searching for something not real. Will lead to lonely hearts. Two lonely hearts.'

Big mama is at the restaurant. She's going to stay at papa's while the twins are with their grandmothers. Ajay had told her he was planning to get reacquainted with Ebony tonight. She didn't object and that was the only seal of approval or cosigning, Ajay felt he needed. He's a lot more frisky after dinner. He can see the passion in her eyes too and he isn't about to let it slip away. He's letting Michel'le do the talking. Or rather, the singing.
'We come to far to let it all end. I've told you over and over again. How I feel inside but if you go. Ooo baby, there's some-thing you should know! Something you should know, Ooo. Something you should know. There's something in my heart, something in my heart, something in my heart. Oooo, that's got me hooked on you.'

He can't hold out anymore. He goes for broke, when he says, "Let's go get in the Jacuzzi, baby."

160

She agrees. But tells him they have to call and hear the twins coo and babble first. He makes it happen and she smiles as she talks to her babies, who make enough noise to let her know they realize it's their mommy on the phone. She has to hang up because she's tearing up. Ajay smiles.

"I made it happen," he says, "Now can I bathe you."
She doesn't answer. She just heads to the master bathroom and he follows.

"Daddy we're gonna get in trouble, being here by ourselves," she tries as they both strip naked and slip into their Jacuzzi tub.

"It's not trouble for me," he whispers as he kisses her with passion immediately and adds, "Baby I miss this shit, *so* much."
He's not planning on her being able to resist him. He's pulling out all the stops. Within minutes, he's all over her in the hot tub. He's licking on her breast, sucking on her neck and aggressively rubbing every part of her flesh his fingers come in contact with.

"Oh daddy," she whispers, "Ssss this is dangerous. You know you can't suck on my nipples too hard......, right?"

"I can't get fed?" he asks jokingly, "I was breast fed too."
She giggles and says, "I know you was and so was I. And no you can't be breast fed by me. All of my milk is for our twins."

"Uh huh. But everything else is mine," he says as he stops smiling and pulls her up on his lap. He asks, "Everything must be cleared up down there. Because you would've never gotten in this tub with me if it wasn't."
He's referring to the cleansing period after birth.

"So you was testing me?" she asks as she giggles.

"Yea and you have no restraint, baby," he says and laughs too.

"Yes it is clear. But my period should start Sunday," she whispers, "And I *want* it to start, Anthony. So let's please be careful and not make another baby right away." She gives him a look of uncertainty.

"We got until Sunday, right?" he whispers back as he strokes her clitoris under the water which drives her crazy.
"You got the lead, baby girl. You know I can't help myself around you."

"Mmm, Anthony. I can't help myself around you either," she says, "We shouldn't be doing this. Until like, September the fifth."

"Uh huh. Yea alright," he says and sucks on her breast anyway.
Not enough to stimulate the milk. But enough to stimulate her. She can't stop him. Or she doesn't want to or whatever. It just feels like a *Jones*.

"Oh baby. Ssss," she moans and that's all it takes for him to go on.
She's already straddling him in the hot tub. He lifts her up and pulls her down on his dick which is exactly where she wants to be.
"Oh! Oh!" she moans as he pulls her face to his and kisses her hard.

"Mmm, I missed my pussy, baby," he whispers as he strokes her gently. "I needed this before I leave for camp. I can't go to work before I get my issue. You understand that, right?"

"Mmm, I missed you too," she says, "Honestly, I was thinking the same thing."

"Baby," he whispers while kissing her and pushing up into her. "I saw two babies come out of here a month ago. This pussy's tight as fuck."

He's pulling her down with force and the sensation is amazing. She feels like a bad girl for having sex before she sees her doctor. But Dr. Weston knows them so well. She knows how hot they are for each other.

"I have to keep it tight for you, Anthony," she purrs, "It's so good. Mmm, you feel so good."

"Oh yes," he agrees in a whisper, "You did that. It's good. It's so damn good."

They make love in the Jacuzzi until he takes her to their bed for more. Ike and Tina scramble for cover from the noises coming out of the master suite.

Rich comes home after midnight. He's looking and spelling a mess. T-baby doesn't even have the energy to argue with him. When he flops into their bed. She jumps up, grabs her pillows and goes into 1 of the guest rooms. He passes out without even noticing.

In the guestroom, she's so angry she puts a pillow over her face and screams into it. Then she cries herself to sleep.

}CrewLand Mall{

After spending a romantic evening at their homes, Rebbie, June, Nina and Tank decide to go to ladies night at *The Chill Spot*. Rebbie and Nina are so sure that Ebony and T-baby are at home having a wonderful evening with their husbands. Since neither of them answered their phones when they called to invite them to go out.

"I hope Ebony and Ajay don't end up getting pregnant again tonight," Nina says.

"Shit," Tank says as he laughs. "My homeboy ain't playing no games around that curve. Twin better have *her* brakes on. Cause he don't."

"You already know," June says with a chuckle. "He's going all in to get at his. And he got camp coming up too! *Ever ready* like a muafuckah," he adds as he laughs.

"I know they're doing the nasty," Rebbie says, "I'd bet my last on that. But Ebony has her hands full as it is, with those beautiful twins. She'd better be careful not to get a stair stepper."

TIME TO KNOW-RELOADED-Time Will Reveal- part 4

"Uh huh because I know their asses are fucking," Nina says with a giggle, "Like jack rabbits."
"We did too," Tank adds as she leans over to kiss him.
They drive on to the club in Tank's Navigator. Her and Rebbie give each other dap.
"I'm not mad at her," Rebbie says.
"Not mad at her at all," Nina says.
Next they discuss T-baby and Rich. June and Tank are quiet during *this* conversation. June knows what the problem is and he's watching his mouth. Tank is watching June because he has a sneaky suspicion, June knows exactly where Rich had been all day. Nina and Rebbie are none the wiser that Rich hadn't spent a quiet evening at home with their best friend.

Tank and Nina check in at *The Spot II*. Al, Greg Sr, Sam Sr and John had opened for them. Brad Sr and Archie Sr had shown up to hold things down and keep an eye on their sons and daughters too. This allows Tank and Nina to accompany June and Rebbie to the VIP of the adult club.

One glance from their VIP balcony and Tank knows he isn't going to be walking through the 1st floor without Nina. The simple whore known as Alana has an eagle eye on him from her booth on the main floor. As he scans the club looking at the packed house, he can feel her watching him. He looks in that direction and tells Nina, "And there that bitch is."
"Baby we're gonna have a good time," she says, "Like I always say. As long as she keeps her hands and everything else to herself. I'll let her live."
"Just let me know if we need to go drag her ass," Rebbie adds.
"Amen," Michelle adds as they give dap again.
Then take their men to the VIP dance floor and party.
Cleveland Browns football players are in VIP. The crew have season tickets already and they are eager for the regular season to start.

ʃJackson Heightsʃ
Laying in each other's arms listening to a CD by *The Roots* called, *Things Fall Apart*. Ebony keeps replaying the track with *Erykah Badu* and *Eve* on it. It's titled, *You Got Me*. She tells Ajay this song was made for them. She's played it 5 times. Enough times to know some of the lyrics.
"That's the only real band in Hip Hop," he says, "*Mint Condition* is R&B. But I think they broke up. Or maybe they don't perform anymore."
"I like how *Black Thought* raps," she says, "It's very natural."
She keeps snuggling closer to him.

163

"Are you cold?" he asks as they snuggle naked under the huge comforter from the back of their large white sectional in the family room.

"Mmmm a little but this is cozy," she whispers as she wiggles to get under his arm. Then she adds, "But I wanna tell you something."

"What is it?" he asks.

"A couple of weeks ago. I asked our mothers to try letting the twins have some formula when they have them," she says and quickly explains why. "It's because I wanna have the option of having a romantic evening with you before you leave for camp. With *all* inclusive sex, Anthony. I miss tasting you too."

"Wow," he says, "You've already made plans for this?"

"Yes," she says, "It's for a good cause and it's not forever. I just wanna be able to have some wine and really unwind with you before you report back. Are you okay with that?"

"What choice do I have?" he asks, "If you've already decided."

"I won't go ahead with it if you're not in agreement," she says.

"We'll see," he says, "We can talk about it. But you convinced me that breast milk is best for them. I know we both had it. But we'll see. As long as it's not a permanent thing."

"It's not," she says, "That's a great bonding time that I have with them. I would never *totally* eliminate it."

He's okay with that response. He says, "We're doing our thing, baby."

"Yes daddy, we are," she agrees.

"You know we never *fully* Christened this house, right?" he asks.

"What do you mean?" she asks, even though she knows.

"While the twins are not here," he says, "I plan to have you in every inch of this place."

"In the basement bedrooms too?" she asks with a giggle.

"Oh nah," he says, "We're not fucking down there. Unless it's on stage. Actually I might need to take you down there and put you on the stripper pole."

"Oh," she says, "I'm in danger. I'm scared, daddy."

They laugh.

"Don't be *scurred*, girl," he jokes as he imitates *Mystikal* in *Shake Your Ass*. He says, "Don't be scared now. If you scared, say you scared."

"I'm kind of scared," she giggles.

"Is it too late to call and check on the twins again?" he asks.

"Yes," she says, "I knew you wouldn't be able to sleep without them here," she says, giving him a doubtful look.

"I'm calling anyway," he says and he does.

TIME TO KNOW-RELOADED-Time Will Reveal- part 4

After listening to their twins coo for another 10 minutes, Jo and Pearl convince them to hang up. His eyes look a little misty after the 2nd call.

"I knew you would miss them too much," she says, "We won't be able to sleep tonight. Watch what I tell you."

"I can. I can,...., if you," he starts pulling her on top of him. He adds, "I can if you wear me out."

They begin another session in the family room.

"Umm. This could be a long week," she says as she takes him into her again and they enjoy the rest of their night.

****

Farah moves her class supplies into her classroom on the 1st day of September, prior to Labor day which is the following Monday. Tuesday will be her 1st day to report for a teacher's work day. By Wednesday, the students return for the fall semester. She can't wait to see what crew members she'll get to meet during the school year. She has plans of quickly becoming the crews favorite teacher. She's even more determined to get big Chill's attention. In true spoiled rich girl fashion, she's in the city now and ready to throw her weight and cash at him. For her to assume that money is all it takes to get her inside of this crew's mix, is a testament to the minimal knowledge and needed experience she has with *real* black men. She'll have some success in the city of Cleveland, with males of the black persuasion. But she'll learn a valuable lesson in the process.

****

On Friday September 3rd, Ebony has her 6 week follow-up exam. Dr. Weston releases her to go back to her normal duties. Weston isn't surprised when Ajay tells her they've been sexually active for over a week.

"I'm pleased to tell you two you didn't conceive another baby while you were being hard headed," she says and smiles.

"I'm pleased to hear it," Ebony says and they all laugh.

"Now we have the green light though, right?" Ajay asks.

"Right," Weston says, "Ebony I'll see you back for your semi-annual in six months."

"Okay."

"How are the twins doing with doctor Mahoney?" Weston asks.

Dr. Susan Mahoney is the pediatrician who cares for all of the crew kids.

"They're doing great," Ebony says.

165

"She's real good with them," Ajay adds.

"They should be getting pretty big by now, right?" Weston asks. She always keeps a check on the babies she delivered. She's into the 2nd generation of deliveries for the crew family. They show her baby pictures.

"Yes indeed," Ajay says, "And Ant junior eats a lot."

"He's taking almost eight ounces of cereal and milk," Ebony says, "Our big mama and mothers say they aren't gonna allow us to starve them by only giving them my breast milk and no cereal to go with it."

"You all have got two more athletes on your hands," Dr. Weston say as she laughs.

"I'm not gonna force them to play sports," Ebony says, "I hope little Ant does. But Lannie will probably fall in love and not wanna play anymore. Like me." She smiles at Ajay.

"No she won't," Ajay says quickly, "She'll play until she's thirty five or so. After that, she can do whatever she wants."

"And lil Ant can play while he loves the girls. Is that it, mister Jackson?" Dr. Weston ask while her and Ebony laugh.

"He'd better do something," Ajay says, "Because he's gonna need a good job and a few women giving him money to support his grocery bill." They all laugh as they finish up their appointment. Ebony gets the date for her semi-annual appointment, then her and Ajay leave.

In the parking lot, she points out to him the exact spot where she had seen Rich and June the day she'd witnessed them cheating. She does it each time they come to the complex. He lets her speak freely about her feelings on that situation from the past. He doesn't respond. He's thinking about the present, where Rich is concerned and possibly June too.

They head home. They'll pick up the twins from *Big Mama's House* later. For now, Ebony wants to get home before anyone calls either of them, bidding for their time. She has a surprise for Ajay, at home. One she'd planned since finding out they would have a 6 week sex drought.

They arrive home. She sends him into the basement and tells him to follow the directions on the cards she'd left down there for him. He smiles because he never knew she had even been down there. He heads toward his sanctuary. He opens the door and enters the basement. The 1st card he sees is on the top step. It reads:

You will see a series of numbered cards. Pick up the next card you see, read it and follow the instructions.

The next card instructs him to:

Have a Hennessy on the rocks and keep the bottle. You may need it later.

TIME TO KNOW-RELOADED-Time Will Reveal- part 4

He smiles. He's definitely interested as he picks up the bottle of Hennessy and the rocks glass which was left on the bar, for his convenience. He pours a glass, grabs some ice cubes from the sterling silver ice bucket and brings the bottle with him as he was instructed to do. He sips his drink as he searches for the next card. It isn't hard to find. It reads:
Put on ONLY the silk pajama bottoms which are placed on your favorite chair. This is the only garment you should be wearing after reading this card.

He places his drink and the bottle of Hennessy on the end table next to his lap dance massage and lounge chair.
"Oh she got some freaky shit going on," he says to himself with a smile as he follows the instructions he's given.
Now he's standing in front of his chair, wearing nothing but a pair of silk pajama bottoms. The next card had been placed under the pajamas. He reads it:
Have a seat in your favorite chair.

He sits in his chair, finishes off the drink and pours another. The number 5 card is turned down on the end table, next to a blindfold. When he spots the blindfold, he says aloud, "What the hell? She's trying to pay me back for the Pocono's."
He laughs and reads the last card:
Place the blindfold over your eyes. "No peeking." Call me only after you've done this. I love you!-Ebony Brown-Jackson.

He follows the instructions. He's very intrigued as he yells for her. She's waiting at the top of the stairs. On his call, she sashays down the basement steps and cues the music.
"You have an addiction to me," she says in a sultry voice. "I'm legally bound to give you *your fix*. As often and thorough as you need it."
Once she's in place on stage, she instructs her husband to remove the blindfold and behold her. He does and his eyes stretch to 3 sizes bigger.
"Uh wow," he says, looking at his wife's attire or lack there of.
She's wearing nothing but a garter belt, tassels on her nipples, a thong, top hat, gloves and a cane. She clicks the remote to the CD player and *UGK*'s, *Take It Off* from the motion picture soundtrack, *The Corruptor*, starts to play. She dances for him just like a stripper. Making her bottom drop, shake, rattle and roll then vibrate. She hops onto 1 of the poles and twist her body around it. Wrapping her legs tightly around it, she lays her body backward, head to the floor, as she holds herself up with only the bend in
167

her knee. She squeezes her size D-cups together as she peers at him and pouts her lips likes she's going to taste her own breast. He likes it a lot. He smiles. She pulls herself up and slides down the pole like the dancers do it on the 2nd floor of *The Chill Spot* known as *The Juice Bar.* He enjoys it to the max. Before her tease is done, he gets up and takes the Hennessey bottle back to the bar. He pours another drink for himself and pours coke for her. He stops her mid wiggle and tells her to have a sip of her coke.

After their drinks, he says, "I think it's time we break this basement in."

"I thought I was never suppose to see the inside of this place. Let alone us having sex down here," she says and giggles. Because yes, she was being defiant by coming down here and she expects him to punish her.

He doesn't answer her with words. But he does give her, his tongue. He puts it as far into her mouth as he can get it. She takes it and sucks it hard as if she's craving the liquor taste. He moans as he rips her thong off. Her clitoris throbs instantly. He starts to massage it and she purrs loud.

He says, "I may hate myself for this later. But you're gonna have to feed my twins formula for a week or so. Because daddy's getting some head today."

"Uh huh," she oozes, darning a huge smile. "Add some Hennessy to my coke, daddy. I'll be sure and cleanse my system."

He adds a shot of Hennessy to her coke and then feeds her a long sip. She escorts him back to his chair and pushes him into it. Her drink starts to take affect as she kneels in front of him. She tugs at his silk pajamas. He lifts his bottom and allows them to slide off. She removes them and takes him into her mouth. He gasp as the sensation of the familiar takes his air. She sucks him in, taking him to her throat. Then sucking hard on the tip of his dick as if it's the best thing she's ever tasted.

"Oh baby," he says, "I missed it."

"Mmm," she moans, "I did too, Anthony. I missed tasting you."

"Do the damn thang, baby," he says, "You're so good baby."

She sucks him until his cum shoots from the tip and into her mouth. She's careful to get every drop before he pulls her onto his lap and makes her lay backward. He pulls her pussy to his face, dives in and devours it.

"Ooohhh!" she screams, "Anthony it's so good."

He double times it and makes her cum hard as her body trembles and gyrates for more than 5 minutes. He can't wait for her orgasm to stop. He wants to fuck now. He tries sitting her on top of him but with each poke, she screams loudly. He knows he's fucking her too hard, too early. He stands up with her, goes around his chair and sits her bottom on the back of it. He finds his rhythm, 1 she likes too. And right there is where he takes her to ecstasy. Sucking on her breast and leaving passion marks along the way.

He goes to ecstasy right along with her. He had plans of ripping her a new one for defiantly bringing her butt into his sanctuary and disguising it as seduction. The same as she'd done the night he'd planted Atlantis and Anthony Jr. But he couldn't today because he was love starved. She was starved for him too. Her hip action which brought his *nut* early, had saved her from a certain pussy lashing. He postpones her discipline, for now.

"I'm tearing this muthafuckah up, later though," he tells her and she smiles.

}September 4{

On Saturday the big kids party at *Granny's house* for the September birthdays is for Brad III, who turns 8 this year. Big Mama's house has a party for Rich III, who will turn 4 the last day of this month. Rich Jr calls and talks to his son during the party. Him and T-baby don't speak at all. Mama Anna notices the hostility in T-baby while Rich and her grandson are on the phone. She calls her into the back office to ask her what has her upset. T-baby gives her enough info to make her aware that she feels Rich is having an affair. Her mother-in-law is familiar, sympathetic and understanding.

"Trisha I know what you're feeling," Anna says, "I'm married to his father and I have been for over twenty five years. So there isn't one emotion I haven't been through with Richard senior. So talk to me."

"Richard just seems like he's still got a chip on his shoulder, mama Anna," T-baby says, "It's like he feels like he's not good enough. I know he feels like he's second to Ajay too. He use to say that to me and I would talk him through it. But nowadays, we don't talk like we did during my last year of high school and during college."

"He's always felt like he didn't measure up to certain guys in the family, Trisha," she says, "He took it the hardest when Richard and I split up. He witnessed his father beating me and cursing me. He saw all of it. But the key to it, is making him face his reality. Whatever that is. It took a lot of years to get his father to come into his own. But he finally did."

"We talked about the abuse and all of that stuff," T-baby says, "During college, he really came out more. Especially since he got MVP for his last college season. He promised he would never do that to our son. I thought he'd gotten passed it. But nowadays, I really don't know."

"Bottom line is, you have to do what's best for you and Richard the third, Trisha," Anna says, "I will never turn on you. Because I know, only too well, exactly what you're dealing with."

T-baby hugs her mother-in-law and thanks her for her kind and on point words of encouragement and advice. Still she doesn't reveal everything. Anna doesn't reveal everything either.

"We'll work it out somehow," T-baby says, "He's still my first and only love. That has to count for something, right?"

"I sure believe it does," Anna says, "His father is mine too and he got it right. After some years, that is."

The 2 of them share a smile and another hug, before rejoining Steven, Alicia and the rest of the crew at the birthday party. Little Ashanti is having a great time.

"Shaunie is having the next birthday party," Ally says, speaking on her and Steven's daughter who'll turn 1 on the 1st of October.

The party is a success, despite the depression T-baby is feeling. She loves her financial career but basketball was always her comforter. Whenever she was down or feeling like she was a step behind. She would pick up her basketball and find a hoop. She's starting to think about the *WNBA* a lot more now. The only thing holding her back is being away from her young son and finishing Grad School with her girls. But still, she's going to start checking into how she can get a tryout. She's going to call Jb, this week.

}*Atlanta*{

Down in Atlanta, Jb has gotten word back from his team of lawyers that the Anthony "Ajay" Jackson paraphernalia which was being sold last year at the Dobbs Flower and Gift shop in Cincinnati, has netted Ajay a settlement. He has to contact Ajay, make him aware of the amounts and see if it's acceptable before he can approve it. Ajay will have Ebony in on the final decision. She was the person who had discover it, protected him and gotten him this money. *His money!*

}*Cleveland*{

T-baby doesn't talk to Rich for more than a week. Not until he calls her at her office and talks to her like he has some sense. This has her even more confused. She really doesn't know how to take him, these days. The more negative things that happen between them. The more she closes herself off. And still, she doesn't share it with anyone. Not even her girls or her mother. Bre's *triple 9's* birthday party weekend and the Labor day celebration starts tomorrow. T-baby hopes to have her husband there with her, like the rest of the females in the family. She closes her side of the office and heads home early. She wants to do some early and extra preparation for the celebration.

TIME TO KNOW-RELOADED-Time Will Reveal- part 4

The next morning the CrewLand mall is all abuzz. Customers are overflowing at all of the shops and stores. From the detail shop to the salon. To the spa and the clothing store. The restaurant is packed too. Many have dropped in to purchase last minute tickets for the party. Only to find that it's sold out. Some want to be in the area, so badly that they get tickets to *The Spot II*, just to hang around until someone leaves the adult club. *Crew Gear* is selling lots of party outfits too. Debbie is expecting her daughter Bre, who's the guest of honor, to come in from Sacramento with her family this afternoon.

"What time does Bre get here?" Anna asks Debbie.

"Their flight is scheduled for three o'clock," Deb answers.

Her and Anna are working at *Crew Spa and Health Club*. It's the busy Saturday morning of Bre's 25th birthday bash and Labor day celebration. The following Monday will be *Labor Day*. The Atlanta crew are coming home as well. Them and Bre's family are coming in today. Not only for the celebration. They'll be staying through Sunday the 12th for the 1st home game of the Cleveland Browns. The team returned to the city for the 1999 season. The Crew are excited to have a home football team again. They all plan to show their support. The entire crew have season tickets.

At the bash, everybody has a great time eating barbeque, drinking and playing cards. All the shops are hosting some facet of it. The restaurant and Stoney's grill provides the food. At *this* event, Ajay and JB get the chance to show off the grilling skills their fathers had passed down to them. *Cash Money Records, Bone & Mo Thugs family* are the performers. Jenkins Jams company provides the music. Que Psi Phi does the photos and video. There are 4 generations of talent at this celebration. Included are Brad III, CJ, Destiny and little Jerica.

By nightfall, the crew have all regrouped, gotten dressed and are at the clubs and ready to party like they know how too. The kids club is packed to the walls. CJ is happy to attend the kids club. She loves *The Spot II* and wishes she could be here daily.

"I like our club for kids," she says to her 1st cousin Brad III. CJ will be 8, next month. Brad III has already made eight.

"I wish I could have my birthday party here," CJ says.

"You have to ask your mama to let you come back," Renee and Chill's daughter Destiny says.

"I miss you being here, CJ," Brad III says.

"I know," she says, "I miss you guys too. All of y'all."

6 year-old Destiny is the youngest in attendance at The Spot II. Jerica

171

and all of the kids younger than 5 are at *Granny's house* with Brenda and Jackie. Pearl and Jo are there, along with Sandy, Anna and Rena. Debbie and Belinda are helping out at the restaurant with their parents and husbands. John and Al have Richard Sr and Brian Sr helping them out at Stoney's, along with Ajay and JB. They had planned well and have all of their basis covered.

Terrell is in town with the huge crew from Atlanta which includes April and Yolanda. His parents, Dr. and Mrs. Jonathan and Jessica Layton are in town from Boston. Ron and Carolyn come from Houston and bring their children and crew. It's truly a large and special family event. Just like normal the celebration, its heavily attended and the talk of the town.

After the Browns game on Sunday, all of the out of town crew have flights. Either this evening or in the morning. Ajay has to fly to Miami to begin preseason conditioning. He finds it even harder to leave, this year then in previous years. When it was only Ebony, it was a real test. But now that he's the father of the most precious twins he's ever seen in his life. It's heart wrenching. Just knowing he's going to miss getting up to the sounds of his babies cooing or peacefully suckling on henny and penny. Well on that part, he wishes he could trade places with them.

Security leaves taking Ajay to the airport. Ebony, Anthony Jr and Atlantis are with them. As they huddle together at the gate, Ajay can't get enough last minute kisses from his little family. Atlantis is a bit restless. It's as if she knows her father isn't going to be there shortly. She doesn't want to leave his arms. Anthony Jr seems self assured. Like he knows he has to be in charge of the 2 females. He looks at Ajay the entire time he's getting his last minute kisses. Then Ajay kisses his son's forehead and looks into his eyes.

He says, "Take care of home. You're the man of the house until I get back. I'm counting on you."

Ebony cries as he hugs and kisses her again. She doesn't want to let go.

"I'm gonna miss you, baby," she says.

"Are you gonna be okay?" he asks.

"Of course I won't," she says and smiles. "But we'll be safe, well taken care of and loved beyond words. That's much better than okay."

"I love you," he says with a final kiss to all 3. He adds, "Take care of my babies. I'll call you when I land."

His eyes well up with tears as he heads down to the tarmac, after leaving Ebony and the twins in the terminal. Ebony cries more while security tends to the twins and gives her some time to regroup. She had held onto her man for as long as she possibly could before he had to board his plane. Bronson and Jacobson had come with them. They help her get the twins back to the Cherokee. Jacobson and McDaniel drive her and the babies to Jackson Heights while Bronson and Teddy Joiner follow in the security car. Ebony will have big mama and the staff at the mansion to help with the twins and the house. But all she can think about is the next time they'll see daddy.

****

Breaking news in Cleveland is a report on a male stripper who has gone missing. Ebony knows it's Angel's cousin James "The Bulldog" Taylor. She also knows her crew had arranged it. She saw Chill, Jb and Ron in mob mode during the celebration. She also saw them fill her husband in on the plan. She knows Ajay will tell her when he's ready. Or if it becomes necessary. But she also knows the latest threat from Angel has been cancelled. James "The Bulldog" Taylor is no more.

TIME TO KNOW-RELOADED-Time Will Reveal- part 4

CHAPTER 42

FATHER AND SON

Something has already sparked the grade school crew's interest and it's only the 1st day of school at MLK. Pam and Roo has a run in with Miss Benson better known as Farah, who seems to be stalking them. She remembers them from Que Psi Phi Studios, back when she purchased her camera and equipment. Neither of these senior girls have Farah's class but juniors Ally and Steven so have her class, as an elective. Chill's son sophomore Lil Kenny needs the class for his college prep. Farah Benson doesn't immediately know Ally and Steven are crew, so she isn't overly friendly with them. Not at first. But she recognizes lil Kenny's name, Kenneth Payne Jr instantly and she starts showing him favoritism from day one. Some might say she's way friendlier than *any* teacher should be with a student. Chaundra certainly agrees. Kenny has been a football star and a celebrity on the MLK campus for 2 reasons. One reason is because he's the starting Quarterback and has been since last year. And two. Not only is he a member of the infamous crew but he's the son of the *notorious big Chill*. Even if he didn't have the same name, someone would've given his identity away as they eventually do with Steven and Ally.

Lil Kenny doesn't know why this teacher is so friendly with him but being who he is, he's going to take *full* advantage of it. His girlfriend Chaundra has a serious problem with how Miss Benson keeps hanging all over *her* man. She's a junior and a year ahead of Kenny.

As Kenny's leaving class, Farah is glued to his arm. He skips quickly to catch up to Chaundra. Still Farah follows him up the sidewalk. Kenny puts his arm around Chaundra. Farah still walks on the other side of him and she's about to start a conversation until Chaundra stops them both in their tracks.

"Who is this teacher?" Chaundra asks Kenny.

"I'm Miss Benson. Farah Benson. I moved here from Pittsburgh."

"*And?*" Chaundra asks dryly.

"I recognized his name because I've been to the spot a *few* times. I love his father's club."

"That's my mother's club too," Kenny corrects her.

He points at Chaundra. Then to Ally and Steven who are standing near with Ruthie and Pam. He says, "And it belongs to all of us in the crew."

He chuckles at the foolish look on Farah's face and says, "Anyway, *bye.*"

Him, Chaundra and the crew leave her standing there and walk away.

TIME TO KNOW-RELOADED-Time Will Reveal- part 4

Kenny's a gentlemen until he feels someone is disrespecting his mother. He knows Farah's after his father just by the way she acts and how she speaks of him. Kenny would've known even if Chill hadn't already told him. He's seen this behavior, many times throughout his life. Women are always going after his dad. But he isn't going to tolerate any advances toward the man his mother loves and is married too. Farah will back off or there will be consequences. For now, he tells his crew to be cool and watch her. "But if she gets out of line," he says, "She can get some chamber action."

****

Debbie and Brad Sr fly CJ back to Cleveland to celebrate her 8th birthday. Ashanti has her 1st birthday party at *Granny's house.* She shares the spotlight with Jerica, who will be 5 this month. CJ has her party at *Big Mama's house.* They share October birthday honors with Archie Jr, who gets initiated to the crew. He's too young to go into the main club and to old to celebrate at Granny or Big Mama's house with CJ and *that* crew. He'd turned 14 on the 4th. His party is at *The Spot II.* The place for 13-17 year olds is the place to be. He's already playing for the high school basketball team, same as Ajay had done. They call each other cousins and he instructs others to do the same. Just as his sister Rebbie has always done with Nina. Their maternal grandparents who live in Europe had started that with Nina and Ajay's paternal grandparents when Archie Jr and Rebbie's mother, Rena was born.

The crew in attendance at The Spot II party are Roo, who won't be 18 until December. Pam who's 17. Steven, Chaundra, Ally and Kenny who are all 16 years of age. Or will be by the end of this year. Charlotte will be 15 soon. Brandon and Brina, who will be 13 next month, go to both the *Big Mama's house* and Archie's party. Sam is over 18 but he opts to go to Archie's party to be with his girlfriend Pam.

Bruce, Kim, Erica, Jesse, Brittany and Greg Jr are all gone away to college. Reaper is in Atlanta, where Brittany attends college, working on his 2nd CD. Venitia is working at CrewLand and taking classes at CSU.

Crew couples who are celebrating wedding anniversaries at *The Chill Spot* are Mr. And Mrs. Brian James Sr and Mr. And Mrs. Samuel Logan Sr. Both have been married for 25 years. Lasting relationships are a normal occurrence in the crew and its something they are most proud of.

****

Ajay comes home for a preseason game against the Cleveland

175

Cavaliers, where Jarvis is playing, on Halloween weekend. He's got another gift for his bride. He surprises Ebony with a 2000, all white Escalade. They sale Ally and Steven her 95 Camry and they're happy to get a vehicle of their own.

Miami wins the preseason game. Ajay scores 37 points has 7 assists and 5 steals. Jarvis did well but not well enough to get a win. After the game, Ajay is happy to be spending the night at home with his wife and twins. But he has to leave again on Sunday.

Before flying out Sunday after church, Ebony reminds him that their twins have to get their 4-month shots the following week.

"Call me as soon as they're done and you get settled," he says, "Or if it's not good news. Call me from doctor Mahoney's office."

She's going to call him before she goes to the pediatricians office because she knows he wants her too.

}*Medical Complex*{

In her new Escalade, Ebony takes the twins in for their shots on November first. She brings big mama along for guidance. Big mama loves her sport utility vehicle.

"This is a fine vehicle Ajay bought for you," big mama says, "It's *really* nice inside."

"Yes it is," Ebony says, "Anthony says Lannie and Lil Ant have to roll in style. That's what he said. Not me."

"Well they are," big mama says with excitement, "This is a *Cadillac!*"

"My caddy from my daddy," Ebony says as she giggles.

"That man loves to spoil you, sweetheart," big mama says, "You had better *stay* good to him."

"I will, big mama," she says, "I promise you. That's one thing you will never have to worry about. I love taking care of him."

They arrive at the complex. Ebony still has to be very careful parking such a huge vehicle. She's still use to the Camry, where she could whip in and out and even the Jeep Cherokee isn't *this* big. They park along way away from any other parked vehicles as Ajay had suggested, to keep from getting any scratches and dents while in parking lots. They go in for the twins visit with Dr. Susan Mahoney. The appointment takes all of 10 minutes. Ebony wasn't squeamish at all. That's Ajay's job. He got outright angry when the twins had their 2 month shots because Atlantis cried. Ajay's eyes welled up too. Ebony told him then that he couldn't come with her for shots anymore and he was fine with that.

TIME TO KNOW-RELOADED-Time Will Reveal- part 4

"Okay we've got the four month shots done early," Dr. Susan Mahoney says, "As long as everything is alright with them. I'll see them back in two months. Where is daddy this time? Is he still angry with us?" she asks with a warm smile.

"He's not mad anymore but I just told him he couldn't come for shots," Ebony says with a smile.

"Well it's okay. He's daddy," Dr. Mahoney says, "And daddy's are suppose to be protective. Especially when the babies are this precious."

"Thanks doctor Susan," Ebony says, "Thanks for taking such good care of them."

"You're welcome, Ebony," Mahoney says, "They're doing great. We're looking really good here. We'll see you in two months."
Her and big mama bundle the twins back up and head for the elevators.

"Shall we get some lunch now?" big mama asks.

"I could eat," Ebony says smiling and pushing the double stroller onto the elevator.

"Let's get something," big mama suggest, "We can sit down and eat at the restaurant and everybody can see the twins too."
The elevator arrives at the lobby, the doors open and Rich is standing there waiting to get on. He's with a woman. It's the same woman Ebony had seen him here *tongue* kissing in June's car, a year and a half ago. Ebony freezes in her tracks initially as her thoughts come rushing to her.

"*What*?!" she tries but no words will escape her.
She's upset as she wheels her twins past Rich and his mistress. Big mama speaks with Rich for a few minutes while Ebony rushes to the exit door. Rich is obviously feeling awkward. Because now big mama has seen him too. Still she makes light conversation and lets him know he can come and talk with her anytime. He says he will but she knows he won't.

Ebony gets just outside of the automatic doors and stops. She can hear Ajay in her head saying not to let someone else's bullshit get her worked up. She can hear him saying he never wants her to be upset and for certain, not when it's not about their babies or them. She's definitely not about to drive her twins while she's angry.

"Oh hell no!" she yells, "I have to say something this time."
She turns the twins back around and heads back inside to where big mama is still standing, talking with Rich while he helps the woman out of her coat. She's wearing maternity clothes.
She's pregnant!

"Rich! What in *God's* name is this?!" Ebony snaps.
177

Rich doesn't reply. Big mama urges Ebony to calm down and come on with her to the SUV.

"Is she *pregnant for you*, Rich?" Ebony has to asks, "Ha? *Is* she?"

"I don't know," he answers and the woman gives him a shocked look as she makes herself known. She says, "Hi I'm Regina Kemp and-"

"So! I'm Trisha's *first* cousin. His *wife*. Do you know her? Do you Rich? How much do you think T-baby's gonna take from you? You're a disgrace. You don't deserve her. Move out of my way. You make me sick!" She turns the twins around and heads for the doors again. This time big mama follows her. Rich gets on the elevator with Regina. He's embarrassed and busted for a 2nd time. He doesn't even look back at them. He does wonder if T-baby will be calling his phone soon though.

Once in the caddy, though Ebony is thoroughly disgusted. She drives carefully to the restaurant while big mama has her say.

"He's not settled in his *mind*. He's got the devil on him."

"Somebody needs to blow his mind out!" Ebony says in anger. But recants immediately and says, "T-baby needs to leave him, big mama Eloise. He's not gonna do right. *Ever*."

Big mama suggests they pray for Rich instead of ridiculing him.

"He's got a lot more problems going on then just infidelity," big mama assures her.

Ebony doesn't comment any further. She doesn't want to pray for Rich at this point. Her big mama has the awesome ability to always find the good in people. Even if what they're showing her is bad and people view them as bad news. She wants to help them do better. Ebony knows Ajay has always felt that way about her. Still Ebony doesn't see herself wishing Rich good luck. Ebony is just plain disgusted with her cousin-in-law, on both sides of her marriage. Instead of eating at the restaurant, she asks big mama if they can take their meals and go to Jackson Heights. Big Mama tells her that's fine. They get their food, then drive to Ebony and Ajay's house to eat. No sooner than Ebony enters the mansion and sits the food down on the daytime table, she says, "I need to call daddy before I can even eat."

She calls Ajay's cell phone immediately. He picks up on the 1st ring. He's been waiting for her call.

"Hey queen," he says with a chuckle "How did the shots go?"

He has a jovial tone, "Are my babies uncomfortable?"

"They're a little cranky," she says, "But I'm gonna feed them and put them down for a nap real soon."

"Okay but that sounds like everything went good," he says.

"It did," she says.

TIME TO KNOW-RELOADED-Time Will Reveal- part 4

"So why do you sound so down, baby?"
"I'll tell you when you get here," she says.
"No," he says, "I'm not waiting. You're gonna tell me now."
She tells him what she witnessed at the complex. It leaves him disappointed.
"Damn. I told that fool to chill out wit that," he says in anger. Then he says,
"Look here. I'm not holding this shit no longer. Tell T-baby I wanna talk to her when I get in, alright? And if that negro trips with you *this time*. I'm killing his ass."
They continue their conversation about their 3-month old twins doctor's visit. Before hanging up, he tells her not to worry about Rich and not to speak a word about what she saw to anyone else. He's going to handle this situation first things in the morning. They hang up after phone kisses.

Chaundra has had her fill of Farah's groping of her boyfriend right in front of her face. She decides to talk to her mother about it before she acts on it. She tells Jackie what's been going on. Even about the stuff she hasn't seen but was either told by Kenny or 1 of her crew.

"Yesterday when Charlotte came up for dance practice at the high school," she tells her mother, "She saw her flirting with Kenny. She said she was trying to rub his face and massage his shoulders but Kenny told her she had to pull up off of him."

"This is a *teacher*?" Jackie asks.

"Yes ma'am. She's new. She goes to the spot all of the time. Kenny said she's really after his dad but he don't like her."

"So she's going for his *jail bait* son?!" Jackie asks in disbelief. "Hold on. Does *Renee* know about this?"

"I don't think she does. Kenny don't want us to tell her though," she says, "Because right now he can skip her class and she'll still give him a hundred for the day."

Her mother says she'll find a way to pass this on to Chill and Renee. She's going to start by telling Jo, then go from there. Jackie tells Chaundra not to worry. She says, "Boys will be boys. But if miss Benson crosses the line. She'll be out of a job."

"That can't come soon enough for me," Chaundra says as her eyes well up. "Why does she have to like *my* boyfriend?"

"He's handsome, honey," her mother says, "They all are. There are some beautiful men in our family. Be proud."

They both laugh as they make dinner together. They became super close when Stoney was killed. Jackie has a great relationship with both of her daughters. Chaundra and Charlotte talk to her about *nearly* everything.

179

TIME TO KNOW-RELOADED-Time Will Reveal- part 4

Jackie had even taken them for birth control pills as soon as their periods started. Sunday dinner is family talk time in their home, as it is with the rest of the crew. Chaundra and Charlotte choose to tell their mother what's on their minds. Unlike the foursome had been. They didn't open up about their sexual activity until they were caught up and forced too.

}Next Morning in Jackson Heights{
Ajay meets with T-baby first thing the next morning. He had told Ebony to call and invite her and Rich III over for breakfast. They show up in 10 minutes and have breakfast with big mama, Ebony, Ajay and the twins. Ebony does the dishes while big mama retires to her parlor. Ajay sends Ebony upstairs to the playroom with the twins and Rich III, so him and T-baby can talk in the family room.

"What's up, T-baby?" Ajay asks, "Come in here and have a seat."
"What's going on, Ajay?" she asks.
He tells her again to take a seat in the family room. Then again, he has to tell Ebony to go upstairs with the twins and Rich III. She wants to be moral support for T-baby. She thinks her cousin is going to be distraught. Ajay insist she go on upstairs and let him handle it. She finally leaves with the children. Ajay talks to T-baby.

"T-baby this is something I really hate to do," he says, "But I don't want you to be clueless and end up getting hurt later on."
"Rich is cheating on me. Ain't he?" she asks, shocking him as he looks at her. "You can tell it straight out Ajay. I can handle it."
"Yes he is and now I hear that the chick is pregnant," Ajay says in a low tone.
T-baby is unusually calm, in Ajay's opinion. Immediately he can sense that she wasn't clueless.

"I've had signs Ajay," she starts, "Every since the night of you and Ebony's reception. After y'all were long gone. So was he. And you're the only one I've told this too so keep it on the *Dee Ell*. Some of what I'm about to tell you, my girls don't even know."
"Talk about whatever you're comfortable with," he says.
"As I was saying. The first time I noticed was the night of you and Ebony's wedding. He disappeared for hours."
"I heard about that," he says.
"He came home at dawn smelling like I don't know what, from liquor and he was high too. He blamed it on the season but I didn't believe him *then*." Ajay listens intensely, as she goes on. "During your honeymoon he was wilding out. Staying out *all* night. I couldn't reach him," she says.
180

TIME TO KNOW-RELOADED-Time Will Reveal- part 4

"Sometimes when I did, his ass would answer the phone, realize it is me then hang up."

"*Fuck*," Ajay whispers.

"That night when my girls had private dinners with y'all. He never even came home," she says, "He didn't show up for his baby's party this year. He just called him. When I try to confront him, he comes close to hitting me. Or worse than that. He comes home stinking and still wants to fuck me." Her voice starts to get loud now as she's becoming upset. "He have me ready to fight women, still to this day. Even though I know it's him that's lying and going after them," she says.

Ebony can hear her from the 2nd floor. She starts to cry as she tends to the twins. Rich III watches her, like crying is a familiar scene. Suddenly he pats her on her back. She picks him up and hugs him tight.

"It's okay, cousin Ebony," Rich III says.

She tries to smile through her tears. He hops down and puts his attention back on his twin cousins. He's okay. Even if she isn't.

Downstairs T-baby and Ajay continue to talk.

"It's not Tameka either, is it?" T-baby asks, "That's pregnant?"

"No," Ajay says, "She's not pregnant but Rich *has* been harassing her for sex. She doesn't want him. I even heard he assaulted her since she's been working for us. But she won't tell on him. She's scared. She's been doing everything to avoid him. He's going after her. Threatening to get her fired if she don't do what he wants."

"We're not gonna fire her. We need to fire him," T-baby says as she laughs.

Ajay doesn't laugh because he knows she isn't happy. She's just laughing to keep from crying. She sits in silence for a few seconds, as he tells her about the complex and Ebony.

"I don't know what to say, T-baby," he says, "I can't stand the way my cousin's life is going. But he don't seem to wanna do right."

"That's an understatement," she says, "Ajay I know you and I have had our ups and downs. Mainly about him. I know you always had my back. You took the rap for Craig's murder. You knew I was shooting too."

"That's nothing," he says.

"So who is the girl?" T-baby asks, "Is she Asian?"

He says no. Then he tells her, he doesn't know her name.

He says, "I would rather not say who it is. Not just yet because it may not be his kid."

"*Whatever*. I appreciate you telling me the truth," she says, "I'm not even gonna tell him I know about his bastard child either. At least, not

181

yet," she says and Ajay looks at her in surprise. Then she says, "I'm for real. I'm thinking of what me and my son's next move is gonna be. Richard ain't right, Ajay. Even mama Anna says it too. He's got some serious issues. Richard is not the same person he was when we started dating in Shaker Heights. Money changed him for the worst. I know our parents bussed us to Martin Luther King high school to make sure we had diversity and all of that. But something was lost with him, way back then. He could've went to Shaker or the Heights. And still it wouldn't have made a difference. It's not about *who* he's around. No more than it is for us. We all have a great foundation and family, Ajay. And we all know that we are loved and we're expected to represent this crew to the utmost. But all of the love and understanding in the world hasn't helped him. He had me ready to beat Tameka down at the spot, one night. He said she was pushing up on him. My heart *knew* he was lying because I remember during you and Ebony's honeymoon when he was trying to kick in her door."

Ajay's looks even more surprised. T-baby continues her revelation.

"See this is how it was. His phone had called me back after I called him and he answered, then hung up on me without saying a word. I heard the whole damn thing. He doesn't know about that *pocket* call. He took the baby to my mama and told her he was coming to Natty to honeymoon with me. She called me thinking we was sleeping in. That's when I knew he didn't have our son. But that was the reason he gave me for him coming back home so early. I didn't tell my mama any of that. Now apart of me wishes I had. But even before I went back to Natty that day. I checked out our secret spot. Some Asian bitch came running out to the Benz thinking it was him, when I approached that house we use to chill at. The bitch ran back inside and hid, when she saw it was me. He don't know that either. Not unless she told him. I don't even hurt anymore, Ajay. I'm so far past that. I'll be okay. I just have to plan. You know how crew do it."

She gives him a forced smile but he can tell she's hurt that her marriage is on the rocks.

"I'll support you," he says, "Whatever you decide to do. I'll support *you*. Just know that."

She thanks him for his honesty. Then goes to get Rich III from upstairs. She tells Ebony she'll call her later and leaves with her son.

Ajay goes to check on Ebony and the twins. He finds her crying her eyes out. He holds her for nearly an hour while they talk and until she starts to calm down.

"I could hear her," she finally says, "The babies monitors was still on and I could hear her. She knew about it all this time. I didn't tell her because I didn't wanna hurt her. But she's been hurting *all* this time and wouldn't even tell us."

"I'll never do that to you and my babies, Ebony," he says suddenly, "You have my word, baby. I'm ashamed of my cousin."

"I know, Anthony," she says, "I know this has nothing to do with our marriage. It just hurts because we've all been together since day one." She tells him she wants to have a talk with big mama. He agrees she should.

"I'll take the twins out for a ride," he says, "We'll go visit Chill." He gives her a tight hug then he seals it with a sweet kiss. Afterwards he gets his twins dressed in matching fall outfits, coats, boots and mittens. He goes and picks up Rich III and Ashanti. Then he takes them all for a ride in the Escalade. After their ride, they stop off at CrewLand mall to visit.

Back at their house, Ebony and big mama sit in the parlor and have a heart to heart.

"Well baby," big mama says, "This week started off with a bang."

"It's insane, big mama," she says, "I barely slept last night."

"I've told you," she warns, "Don't let anybody else's problems become you and Ajay's. I won't stand for that."

"Big mama you're so wise," she says, "I hope to have *half* of the wisdom you have, one day."

"I've been living longer," she says with a chuckle, "Experience is the best teacher."

Big mama finally tells her about the whole situation with Sonya and Shuntay. And why her and poppa had allowed them to hang around them.

"They needed to be around you to see what true love, commitment and real family values was about, baby girl," she says, "That's the only reason I tolerated them and let them come around my home."

"You knew they was loose, *right*?" Ebony asks, "And that they danced until their butts and everything else falls out of their clothes?"

Ebony laughs. She had just repeated a saying big mama and granny had etched in the minds of her and her girls.

"Oh honey hush. Of course I did," big mama says as she laughs too. Then she tells Ebony she'd realized those girls didn't have any guidance and that was what she was trying to be for them.

"They needed to leave that Raymond alone and find somebody to treat them the way Ajay treated you. And still treats you, baby," she says, "But after he attacked you. Me and Percy didn't give a damn how they got along. We knew they were accessories to him attacking you."

She knows about another of Raymond's victims but she doesn't go into it.

183

TIME TO KNOW-RELOADED-Time Will Reveal- part 4

Just hearing Raymond's name again sends a cold chill through Ebony. Today she feels like she needs to cleanse her soul. So she does.

"Big mama I wanna tell you something," she says in a soft tone.

"What is it, sweetheart?" she's looking at Ebony with sincerity.

"It's about Raymond. He-"

"He's not coming back?" big mama offers.

"No ma'am. He's dead, big mama," she admits.

"I know that already," she says, stunning Ebony.

"You do!?"

"Oh yes. I know that," she says, "Ajay told me that awhile ago."

"Did he tell you how?" she asks.

"No. He said he did it," big mama says, "I didn't believe him but I didn't push."

"I did it, big mama. I'm so sorry but I was scared-"

"Who cares *why*?" big mama interrupts her again, "He tried to kill your spirit. Big mama wanted to take his life myself. You repent baby. Ask the Lord to forgive you for your sins."

"I did and I still do," she says, "Everyday. Every time I look at our babies. I pray that I'll be able to watch them grow up and be here for them. For along time I had nightmares about that night. But Anthony has filled my life with so many good memories. He makes me feel so safe. With that and then the babies coming, I hadn't thought about it in a *long* time."

"Good for you," big mama says, "God forgives us because the flesh is weak. Only the soul is immortal. With all of the blessings you and Ajay have had since. I'd say God has forgiven you *and* him. All of you. You getting rid of him was God delivering you from evil. That's how I see it."

Ebony says, "That's so much pressure off me, just telling you that."

"I knew you could do it, baby girl," big mama says, "I mean. I knew about Neal too."

Ebony listens in surprise as her grandmother tells her of how Al had told her the story years ago.

"Folks in this crew have always told me their deepest secrets for some reason," she says with a smile.

"Because you're the *best*, big mama," she says, "That's why we all confide in you and love you so much."

"Richard and June are not doing right by their wives," she says, "God's gonna punish them if they don't get it together."

"Anthony treats me so good," Ebony says, "If he was cheating. I wouldn't even know."

"Yes you would," she says, "You would know. Just like T-baby and

184

Time To Know- RELOADED-Time Will Reveal 4   Black Coffee

Rebbie knows something ain't right. They're not ready to deal with it yet, is all," she continues, "You and Ajay are my vision of love. Y'all are me and Percy, forty five years ago."

"Really?"

"Uh huh. You two have been through more *together* than anyone else in *your* generation of this crew. And y'all managed to stay together and in love with each other," she says, "That's something special. Everybody can't have that. Only a few have that kind of love and dedication. Many people stay together for life. But every couple don't have that true bond."

"I know he loves me and I love him," Ebony says.

"Oh yes ma'am and he'll lie, cheat, steal and kill to protect you, baby," big mama says, "That's Percy for ya."

Ebony laughs and big mama continues, "You know you're marked by me from birth."

"What do you mean? I know I got your name. Me *and* Jerica."

"You have my passion too, baby girl," big mama says before an admission of her own. "You're not the only one who killed someone at an early age," she reveals, "I did also."

"You *did*?"

"Mister Prescott," big mama confesses.

"Your *real* daddy?"

"He was my biological father," big mama corrects her. "Johnny Wilkes was always and will always be my daddy. My *real* daddy! See your mother married a man with the same name as her *real* granddaddy. Just like Joanna married Allen. The same name as *her* daddy. We always saw symbolism in names. You're Eloise and you was born to be a wise person. But I killed Edward Prescott myself."

"I thought his wife killed him," Ebony says.

"Misses Clara Prescott was his wife's name," big mama starts, "She didn't kill him but she told the sheriff she did. She said that to protect me and my family."

Ebony listens.

"Misses Clara told the sheriff he'd come in beating on her like a mad man. And he had because she caught him trying to rape *me*. She gave me the rifle and helped me hold it. We waited for him to come back into my room. It was later that same night after he had tried to rape me and she caught him. She lit into him and he beat her up pretty bad. Then he left to go to the local juke joint. He came back drunk as a skunk and wanted to have me. She didn't let him."

"I had no idea about this part of it," Ebony says as her eyes well up

185

with tears. Then she says, "So you do know what I went through."

"Yes honey I do," she says, "Like I told you. I would've killed Raymond myself, if I'd ever gotten my hands on him."

Ebony is crying now as her big mama reveals the story of her own attack.

"Pain like that never leaves you. *Really*. It haunts you until you get relief from it. Your crew chief Chill. He understood. That's why he made sure Raymond was found and handled. But every time he does something where someone's life is taken. He's most likely avenging the deaths of his parents."

Ebony hadn't been told any of this but she knows it's the truth because big mama knows every secret there is in this family.

"Why would he try to rape you? Did he know he was your father?" she asks.

"Yes he knew," she answers, "He knew he had been raping my mother for years. He knew I was his child but he didn't care."

Big Mama talks about how whites viewed blacks, back when she was a girl.

"We was property to the white man," she says, "The bigoted man, that is. Property and nothing more. They felt like they could treat us in any way they wanted too."

"That's *so* wrong," Ebony says through sobs.

"Well it's not a whole lot different now," big mama says, "They just have other ways of treating us like second class citizens."

"I know that's true," Ebony agrees, "Like joining the police force so they can further their cause, in some cases."

"Misses Clara took that upon herself because she knew those bigoted folks would've lynched our entire family if they had known some Negros killed a white man," she says, "They would've killed us, for sure."

"Misses Clara took that to her grave?" Ebony asks.

"She sure did. She took care of us like we was her family, after his death too," big mama says, "She paid for your mama and your aunt Brenda to go to college. She paid for their weddings too. And when she died, she left us everything. See mister Edward Prescott was very well off. Him and Clara didn't have any kids of their own. She left us all of his possessions. She said it was the least she could do after what he had done to our lives and after what he'd put my mama through. My mother could never bring herself to have any more children. I don't even know if she ever let daddy Wilkes get that close to her again. The rape which created me, damaged my mother's heart. I was told by many that she was one of the nicest and most giving people you could ever meet. She cooked for the church and the men who worked on the railroad. That's how she met daddy Wilkes. She was a late bloomer for those days. She was nearly sixteen before she met daddy.

TIME TO KNOW-RELOADED-Time Will Reveal- part 4

She could sew, cook, garden and she could read and write too. She taught me everything she knew and misses Clara is the one who gave her the books for me. She also gave her, her first job. Which was subsequently her undoing. I heard she was never the same after that rape. But I only got to know my mother, *one* way. Impatient and short tempered. Misses Clara called her, *her* daughter. My mother took care of misses Prescott like she was her real mother. She loved her. We all did and when she fell ill. That's when me, my mama and daddy took care of her."

"So that's where you and poppa got the money to move to Cleveland?"

"Well that's how mama and daddy bought the land and built the house in Houston first," she says, "To get away from the hateful sneers in Beaumont Texas. And yes that's how me and Percy was able to build here when we escaped north during the sixties. Misses Clara had already given my mama all of their worldly possessions and left us everything in the will. But bigots still wanted to take it. That's when my ability to read and write became very valuable. Misses Clara gave me her grandmothers pearls, *personally*. That was the night mister Prescott died. She said she wanted me to pass them on to my very first granddaughter when she got married. Cause that would be her great-granddaughter. She always called my mama, *her* child and me, her granddaughter."

"Those are the pearl's you gave me at my bridal shower, for my wedding?" Ebony ask in tears.

"The very ones," big mama says, "I want you to give them to your first granddaughter on her wedding day. But let your daughter's borrow them. That's what she told me to do. Then pass them on too....well, to *you*."

"I will big mama," she says, "I'm gonna go put them on now."
Big Mama smiles as Ebony runs to the safe in the master bedroom to get the string of pearls. She returns with them.
"Will you fasten them for me?" she asks.

"Sure honey," big mama says and she does.

"I guess I don't have to tell Anthony about that story either, ha?" Ebony asks smiling through tears.

"No," big mama says, "He knows. We talked about it a long time ago. After your attack, it was the only way I could keep him from coming back to Houston to look for that boy. I wanted him to know that you would come back around. He just had to find the way. I knew *only* he could. So I advised him to talk to both your parents and speak from his heart. I called the parents beforehand too. But he did a great job from what they tell me. He had to know whom he was trying to love. That's the only way he could

187

do it correctly. And baby girl I have to say. He got it right!"

"He sure did," Ebony says and smiles. "Now I understand why Anthony knows me so well. He's always talked to you, hasn't he?"

"Yes he has and he still does," big mama reveals, "He's always liked you. Even when you use to fuss at him for just coming *near* you."

"I sure did," Ebony admits as she laughs. "And he would just look at me and smile. That was back when I could beat him. I know he just let me beat him up though. I was mad at him because he broke my bike."

"No he *did not* Ebony Eloise" big mama says as she chuckles, "He just *souped* it up so it could keep up with his. He wanted you to go bike riding with him and you wouldn't give him the time of day. You told him a lie too. You said you wouldn't ride with him because your bike was too slow. So he reacted like a boy with a bruised ego. He got all of that out of his system though. He use to tell me every time I came here to visit, that he liked you and you was gonna be his wife."

"He did?!"

"Oh yes child. He would have Jo and Al calling me all the time. Every since he was about seven or eight years old," she says, "He would tell me then that he liked you. But you treated him mean," big mama says and laughs out loud. "I thought it was the sweetest thing. I never worried about the two of you, once y'all *got* together. But that made the others your age, think they could get together early too. The other boys wasn't as mature as Ajay. Tank, June and Richard. Nor John junior either."

"We went through a lot to be together, back then," Ebony says.

"Yes but y'all had me and Percy on y'all side. John and Al was too. We stayed on Jo and Pearlie. They finally gave in and just let y'all be."

"That's so beautiful," Ebony says, "I never knew all of this stuff."

"Well now you do," she says, "I was going to see to it that Ajay had his princess. Because I knew he would take care of you. That's all he ever wanted to do. When he got to be a teenager, he started calling me on his own. When you came to stay with me. He was more relieved than upset."

"You think so?" Ebony asks her.

"He knew I wasn't gonna let you date anybody," big mama says with a smile. "He hated the distance but he never worried about anyone visiting you while you was in my care."

"Wow. I'm just thinking about a letter I sent to him from your house. He already knew I was lying. But he never told me how he was so sure."

"I remember that letter story," big mama says with a smile. "That was during that holiday when Shuntay and Sonya came up here with us,"

TIME TO KNOW-RELOADED-Time Will Reveal- part 4

she giggles. "He was so upset that you had the nerve to tell him a lie."

"He sure was," she says with a smile, "Oh boy. He went off on me. That was the first time I saw him hurt. I never wanted to see that again."

"I knew he was a sexual young man. His father and yours. Jackson and Percy are too," big mama says, "We knew what kind of man you would fall for. So me and Percy decided to get you on some pills. So that you all wouldn't end up with a baby before y'all became superstars."

"Big mama we always said to each other that we was born to be together," Ebony says, "Because that's how it seems. I remember when granny and papa told us that before I moved with you. They told us that but I didn't know you and poppa was pulling the strings."

"I wanted the best for my namesake and heiress," big mama says with a wink. "And they also knew Ajay came to see you in your room too. And they know you told him too."

"Oh my God!" Ebony screams as she burst out laughing, "They didn't say anything!"

"No they didn't," big mama says as she chuckles, "They knew y'all were gonna find a way to be together. Jackson knew y'all was acting like dogs in heat," she laughs hard. "But he also knew it was gonna last too. So you see. Y'all had chances that most kids *your age* would never have. And look where it brought you."

They smile at each other and hug.

"I love you, big mama," Ebony says.

"I know you do, lil Ella," she chuckles, "I love you too, honey."

They prepare to leave. Ebony takes her in Ajay's Jaguar, to meet papa and poppa at CrewLand. Big mama will stay in the Point while Ajay is home.

"We'll take the Jag," she says, "Anthony and the twins must be having a good time."

"They're out with their daddy getting spoiled," big mama says, "And I'll bet you, you get something out of that trip too."

****

It's mid November 1999 and Ajay is back in Miami while Jarvis is on the road. Gwen hangs out with the foursome and works at CrewLand mall, along with Tonya's sister Venitia. Wesley's house is ready to move into by mid November. Renee is overwhelmed with excitement when he comes and reveals to her that the house on Payne's Lane is for him and his daughter Jada Renee. The crew get together to help them move their things in and get set up. From day 1 of the move-in party, Wesley shows that he's

189

still sweet on T-baby. He has barely taken his eyes off of her. Even his daughter Jada seems to take to T-baby instantly. She follows T-baby around the house all day.

"You're pretty," Jada says to her.

"Thank you miss Jada," T-baby says with a smile, "So are you."

"My daddy says you're pretty too," Jada says.

"Okay," T-baby says while blushing, "I think he's handsome." Nina, Rebbie and Ebony smile. The 4 of them had discussed some of the things T-baby had talked to Ajay about. So by now her girls know her situation enough to want it better. They're happy to hear that Wesley is sweet on her and vice versa. They haven't seen her smile like this in awhile. They know about the baby Regina is having. Neither of them have spoken a word about it to anyone other than each other. Ebony, Rebbie and Nina haven't spoken to Rich since finding out either. Him and June are away a lot now playing football. Not seeing them daily makes it even easier for the Awesome Foursome *not* to speak to Rich.

"Do you ladies want to get a dinner order in?" Wesley asks, "My treat."

They accept his offer.

"Thank you," T-baby says, "That's really sweet of you."

"Oh you're very welcome, Trisha," Wesley says, "It's the least I can do since you all worked so hard getting us up here and settled in."

"It's our pleasure," she says with a warm smile.

"Mine too," he says returning the smile. "Well Chill and myself are going to go pick up the food. We'll be right back."

"Alright," she says.

Wesley catches up with Chill and Renee at the door and they leave.

Inside the house, T-baby's girls love what just happened and they're ribbing her about it already.

"*It's our pleasure!*" her girls tease.

"T-baby he likes you," Ebony says.

"Uh huh," Nina says, "And she likes him too."

"I'm not mad at you," Rebbie says.

"We're not either," Ebony and Nina say together.

T-baby just grins from ear to ear. They can tell she's interested. *Very* interested. He's Renee's younger brother. So *technically*, he's crew already.

On the way to the restaurant, Renee, Chill and Wesley are having a similar conversation. Wesley tells Chill and Renee he still likes T-baby.

"She's beautiful," he says, "And her personality is strong. That's the kind of woman I need in my life."

"Yes she is brother," Renee says, "But she's married."

"But she's not happy Renee," Chill adds.

"I know but she's still *married*," Renee reiterates.

"I don't care what happens at this point," Chill says, "My boy Rich is not doing his job. And he already knows how I feel about the shit."

"Well if she would talk to me," Wesley says, "I'd like to get to know her. She really has me shook."

"Well you got my vote Wes," Chill says, "T-baby deserves to be happy. And Renee you have to admit. Rich hasn't been taking care of his home."

"Wes, you and T-baby's lives are *so* similar," Renee says, "You would be amazed."

"Well my now ex-wife was pregnant for her lover when we divorced," he says.

Chill says, "Well her husband has his mistress pregnant, right now."

"Kenny!" Renee tries.

"No Renee," Chill says, "I meant to say it and as much as I love Rich. I can't forgive him for that one. It's unnecessary and disrespectful. T-baby is his crew and he's treating her like an outsider. Like they didn't grow up together. Like he's not her first and only."

Renee has to agree with Chill on that point. Rich is very much disassociating himself with not only his wife but his whole crew too.

}*Thanksgiving*!{

This Thanksgiving the crew gather at Renee and Chill's house for dinner. Jarvis and Gwen are there with Jarvis Jr. Nickeia came up for Thanksgiving. Something she's planning to do for Christmas and summer break too. She's going to attend CSU in the spring and stay with Gwen and Jarvis. Just so she can be closer to Ajay. Ajay still hasn't noticed her. Not anymore than he had when she'd visited her sister in Natty. But she's determined to change that.

The men have their party in Chill's basement this year. But the ladies crash it immediately. Instead of a stripper show. They view the video's and pictures from the previous Thanksgiving celebrations. When they get to the video and pictures from last year's celebration, everyone comments on how pale Ebony was.

"Yea I was pregnant that night and didn't even know it," she says.

"You know it now though," Chill says and they all laugh.

"I knew it then," Ajay says, "I told her that same night. But she was out cold."

TIME TO KNOW-RELOADED-Time Will Reveal- part 4

"From sex," Nina adds, "Cause the both of you looked like warmed over dead people when me and Jeremy dug y'all out of that room."
They all burst out laughing while Nickeia just listens. She doesn't say anything. They continue laughing at Nina's comment and still Nickeia is quiet. They reminisce about all of their Thanksgivings. And even more, about how much more they have to be thankful for. They all vow to teach their seeds how to keep the crew spirit alive. The men make them promise to allow them to have their male party.

"I'm not gonna interfere when my husband has to host again," Ebony offers, "I realize it's a tradition. So I want interrupt it. Unless I'm trying to get pregnant and I'm ovulating."
They all laugh hard again. Even her mother has to give her some dap on that statement.

"That's my daughter right there," Pearl says.

"She's the only one who could tame my son," Jo adds.

"And get us in at the same time," Lynn says and laughs hard.

"Yea," Ajay says, "Alright but y'all gonna stop *using* my baby. I told you that already sis. She don't ever have to scheme to get this. I'm her husband and I'm willing."
Nickeia was imagining herself in Ebony's place as the family continued their talk.

"Oh shit, dog," Jb says, "Who don't know you're always willing?"
They laugh again and Jb adds, "We better get our coats and get him and baby girl on the road before they be missing in action real soon."

"No shit," Tank adds as Pearl checks him and Jb on their language. While everyone is still laughing, Jb says, "See we was just checking to see if you was gonna check us, mama. We thought we was grown for a minute there."

"Y'all old enough to go out," Jo says, "That's it."
They laugh before Nina says, "Okay good. Cause we *own* clubs now."

"Alright then y'all!" Tank yells, "Let's take it to *our* clubs!"

"I'm wit it," Nina says as the rest agree except Jan.

"I don't think I'm gonna stay that long," she says.

"Baby we can leave whenever you get ready," Rob says, "Because you're the one pregnant *this* year."
They all laugh as they load up into their vehicles to go to The CrewLand mall and party at their clubs. Nickeia ask if she can ride with Ebony and Ajay. But Gwen says, "No. We're already riding with Nina and Jeremy."

"Call him Tank," Nina says, "Only *I*, call him Jeremy."
Everybody laughs again. Only no one notices Gwen and Tank don't.

192

CHAPTER   43

ON BORROWED TIME

T-baby still hasn't found out anymore about Rich's mistress. And unless she ask *him* who she is, finding her doesn't look promising. Asking Rich isn't the route she wants to take. She's going to play it smooth, low key and work the sources she has. If she has to, she'll camp out at the medical complex until she can catch them together.

Today starts off like any other normal day at *Williams Accounting Firm*. T-baby's going over clients files, taking new clients and giving tax advice. She handles taxes for CrewLand Enterprises and CrewLand Mall. Her and Claudia are making files and folders for all of her clients and getting things ready for the tax season, when she receives a phone call. It's her youngest brother Steven, now a junior at MLK. He's calling her for assistance.

"Tee can you come check me out before second period?" he asks.

"Are you sick?"

"No," he says.

"Then why do you need to be checked out? And don't lie to me," T-baby says, "Or I'll call mama *myself*."

"I have computer tech next period. That teacher gets on my nerves," he says, "She's always in our face. Asking about the crew."

"Is that the white girl who be with Alana?" she asks.

"At the main club?"

"Uh huh."

"Yep," he says.

"Okay. But what is she doing? And why can't you go to the office?" she asks.

"She flirts with me and Kenny *real* bad," Steven says, "Big Chill don't want us to report her yet. He said he's got a cake baking."

"Okay. I'm on my way," she says, figuring Chill already has a plan in action for Farah Benson.

She tells Claudia and Ebony about her errand. She says she'll be right back and then leaves. She's focused on helping her brother and crew right now. That's enough to take her mind off of her wayward husband. At least for awhile. She calls Renee from her cell phone as she pulls up in front of the main club.

"What's up, T-baby?" Renee answers.

"Ride to MLK with me," T-baby says.

"Come through."
"I'm out front," T-baby says.
"In a minute," Renee says.
"See ya."

Farah looks forward to 2nd and 5th period everyday. She questions and sucks up to Ally and Steven in 2nd period. Then throws herself at Kenny during 5th. All the students know and are starting to talk about it around campus. She says she'll pull back. Her 1st period class is in session and students are talking *in code* about her and Kenny's situation. Farah knows some of the code. Still she makes no real attempts to smother the rumors. She thinks it's *quite* funny that they're *so* wrong. She doesn't want Kenny. Well at least, not Kenny Jr. She wants his daddy and she has plans on getting to him through his son. That's the typical mistake outside stigmatic women make when trying to get the attention of a crew man. It often leaves them at the whim of the crew women too.

T-baby and Renee arrive at the school while 1st period is still in session. They go directly to Principal Myers office. First they get Steven, Ally and Kenny checked out. Then Renee requests a schedule change or another computer technology class for the 3 of them. Myers is going to do his best to move them.
"I need you to make it happen or just give them all another class, all together. Do you have another teacher?" Renee asks.
"We do. The same period as a matter of fact. Misses Burnett. You had her for-"
"General Business," Renee says, finishing his sentence, "I sure did. My senior year. I want her to teach my son too."
"I'll make the changes. Tomorrow when they come back, they need to report to misses Burnett's class at the same periods. For that same elective," Mr. Myers says.
"Perfect," Renee says.
Her and T-baby thank him and tell him what they're up too now, as they wait for Ally, Steven and Kenny to come up for check out.

Farah Benson doesn't immediately know of their schedule changes. She's disappointed to see that Ally and Steven have checked out early. She gets the list at the start of 2nd period. She sees that Kenny has checked out too. But by the end of 3rd period, she gets the class switch list and realizes she doesn't have either of them in her classes anymore.

194

TIME TO KNOW-RELOADED-Time Will Reveal- part 4

"Oh no!" she says, "Why would they want *old ass* misses Burnett?" She's talking to herself as she prepares for her free period which is 4th period and all lunch breaks. She heads to the cafeteria to eat and tries to think of a plan to still see the crew members.

I'll bet you his wife had them moved from my class. Okay bitch. How are you gonna move your fine ass husband? Because I'm gonna get with that and I'm not sorry for you.

Meanwhile Renee and T-baby have Ally, Steven and Kenny in the Navigator with them. Their driving back to CrewLand Mall.

"Kenny is that teacher still being inappropriate with you?" Renee asks suddenly.

"I guess so. Yes ma'am," he says, "She just lets me have my way in there. She tries to kiss up to me. Like, I can say *anything* to her and she won't even write me up. I can *not* do the assignment and she'll still give me a grade. The other students already think we're doing the..., *you know.*"

"I hope you're not," Renee says.

"No ma'am. Not with her. But I could if I wanted too," he says, "I just don't want too. She wants daddy, ma."

"I know that and I'm trying not to go to the principal with this," she says, "But your daddy had better get this plan off the ground real quick."

T-baby parks in front of *The Spot.* Ally, Steven and Kenny get out and head to Crew Cuts to help out for the rest of the day. That's when Renee tells T-baby she has some tax info she wants to add to the club's file. And also some employee folders for the file room. T-baby accompanies her inside.

As they step in, 1 of the dancers wants to speak with Renee. She's a stripper who works in their strip club, *The Juice bar* on the 2nd floor.

"Come on up to my office, Regina," Renee says, "Are you okay?"

"I am but I need to tell you something," she says, "I have to stop dancing for a few months."

"I noticed you're getting a little thick in the middle. Are you pregnant?" Renee asks.

"Almost seven months. Yes," Regina says, "I do wanna come back after I have the baby though. I hope that's okay. I just don't feel I can suck in enough to keep going now. But I need to keep this job."

T-baby's mind goes wild as she looks at this woman whom she's never met and has never noticed. Yet this woman works for her. She doesn't say anything as Renee asks Regina to wait in reception, just outside of her office while she squares T-baby away.

195

She doesn't act like she knows me. I wonder who she's pregnant for.

"Who is she? Regina who?" T-baby asks Renee, after they're inside the office.

"Regina Kemp," Renee says, "She's harmless. She's been stripping for awhile locally. She came to us in January. Almost a year now. But she works a day job too."

"Do you know where?" T-baby asks, "She looks familiar."

"I don't know, right off hand," Renee says, "But it's in her file. And you're about to take those to the file room and get everybody's W-2's out. So you'll see it."

Renee gives her an intentional heads up on the personnel file. She can sense that T-baby is suspicious of this employee. She has a sneaky feeling this is the woman Rich has been cheating with. Just from T-baby's reaction. Of course none of the guys ever let it out. And Ajay made Ebony promise she wouldn't tell until after the paternity test.

"Oh okay. Give me what I need and let me get back to my office," T-baby says.

She puts the file boxes on a dolly, takes them outside and has Steven and Kenny to load them into her SUV. Then she drives back down to her parking spot. Kenny and Steven unload the boxes of files and take them into her office. Her and Ebony's duplex office is where the CrewLand Enterprise file room is located. She has Regina Kemp and Tameka Robinson's files tucked under her arm. She wants to read those first, for personal reasons. She had overheard Tameka yelling at Rich when his phone had called her back, that he had no business going into her employee file to find out where she lived. She closes her office door and locks it. Then puts the 2 files on her desk. She starts with Tameka's.

If his dumb ass can find what he wants from a file. I sure as hell can too.

Farah is still at school. The class day has just ended and she's waiting for teachers to be dismissed. While she waits, she calls Alana. She tells her about losing her 3 favorite students. Alana has finished classes for today and she's home from CSU.

"Why do you think they got moved?" she asks Alana.

"I don't know. He probably told his mama how nice you've been. And her ass don't like it," Alana says.

"It must *really* suck to be a loser like her," Farah says, "Why would you deny your son a guaranteed *Ay*. Just because you're insecure?"
She laughs.

"Be careful partner," Alana says, "The crew are slick. They may have something in the works *already*. And knowing them, they do. So be careful and don't push them. Just cool out for awhile. See what shakes."

"I hope that fine ass Chill moves something *this* way," Farah says, "Kenny is almost sixteen. I should've told him I was giving him some head for his birthday." They both laugh.

"I'll bet you he would still be in your class if you would've said that," Alana says.

"But that was during school, girl. I didn't wanna go there, at work. I need to get him out to the house, one day," Farah says, "Now that football season is over. He's the number one player in the state. I'll bet he gets a lot of head from the school girls."

"You know he does," Alana says.

"But I'm a grown bitch with a PHD in dick sucking," Farah boast. They laugh loud. Teachers are dismissed and Farah tells Alana she's about to head home.

"Pass by the mall and see if you see him," Alana suggests.

"I think I'll do just that."

Renee allows Regina leave without pay until May 1st of next year. She's due to have her baby in late February. She thanks Renee, takes what she needs from her locker and leaves.

T-baby finds Tameka's new address in her file. She can ride by there on those late nights when she can't find her husband, to see if he's there. Regina's file reveals a bit more. This stranger she'd met today, she now believes has 1 thing in common with her. The father their children is the same man. She's sure of it. Regina listed each of the crew men bachelor parties as experience for her application to *The Juice Bar*. She had also worked, not only in a strip club in Cleveland. But Cincinnati and New York too. Every city Rich has lived in. Regina has *worked* in. The most revealing item in the file is her day job. She works as a nurses assistant for Dr. Kathleen Palms, a general practitioner at the *Medical Complex*. Ajay had told her that Ebony had seen him there almost 2 years ago.

"Rich is meeting her at work. That bastard! I wonder how long he's been fucking with her? It seems like since sometime during his college years," she says to herself as she drops her head on her desk and cries to herself. "When was he ever faithful to me?"

Farah comes through the mall. She sees Kenny and Steven standing just inside, The Spot II. They're talking to other students. They don't notice her, so she contemplates going in to ask them why they switched from her class. But she thinks better of it. She parks at Crew Cut & Styles, then goes in to make an appointment. Tonya puts her on Matthew's clients list. He's going to take a chair in the shop, starting next Saturday. He'll surely bring in even more clientele.

"He can work with any grade of hair," Tonya tells Farah.

"Okay," Farah says, "Thank you so much. I'll be back a week from Saturday. Thanks again," she says as she leaves.

"That bitch is becoming a bad rash," Justine says as she laughs, "And I'm a white woman who can do any grade of hair. I just didn't want the bitch in my chair because I know she's on some dumb shit already."

"I knew you didn't," Tonya says as she laughs too. "That's why I didn't even go there. She's too pushy. She don't get it at all. We don't wanna be her friend. But she can spend all the cash with us that she wants too."

"Tonya, you and Nina can do any grade of hair too," Justine says, "I was about to burst over here."

"I don't want her, her hair nor her or Alana's cash," Nina offers, "I want that Alana bitch's *ass*. I have a feeling I'm gonna be kicking her ass again *real* soon."

"For the *new* Millennium!" Justine screams and the entire shop explodes with laughter.

Farah and Alana are at home in Parma, thinking of any excuse they can come up with to go back to CrewLand. Just then, Rodney and Jamal show up looking for their mother Darlene. She'd moved into the house in October. Her sons haven't moved with her but Farah is considering asking them too. They visit the Spot II every day. They'd been banned for 30 days after the discharging of weapons incident. Farah has to bring that up because she wants to use them to get in better with the crew.

"They didn't even file charges on us, man," Jamal says.

"The crew is the shit," Rodney says, "I've been wanting to be down every since Ajay use to be by our apartment, back in the day. Dude is a NBA superstar now. Me and Jamal, we knew he was going. You see I call him *dude*. He told us along time ago. Never call him nigga. I remember that shit and respect it. The crew is as real as they come. You *heard*?"

"The crew is gangster, for real though," Jamal says.

Farah hears the conversation and smiles. She's going to find a way to spin their fascination to her advantage.

"You guys still go to the arcade everyday?" she asks.

"Every time they have something. I'm in that joint," Rodney says,

"I be off up in the big club too. When mama don't go in there."

"Fasho!" Jamal agrees.

"So why aren't you guys there *today*?"

"We need to see if we can use mama's car," Rodney says, "Or I need to get a battery for mine."

"So you guys need a ride over there?" she asks.

"I mean, yea," Jamal says, "We got to get in that tournament tonight. The prize is two grand. We win that cash we can buy a battery. No problem."

"I can take you guys over there. If Darlene and Alana will go to happy hour with me," Farah says.

The girls say they'll go. The 3 females get dressed for happy hour and head to CrewLand Mall with Rodney and Jamal.

They arrive early enough for the guys to enter the *EA Sports* tournament. Farah, Alana and Darlene stay about 15 minutes until the competition kicks off. Then they walk across the street to the Chill Spot. Happy Hour was about to kick off when Alana gets an idea.

"I know what I can do to earn some money for school and the house too," she says.

"What?" Darlene and Farah asks.

"I can work at The Juice Bar."

"You're still on *that* dream?" Farah asks, "I thought about doing that on guest night. But I'm a teacher."

"I don't have the body for it anymore," Darlene adds.

"Come go with me to see how do I apply," Alana says, "I just saw a girl going up there. I can ask her."

They 3 ladies go to the 2nd floor. Alana is told to get an application from the DJ booth and she does. They go back to the 1st floor and enjoy happy hour while she fills out the application. When she's done with it. She turns it in to the DJ. He'll pass it along to Jr, who handles *The Juice Bar*.

Before club time, Renee and Chill meet in her office. She tells him she switched their son and the crew out of Farah's class today.

"Good," he says, "First she wanna fuck me. Then she come at my son. She's a trifling muthafuckah. We had to bake a cake for her ass."

"What's in that cake exactly?" Renee asks with a smile.

"All the ingredients needed to familiarize her ass with the real crew," he says.

The discussion is closed and Renee doesn't ask anymore about the cake. She knows not too. But she has a pretty good idea that whatever is going to happen. Her son will be apart of it. She just doesn't know how big of a part

TIME TO KNOW-RELOADED-Time Will Reveal- part 4

he'll play. Some things the men do in this family, the women are not privy too. Like the Johnson beef. And this, she feels is 1 of those sorts of things. So she leaves it at that and they go on to work.

****

The crew are preparing for the Christmas season as they get their gift list together.

"It's nineteen ninety nine y'all," Nina says from her station at the salon, "The world is coming to an end on New Year's eve!"

Everyone laughs.

"Girl don't believe the hype," Tonya laughs, "We're gonna still be up in here dealing with the same madness, after New Year's Eve."

"Prince said; *two thousand zero zero, party over, oops, out of time*! Right?" Justine asks as she laughs.

They all have their jokes about the new millennium.

In addition to Farah, Matthew met another new client today by the name of Ellen Barnes. She's very attracted to him from the start. He likes her too. He's 1 of the few males in the hair industry, whom Tonya knows who *isn't* gay.

"I'm all man, baby," Matthew says, "Don't get it confused. I like pussy. The only penis I'm handling is my own and I'm handling it well."

"Do you get that question a lot, Matt?" Nina asks.

"*Hell* yea. All the damn time. And I set them straight, each and every time," he answers.

Ellen Barnes gives him her phone number before leaving the salon.

"I'll call you later tonight," he says, "Is that good for you?"

"That will be just fine for me," she says while blushing.

Then she books her follow up appointment and leaves the shop. The ladies take this opportunity to poke fun at Matthew.

"Matt you just be pulling the women, don't you?" Nina jokes.

"Best job in the world to pick up women," he says and they all laugh as he calls Farah over to his station to get started on her.

"I need to go to Granny's House to check on Jerica," Nina says, "She wasn't feeling to good this morning when I dropped her off. Can y'all cover for me?"

Tonya, Matt and Justine say they can. Nina trots over to the preschool to check on her daughter.

"Hey mama Brenda," Nina says as she enters, "How's Jay doing?"

200

TIME TO KNOW-RELOADED-Time Will Reveal- part 4

"She's sleeping right now and we got her temp down."

"Good. Thank y'all so much," Nina says, "I'm taking her to doctor Mahoney this afternoon."

"Brenda has been feeling bad today too," Jackie says, "Must be something going around."

"I do my pap today," Brenda says, "I'm gonna have Gladys check me out *thoroughly*."

She's scheduled to see Dr. Weston at 2 o'clock.

"Big mama told me you was feeling bad yesterday," Nina says.

"Yes and mama wants me to have a mammogram," Brenda says, "She says my symptoms are like those *early signs* of breast cancer that she went through."

"Oh Brenda. I hope it's not that serious," Jackie says.

"We're doing all the test. I'll know something by Friday."

After seeing that Jerica is okay, Nina heads back to work. Brenda prepares to leave for her doctor's appointment. Pearl is going with her while Annabelle and Mrs. Green come over to help Jackie out.

****

T-baby and Renee are at T-baby's office going over the crew's business reports from the month of November. All of their business profits are still very good.

"We're doing *real* good!" Renee exclaims.

She's very excited to see how profitable the entire CrewLand mall has been.

"It's a lovely thing," T-baby says as she laughs.

All 19 businesses including those in Atlanta are in the pink and have been since their openings.

"Do you know Farah is still chasing Kenny and the crew around school?" Renee asks, "Even though we moved them from her class?"

"Even after you changed their *schedules*?" T-baby asks.

"Yes girl. She's still doing it," Renee tells her, "Just to see them, she's been sending other students to bring them to her class. All kind of shit."

"She's a pest. That's all it is to it," T-baby says, "So what does the crew have planned for her?" T-baby asks, "I wanna know."

"I don't know for sure. But I'll bet you my son is a huge part of it. Kenneth keeps saying he's baking a cake for her," Renee says and sighs.

"Oh shit," T-baby says, "She may or *may not* see the new year."

"It'll be a happy one for me, if she don't," Renee says, "I hate to

201

say it. But I sort of miss the old days. The days when we use to get rid of this type of bullshit, early in the game."

"I know that's right, girl," T-baby says, "When we was innocent, young and impatient." They both laugh.

"This woman is after my husband *and* my son," Renee says, "I'll kill her myself before I allow that to happen."

"I feel you, Renee," T-baby says, "And I'll help you with that if you call. I feel your pain. God knows I do. I hope Chill do the right thing and I'm sure he will. I can't say the same for Richard though."

"I am so hurt over your whole scenario," Renee says, "How are you holding up. *Really*."

"I think I found out who my husbands mistress is," T-baby says.

"For real? Who is she?" Renee asks.

"Regina Kemp."

"From *Juice bar*?"

"And the Medical complex too. Where he use to meet up with her."

"I had a feeling the guys know or knew more than they was telling us," Renee says, "I know Chill don't agree with it. I feel they've been trying to get him right. Instead of telling the females. But he didn't get right, as all can see. I just want you to be happy, T-baby. Whatever that takes I will support you. Okay?"

"I know sis and I appreciate you," she says, "And all of my crew. I know all of you have my back."

"T-baby, Wes is so sweet on you, girlfriend," she says with a smile, "I just wanted to let you know. He still is. From childhood."

"I know," T-baby says, "I think he's sweet too."

"Well you know. If you and Rich don't work out," Renee says, "He would be *more than* happy to step in."

T-baby blushes as Renee adds, "You like him. Don't you T-baby?"

"I must admit," T-baby answers, "It's been a long time since a man looked at me with those kind of eyes. The kind with desire in them."

"That's not good," Renee says, "You and Rich been together since eighty six. I remember the night y'all took it to a sexual level."

They both laugh and she continues, "Rich should be ashamed of himself."

T-baby agrees with Renee as they finish the last report just in time for lunch. All of the females are meeting at *The Crews House of Soul Food*. T-baby calls Rich, who is at home today.

"Hey baby," she says, "Do you want me to bring you some lunch?"

"No I'm getting ready to eat, right now," he says dryly.

"Oh okay," she says, "We're going to the restaurant to eat. I'm

202

going to bring dinner home for Richie and I. You too, if you want."
"Alright."
They hang up. Then T-baby and Renee hurry to meet the girls for lunch.

At the restaurant, Wesley walks in as the females are enjoying their lunch and a lot of stimulating conversation.
"Hey," Wes says to the females, "Mind if I join you ladies?"
"Not at all, lil bro," Renee says, "Sit down and eat with us."
He does. Nina and Renee make sure he sits next to T-baby. Intentionally the ladies start other conversations amongst themselves. T-baby and Wesley are left out of the conversations. The ladies want them to talk to each other. Wes and T-baby fall in line and exchange pleasant talk. He asks T-baby if she's interested in interviewing him for a job at her firm.
"Sure. Can you come in tomorrow?" she asks.
"I'll be there," he says as they trade smiles.
The other ladies are smiling. They're just happy to see T-baby smiling for a change.

After lunch, Wes walks the ladies back to their jobs. T-baby and Ebony's office is the last stop. Again that was intentional but an innocent act which brightened T-baby and Wesley's day was about to be soured royally.

Rich had shown up at Stoney's. He watches as his wife walks with Ebony and Wes. He feels jealous instantly. Wes walks them inside, says his goodbyes and then goes on over to visit with Renee at the club. After he's out of sight, Rich storms into T-baby's office and slams her door in a rage.
"What the fuck was that?!" he yells.
"What was what?" T-baby asks calmly.
"Who the fuck is that nigga you was wit, Trisha?!" he yells.
"Oh baby that's Wesley. Renee's brother," she says, "You met him at Thanksgiving. You don't remember?"
"Are you fucking him now or something?"
"No Richard," she says, "He was just walking me and Ebony back to work."
"She's probably trying to hook y'all up," he says as he continues to yell.
Ebony can hear him, over on her side of the split office. Rich is furious. He grabs T-baby out of her chair and slaps her before she can defend herself.
"You need to let me know you want out of our marriage. Before you start fucking another nigga!" he screams.
Then he storms out of her office, out of the building, jumps into his Benz
203

and peels away, just as Ebony and Claudia are coming to T-baby's aid.

"Are you alright?" Ebony ask as her and Claudia run into Williams accounting's office to check on her.

"I heard some bumping and I saw Rich peel away," Ebony says.

Claudia is straightening T-baby's desk and fixing the papers Rich had knock on the floor.

"He slapped me, Ebony," T-baby says, "Just for walking with Wesley."

Ebony is angry. She says, "I'm calling Chill right now," and she does.

Within the hour, Chill and Jr are out looking for Rich but aren't able to find him. Chill comes by T-baby's office to check on her.

"I don't believe this dude," Chill says calmly, "He's constantly fucking up."

T-baby is still upset but she tries to veil it from all 4 of them.

"As soon as you see him, let us know," Jr says, "We'll get in his ass." They all leave and T-baby goes back to work.

"I'm gonna end up killing him," she says aloud, "I swear I am."

****

Matthew makes a play on Farah and she's mildly interested. But only after finding out that he's a professor at CSU.

"I'm a first year teacher at MLK," she says.

"I've been teaching hair for twenty years and doing hair for thirty," he says.

"I would love to have you come and speak to my class for career day," Farah says.

"When is it?" Matthew asks.

"It's in late March," Farah answers.

"It's a date."

The next afternoon, T-baby hires Wes despite Rich's objections the night before. Chill and the guys have grilled him thoroughly. T-baby isn't concerned with his jealousy. She has become numb to any and everything *Richard*. She has began to look past this relationship because she isn't going to stay with him. Not after he has made a child with another woman. Wes has plenty of experience, a great resume', he needs a job and she has money to hire him.

"I think we'll do great together, Wes," she says after the interview.

"I agree," he says with a smile, "Thank you for hiring me. Now I don't have to worry about just living on my retirement and only that."

****

Brenda's mammogram results come in on Friday. Big mama and Pearl go with her to the complex, where she finds out that she's in the early stages of breast cancer.

"We can treat this, Brenda," Dr. Weston says, "And reverse it before it goes too far."

"It's a good thing you caught it early," big mama says, "You won't have to endure what I went through, baby."

Brenda is still upset as she calls Brian Sr. But she's happy that the cancer can be cured without surgery.

"I'll call June and Brittany and let them know, honey," Brian Sr says, "You'll be fine and we'll make sure you're taken care of."

****

The crew fly to Sacramento the following Friday. Bre graduates from OTS on Saturday. Her, CJ and Cedric will move to Atlanta, in early 2000. They have already built a home in Smyrna, on the same block as Lynn and Jan.

****

By mid December, the next generation of the crew has formed and Bruce is the head of it. It includes Kim, Reaper, Brittany J, Greg Jr and Erica. Jesse and Ruthie plus Sam Jr, Pam, Steven and Ally. Also Kenny, Chaundra and Archie along with Brina, Brandon and Charlotte. They are the next generation who will follow Chill's crew.

"Another generation of crew is already in full effect!" Chill says later that evening, at The Spot II, "The crew will go on forever!"

Everyone cheers and toast the new crew. 18 strong just like Chill's crew and the males are already aware of big Jake Johnson.

"Lil Brad will head the next crew," Jr says proudly, "He'll be thirteen in five more years. Time is flying man!"

Chill notes how the dynamics of the crew changed with Bruce's generation. For instance, cell phones are much more prevalent nowadays then they were when he got his 1st cell phone and needed a whole suitcase just to make a phone call and the phone plans were very expensive then too.

205

"Now all of them have a cell phone already," he says.

"That's why their asses keep getting caught up with their females too," Jr says and they all agree with laughter.

"They're more flamboyant then we was," Tank says, "They all want to show off things, cuz. They got to have *Bling Bling*. The Polo gear, the rims, jewelry and clothes. They're listening to the *Big Tymers* and getting they stunt on."

"We have to stay on their ass though," Chill warns, "Because that stunting is gonna draw too much attention."

The others agree that even though the crew is legitimate, for the most part. All of them still dabble in the underworld, just like big Brad's crew and the crew before them had done.

****

It's 2 days before Christmas. Nina's birthday party is tonight and Ajay is home for their Christmas Eve game against Jarvis and the *Cavaliers*. The crew are done with their Christmas shopping and looking forward to the celebration. June and Rich are home. So are Greg Jr, Jesse and Erica.

Erica and Greg Jr's relationship has been on the rocks more during their freshman year of college, at separate schools. As if they aren't already having enough trouble. Mya Dean shows up at the party. Greg has been alternating his time between the 2 of them. He thinks no one has noticed him until June pulls him into the bathroom for a 1-on-1.

"Man, what the fuck do you think you're doing?!" June explodes.

"Crew what? Getting my mack on! I thought you *knew!*" Greg Jr yells back.

"Greg you must be fucked up! How you gone be playing on Erica like that?!" June continues shouting.

"Oh dude please! How you gonna scream on me?!" Greg asks, "When you're married and yo ass cheat! At least, I ain't married!"

"You don't even know what the fuck you talking about, Lil nigga!" June yells.

"Who you callin a *nigga*?!" Greg Jr charges as he starts to get heated, "Dude get a grip! You and Rich both some cheatin muafuckaz! So how you think I'm gone allow you to check me?!"

The dynamics of the crew have definitely changed. Crew arguing like this is something that would've never happened between Brad Sr or big Chill's crew. Let alone Allen and Paul Sr's crew. But Bruce's crew are some young knuckleheads, for real. They see any *checking of their stance* done by a

206

hypocrite as bogus. The only crew trait many of them seem to have picked up, is the dog side of it. Being that his cheating ways have already been exposed amongst the males, June isn't the 1 to give the younger ones any chastising about how they should treat their girl. They don't have respect for him in that department. Simply because they know and have witnessed how he cheats on Rebbie. It's going to take Bruce or someone from the crew who are not doing the dog game, to reach Greg Jr.

Jesse walks into the men's room and witnesses the confrontation. He goes back to the VIP and alerts the crew. Chill and the guys rush in, just as June and Greg Jr are about to tie up. Chill, Jr and Tank manage to calm them down enough to get them out of the bathroom and to Chill's office.

T-baby who had gotten wind of the argument, follows them. June and Greg Jr continue to argue and act out aggressively. Greg is angry with June anyway. Because he knows June was always aware of Rich cheating on his sister. He had witnessed them both cheating and egging the other 1 on, at Ajay's bachelor party. So Greg keeps making references to June's part in keeping Rich's secret. He doesn't know his sister is aware of it already and that Ajay had told her. What he's doing is called *dry snitching*. But hell, this is his only sister who's being cheated on. Greg Jr is going all in for T-baby, trying to give hints to the ladies about what he knows without just saying it. At the same time, T-baby doesn't want her brother to give up all of the information. Because she doesn't want Rich or June to know *she's* aware. So she jumps into it and starts screaming obscenities at June. June lashes back at her.

"You don't take care of your husband, T-baby," he yells, "That's why he's so fucked up in the head. Because you don't take care of the man." That pissed T-baby off. Rebbie has made it to the office. She's trying to calm them both down but after that stunt by June, T-baby has to counter.

"So is that your reason for fucking up too?!" she yells, "Ha?! Is it?! Is that why you're fucking up, along with him?! Ha June?! Is that why you're chauffeuring y'all ho's around in the Legend?! Is that why you fuck up because Ree Ree's not taking care of you?!"

"Ah fuck you! You rank for that shit!" June yells, "Just because yo shit's fucked up! Yo inadequate ass wanna go in on me with dumb shit!" June explodes on her, just as Rich comes into the office. He tries to calm T-baby down but she stays on hers. Finally Chill manages to calm all of them down, with help from Ajay, Tank and Jr. June and Greg Jr are hell bent on fighting, so Chill suggest they end the party, close up and leave. That doesn't make Nina happy. She's angry with them for ruining her party.

At 2am, they shut it down and leave, leaving Chill, Jr, Tonya and

TIME TO KNOW-RELOADED-Time Will Reveal- part 4

Renee behind with Tank and Nina to close up the clubs. Ajay, Ebony, June, Rebbie, T-baby and Rich all head to Jackson Heights, in 3 separate vehicles. Rebbie and June plus T-baby and Rich argue all the way home. In Ebony's Escalade, her and Ajay discuss how tragic the whole incident is.

"That shit was stupid, baby," Ajay says.

"It's crew on crew lately," she says sadly, "What is *going* on?"

"June was out of line," Ajay says, "I told him I was gonna speak to Greg. Erica is my sister. I would've done it different. Greg don't see me fucking up like he do with June. But June don't get that. He thinks his age is gonna trump shit. He shouldn't have said shit. Trying to cover for his own guilt and got busted. Because now, Ree Ree knows about his shit too."

"Erica don't know Mya visits Greg down in Baton Rouge."

"*Visits*?" Ajay asks in a surprised tone, "She's in school, baby."

"What?" Ebony asks in shock.

She hadn't heard anything about it until now. She figures her girls hadn't either. So before they arrive home, she calls Nina on her cell phone to tell her about it. And ends up getting shocked again. She finds out Nina already knows and just hadn't said anything to her. She didn't because she was trying to protect her sister's feelings. Ebony feels as if she's been in a bubble. All the drama going on with her family and she knows nothing of it.

"You kept it a secret from me too Nina?" Ebony asks.

"I kept it from everybody," she says, "T-baby knows what Greg juniors been doing and she never said anything about that either."

"How do you know she knows?"

"Come on, Ebony. T-baby and Greg Jr talk about everything. They're just like you and Jeremy, on that," Nina says frustrated, "You think she don't know about Mya living with him?"

"Nina, we all have to get together and talk," Ebony suggests.

"Oh baby girl, why bother? I want Erica to leave him alone. He's no good anyway and neither is Mya. Greg will get what he deserves, for messing over Erica. You'll see. That Lil ho is gonna put him through what he's been putting my Lil sister through. This ain't like that Alana shit or any ho Ajay ever fucked with. Deep down, we knew they didn't give a shit about those ho's. But Ebony, Greg junior got that ho living with him and Jesse. Asks your little brother, baby girl. He's treating Ruthie straight and she ain't even down there. But Greg junior took that ho to college with him. And he did it because my sister wouldn't let go of her scholarship to follow him. I'll call you a little later, baby girl. Jeremy needs me to run tickets so we can come home. I'll call you later and we can discuss it, if you want too." They hang up. Ebony is sad. Ajay gives her a pep talk.

"Don't let it worry you, baby," Ajay says, "*Our* thing is solid. All I want you to be concerned about these days. Are our twins and us."
How is Ebony going to do that? That's not the way it's been all of her life. Her girls have never kept secrets from her. *Have they?*
I kept a secret from them. I saw their husbands cheating and I didn't say a word to either of them. And I avoided them. But I didn't do that because I wanted to keep the secret. I didn't want to hurt my girls. Oh my God! Is cheating gonna be the action that brings down my crew? My family?

"I know I've sheltered you, Ebony," Ajay says suddenly.
She's tripping because she realizes how weird it sounds when he says her government name. She smiles and mentions it.
"You've hardly *ever* called me by my name," she says, "It sounds funny."
They laugh and he says, "I'll call you whatever you like best. I put it down for you, baby. I always have. Anything that didn't bring you closer to me. Or make you run to me. I stopped doing. I accepted being a man. *Your* man. We knew we had something way more special than them. Even Nina and Tank. Or Jb and Lynn. I love the woman *and* the pussy I come home too."
She blushes as he continues, "I don't want my son to check me at the damn *door*, one day. I learned that from my pops. He told me, *'Don't ever allow my son to lose trust in me. Because he would never give me a reason not to trust him.'* He adores my mama. So he's good with me. I have to be good with my son too. Because we love our mama's. That's the way we learn to love our woman. By watching our fathers. That's how I've always looked at it. Outside pussy will never cost me everything I was born to have and do. So I'll call you Ebony or baby girl. Or misses good pussy. Whatever it takes to keep your beautiful ass *smiling.*"
He has to chuckle to himself because Ebony is giggling.
"Just call *me*," she says, "I don't have a preference, daddy. As long as you're calling *me*. I'm just gonna have to accept what I saw coming a long time ago. All of us are not gonna make it as couples. But I won't deal with the arguing, cursing each other out, fighting or my girls and me not being open with each other. That's a wall that will have to come down and right now."
"I hear you baby," he says, "We'll try to be the example for the next crew. That's all I can promise. But our thing is gonna stay tight. I don't give a fuck what else happens. I'm gonna keep your world *untainted.*"
"I just love you, Anthony," she says.
"That's how we got here," he says, "I love you too and it's easy."
209

TIME TO KNOW-RELOADED-Time Will Reveal- part 4

They *are* family. *All* of them. But the dynamics are changing right in front of their eyes. Ebony use to think getting Ajay on the right track was the ultimate challenge. That mission was completed and recognized 6 years ago. But during those same 6 years, a lot changed with her crew. While her and Ajay's relationship grew and blossomed into something so beautiful and real. Two of her closest friends have lost their happily ever after. And still, some of their younger siblings seem to be from a totally different family.

"How did this happen?" she asks and drops her head.

She's in tears. Ajay pulls over by the guard booth to comfort her. He can't stand it and never could deal with seeing her bothered. He had told Jarvis he would visit before they have to report to Gund Arena tomorrow. Him and Gwen had stayed home, instead of going to the party because Jarvis Jr had a high fever. But with his wife in pain over this drama in their crew. He knows his every moment at home will be spent with her. Making her feel better and putting a smile back on her face.

Rebbie and June drive into their driveway. Just before T-baby and Rich drive into theirs. T-baby and Rich are having a very heated argument. Rebbie and June can hear them over their own argument.

"Trisha will you please stop wit the bitchin! *Damn*! *Please!*" Rich screams.

"Oh! I'm *bitchin* now?!" T-baby yells back, "You think I'm bitchin now?! You haven't seen nothing yet! If I'm so much of a bitch. Then why do you even come home, Richard?!"

"I don't know why *the fuck* I come home!" he yells.

"Why don't you just take your ass on over to your pregnant bitches house then!" T-baby yells.

Rich pauses. She lets the cat out of the bag and he realizes. She knows not only of his infidelities but of his pregnant mistress too. He's startled by her last comment. But after a few seconds, he regroups. His shock and surprise, soon turns to embarrassment as he goes into defense mode. He has to save face because he has no idea of how to lie to her this time. How can he fool her into believing she's the 1 who's wrong. Like he's done, numerous times over the years? He can't and he knows it.

"What?" he asks as his voice is lower now.

"Oh wait! You didn't know I *knew* you had a baby on the way!?"

"Bitch you're stupid," he lashes out.

"I'm not the stupid one Richard! Not anymore!" she yells as she heads toward her front door, "You are!"

She's searching her purse for the house key and has taken her eyes off of

210

him. June and Rebbie are witnessing this from their driveway.

"What's that suppose to mean?!" Rich asks, coming up behind her. T-baby talks over her shoulder as she digs and finds her keys.

"Nothing Richard. Other than you think I'm stupid. But I'm not," she says, "You've always played me *stupid*. But I helped you graduate high school *and* college! I allowed you to treat me like I was dumb. You took advantage of someone who truly loves you! So if either of us is stupid. It's you!"

She unlocks the front door, just as he grabs her arm and yanks her to him.

"You're fucking that Wesley nigga now! Ha, bitch?!" he yells as he grabs her by the back of her neck.

In an instant, he slams her down on their concrete landing.

She struggles to get up and fight back but he jumps on top of her and starts beating her about the face and head.

Rebbie and June run over to intervene, just as Ajay and Ebony are driving by. They notice the commotion and pull into T-baby's driveway. Ebony sees June and Rebbie trying to pull Rich off of T-baby. She jumps out and runs up to help.

"Rich get off of her!" Ebony yells as she tugs on him.

Ajay and June grab him and sling him off of T-baby and across the yard. Rebbie and Ebony try to help T-baby up but she's not moving.

"She's hurt!" Ebony screams, "Ree Ree, call an ambulance!"

"Rich what the fuck is wrong with you, *Cuz*?!" Ajay yells as he charges at him.

Rich doesn't answer. He runs from Ajay and jumps into his Benz. He speeds away. He left his crew there with his wife who's barely clinging to her life. T-baby is unconscious. Rebbie yells that the ambulance is on the way while her and Ebony talk to T-baby. T-baby never responds. Ajay gives June an angry stare. He's been assisting Rich with this nightmare which has left their sister in dire straits. She's bleeding profusely from her head. T-baby had hit her head on the concrete when Rich slammed her down.

"Tee, please wake up!" Ebony cries but T-baby never responds.

The ambulance arrives shortly afterwards. Jacobson sends out Rich's tag and license numbers to the police, once he gets wind of the incident. Ebony calls aunt Sandy to tell her, T-baby is hurt and going to the hospital. Sandy and Greg Sr will meet them there. The paramedics revive T-baby briefly and load her into the ambulance.

"We're following them to the hospital," Ebony cries.

Ajay starts up the Escalade and they all hop in. Rebbie calls Nina and the crew, who have just finished closing the clubs.

TIME TO KNOW-RELOADED-Time Will Reveal- part 4

"We'll be right there," Chill says after overhearing the news.
He takes the phone from Nina, who's crying hysterically.
"We'll all be there!" Renee yells.
The 6 of them head to the hospital. Erica is riding with Kim and Bruce. She tells them, after she gets the news from Ebony via her cell phone. They head to the hospital too. Erica calls Greg Jr to tell him. He's at Mya's house. He leaves immediately going to get Steven and they head to the hospital.

At the hospital, T-baby's in critical condition. She has suffered severe head trauma and had 2 convulsions on the way in. The staff manage to stabilize her. For now, she's in a comatose state in intensive care.

Greg Sr is upset beyond belief. Him, Greg Jr and Steven leave the hospital and go looking for Rich. Richard Sr and Anna show up to check on T-baby, after Roo and Jesse called to tell them. They're in total support of T-baby. Anna tells the police to arrest her son.
She says, "He needs to be punished for what he's done."

"Oh he will be. If Greg and the boys catch up to him," Sandy says.
She's upset with Rich. But her and Anna are friends to the end. They've been here before. Maybe not this severe. But this isn't the 1st fight T-baby and Rich Jr have had. And it won't be the last as *Time Will Reveal!*

After spending 3 hours at the hospital, Ajay decides to take his wife and go home. He tells Erica to come with them and he'll see to it that she gets to Shaker Heights. On the way to their mothers house, he has a heart to heart talk with his 2nd youngest sister.

"Erica you need to move on, lil sis," he suggests, "It's time for you to get your life and future going. In the best direction *possible*."

"I know, Ajay. I know that," Erica says.

"Lil Greg is not gonna do right either," he says, "I'm not gonna sit by and watch my sister get dogged out. I know he's been hitting you."
Erica is stunned. She had no idea her big brother knew Greg had slapped her around.
"Yea I know about it," Ajay says, "You and Greg are the T-baby and Rich of y'all crew. That *will not* work for me. Erica I will kill a stupid ass muthafucka over dumb shit. *Punk shit* like that. Do you hear me?"
Ebony joins the conversation.

"Erica you can't let someone beat on you and think that he loves you," she says, "You once told me that you wanted your love to be like ours. Your brother has never hit me. *Ever.* And you know how stern *he* is."

"I'm a fuckin man," Ajay says, "I'm not some punk ass lil boy. A real man can handle his woman like a woman and still be the man, Erica.

212

TIME TO KNOW-RELOADED-Time Will Reveal- part 4

Either you leave his ass. Or I'm gonna have to tell pops. And you know that's the shit *hitting* the fan."
By the time they arrive at Jo's house, Erica has made her decision.

"I'm not gonna talk to him anymore, Ajay," she says, "I promise. I know it's gonna be hard. But I know y'all are right. He's not gonna do any better. I'm not gonna end up like T-baby. That's his sister. You would think he would do better. Especially with what he sees her going through. But he's out of my life as of this year. I'm moving on for the new year. I just made that my New Year's resolution. I can't let my brother kill him and go to jail. I still want my Benz."
They all laugh. She gets out of the Escalade and hugs Ebony and Ajay. They walk her inside. They go in and kiss the twins goodnight, then head home. During the ride, they talk about T-baby and Rich's fights of the past.

"Ain't this the same way the nineties came in, baby girl?" he asks, "Same old shit. Ten years later."
Ebony agrees with her husband.

****

T-baby is finally awake and doing well by Christmas morning. She gets released to go home, 2 days later. Instead of going to Jackson Heights, she goes to her parents house on Sandy's insistence. Greg Sr and the boys haven't found Rich and it's been 4 days.

"It doesn't matter y'all," T-baby tells them, "I'm not going home until he moves out. I want a divorce. I'm so sorry but this will be one crew marriage that will not stand the test of time. I'm gonna end up killing him."
Sandy is happy to hear her daughter say that. She doesn't want T-baby to stay with Rich any longer, after all he's done to her. To top it all off. He has fathered a child outside of their marriage. That's far to the opposite of what the crew's family values are. Nowhere in these moves Rich has made, can you fit the quote;
Respect your wife and the females of this family to the utmost. Raise them to be strong, loyal and wise. They are our backbones, our child bearers, our rocks and our partners for life.

Those very words had been spoken by his own paternal grandfather, Allen Saul Williams, who has to be churning in his grave knowing the pitfall his 3rd grandson is headed for. Rich hasn't been home to any of the crew's knowledge, since he assaulted and nearly killed his wife. But after all she knows and all that she's gone through. She still won't cooperate with the police on the matter. Nor has she offered them any assistance.

"I've already spent Christmas in the hospital," she says, "I'm not going to let him ruin my New Year's. Let's just put it in the past."

Sandy is upset with her for not pressing charges. However the state still upholds the domestic violence and assault charges. They indict Rich. The family still tries to figure out the cause of his erratic behavior.

In the beginning of this mess, Rich blamed the disappointing 9-7 season as the reason for his depression and inattentiveness. Last season the team had gone to the AFC championship. 1 game shy of the Super Bowl. But his attitude has only gotten worse. This year his team had lost their quarterback in the 1st half of the 1st game of the season. They had finished with an 8-8 record. This years record was the worst of the three. But the crew aren't going to accept that as an excuse. Rich hasn't tried to explain anything to any of his family. Instead he'd gone back to New York and didn't even stick around Cleveland. He was arrested there, extradited back and held in central lock up. His team furnished a legal team and his Jets attorneys gets the charges reduced. He has to pay major fines but he won't serve anymore jail time. He gets off easy because of his professional status and the prosecutor's weak case. T-baby had refused to be a witness for the prosecution. The crew were hoping Rich would ask for help but he doesn't.

∤New Year's Eve, 1999∤

Ebony and Ajay's 2nd anniversary is a subtle one. They don't want a celebration due to how tense everything is within their crew. They plan to spend it at home with their twins and Ike and Tina. Ajay won't be home until the late morning. But Ebony is up early with the twins, who made 5 months old on her 24th birthday. She's looking forward to having Ajay home, after just 5 days. Miami had beat Cleveland on Christmas eve and Ajay stayed with his family for Christmas day. He went back to his team, the day after Christmas. Ebony isn't returning to her office until Monday. She has a full day planned. She's preparing for her own little family celebration tonight. She's cooking a soul food meal for her husband and herself with his favorites; Fried chicken, macaroni and cheese, cabbage, sweet cornbread and yams. She's baking him a chocolate cake for dessert and sweet ice tea to drink. After dinner, her and Ajay will have chocolate syrup, strawberries and champagne while watching the complete box set of their lives together. This is their way of reflecting on their honeymoon, each anniversary. She dressed the twins early for Big Mama's house. Now she can attend to her cooking duties while they watch her. She places them in their twin swings. She's about to go and get dressed herself, when she hears loud banging at the kitchen door. Her cell phone is ringing too. It's Jacobson at the guard booth. She goes to the peep hole. *It's Rich.*

Today is the 1st time he's been near family or crew since pleading out and getting fined. None of the crew have seen nor heard from him until now. Ebony figures this must be his 1st time coming back to Jackson Heights. She wonders why he's not seeking out a male crew member. He has to know Ajay isn't home yet. He's still a pro athlete so he's familiar with the scheduling.

Why is he coming here first? He should be talking to his wife!

She answers her cell phone and asks Jacobson to hold on while she opens the door.

Immediately she asks, "Rich where have you been?"

But once she opens the door and sees what bad shape he's in. She tries to slam it right back. She doesn't want him near their twins in his condition. But he barges his way in and starts verbally attacking her. This time is even worse than before. Jacobson heads to a security car and heads to Ebony's aid. Meanwhile Rich is on another rant.

"You lil sneaky ass bitch!" he snarls, "You told Trisha about Regina's baby! You just had to tell her! Didn't you?!"

"Rich you've got it all wrong and you need to leave," she says, trying to appear calm.

She doesn't want to upset the twins who are in their swings, just a few feet away.

"Nah muthafucka! You got it wrong!" he growls, "You're gonna learn once and for all to stay out of my *fuckin* business!"

The twins become alarmed instantly. This isn't something they're use too.

"What? What does *that* mean?" she asks, keeping her voice low.

"For your information. I met Regina through Ajay!" he yells, "I met her at *his* bachelor party. And he was with somebody too! Deal with your own marriage and stay the fuck out of mine!"

"Why do you always do this?" she asks, "Don't try to make this about Anthony. He's not having an affair or a baby with another woman. You are."

"You think that nigga not fuckin-"

"Don't you *dare* come in our home calling my husband out of his name, Rich," she spits, "He's a man and you will address him as *such*. And you will stop with the cursing and yelling. Or this conversation is over."

"Whatever Ebony!" he continues to yell. "You think Ajay not fuckin nobody but *you*!? You're so fuckin dumb, bitch!"

"Get out of my house!" she screams and Lannie screams out too. Lil Ajay gets upset. She goes to console them. At the same time and a little calmer now, again she tells Rich he needs to leave. Gwen and baby Jarvis arrive to see if she needs help with dinner. They're just in time to witness Rich's rant.

"Fuck you! I'm gonna do what my cousin should've done years ago!" he yells, "And that is to put your ass in line!"
The twins start to cry. Rich has come closer to Ebony as she's tending to them. They're upset from his loud screaming and ranting. They cry louder.

"Rich you're upsetting my babies," she tries, "Please stop with all of this screaming. We don't do that here. We talk in this house. Not yell."

"Fuck that!" he yells again, "You're gonna learn to respect me!"

"What?" she asks in disbelief, "Leave now Rich. Right now."
He lunges toward her. First he seems like he's confused and disoriented. She takes another step back and shields her twins. Then when his senses return, he lunges at her again. She steps toward him, staying between him and the twin swings. She doesn't even want them to hear him like this. Let alone see him. But he seems determined to have an affect on her and the kids. He's not successful in making her afraid which seems to piss him off more. Suddenly he raises his fist at her. She knows he wouldn't dare risk crossing his 1st cousin by hitting her.

"Don't you dare," she says very calmly, "You don't want it with Anthony and you know you don't."
He thinks about it and changes his mind about punching her. Instead he back hands her with all of his might. Which sends her flailing over and into the double swings, knocking the twins over. She lands hard on top of them and then tumbles to the kitchen floor.

"Why would you do that?!" Gwen screams and panics her son, who starts to cry along with the twins.

"Shut up you *outsider* bitch!" Rich yells at Gwen, "Don't you dare speak to crew like that! This bitch is gone learn some respect for a real man today! You just worry about what Nina's gonna do to *you!*"

"Ahhhh!" Ebony screams like a mad woman after seeing her twins lying on the floor, still in their swings and frantic, "You son of a bitch!"
She pulls herself up. Immediately she picks up her twins. Gwen, who pushed her son to a safe distance in his stroller, helps her get the twins and their overturned swing up off the kitchen floor. Rich knows Ebony as this mild mannered girl. Because that's who she is with Ajay. He must've forgotten that she taught T-baby how to fight in 2nd grade. He thinks she's soft but he's wrong. She's a fighter when threatened. He calls her a few choice

216

names, thinking she'll be afraid and just back off. But once the twins are off the floor, she turns around to handle him. While Gwen tries to assess the twins injuries. It's when Ebony turns to face Rich that he realizes he's fucked with the wrong woman. He can see the look of rage in her eyes. That's when he recalls the fact that he had watched her kill the 1st and last man who ever hit her. He makes his way to her door to haul ass but she's on his back before he can clear the kitchen porch. He had parked in her driveway. Before he can get to his car, she's on his back, digging her nails into his neck and whacking him in the back of his head with her cutting board from her kitchen counter. It's all she could find quickly. She gives him and few hard clunks to the back of his head and neck as he struggles to shed her like a bad coat. Jacobson is pulling into the driveway as Rich jumps into his Benz. He'd left his motor running like he had planned to have to make a quick get away. His tires squeal as he starts to back out, narrowly missing Jacobson's security car. Jacobson is trying to halt him. Ebony picks up 1 of her potted plants, throws it at him and hit's the front of his car. He gets turned around, speeds out of her driveway and around the small curve, heading back out of Jackson Heights. She runs back inside to check on her crying babies while Jacobson calls the gate. Gwen assists her in trying to console the kids. They're crying out of control. This mayhem has terrified them. Ebony wants to catch Rich but she's more concerned with her twins.

"Are you okay?" she asks as she cries and hugs lil Ajay.
He took the brunt of the fall. Lannie's swing had landed on top of his. He's crying even more than Lannie is because he's hurt. Lannie is afraid.

"He's a crazy man," Gwen says, "He's always so *rude*."

"He's going to lose it for real when Anthony gets to him," Ebony says, not wanting to alert Gwen that her husband is going to be in a killing state when this news reaches him. "Can you keep an eye on the house for me? I have to call my mom and go get my babies checked out before their daddy gets here."
Gwen tells her she'll keep watch as she gets her son and prepares to head back home. Before she makes it to the street, she calls Renee and lets her know what she's just witnessed.

Inside Ebony calls her mother at *Big Mama's House* and tells her what's just happened. Pearl is upset as she tells Jo.

"Ebony call Renee and the girls," Jo says, after taking the phone from Pearl, who is fussing plenty. "Tell Nina to bring the babies in for you. We'll get Mahoney out here so she can check them out for any injuries," mama Jo says, "Before Ant gets here. We're gonna have to tie him down."

Pearl had already called Renee and learned that Jacobson and Gwen had called her too. She's arriving at Ebony's house as she hangs up with Pearl. She'd already called Nina and Rebbie. The 3 arrive simultaneously. Ebony hangs up with Jo as the 3 ladies run inside.

"Ebony are you guys alright?" Renee asks as she runs in through the kitchen door which is still wide open.

Jacobson has gone back to the booth to file reports. Ebony is consoling her twins. She has managed to get them to calm down and stop crying.

"What the hell is on Rich's mind?!" Nina asks, "Ajay is gonna kill that boy!"

"I know that's right," Rebbie says as she shakes her head.

"He's on that shit," Renee confesses, "He's not even giving a damn right now."

"He must wanna die. Doing shit like this," Rebbie says.

She doesn't usually use such colorful language. But they're all familiar with Ajay's short temper when it comes to those he love. And today, Rich had attacked the 3 most important pieces of his heart. Ebony is still crying as she sits at the breakfast nook cuddling her babies. She wants to call Ajay. But she knows he's in flight. Besides this isn't something she wants him to hear over the phone.

"Ant junior fell the hardest," she cries, "I think he broke his arm." She breaks down crying.

"Ajay is gonna kill Rich," Renee says, "Oh my God. Nobody will be able to hold him back. And I don't know if they'd want too. This is insane."

"I'm mad y'all," Nina says, "But I don't want my brother to go to prison. And not for killing my first cousin. Even though he *is* acting like a piece of shit."

"I hear you," Rebbie says.

Just then Jo calls back to tell them Dr. Mahoney will be at aftercare in minutes and to bring the twins on down.

"Ebony we'll take them for you," Rebbie offers.

"Are you crazy?! They're not leaving my sight," she says, "Not until I know they're okay. Can't you see how confused they are?"

"Ebony you need to get you lip checked out too," Nina suggests, "It's bleeding pretty bad. That's what the babies are looking at. *You*."

"Your face is puffy too," Renee says.

"Ajay's gonna lose it," Rebbie says, "He'll kill him. I know it."

"I don't want my brother to go the jail," Nina says as she cries.

"I'm gonna call the house and tell Kenneth," Renee says, "So him Jr and the guys can be ready to intercept Ajay."

TIME TO KNOW-RELOADED-Time Will Reveal- part 4

"They'd better be prepared to tie him down," Nina says, "He'll want Rich and so will Jeremy. And he's picking him up from the airport. That's the recipe for a nuclear weapon."

She calls Tank to inform him of what has happened.

"I hope he does fuck him up for hurting our babies," Ebony says, "We worked too hard for these kids. He comes up in *our house* and hurts all three of us. Daddy is gonna take care of him. He won't kill him but he'll wish he was dead."

"I know Tank is gonna want his head," Renee says, "But I'm glad Jb ain't here."

"Oh my God. For *real*," Nina says, "He would be pushing Ajay out the way to get to Rich's ass. Let's get these babies to CrewLand."

"Quickly," Rebbie adds.

The girls help her get the twins in her Escalade. She's limping. Her knee and her ankle is hurt.

"Ebony is your leg hurt too?" Rebbie asks.

"I fell on my hip," she says, "I was making sure I didn't fall on my kids. Then their swing fell on me. That's what stopped their heads from hitting the floor. *My body*. Their heads landed on me."

"Jeremy is picking up Ajay in *two* hours," Nina says as she hangs up with her husband. "Rich has two hours to get his ass out of town. Cause now Jeremy wants to whoop his ass too."

Nina and Rebbie get in the Escalade with Ebony. Nina gets into the drivers seat and they drive the twins to aftercare. Renee follows in her new Benz S600. In 10 minutes they're at The CrewLand mall. Jo and Pearl run outside and help get the twins inside.

An hour later, Mahoney has checked them out. Ajay Jr has a bruised right forearm and upper thigh. Atlantis doesn't have any apparent injuries. Ebony has a black eye, a busted lip and a bruised hip. Mahoney wants the twins x-rayed.

"I'm calling big Rich," big John says.

He had come over to the nursery with Al when Jo called them with the news. "We're gonna have to get him some help. *Quick*."

"You'd better get him out of Ant's sight quicker," Al says, "He's gonna tear him a new asshole over these three."

"He might just have some help," Jo adds, "Rich is not gonna be beating on my family like he's some damn fool."

John and Al take that as a hint to walk up to Crew Details and speak with Rich Sr.

He's fully cooperative as they knew he would be. He wants to find

219

his son and get him some help too. He suggests they get Rich's crew to assist in finding him.

"I've been looking for him since he jumped on Trisha," Rich Sr says, "And I haven't seen Hyde nor hair of him."

"If you don't want a dead son," Al says, "I suggest we find him before Ant does."

"He decided he had beef with baby girl and went straight there," John says, "Only I don't think his addiction allows him to add in the Ajay factor. Or that I don't want nobody putting their fuckin hands on my daughter."

"Or maybe the addiction does," Brian Sr adds, "You know that's how I lost my mother and subsequently, my only sister."

His only sibling who was older than him, had an addiction to heroine in the early seventies. In a fit to get a fix, she confronted their mother for money. Money her mother either didn't have or wasn't willing to give to her. His older sister had left their house and came back with a male who she had been shacking up with. He'd helped her take her own mother's life. After killing her, she found out that her mother only had $14. And she had killed her for it. Brian Sr never knew his father. But he knew drug addictions. It was a drug addiction that sent him to foster care at the age of nine.

"So y'all know, I know the ups and downs of this issue," he says.

"We don't have to open the grill for another five hours," Al says, "We can go with you to look for him, Rich."

John, Al and Rich Sr leave Brian Sr in charge of Crew Details and they set out to look for Rich Jr again.

Tank stops by the nursery on his way to the airport. He wants to check on his only sister, his niece and nephew before bringing his best friend to see the horror that will shake him like little else can. Jo and Pearl demand to keep the twins there with them as Ebony is about to head back home. She knows Ajay has told her that's where he wants her to be, whenever she's been harmed and he's not around. Jacobson has been on the phone constantly since the attack. He has several of his security team at aftercare.

"Are you okay twin?" Tank asks Ebony.

"No I'm not," she says, still crying.

She gets into her SUV and leaves. She needs to make herself look a little better before Ajay gets home. If he sees blood dried all over her face and clothes, he won't even care about making the news. Tank checks on the twins, then heads for the airport. Nina goes on to open up the salon. Renee

220

goes to open the Spot II for Tank. Both clubs have major New Year's Eve celebrations going on tonight and the crew could've done without this mess.

Ebony goes home and tries to resume her anniversary dinner. As soon as he lands, Ajay calls her while she's still cooking. She's still sniffling.
"Happy Anniversary," he says, "What's wrong, baby?"
"I'm okay. I'm peeling onions, Anthony," she tries.
"You don't sound okay," he says, "Are my babies there?"
"They're at aftercare, so I can cook," she says sadly.
"Okay. I'm going by there first," he says, "Then I'll be on home to make whatever it is better. Okay?"
She says okay and they hang up. Then she thinks better of it. She turns off her dinner again. She grabs her handbag, her keys and heads back out to her Escalade. She heads back to aftercare.
"I'm gonna be there when he sees the kids," she says to herself, still sniffling. "He's gonna rip something for sure, if I'm not there."

Tank and Ajay leave the airport heading to Big Mama's aftercare. Ajay noticed the stand offish manner Tank had inside of the terminal. Security had taken his bags and escorted them back to the vehicles. As they head back, Ajay is curious about what has Tank bothered.
"What's up partner?" Ajay asks.
"Shit," Tanks says, "I'm just not having a good day. We'll talk on it in a few. Just not right now. Check on my niece, nephew and twin. Then we'll talk, alright?"
"Alright," Ajay says, "If you're sure."
"I'm positive we will," Tank says as he pops in Big Pun's CD and they head to CrewLand with no more words.

}Shaker Heights{
T-baby has gotten word about Rich attacking her 1st cousin and the twins. She knows this spells trouble for the man she loves but never bothered to hold accountable for these same deeds done to her. She has to get in touch with Ebony as soon as possible. She gathers herself before calling. She feels guilty for not just telling Rich who had told her about his whore's pregnancy. He'd confronted her over the phone last night. Asking her how did she find out he'd gotten someone pregnant. She never told him it was Ajay who revealed it to her. With Ebony having seen him at the complex with his mistress and knowing that she's very tight with her girls. He blamed her automatically. He just assumed she told T-baby. T-baby and

221

TIME TO KNOW-RELOADED-Time Will Reveal- part 4

Ebony still haven't discussed what Ebony saw at the complex. She only knows Ebony didn't tell her because she wanted to spare her feelings. Though Ebony knew Rich was a cheater. She never told exactly what she saw. T-baby had suspicions of her own. She never told her girls either.

Ajay is the one who told me so why would he attack Ebony? Because he thinks she told me. I need to get my nerves together and call my cousin.

}CrewLand Mall{

Tank and Ajay arrive just minutes before Ebony does. Ajay walks in and speaks to his mother and mother-in-law in his usual chipper tone and manner. But that mood changes as soon as he reaches to pick up his baby girl and looks at his son. He notices scratches on his left ear.

Immediately he asks, "What the hell happened to my son?"

He reaches for Ajay Jr, who pouts his lips as if he's about to cry. He sees his protector. Seeing his son about to cry makes Ajay instantly angry. Pearl and Jo are hesitant in telling him what happened. They see Ebony outside, parking her SUV. They decide to wait for her to come in and let her tell him. Ajay notices the bruise on his son's leg and his eye starts to twitch.

"How did my son get these bruises and shit?" he asks as his voice starts to rise.

Before Jo can answer him, Ebony runs in wearing her *Chanel* sunglasses. He whips around to ask her the same question. But he notices her lips are swollen and there's a bruise on the side of her face. He loses it.

"What the fuck is going on?!" he yells, upsetting all of the children except his own as his daughter lays her head against him.

He's upset right now. So Tank grabs Atlantis from his arms. Ajay removes Ebony's sunglasses. The anger in his eyes is visible to everyone.

"Somebody better tell me what the fuck is going on," he warns, looking directly into Ebony's eyes. "Baby did you wreck your truck?"

"No," she says as the tears return. "It was Rich. He hit me with his back hand and knocked me over. I fell on the twins while they was in their swing. Lil Ant fell on the floor. Lannie was on top of him. Their heads landed on me."

She cries harder. He hugs her. He's still holding his son as he turns to Tank, who's still holding Atlantis. He says, "Give her to her mama."

Tank gives Atlantis to Ebony.

"Baby let's go," he says, "Let's take my kids and go home. I want y'all to wait for me there like we planned it before this mess happened." He gives her a kiss, then in his usual calm or more like callous way, he says, "Everything will be alright in a little bit. I'll see to it. You know I'm gonna

222

protect my family. My kids look like they've seen a damn ghost. I ain't having that."

Chill and Jr, having heard that Ajay had arrived, pulls into the parking lot just as he's helping Ebony put the twins into their car seats.

"We're with you," Jr says as he and Chill hop out of Chill's Blazer. Ajay gives each of his twins a kiss, then he hugs and kisses Ebony again. He looks her in the eyes and says, "I can't just go home and stay there. You know I can't stay home just yet. And you know why."

He has that same stare in his eyes he'd had when Ray was at the chamber. *Blank.*

"He's crew, Anthony," she says in an almost whisper.

"Not today he ain't," he says, "Crew wouldn't do this to family." She knows anything goes for Ajay right now. As protective as he's always been of her. He's a thousand times more protective of his kids. Add in the fact that Rich had gone to his home to do it again, after being punched 2 times and let off the hook the 1st time. Ebony can't even measure the amount of anger her husband is feeling at this moment. No matter how eager he is to have fun time with his kids. She knows he's focused on only 1 thing. Finding Rich Jr and making him feel the pain and fear that he'd most likely caused his kids. Or whatever comes to his mind at the moment he sees him. She can't see any emotion in his eyes. This frightens her because she knows *this* zone. The target of the anger that brings forth this stare, rarely lives to tell about it. She needs him to have her and their kids on his mind. And not just protecting them.

"I love you, Anthony," she says, "And we *need* you."

"I love you too," he says, "I love all of you."

He puts her in the passenger seat, then he hops into the drivers seat of the Escalade. He's going home to get his guns. Chill, with Jr in the Blazer and Tank in his own vehicle, follow closely.

They get to Jackson Heights. Ajay helps take the twins inside and puts them in their play pen. He kisses his son and daughter again. He looks into their eyes. They look up at him as if they know everything is going to be okay. They give him their smiles. The thing he always ask for when he gets home. The twins will live this down. But will their father? He goes to his safe and grabs 2 of his 9mm pistols and an extra clip for each. He turns to see Ebony standing next to the door of his walk in closet where his safe is installed. She looks stressed beyond belief.

"Stay home and wait for me," he says, "Don't go anywhere. I have to find this nigga right now."

Ebony will do exactly as she's told. She follows Ajay. He meets Jr, Tank and

Chill on the driveway. They all get into Chill's Blazer. But before they can pull away, Al, Rich Sr and John pull up in Rich Sr's vehicle.

"Where is he?" Ajay asks them.

"We couldn't find him, son," big John says.

"We're gonna find him," Ajay says and they pull away as Rich Sr, Al and big John follow them.

"Chill," Ajay says, "Call Arthur and Kilo. They know where that crack head ass nigga is."

Jr calls Arthur. Him and Kilo tell them Rich was in The Point earlier. Ebony calls Chill's cell phone while they're driving to The Point.

"Hello."

"Hey Chill. This is Ebony," she says, "I know my man's with you."

"Yep."

"Chill please don't let him kill Rich. *Please*," she pleads.

"I won't," he hangs up immediately and they drive in silence.

Meanwhile T-baby calls Ebony so she can check on the condition of her and the twins.

"Hey Ebony. How are you?" she asks.

She's calling from Sandy's house where she's been staying since she was released from the hospital. "I heard what Richard did," she says.

"Yes," is all Ebony says.

"Are you and the twins alright?" T-baby asks.

"We're not critical like you was," she says bluntly, "But he crossed the line this morning. One that he may never get back over."

"I know he did. But Ebony he's on drugs."

"So!" she says as her voice rises.

"I know that's not an excuse but he is," T-baby says.

"Anthony is home and he's out looking for him," Ebony says, "He hurt me and our babies, T-baby."

"He thinks you told me about Regina being pregnant," she says.

"How do you know that?" Ebony asks.

"He called over here last night," T-baby confesses, "And he was blaming you. I told him you wasn't the one who told me but he didn't believe me."

"That's *obvious*," Ebony says dryly.

"I really do hope Ajay beats his ass good though," T-baby says, "He needs it."

"Well he's gonna get what he needs just in time for the new year," Ebony says, "T-baby I've got so much more cooking to do."

"Okay. I'll call you later, alright," T-baby says, "I know you're on edge about what Ajay might do. But I'm not. He loves his wife and kids too much to ruin his life. Kiss my cousins for me and tell them I love them."

"Okay, Cuz," Ebony says, "We love you too."

They hang up. T-baby knows there is a hunt on for her husband now. She wonders if her crew blames her for not pressing charges on him. Or does Ajay blame her for Rich coming to his house today. She feels guilty as she thinks about calling Ajay's cell phone.

}The Point{

The guys arrive at the house in The Point that Arthur and Kilo had suggested. It's the same house Ajay parked Chill's blazer at when he'd gone to granny and papa's house to sneak in Ebony's window, the night before she first moved to Houston. The girl that use to live there is now incarcerated on drug charges. She had become addicted to crack in 1992 and has been in and out of jail every since. She's serving the last year of a 5 year sentence. She owed a debt the her front man and as the game goes. They took over her house as collateral when she got locked up. Her house has gone to the streets, pretty much and her roommates have been prostituting themselves to support their habits. Rich use to sell to these very women. Now he's a junkie as well. But Rich isn't at the house when Ajay and the guys arrive. The house is barely there and is being demolished due in part to the activism of papa and their senior crew. Ajay is heated at not finding Rich there. His cell phone rings.

"Hello!" he says impatiently.

"Ajay I know where he is," T-baby says.

"Where."

"Mentor. Madison on the lake. Rhodes drive," she tells him.

Ajay tells Chill where to go, then he gets back to T-baby.

"Who the fuck does he know out there?" he asks her.

"A Clydesdale owner and trainer that everybody calls Clyde. He's part owner of the Indians. They have big drug parties out there and always have. Rich use to sell his whole stash at that *one* mansion. That's where I think he goes now when no one can find him. It was our secret place. The place where he eventually got hooked on his own product. I was thinking he had a mistress out there. I thought his bitch was hanging at that mansion and having him there. But he was bringing her with him when he went there. Just like he had done with me. Crack is his *real* mistress. And instead of selling her. He started smoking her."

Ajay tells her he's going to find Rich and get rid of his and her problem. Before she can talk him down, he hangs up on her.

225

When they arrive at the mansion on Rhodes drive, it's just as T-baby had said. There's a party going on in the middle of the morning. Rich's Benz is there. Which means, so is Rich. Ajay pulls 1 of his 3 pistols as soon as he jumps out of Chill's SUV. But his father Al is there to help Chill keep him from committing murder.

"Hold on son," Al says, "I know you're mad as *hell*. I am too. But I'm not gonna let you kill him."

Ajay pushes past his father. Then John, Chill and Jr step in front of Ajay.

"Man we're gonna let you beat his ass until you get tired," John says, "But there ain't one of us *out* here that wanna see you go the jail. Or that wanna see Rich junior *dead*."

"Daddy's right," Tank says, "That's my twin and *his* daughter. You and Rich are *my* brothers. He deserves to get his ass beat *real* good for fucking wit twin *and* the twins. But I ain't letting you go the *jail* man."

"What about your family, Ajay," Chill asks, looking into his eyes.

"That's who I'm protecting," Ajay grunts.

"Do you wanna sentence Ebony and those twins to visiting you in jail? For the rest of your natural life, Ant?" Al asks as he steps back to him. He looks at his father and the guys finally notice him blink. Ajay, after much coaxing, gives Al his gun. Tank searches him to be sure he doesn't have a back up. He has 2 more guns and Tank takes those as well.

"I know you bro," Tank says, smiling slightly, "You've always got a spare."

Ajay gives him an impatient look as he makes his way to the door. They follow him into the *crack* mansion.

Eventually Ajay locates Rich in the far back room on the 2nd floor, in a corner. He's stoned out of his mind. Ajay grabs him and slings him across the room. The other addicts run for cover. Most of them left the premises when the crew barged in. Those who remain, become scarce when the beating starts. Ajay starts to whip Rich as if he'd stole something. For the next 15 minutes, he punishes him. He whips him good. Then he drags him out of the room and down the stairs. Just like *Scotty Appleton* did *Nino Brown* at the end of *New Jack City*. Ajay drags Rich all the way to the car, slamming his head into it once he reaches big Rich's vehicle.

"Nigga you're gonna get your shit together," Ajay oozes, "You fucked with *my* wife and kids. I know it's because you're trying to die."

Rich is trying to explain but Ajay punches him again.

"Nigga I told your wife about you fucking up. *Not* my wife!" he yells, "Do you understand me?! I told T-baby about your kid that's on the way! Not Ebony! T-baby still don't even *know* you was fucking with that bitch while

226

she was still in Natty! Ebony didn't tell her! I did! Now! Fuck with me, nigga!" He's choking Rich at this point.
"I told you not to fuck with mine, Cuz," he says in an eerily calm voice.
Rich is gurgling for air. Ajay only tightens his grip. Al and John grab him.
"Let him go son," Al says.
"He's done man," John says.
But Ajay continues to strangle him. Al, John and Tank work to get Ajay's hands free of Rich's throat. Finally they succeed. Ajay swings on Rich again. Knocking him against Chill's SUV. Rich finds some air.
"I'm sorry Ajay, man," he says, sounding as if he's down in a hole. *"This shit got me. It's got me so fucked up, Cuz."*
Ajay goes after him again and gets another lock on his throat.
"I may as well kill you now then!" Ajay yells, "You're slowing killing yourself anyway! I should've told T-baby a long time ago! She wouldn't be going through this hell with you right now!"
"Son, let him go," Al insists.
But Ajay's hands are like vice grips on Rich's neck and he has no plans of letting go this time.
Al and John get help from Rich Sr and Jr. Again it's a struggle but finally they get Ajay's hands from around Rich's throat again. Ajay kicks Rich in the head on release. Rich slams into the side of his fathers car and passes out cold.
"Let's get him to the hospital," Al says.
John and Chill puts the *unconscious* Rich in his father's car. John and Rich Sr get in with him while Al drives Rich's Benz. They drive him to the ER. Tank, Jr and Ajay ride with Chill. On the way to the hospital, Ajay has a revelation for Chill, Tank and Jr.
"Rich visited Tameka in jail. Numerous times," Ajay says, "And he kept money on her books too. That's why he feels like he can have her now. He never did stop seeing any of the women he was fucking with in high school. Even the girls from Houston. They cracked out too. This nigga don't wanna do nothing good. He don't give a damn if any of us have a good thing either. Rich counted himself out when he was seven years old. I remember all of the shit his use to tell me. I seriously thought he was gonna be a serial killer. He use to kill puppies and kittens and shit."
Chill, Jr and Tank say nothing. But they agree with Ajay on every point. It hurts them all to see their family bottom out. They know it's now or never for Richie Rich.
At the hospital, they patch Rich up and release him immediately. Rich Sr contacts Jb and tells him to get Rich a flight scheduled.

227

"So he can get his ass *back* to his football team immediately," Rich Sr says.

Rich has been home since the season ended. Doing drugs mostly and just messing up everything he puts his hands on. He hasn't even been in contact with his team to sign in for next season.

After leaving the hospital, they take Rich to his home in Jackson Heights. They're surprised to see T-baby when they get to the door. Rich hugs her, cries and apologizes, over and over. She tells him to come on in and go take a bath. She has made dinner and their son is there as well. Rich seems to appreciate it. He goes to the bathroom to take a long bath. Jb calls Rich Sr back before the crew leaves. He tells them Rich has a flight to New York. Its scheduled for tomorrow morning at ten.

"Make sure he gets on that *damn* flight," Jb warns, "Because the GM is fuckin annoyed with him, as it is."

After everyone leaves, T-baby goes into the bathroom with Rich. She gives him some ice water to drink. His drug problem is apparent to everyone now. He's on a downward spiral and even though he had beaten her critically, just over a week ago. T-baby can't help but cry and feel sorry for him. She's loved him all her life. Though she wants to hate him right now. She can't. She just keeps hearing her wedding vows, *"Til Death do us part."*

}Jackson Heights{

Ajay and Ebony manage to have a nice quiet anniversary dinner at home with Ant Jr, Atlantis, Ike and Tina. Ebony is happy her husband didn't commit murder. But she's pleased he'd avenged Rich's assault on her and their twins.

"I love you, Anthony," she says.

"I love you too," Ajay says, "Busted lip. Black eye. Bruised hip and all," he has a slight smile on his face as he says, "Come on over here."

She knows he's still upset. But if he can joke about it, then she knows he'll be okay. It just something inside of her that tells her this Rich situation isn't over with. Not by a long shot. Ajay plays with his 5-month old twins. She joins him while their personal DVD plays. Her and Ajay do a lot of passionate kissing. He moves his fingers over her bruises as if he's trying to make them disappear. She closes her eyes for several minutes while he does this. Without speaking any words, she knows he's wishing it could all go away. She opens her eyes and smiles *big* for him. He smiles back at her. For now, his family is okay. He can relax. Ike and Tina play tag with their squeeze toys while Ajay plays peek-a-boo with the twins. They giggle a lot. Showing that they're having fun and their spirits are not broken. That's what Ajay had worried about. He didn't want them to be afraid. Nor to feel unsafe. Especially not in their own home. They don't appear to be affected. All he cares about at this moment is another lovely anniversary.

****

In the late evening, Belinda calls Pearl from Atlanta to tell her, Jan is in labor. Belinda and Kim have been in Atlanta since Christmas Eve awaiting the birth of Jan and Rob's 1st baby.

Jan has a cesarean section delivery. Their baby boy is the 1st baby born to that hospital for the New Year.

"We got baby New Year!" Sam Sr exclaims and laughs.

He's in Atlanta as well. Sam Jr and Pam are in Atlanta with them. Kim is flying back today and meeting Bruce and the Ohio State team at the Columbus campus. She's going to watch Bruce play his 4th bowl game in 4 seasons. They're going to host Erica in their place during the weekend. But at Grady hospital in Atlanta, Rob and Jan are finally parents.

"He's so fine, baby," Rob says, "I got *me* a junior now."

"Yes you do, baby," Jan says, though she's still groggy from the anesthesia. "We did it. We finally did it."

NAME: Robert Leon Jenkins, Jr
BORN: January 1, 2000
TIME: 12:00:05AM
WEIGHT: 7lbs, 7ounces
LENGTH: 20inches

Welcome to the world...........................Robert Leon Jenkins, Jr!

HAPPY NEW MILLENIUM, FROM THE CREW!
#CREW4LIFE

CHAPTER   44

CREW Y2K

It's the new Millennium and crew are still holding things down. Bre, Cedric and CJ stop in Cleveland to go with the crew to Bruce's bowl game on the 3rd against Oklahoma. They're in the process of moving to Atlanta where they'll take over management of *The Hideaway Bar-n-Grill.* Plus assist with *The Sports Complex,* as soon as they touch down. Bre is a member of the Army reserves and will report once a month to *Warner Robbins* for drill.

Wesley, who's also a member of the Army reserves in Cleveland, begins work with T-baby at *Williams Accounting firm* the day after they return from the game. Jb is in Cleveland this 1st week to open his Sports Agency office at CrewLand Mall. He attended the bowl game as well. After the game, Eric McNair, an all-American special teams player from Oklahoma had shown interest in hiring Jb as his agent. Jb signed him on immediately. Eric McNair is a top football player from Chicago and a good friend of Erica's at Oklahoma. While at home, Jb starts negotiations with the *Browns* to get Eric in the upcoming NFL draft, along with Bruce. Bruce still has another year at *Ohio State* before he gets his degree. Eric, who's ready this year, had come on into Cleveland with Erica to meet her family. He stayed in town for his 1st meeting with Jb. It's during this meeting that he confides in Jb about his secret crush on Erica Jackson.

"I really like her a lot," he says, "That's one reason why I wanna come to Cleveland to play. I wanna meet her family and crew. I wanna date her if she'll give me the chance. What do you think?"

"She's a great girl," Jb says, "She's like a little sister to me. Our parents live next door to each other and have for all our lives. I've known Erica since birth. I'm married to her oldest sister Lynn. My brother Tank is married to her second oldest sister Nina. And my *only* sister Ebony is married to her *only* brother Ajay. As you know, he plays for *The Heat.*"

"Wow! That's some ties right there," Eric says, "But do you think I should ask her *out*?"

"You'll need to ask her pops first," Jb says, "And her brother too. In this crew, we see our females as queens. *Royalty.* They don't usually date outside the crew. You'll have to ask her male leaders before you ask her."

"I will," Eric says, "Where can I find them?"

"Her pops will be at Stoney's shortly. He runs the grill with my dad. Ajay plays with Miami so he's not always here. But you can meet big

TIME TO KNOW-RELOADED-Time Will Reveal- part 4

Al *today*. I was gonna take you by there to grab some food. So when we finish up the paperwork, I can introduce you to the family."
Eric is happy with that plan as he looks through the front window of Jb's office. They'll take the tour and Jb will introduce him to the crew family in each of the businesses they own, along the way.

"We own all of this and we're building more," Jb says, "This whole strip here. And that one over there," Jb says while standing in the front window next to Eric, pointing across the parking lot to the adjacent strip. Which houses; *Stoney's Sports bar and grill, Jackson's Real Estate, Williams accounting firm, Big Mama's House aftercare, The Spot II, Crew Spa and Health club, Crew Gear & Alterations* and *Jacobson's security office.*

"*Man* y'all got it going on in Cleveland. Don't you?" Eric asks as he still admires the businesses through the store front window.

"We're doing pretty good," Jb says, "Actually this is opening day for *this* office. This is *Brown's Sports Agency*. It's the eighth business to open on this side. We have my uncle Greg and big Sam, who do all of our construction and they haven't even opened an office yet. They're waiting on my dad to open an office for his trucking company. Then they'll have a dual set up, like my sister and my first cousin have for their real estate and accounting offices with one entrance. People can get their credit in order first. Then have my sister help them to get property. My dad and my uncle will be similar. Uncle Greg can build it. My pops can truck in all the supplies and move the families in too. Come on. Let's go have a closer look."

"I'm ready," Eric says as he goes out the door behind Jb.
Jb takes him down the sidewalk to view *Crew Details, The Chill Spot, Crew Cuts and Styles I, The Crews House of Soul Food, Granny's House preschool, Jenkins Jams Studio & Record Store* and *Que Psi Phi Video & Photography.* His sports office is number 8 in this strip. He takes him to *Crew Details* too.

"This was our *very* first business," Jb says, "For most of the males in this family. This was our first job."
They go across the catwalk to view the 8 businesses on the other side.

"So your family has eighteen businesses that y'all own and run?" Eric asks.

"Actually it's twenty three when you count the ones down south. *The Dirty South Chill Spot, Southern Exposure restaurant, Hideaway Studio, Jenkins Jams South record store and the Southern Sports Complex.* Those are in Atlanta," he clarifies with a chuckle. "*Hey* there's a lot of us."

"That's awesome, man," Eric says, "I hope to add a business to the family too. That is, if I can become apart of this awesome crew. You know. If I can get Erica to go out with me."

"Talk to her daddy and her brother before you ask her out," Jb advices. "That's how we get down in this family. Your relationship won't be respected if it's not done that way. And believe me. A lot of us tried to get around it. It's impossible. They have to know and *then* approve of it."
Eric agrees to follow crew code.

Eric's Cleveland Browns meeting has been set up. It's ready to go. Jb and Eric head to the Cleveland Brown's offices to see what deal they can get for the new season.

The Browns agree to draft Eric McNair and Bruce Wilson in 2000, if they're still available. Eric and Jb go to Stoney's to celebrate.

Jb introduces Eric to Al and John. That's when Eric starts to make his case with Al. Al tells him, he would like to know him better before he can give him an answer about dating his daughter.

"Whenever you can get back in town," Al says, "We'll get together at my son's house. The three of us can talk it over."

"That's fair sir," Eric says.

"You'll have to be a strong and stern man," Al tells him. "Because if you date Erica. You're getting a version of my wife. She's head strong and very intelligent. So you have to be a strong man and take care of things. I look forward to getting to know you, either way."

"Hopefully you'll get that chance," Eric says, "If I get drafted to Cleveland."
Al wishes him luck. They celebrate his success over a few beers. Al likes what he sees in Eric, so far.

The next morning before Jb can leave Cleveland, he gets a call from New York. It's from Rich Jr. He's been released from *The Jets*. He failed a substance abuse test. Jb isn't happy with the news he has to tell Rich's parents. But he finds Rich Sr and Anna and makes them aware.

They're both hurt and disappointed but they tell Rich Jr to come on home. He barely has money left for a ticket so T-baby reserves the ticket to Cleveland for him, from her office. She tells Ebony the news. Ebony is sorry for Rich's troubles but she hasn't forgiven him for attacking, not only T-baby but her and her twins too.

"He'll have to work with me for awhile, I guess," T-baby says.

"I don't like that T-baby," Ebony says, "He don't need to be working around *anybodies* money."

"What do you think I should do?" T-baby asks her.

"We have all of these businesses, Cuz," Ebony says, "He needs to be in one where the men are. Like Stoney's or Crew Details, with his daddy. Let them deal with his attitude. Maybe they can handle and fix him."

"Will you help me get him set up?" T-baby asks.

"Sure Tee. I'll call my pops right now," Ebony says.

She calls John at the bar and grill. Him and Al agree to let Rich work with them. Rich Sr and Brian Sr also say they can use his help at the detail shop. The men hang up. Ebony and T-baby continue their talk.

"So now he has two jobs," Ebony says with a smile. "Anthony is not gonna be okay with him working in our duplex anyway, T-baby. He needs to be around the men in case he goes on another tear."

"But those are hardworking jobs," T-baby says, "He did help start many *these* businesses. He should be the CEO of something. Even if it's just cosmetic."

"Yes he did invest some of his salary to grow CrewLand," Ebony says, "But that doesn't mean we give him a license to end them. Cousin, he's a crack head and the sooner you accept and face that. The better it will be for you and him."

"I wouldn't actually give him access to any of the clients money, Ebony," she says, "You know I know better than that. I was gonna see how the other jobs worked out anyway."

"We're due for a nice surprise, don't you think?" Ebony asks.

"Yes and hopefully he won't fuck this up," T-baby says as her and Ebony share a smile, then return to their offices.

Ajay will be home on the 8th for a 2nd game against Jarvis and the Cavaliers, this Friday. Ebony's excited as usual. Her, Gwen and her girls are having lunch at Crew's house.

"I miss my daddy y'all," Ebony says to her girls.

"She *really* does," Gwen adds, "She's been a bit much to take around that curve."

They laugh and have lunch at Crew's House the afternoon of the 7th. Things are tense for Gwen but she's learning to relax with the foursome.

"The twins get to see their daddy play tomorrow night," Nina says.

"It's their first game," Ebony agrees, "That's how he wanted it."

"Oh that's gonna be great," Rebbie says, "They're gonna put the camera on y'all."

"They sure are," Gwen agrees, "Me and Jarvis junior will get a break. I'm glad about that part."

"Well we had all better be camera sharp then, right?" Ebony says as she laughs.

"That's right," T-baby says and laughs. "Y'all have to look good for the media. Mama got some sharp outfits made for y'all too. She said

TIME TO KNOW-RELOADED-Time Will Reveal- part 4

Ajay had her to make them and get our salon to style you and Lannie."

"Lannie don't need any styling," Nina says, "Her hair is still slick. She got that Pocahontas look, like her Nana Jo."

Ebony smiles brightly. She had no idea her husband had ordered special outfits for them to wear to his kids *1st* NBA game. She agrees that her daughter favors mama Jo, Nina and Erica.

"Lannie's got light skin like the bright Jackson's. And Ant Jr is dark like Anthony, papa big Al and his aunties Lynn and Pam," Ebony says with a smile. "The media will make a story out of that, just to keep camera's on us. But really I hate the media part."

"You always did, kid," T-baby says as her girls agree and laugh.

}Parma{

Darlene had convinced Farah to get them tickets to the Cavaliers-Heat game tomorrow night. They have awesome seats near the floor. But of course Ebony will be *on* the floor in the elite seats with security, assistants and caterers who will be catering to her and the twins every need.

"I can't wait to see Ajay's sexy ass," Darlene says, "I will never get over that boy's dick."

"He's a man now auntie," Alana jokes, "He's all man *now*."

"He was all man *then*, shit," Darlene says and giggles, "Ajay had a twelve inch dick at thirteen years old. Just in case y'all are wondering why would a twenty three year old be fucking with a thirteen year old? His dick was thirty five. *Okay*?"

"Oh shit! That muthafucka is packing the heat!" Alana yells.

"The meat, you mean," Farah says with a laugh, "I wonder what Chill is holding?"

"Jeremy got ten, *easy*," Alana offers, "And I heard that the whole crew is some big dick *muthafucking* men. Well not the females."

They all laugh as they prepare to go shopping for game outfits. They have to get their hair and nails done too. There's going to be an after party at The Spot and they want to look *faceable*, to any takers. All 3 of these ladies have their sights on a crew male who's already married and has a family. Nothing says *ass out* more than that. There are many myths and sayings in Cleveland about the crew man. But leaving their wives for another woman isn't 1 of them.

}Gund Arena{

The next evening the Gund Arena is filled to capacity. Ebony is courtside, seated with Gwen Russell-Rhodes. They're surrounded by crew and employees from CrewLand. Ajay plays a great game. He led all scores

234

with 39, assist with 11 and he had 4 steals. He was 3rd on the boards with seven. Miami won the game easily. Jarvis played well but not well enough to get the Cav's passed Ajay and the Heat, this time either.

Darlene watches as Ajay goes over to his wife and twins after the game.

"Those *are* some cute babies," Farah says.

"They sure are," Darlene agrees, "The media's eating them up."

"We'll see them all over the TV," Alana laughs, "Jeremy's little girl is pretty too. The one sitting by Ebony."

Alana loves being salty when it comes to Nina. However she'll never be forthcoming with it when in the presence of Nina. They continue to watch with envy as Ajay puts his twins in their stroller.

"Great game, daddy," Ebony says with a smile as she gives him a kiss and escorts him up the tunnel to the dressing room.

He pushes the twins stroller. Gwen, Jarvis and Jarvis Jr are with them.

"Did y'all enjoy daddy's game?" Ajay asks playfully to his twins as they giggle at him.

"Baby y'all wait in the family room," he says, "While I do post game and get a shower. Then we can go by Stoney's for some food while I get my game grade from pops and big John."

"Okay," she says as she wheels the twins into the waiting room and out of sight of the prying media. Gwen had gone in ahead of her.

Outside in the tunnel, after he finishes 3 courtside interviews, Ajay is approached by an adoring fan who has a shocking revelation for him.

"Hey Ajay. How are you?" the fan asks.

"I'm fine, man," Ajay answers, "How are you doing?"

"I'm doing okay. My name is Corey Grey," he says, "I was wondering if I could talk with you, man to man. If you have a minute."

"What's this about?" Ajay asks.

"It's kind of a long story. But I think we have a father in common."

"What?! A father in common?" Ajay repeats in shock but still in his usual calm. He says, "You got the wrong guy, Corey."

"Your father is Allen Jackson, right?" Corey presses.

"Yea *mine* is but yours isn't," Ajay says as he grows impatient quickly.

He looks back toward the end of the tunnel, thinking that's the way Corey should be headed. He sees Darlene standing there waiting to talk to him. He moves further up the tunnel and away from her. He wonders if she's behind this Corey claim but not enough to ask her. He has no interest in anything she has to say. Meanwhile, Corey continues his case.

"Can you give me a few minutes, so you can clear it up for me?"

"Alright. Look you can wait in here while I finish post game," he says, "But I'm sure you're wrong."

"Ok and maybe I am. I really am just trying to meet my father."

"Wait in here," Ajay says and Corey goes into the waiting room. Ajay is a little perturbed by Corey as he goes to take a shower.

Corey introduces himself to Ebony and Gwen as they all wait in the family area, along with the families of the other players. Corey tells Ebony, he's waiting to talk with her husband about her father-in-law.

"What about big Al?" she asks curiously.

"Well like I was telling your husband," Corey says, "I think we have the same father."

"No way in hell y'all do," she says as she giggles. "You don't even look like big Al *or* Anthony."

"Well that's what my mother told me before she died," Corey says, "I just wanna know who my dad is. I don't mean any harm. *Really.*"

"How old are you?" she asks.

"I'm twenty now but I'll be twenty one in July. July twenty fifth. Same day as your twins."

"No way big Al is your daddy," she says, "He hasn't cheated on mama Jo. No way."

"I'm just trying to follow up on what I was told."

Ebony is silent as she surveys Corey.

He looks nothing like my man. He favors Nina and Erica though. But that could just be his light skin. It's probably just somebody trying to come up on some money. He's fucking with the wrong man. Anthony is gonna hurt him for even starting this mess.

"I don't wanna offend you, really," he says, "I'm just trying to get some answers."

"Uh huh," she says, "Well Anthony will definitely get to the bottom of it. That's for sure. Otherwise, he wouldn't have sent you in here."

Ebony moves over for privacy and calls Nina from her cell phone. She tells her Corey's claim. Nina is upset immediately. Ebony knew she would be.

"I'm gonna call daddy at Stoney's," Nina says, "Tell Ajay to bring him by there. I'll meet y'all there."

Nina had just left the game and made it to the Spot II with Tank. They sent Jerica home with Pearl. Nina tells Tank about Corey after speaking with Al. Tank isn't buying it either.

"Baby just help me get things opened up and running," he says, "You go on over there and handle your business."

TIME TO KNOW-RELOADED-Time Will Reveal- part 4

Al has already called Jo to come down to Stoney's, by the time Nina makes it over there.

"Come in Nina boo," her father says, "Your mama is on her way."

"This is some crazy shit, man," John says, "Where in the hell did this boy come from?"

"I don't know but not from me," Al says confidently.

By the time Ajay, Ebony and the twins make it to Stoney's with Corey, who trailed them. Jo and Nina are already there. Nina has Lynn on the phone too.

"Bring me my grandbabies," John says.

He grabs Anthony Jr and Al grabs Atlantis. Corey comes in and introduces himself to everyone else.

"Would you like something to eat?" Jo asks.

"Yes ma'am. I was gonna order-"

"-Just tell us what you want," John says, "We'll feed you, tonight."

"It's on the house this time," Al adds with a laugh.

"Oh well, thank you. Thanks so much," Corey says, "I'm going to college at Cleveland State and money does get tight. So I do appreciate it."

"Are you from Cleveland?" Jo asks.

"Yes ma'am. Well I was born here, out in the point. But my mom moved to Toledo when I was in first grade," he says, "I've always wanted to come back to Cleveland to try and find my father."

"So what makes you feel like I'm your father, Corey?" Al asks.

"My mother told me that my father has a crew in Cleveland. In Shaker Heights. She told me that my father had one son before me," Corey says, "And just before she died. She told me that my older brother was a professional ball player and he had gone to college at Cincinnati."

"So you just figured it was me, ha?" Al asks.

"Yes sir."

"Who was your mother, son?" Jo asks.

"Her name was Lisa. Lisa Grey."

John and Al look at each other. They remember Lisa Grey. *Well.*

"She died?" John asks.

"Yes sir."

"What did she die from?" Nina asks.

"She had *Lupus*. She was only forty when she died," he says, "She would be forty three now."

"I remember her," Jo says, "She was in the same class as Sandy, Brian and big Archie."

"So y'all *did* know her?" Corey asks Al, John and Jo.

"Oh yes we knew her," Al and John say simultaneously.

Ebony and Nina can tell by their father's reaction. That Corey's mother must've been *a shared experience*.

"Well son. We'll definitely try to help you all that we can," Al says as he gives Corey his food. "Here's my phone number. Call me tomorrow and we'll get you started with getting some answers."

No one else speaks on the issue while Corey is still present. But after he's gone, Al and Jo along John tell them about Lisa Grey.

"Back in the day we all probably slept with Lisa," Al says and John agrees. "But that boy was born in seventy nine. There's no way he can be mine."

"I know that's right," Jo says, "Let's clear that up right now."

Nina and Ebony smile but Ajay doesn't. He wants to know more.

"Why is he saying it's you, pops?" Ajay asks.

"I don't know. Maybe Lisa didn't tell him she had all of us," Al says, "And I'm the one with one son that went to UC and went pro."

"Ah and *Richard* too," Jo says as they all look at her. She adds, "That young man that just left out of here, looks like my brother."

"I know he does," Al says, "I was thinking the same thing. But I didn't wanna say it in front of him."

"I said he looked like Nina and Erica," Ebony says, "But I didn't think about Roo and Rich. All of y'all have light skin."

"Like me and my family," Jo says, "Allen, all of y'all need to take a paternity test. But I'll bet you Anna can tell me more about this."

Just then Darlene, Alana and Farah walk into Stoney's and take a booth. Ebony and Ajay take the twins and leave. Nina leaves and goes back to The Spot II. Jo hangs out with Al and John for awhile longer.

2 weeks later, all of the fathers of the 2nd generation of crew and Corey take a paternity test. They get samples of Lisa Grey's DNA supplied by Toledo General. The test results will be ready in 2 days. Needless to say, Corey questions why all 8 men was there. They tell him the truth. They'd all been intimate with his mother at one point and time. But only 1 of them had been intimate with her after he was married.

After the paternity test are finished, Corey comes to Crew's house to apply for a job. Big mama and papa do the interview. They're familiar with him from the talk amongst the crew. Big mama hires him as a busboy, part-time. Corey needs the money to maintain while he attends school. He meets Tameka, the same evening. She's in need of a roommate and had it posted on the employee board in the break room. Corey needs a room he can afford. She tells him she'll need some time to get to know him better. But if everything checks out. She'll be happy to let him room with her.

"That's very nice of you," Corey says.

"You got the job," Tameka says, "Why do you look so down?"

"I have to wait until Wednesday to find out who my father is," he says, "It's driving me crazy."

"I heard about that," Tameka says, "You think it's Ajay's daddy?"

"Yes but he doesn't think so," Corey says, "Then it doesn't feel good to know that my mother has been with all of the fathers in the family."

"Oh I know," she says, "I have sort of that same reputation, from back in the day. I was with five of them from Richie's crew. But mainly him. I can't stand him nowadays though. He's the reason I felt so uncomfortable here, for a long while. But their grandparents, parents and the crew are really good people. They are strict and they're very particular about letting people into their mix."

"I don't wanna upset anybody," he says, "I just wanna know who fathered me. Especially since my mother's gone. I feel so alone these days."

Tameka and Corey talk a lot during his 1st night at the restaurant. By closing time, they're already becoming fast friends. Tameka familiarizes him with the does and don'ts and how to get extra work at the clubs. They find they have similar personalities and are making plans to be roommates.

On Wednesday, the test proves Richard Williams Sr is Corey's father. Corey is both relieved and apologetic. He apologizes to big Al for accusing him. Big Al excepts his apology with a smile.

"You can still come by and talk to me, son," he says, "After all. I'm still your uncle. Richard is my brother-in-the-law."

Corey tells him he appreciates the offer and he'll definitely be around a lot since he works for them.

As soon as she hears the results, Ebony calls Ajay and shares the news with him. He isn't a bit surprised.

"I knew I was pop's only son, baby," he says, "I never had a doubt. I knew my daddy hadn't lied to me nor cheated on mama."

"I knew it too, Anthony," she says, "It was just crazy how all of the fathers had to be tested."

He laughs. Then he says, "I know it had to be like *The Maury show* up in that bitch."

They laugh hard.

"I see our fathers crew was just like yours," she says smiling.

"I don't have no babies out there," he says.

"You'd better not."

He says, "You know where all three of my kids are."

"Yes daddy, I do," she laughs, "And two of them are trying to get the phone right now."

"Put it on speaker," he says.

She does and he talks to his 6 month old son and daughter for several minutes. They always count the daughter that was murdered too.

"They're looking around the room for you, Anthony," Ebony says and laughs, "They hear daddy's voice but they can't see you."

"They know this is daddy!" he says as he laughs too.

They make plans for the twins 1st trip to Miami on the weekend.

"Y'all staying for a week, right?" he asks.

"Yes daddy. If you can tolerate us for that long."

"I can handle y'all for a lifetime, baby," he says, "You know that."

Then she tells him about the strange letter he'd received at CrewLand security office.

"What letter?" he asks.

"From Darlene's boys. Rodney and Jamal," she says, "That's what they wrote on the envelope. Jacobson said he called you."

"He did," Ajay says, "I told him to give it to you so you can read it to me. So what do they want?"

He tells her to open it and she does. Then she reads it aloud.

She says, "They wanna be in the crew. *Basically*." She laughs.

"Darlene was at the game that night when Corey came in the picture," he says, "I seen her in the tunnel, looking dumb."

"I didn't see her. Where was I when you saw her?"

"In the family room where you belong," he says, "Not standing by the tunnel like some groupie." He laughs.

"Oh okay," she says and laughs too. "Well they said they wish you was still coming around. They think of you like a role model and they want to know if they can talk to you again, one day."

"As long as it ain't about being out with their mama," he says, "Sure."

They laugh. The twins are getting sleepy. Ebony tells him she has to feed them, give them baths and get them ready for bed.

"Damn. My kids are *so* lucky," he says as he chuckles, "They get henny and penny and I can't get either one of 'em."

"Oh my God," she says as she giggles, "You're crazy."

TIME TO KNOW-RELOADED-Time Will Reveal- part 4

"I miss you, baby," he says, "I can't wait until you get here this weekend, so I can see my babies and tighten my pussy up too."
"I'm looking forward to it," she says blushing.
"You'd better be," he says, "I'm full."
"So am I," she says.
"So how long will your breast be off limits?" he asks.
She laughs first, before attempting to answer him. He starts to laugh too. Which makes her laugh harder.
"Are you gonna answer me?" he asks, this time with a longing in his voice.
"Our babies are breast feeding," she says, "You want them to be healthy and strong, correct?"
"Of course," he says, "And I need to stay healthy and strong too. And those full on sex episodes is what keeps my three pointers dropping."
She cracks up laughing, which makes him laugh hard too.
She says, "You can have them, Anthony. You just can't pull on the nipple."
"So I can just lick on em?" he says, "And run my tongue around em?"
"Yes and you're making me horny," she says suddenly.
"Uh huh," is all he says.
They laugh a lot and soon they hang up so she can tend to their kids.
On Friday, Ebony and the twins fly to Miami. The heat have 3 home games this week. Ebony and the twins will be Ajay's special guest at all 3 of them.
On Monday the Hip Hop community mourns the lost of another major figure. Christopher Rios also known to the Hip Hop world as *Big Pun,* died of heart failure. Big Pun was the 1st Hispanic rapper to sell a million records. He had huge success with the release of his CD, *Capital Punishment.* Which released the smash single, *Still not a player* that features *Joe.* Chill's favorite song by him is *Dream Shatterer.* He had *Big Pun* scheduled to perform at The Spot, this spring. Just as he'd had *Tupac* scheduled for the Thanksgiving after he was killed.

REST IN PEACE TO:
CHRISTOPHER "BIG PUN" RIOS
FEBRUARY 7, 2000
WE PRAY FOR YOUR FAMILY AND THE TERROR SQUAD FAMILY
DURING YOUR TIME OF GRIEF.
THE HIP HOP NATION GRIEVES THIS LOSE, WITH YOU.
BIG PUN WILL LIVE ON, WITH THE CREW.
"THE DREAM SHATTERER!"
241

TIME TO KNOW-RELOADED-Time Will Reveal- part 4

On the following Friday, Chill has a farewell celebration for *Big Pun*. It includes special guest *Fat Joe and the Terror Squad*. The entire Crew come home for this event. Ajay is home this weekend as well. He has the opportunity to speak with Corey again at the restaurant.

"So I hear you got that situation straightened out," Ajay says to him. "I'm happy to hear you got some closure, man."

"As it turns out, you're my first cousin," Corey says humbly, "Instead of my brother."

"Well we're still family," he says, "Uncle Rich is my mama's only brother. He has one son, Rich Jr. And well…., and you now."

"He has a daughter too, right?" Corey asks.

"Yes. Ruthie but we all call her Roo," Ajay says, "She's eighteen."

"Is she in college?" Corey asks.

"She graduates high school this May and she's going to Southern Baton Rouge, in the fall," Ajay says, "That's where my wife's youngest brother attends. He's Ruthie's boyfriend. If you haven't noticed. We're a tight knit group. Everybody has known each other for life."

"I hope I get to meet Roo and Richie soon," Corey says, "I'm an only child."

"They should be at the club tonight," he says, "The crew will make sure y'all get introduced."

"I heard that my brother isn't the most friendly person," Corey says, "Is this true?"

"He's been having some problems lately," Ajay says, "But yes, he can be an ass. But then again. When you stepped to me saying you was my brother and you was only *twenty*. I was angry, myself."

Ajay is signing autographs while sitting at the restaurant. Security are always present with the entire crew nowadays. Jacobson does a great job keeping danger away from them and their businesses.

"I knew you was mad," Corey says, "I could tell."

"I mean, that's straight out acknowledging that his father cheated on his mother," Ajay says, "For me, that would be hard to swallow, Cuz."

"I understand where you're coming from," Corey says, "And I'm sorry about that, man. I already apologized to your father for my mistake. I was only going by what I was told and I was mistaken."

"So you'll be twenty one on my twins birthday, right?" Ajay asks.

"July twenty fifth."

"My wife told me," Ajay says.

"She's wonderful, Ajay," Corey says, "She's really beautiful."

"I agree with you," he says, "But not only do I refuse to share my

242

father with you. I *definitely* don't share Ebony. It's only because you're new that I'm being calm about it. The crew will tell you. I don't even play nobody *looking* at my girl."

"I didn't mean to disrespect you. It's just an observation."

Ajay is done with the autograph signing. He invites Corey to have a seat at his table and he does. Ajay comments about how articulate his speech is.

"Did you go to private school or something?"

"Yes in Toledo," he says, "My step dad was wealthy. He had other kids that was going to that school. So him and my mom put me in it too."

"So you have a step dad in Toledo?"

"Not anymore," he says, "Him and my mom split up when I was almost thirteen. She divorced him before she died."

"I was sorry to hear about your mother," Ajay says.

"Thanks man. That's the reason I wanted to find my father," he says, "I'm alone right now."

"Well you've got plenty of family now, Cuz," Ajay says, "And if you want to be apart of the family businesses. You'll have to do your part."

Corey says he understands.

"Do you know how I got confused, Ajay?" Corey whispers.

"How?"

"My mother told me about this time, back in the day when uncle Al and big John got into some racial incident with two *policemen*," Corey says with a questioned tone to his voice. "Do you remember anything like that?" He's still whispering.

"Yea," he answers, lowering his tone also. He says, "Some crooked ass cops took daddy and big John to a deserted area and was planning to kill them. But it didn't go down like that."

"Big John and uncle Al ended up killing those cops," he whispers, "Then they called my mama to come and get them because they was out by where she was living during that time."

"Yes but I also heard they had called uncle Richard, who was with your mama at the time," Ajay says, "And they both came."

"My mama said she helped them bury the bodies and everything," Corey says, "I remember Al because she was really in love with him. But he apparently wasn't in love with her."

"I'm sorry man. But all of them shared her," Ajay says, "Me and my crew went through some females that *same* way. But it ended for most of us when we got married."

"I heard y'all did the same things," he says, "But just like uncle Al, you stopped. I heard my brother hasn't though."

243

TIME TO KNOW-RELOADED-Time Will Reveal- part 4

"Yes. I did just like my pops," Ajay agrees, "And Rich hasn't. Just like his daddy. Uncle Brad is really the one that called uncle Rich though," Ajay continues, "He knew he was at your mama's house."

"I heard Rich is a lot like our father," Corey adds, "I mean with the infidelity thing."

"He's got a kid coming real soon," Ajay reluctantly admits, "Outside of *his* marriage."

"Like father, like son," Corey adds.

"Unfortunately," Ajay says, "Hopefully you don't have any stray kids out there."

"Oh no man," Corey says, "And I'm sure about that. But Rich junior isn't anything like you. I've learned that and haven't even met him." Corey is trying to hint to Ajay about the way Rich is terrorizing Tameka. But he isn't sure how. Besides, Ajay is ready to leave so Corey thanks him for the talk and goes back to his duties. Ajay pays for his lunch. He signs a few more autographs for patrons who had come in during him and Corey's private talk. Then he leaves.

Jo is keeping the twins tonight, so Ajay and Ebony can attend the farewell to *Big Pun*.

Jo calls Anna to come over and she tells her, "Bring Richard the third with you too, sister in law. Pearl is coming over with Jerica."

Anna tells her, she'll be there shortly. Jo wants to talk to her about Corey.

When Anna arrives, her and Jo sit in the living room to talk.

Jo says, "I'm sure you're aware that you're a step-mother, by now."

"Uh huh. I heard," Anna says dryly.

"Well let's remember that it's not Corey's fault, okay?" Jo says.

"Oh I know that, Jo," Anna admits, "I always knew that."

"So you *did* know about this boy?" Jo asks.

"*Hell* yes. Lisa Grey came by my house *with him* when he was first born," Anna says.

"Anna you never said a word about him," Jo says, "You know I'm always here for you. We've been to hell and back with my little brother."

"I know, Jo," she says, "I was devastated. But Richard was denying him then."

"So Richie knew too?" Jo asks.

"Yes he knew she was *saying* it," Anna admits, "But he was locked up at the time. Then when he came home. He didn't wanna hear about it. I tried to talk about it and he beat me up. *Badly*."

"When Roo was a baby?" Jo asks, "This is what that last fight was about, wasn't it? Him being in denial?"

244

"Yes and that's when we split up for a long time," Anna says, "I thought he had gone to see the child at some point. I promise you I never knew that he didn't *ever* go see about him."

"Well has Richard ever said anything about him since?"

"He said he had a test done and the child wasn't his," Anna tells her, "It still took me years to take him back. And now, here it is again almost eighteen years later. It turns out the boy was his all the time. He lied to me again."

There's a knock at the door. Jo goes to answer it. It's Pearl. She's come to help out with their grand twins and she has 5 year old Jerica with her.

"Hey girl. How are y'all doing?" Pearl asks as she notices the somber look on Jo and Anna's faces. "What's going on?" she asks.

She knows about Corey being Richard's son. So she figures this is the reason Anna is looking down. But Anna has much more to confess. After laying a sleeping Jerica down to bed, upstairs. The ladies meet back in the living room to talk more.

"Girls listen. Lisa had contacted us several times, throughout the years," Anna says, "So I don't know how come Corey didn't know it was Richard. Unless *she* never told him the truth."

"Well he was claiming Allen," Jo says.

"The last time she called, it was right after Rich Jr signed that scholarship with Cincinnati," Anna says, "And Richard said she was just smelling money."

"Well if that was the case. She could've claimed any of our husbands," Pearl adds, "Because all of our kids have done extremely well."

"All I had to go on was what my husband told me," Anna says, "And I wanted *so much* to believe him."

"Well Anna you two have been doing great for the past decade," Pearl says, "And y'all can work through this too."

"We'll definitely be here," Jo says, "You know that, right?"

Yes I know," Anna says, "But it still hurts to hear it. Even now."

Jo and Pearl both say they understand and she's certainly human for feeling betrayed.

By the last week in February, Tameka and Corey have gotten to know each other pretty well. They have become good friends. Good enough friends that Tameka agrees to let him move into the apartment with her. Corey signs the lease and moves in immediately.

"It's gonna be great having someone to room with and split the bills too," Tameka says to Corey as they move his last box into his room.

"You just don't know how much I appreciate you for letting me room with you, Tameka," he says.

"We're both outsiders, basically," she says, "So we can relate and be here for each other."

Corey agrees with her. He had shared a secret about himself, 2 weeks ago. A secret he hasn't told anyone in the crew.

"I just don't know how they're going to feel about it," he says as they unpack and place his things.

"I don't have a problem with it," she says, "You're genuine and that's what counts."

The next day Ebony and T-baby meet Rebbie and Nina at the restaurant for lunch. Gwen is on the road with Jarvis and the Cavaliers. Tameka and Corey are both working the lunch shift. Corey doubles as a server for extra money. He waits on the foursome today.

"Hi Ebony," he says, "And how are you ladies doing?"

"We're doing great, Corey," she says, "Did you get settled in yet?"

"Yes. We finished moving yesterday," he says.

"We would have helped you, if you had said something," Nina says. T-baby looks doubtful. She isn't thrilled with Nina for offering her services to help out Rich's ex-lover with anything.

"We took care of it, Ebony," he says as he smiles at her. "But thank you ladies anyway. Now what can I get for y'all?"

They order their meals and go back to their conversation while he turns in their orders. Then him and Tameka have a short talk in the break room.

"Roomy, you'd better stop acting like you're flirting with Ebony," she warns, "Ajay is a jealous man."

"Oh I know," Corey says, "He already warned me."

"Then you'd better listen," Tameka says, "Anyway, that ain't even your flavor."

They share a laugh and go back to their stations while the foursome seem to be having a similar conversation, along the same vibe Tameka was on.

"Corey just be kissing your ass, Ebony," Rebbie says, "He just be smiling at you."

"Yea I noticed it that night at the game when we first met him," she says, "But I don't think he likes me. Not like that."

"He's *sure as hell* watching you a lot, Cuz," T-baby says.

"Ajay is gonna bust his damn head," Nina says, "He already came into the mix *wrong*. He don't *wanna* go there."

Ebony laughs, then says, "I really don't think he's into girls y'all."

"What?!" Nina says aloud, then she lowers her voice as she asks, "He's gay?"

"I think so," Ebony says, "His mannerisms suggest as much."

"Just another reason for our crew *not* to accept him," Rebbie says.

"Really though," T-baby agrees, "Y'all know how the men are about switch hitters."

They share a laugh before Corey comes back with their meals. He smiles flirtatiously at Ebony and places her entrée down in front of her.

"Thanks Corey," they all say.

"You girls are all so welcome," he says, "Enjoy now."

He smiles at Ebony again before leaving their table.

"Well cousin, maybe he wants you to help him hit it to right field?" T-baby jokes, "Get his pitch straightened out?"

"Please stop, Tee," Ebony says and laughs, "Don't give daddy no excuse to split his wig."

The foursome share a few laughs. They aren't at all biased about Corey's sexual preference. Neither are their parents or grandparents. It just seems like the guys from the second generation down, like most males between the ages of 13 and 45, are homophobic.

"So Tee, how's Rich been doing at CrewLand?" Nina asks.

"Bad," she says, "He barely shows up and sometimes, not at all."

"He has to get some help," Rebbie says, "He has too. He can't kick the habit on his own."

"Yes but we can't force him to go in," Nina says.

"He's already lost his place with the Jets," T-baby says, "It seems like that should have been enough."

"He'll be worse now because he knows he owns part of the businesses, he works in," Ebony says.

"Uncle big John told daddy that he caught him out in back of Stoney's the other night, getting ready to blaze a rock," T-baby says, "Then he wanted to go off on uncle John for getting on his case."

"He has to get clean and stay clean," Rebbie says.

"He has to want too," Ebony adds, "And if he says something else to my father. My father's kids are gonna whoop his ass."

They notice Corey staring at Ebony again.

"I don't know y'all," Nina says, "The way he's staring at Ebony. Maybe he's bisexual."

"He's gonna be *bye-bye* if he don't check his self before he wreck his self," Ebony says with a laugh, "Big Anthony don't play that."

They all laugh.

TIME TO KNOW-RELOADED-Time Will Reveal- part 4

Later that night after closing, Corey and Tameka head home. They finish their showers, then sit down in the living room to watch some movies. They hear a knock on the door. She isn't home alone. So this time, Tameka answers the door. It's Rich again.

"I've told you not to come here," she says, "I've told you many times."

"You got a *nigga* up in here?" Rich asks, looking at Corey, who's seated on the couch.
He hadn't met his brother, due largely to the fact that he hasn't been around the crew long enough for anyone to introduce them.
"You're fucking this nigga?" Rich asks.

"Not that it's your business. But yes and he's my new roommate and coworker," Tameka tries.

"I work at The Crew's House," Corey says.

"You work for me," Rich says very obnoxiously.

"For the *crew*. Yes, of course," Corey says.

"Oh I get it. You the nigga that claim to be my brother, ha?" Rich says rudely.

"I'm Corey. It's nice to meet you."

"You got me fucked up, nigga," Rich says, "You think you can just show up here and we're gonna automatically make you family?"

"No I don't expect that. I know it'll take time. But I *am* your brother. Like it or not."

"Man your mama was a ho," Rich blurts out, "All of our daddy's use to pass her around."

"That may be true. But your father and mine, Richard Williams senior, *your father and mine*, is the only one who made a child with her," Corey says frankly, "And that child is me."
Rich continues with the rude comments.

"Nigga please," Tameka finally says, "You're a fucking crack headed ass loser. Get the fuck out of my apartment before I call them folks on your wasted ass."

"Damn," Corey says, "I would've rather had Ajay as a brother anyway. He's got it going on."
Rich continues to rant until Corey and Tameka order him to leave. He's reluctant until Tameka picks up the phone and threatens to call the police. Rich shouts a few other obscenities before he leaves. But he does leave. He goes to get high once again. This time, he has to find a different crack house to lay low in. He doesn't want the crew to be able to find him. He's gone for several days.

248

TIME TO KNOW-RELOADED-Time Will Reveal- part 4

****

On March 3rd, Pearl is at work at East General. She notices a name on a new patient chart and calls Ebony at her office.

"Hi baby girl," Pearl says.

"Hey mama. What's up?"

"I think Rich's mistress is here and she's in labor," Pearl says, "Do y'all know where he is?"

"I don't, mama," she says, "He's been gone, for four days."

"Well big Richard and Anna are here with her," Pearl tells her, "If y'all hear from Rich. Will you please tell him that he should be here."

Ebony hangs up. Then she calls Chill to let him know. He says he'll go over and see if Arthur has seen or heard from Rich.

"*Money shot* always seems to get the information first," he says.

Chill heads over to Arthur's. Coincidently Rich shows up at Que Psi Phi studios to speak to Arthur, just as Chill is headed over there. Rich is trying to get some drugs on loan. Arthur opens the door for Chill. As soon as Chill sees Rich, he goes in on him.

"Rich we're gonna get you cleaned up and get you to the hospital," he says, "You're about to be a father again."

"You need to get your shit together," Arthur says, "You know better then to be coming up in here to *score*. What the hell are you *thinking*?"

"He's not thinking," Chill adds, "Let's go Rich. So you can get a damn shower and go to the hospital with this girl."

Rich makes it to the hospital for the delivery. Regina has a little girl, whom she names, Richanda Trenice Kemp. Rich refuses to sign the birth certificate and demands a paternity test. Regina agrees. The test is done. By discharge day it is determined that Rich is the father. He signs the birth certificate so his daughter can receive his last name. Richanda Trenice Williams weighs 5lbs and 5 ounces.

Later with Ajay on the phone, Chill has a heart to heart talk with Rich Jr. He and Ajay talk to him for hours until he admits his problem.

"I wanna kick this habit," Rich says, "I really do. I wanna tell my wife I'm sorry. For *all* of this."

After hanging up, Chill drives Rich to Jackson Heights. Rich and T-baby have a long talk. She agrees to stay by his side if he goes to rehab.

"I'm going," he says, "I'm going tonight. Will you go with me?"

She agrees to go with him but he doesn't leave tonight. It's 1 week later, on March 10 when T-baby and Chill admit Rich into rehab in Cincinnati.

249

Mr. Parkwood had set it up. The entire family is happy to know he's gone to get clean. Rich is going to try to get help for his drug addiction and they all vow to support him. Even Ebony.

****

"Hello?" Ebony says, answering the phone.

"Hey baby. How are y'all doing?" Ajay asks.

He's on the west coast with his team. They've just finished up a game against the *Los Angeles Lakers*.

"Not to well. We're missing you, daddy," she says, "I've been keeping up with the road trip stats. You do know that?"

"So how am I doing?" he asks, knowing she'll answer him honestly.

"The first three games was great. But you could've done better tonight."

"I know and I will," he says, "Are my babies asleep?"

"Okay and no," she answers, "They watched the game with me. Then crashed. They was played out. We had company over. I hope you don't mind. Tameka and Corey came by to watch the game with us."

"Corey was in my *house*?" he asks.

"Yes. I thought you would be okay with that," she says, "The twins and I had dinner at the restaurant. And they were both getting off work, as we were leaving. I ask them if they wanted to come out here and watch you play the Lakers."

"I don't trust him, baby girl," Ajay says, "He got the hots for you."

"Anthony. Corey is gay," she tells him.

"What? He's a faggot?"

"No he's not," she says, "He's gay and Anthony, that's not nice."

"Being a homo ain't nice either," he says, "I know that's *definitely* not my daddy's blood right there. Grandfathers either."

Ebony tells him it isn't right to discriminate against Corey's sexual preference.

"That's between him and God, Anthony," she says, "Not us."

"Well as long as he don't like my wife," Ajay finally admits, "I don't really care *who* he fucks. Hell, that might be better that he is."

Then he changes the subject, "So Rich is finally getting help."

"Oh yes and I'm so happy too," she says, "I hope he gets his act together because he's got a son and a daughter to think about now."

"Yes I agree," Ajay says, "He needs too."

"Will you forgive me for having company without asking you?"

TIME TO KNOW-RELOADED-Time Will Reveal- part 4

"This time. But from now on. I wanna know who's around my wife and my kids," he says, "And who's in my house too, woman."
He chuckles but she knows he's serious. She says she understands. They talk a little longer until it's time for his flight. Then they hang up.

CHAPTER 45

WHAT GOES AROUND......

Erica and Greg Jr are *officially* over. He's dating Mya Dean, who announced last week that she's pregnant. Erica was hurt and though her and Greg have been broken up for a long time. She still feels cheated on. She admits to Nina and Tank over the phone, that she always thought he would get his act together and stop messing with Mya but he didn't. Now he and Mya could be connected forever.

****

March brings on the NFL draft. The crew have 2 players going in. Before the draft, Bruce has a special trip planned. He and Kim are still in class at Ohio State when she finds out about the trip. To celebrate his bowl win, Bruce takes Kim to Hawaii for the week. Eric McNair is entering the draft also and he wants to take Erica to Hawaii. But he knew it was too soon to ask her to go on a trip with him. They've had a *couple* of unofficial dates but it's nothing to serious for Erica yet. She does enjoy his company and feels like he's very respectful of her. She feels Eric is more understanding also. In late March, Eric and Bruce enter the draft with Jb as their agent. After being drafted 1st round 13th pick to Arizona, Bruce gets traded to Cleveland. He wanted to go to his home team. His salary is $35 million over six years. Eric is a lottery pick of the Browns. His contract is $45 million for 6 years. He goes 1st round, 9th pick. Jb is making huge commissions. The crew celebrate at the spot with all 3 of them.

In early April as Rebbie drives to work, she spots June's car parked at the U apartments. She pulls into the far end of the parking lot and calls his cell phone. When he answers, she asks him where he is and he lies to her. He says he's at the high school about to sit in on Steven and Lil Chill's morning football practice. Rebbie knows he isn't telling the truth but she decides to wait until they get home to confront him.

"Okay honey," she says, "I'm going on in to work. I'll see you at dinner. Thanks for dropping Orian off at big mama's house this morning."

"Oh you're welcome, baby. No problem," he says, "That's daddy's girl right there. There ain't nothing daddy won't do for his baby."

Rebbie pulls out of the parking lot and goes on to work. She doesn't say a word about it to her mother or anyone else at the mall. She just floats from business to business as needed, like any other normal day. *This is something for me and my husband to settle first.*

During Rebbie's work day she does some investigating of her own. She feels like June and Rich have more of a connection then just football. She knows June isn't doing drugs. But he does know a lot more about Rich's cases, addictions and infidelities then anyone else in the crew. And he knew *before* they did. So she starts with Rich's mistress and looks for a connection. She soon finds out, not only does Rich's mistress live in the U apartments. But so does her husband's mistress Diana Keyes. She'd gotten the name from a lease she'd dug up. She isn't sure if Diana is sleeping with her husband but she's going to work with what she's got.

After work T-baby, Anna and Richard Sr go visit Rich in Rehab. Rich III stays with Ebony. T-baby doesn't want him to see his father in his present condition. Rich looks a lot better after only 30 days. He's anxious to come home but neither his wife nor his parents will agree to sign him out.

"You need to stay the full term, son," Anna says.

Rich isn't trying to hear it but they are not going to budge.

"So how have you been, honey?" T-baby asks.

"I've been alright," he says, "I'm just missing everybody."

"That's the price you pay if you wanna beat this," Anna says.

"We're gonna support you, son," big Richard says, "We want you to come out of here clean and *stay* clean."

His father explains to him how he'd had an addiction to cocaine and how it had cost him so much time with him, Ruthie and their mother.

"I guess that's when you made the other son, ha?" Rich asks.

This is his 1st time confronting his father about his infidelity. Richard tells him yes. Corey had been conceived during the time when he was using. Just as his daughter with Regina had been. Rich tells his father how hurt he was to find out that he had fathered an outside child.

"How do you think that makes my mama feel?" Rich asks.

"The same way Trisha feels," Anna interjects, surprising him.

He seems to have forgotten that he had done the same thing. Then realizing that he's in the same position, he quickly makes an admission.

"I guess drugs do make you careless," he says to his father apologetically while he looks at T-baby.

"Rich we'll deal with this another time," T-baby says, "What's important right now, is that you kick this habit and get better."

They all agree on that point.

253

"I'm ending it with Regina, Trisha," he says, "I hate I put you through all of that mess, baby."

"We'll deal with it later, okay?" she says again.

He agrees to discuss it later. He knows they don't want to upset him with anything negative and he appreciates it.

"I just regret the day I met her," he says, "And I know June regrets meeting Diana too."

Just like that, he tells on June. Rich was never a stand alone guy. He always had to have a crowd with him. If he's going to be caught up for cheating. Then someone else has to be caught too. He isn't going to confess alone.

****

At Rebbie and June's home this evening, June sits down in the living room to watch the NFL predictions after the draft. Rebbie is in the kitchen making dinner. June has almost 3 year old Orian in the living room with him. Rebbie tries to hold off until she's done with dinner but she can't. She walks into the living room and sits down next to her husband. It's time to confront him.

"Baby I have something to ask you," she starts.

"Okay."

"When I called you today. I know you wasn't at MLK," she says, "I know you was at the U."

He looks stunned as she continues, "I know why you was there too. I just wanna hear it from you with no lies this time."

He sits in silence.

"Were you with Diana Keyes?" she asks.

He hesitates. He didn't even realize his wife knew his mistresses name.

"Well Brian?" she asks again.

"Yes Rebbie," he admits, "I was but it's not like you think."

"Not like I think?" she asks, "Oh well, just how is it then Brian?"

"I haven't been seeing her. Not all of this time-"

"-All of what time? Is this the woman you was with when Ebony saw you?"

Ebony had finally told her girls what she's witnessed. But only after she learned about Erica and Greg Jr. And after Rich went to rehab.

"Yes but I haven't been seeing her all of this time," he tries again.

"Brian you've been married to me, all of this time," she says, "You wasn't suppose to be seeing her at any time."

He decides to come clean and tell his wife all the details. He explains that

254

he'd met her when he attended UC. They had been seeing each other up until 1998 when Ebony discovered them at he medical complex with Rich and Regina. He says he ended it then and had just recently started back up with her after the 2000 season ended.

"So do you think I'm gonna sit here while you go out there and make an illegitimate child too?!" she screams.

Orian starts to cry and June calms her down. Then he admits openly that he had the affair. He promises to break it off for good.

"Do it. Do it right now," she says, "Or pack your shit and get out!"

He doesn't even try to resist when she asks for Diana's phone number. He gives it to her and she dials the number from his phone, knowing Diana will pick up and she does.

"Hello baby," Diana says.

"Not baby. Rebbie is my name. Misses James and you're his ho."

She has her *Janet Jackson, Nasty Boys* attitude. If she wasn't so angry, she would've broken into a dance then laughed. But this is no laughing matter.

"Excuse me?" Diana asks.

"I am speaking to my husbands mistress, right?" Rebbie asks.

"Who's calling?" Diana asks.

"This is misses Brian James junior," Rebbie answers, "If this is Diana, then I'm the woman you wanna be."

"This is Diana," she says hesitantly.

"Hold on mistress," Rebbie says as she hands the phone to June.

"Diana?" he says.

"Yes June," Diana answers.

"It's over. I love my wife," he says, "I can't see you anymore."

"Oh, just like *that*?"

"Just like that," he says, "Don't call me and I won't call you."

"Fine then, June," Diana says, "Have a nice life."

"You too," he says and hangs up.

And as Diana had said it. Just like that, it was over. Rebbie still has doubts and insecurities but June has been shocked into reality.

"Just so you know," Rebbie says, "If I ever get proof that you're cheating with anyone, ever again. We're gonna see which one of us can get the most fucking done *outside* of our marriage."

She returns to her kitchen duties. June doesn't say another word. He doesn't want to loose his girl of 12 years. Not for any fling. June has always been the last guy in the crew to cheat. Even with a girl all of the crew had. At the same time, he hates the way it feels now. He's truly humble and sorry for cheating on his wife. Had he thought it through beforehand. It might've never happened. From this day forward, he'll never cheat with Diana Keyes again. He ended it. If only all affairs could end this clean. Him and Rebbie have a long talk after dinner. She loves him with all of her heart. June knows he loves only her. He apologizes to her and begs for her forgiveness. She agrees to forgive him and they vow to work through it.

"But I meant what I said before I went back in the kitchen."

}*Atlanta*{

Lynn turns 27 in April and retires from Track and Field. She's going to dedicate herself to her son, husband and her Air Force reserve unit fulltime. Chaundra turns 17 at the end of the month. While big mama and poppa celebrate 46 years of marriage on the 3rd day of April. Ebony and the twins travel to Atlanta to watch Ajay play. They stay for a week with April and Yolanda. The twins will be a year old in a few months. They have a blast with their 1st cousin lil Jb, their Godmothers and crew in Atlanta.

In May, Jo and Allen celebrate their 28th year anniversary on the 15th. Grandma Sally and grandpa Joshua Logan celebrate 45 years of marriage on the 21st of May. Ruthie and Pam graduate with honors from MLK. Ruthie will attend college in Baton Rouge with Jesse. Pam is going to CSU with her boyfriend Sam Logan Jr.

Terrell comes up from Atlanta in June. He's here to help Ajay open up his newest business venture and the latest CrewLand family business. *Allen Saul Williams Sports and Recreation facility* has it's grand opening on Chill's 31st birthday, June 14th. He named it in honor of his Maternal grandfather. Ajay's sports complex has an auditorium, 2 basketball courts, a soccer field, 2 tennis courts, a baseball and softball field, 2 swimming pools (1 indoors and 1 outdoors) and a huge exercise facility. He and June are also sponsoring teams for all sports. The city of Cleveland has acquisitioned the facility as the site for their inner-city youth and adult leagues. Ajay and June stand to make healthy profits. Terrell brings his beautiful girlfriend for the crew to meet. Her name is Christina Hayes. She's a corporate attorney in Atlanta but her home is Detroit. Christina or Chrissy as she prefers to be called, helps Ebony do all of the paperwork for Ajay's facility and all deals are finalized. Ajay and June receive a 5 figure advancement check for equipment and uniforms for their 2000-2001 city league teams.

Celebrating birthdays in June are Ally, who turns 17 on the 3rd. Chill makes 31 on the 14th and June turns 25 on the twenty sixth. June and Rebbie, T-baby and Rich have their 4 year anniversary on the twenty second. Jb and Lynn, Rob and Jan, Bre and Cedric celebrate 5 years of

256

marriage on the twenty fourth. Chill and Renee, Jr and Tonya have been married 9 years as of the 28th of June. Where Jarvis and Gwen have been married 2 years on that same day. Little Jarvis spends a lot of time at the mansion playing with Lil Ajay and Lannie. But there isn't any obvious chemistry between Lannie and him. Lil Ajay doesn't seem to want him to even play with his twin sister.

June 30th would've been 47 years of marriage for papa and granny, who died September 1991. The crew do something special for them.

Ebony has planned a huge July birthday bash for her husband and their twins. Gwen, Venitia and her girls are helping her plan it. Chrissy, Terrell and the Atlanta crew are coming back for it. The birthday bash will be on the 24th of July at The Chill Spot and The Chill Spot II. Brad Sr and Deb, along with Richard Sr and Anna, will celebrate 26 years of marriage in July as well.

Terrell and Chrissy arrive from Atlanta for the big party. April, Charles, Yolanda, David and all the crew members from Atlanta are with them. Ron, Carolyn, their children and crew come up from Houston too.

"Ebony it's been too long since I've seen you," April says, "And my god twins too."

Her and Yolanda had christened the twins when they were 2 months old.

"Before *this* spring it have been almost a year, April," Ebony says with a smile. "But we won't wait this long again. The twins and I are coming back to visit y'all before this year ends. I promise you that."

They have a blast at the celebrations. Lannie and Lil Ajay are really active at their 1st party. They get into everything. Ajay allows them to cut their own cakes and they make twin messes of them.

"It's okay," he says, "It's their cake. They're suppose to cut it."

Everybody laughs at the twins as they slice up their cakes. They wear more than they serve. Ebony and April steal away up to Renee's office to talk before April has to return to Atlanta tomorrow.

"Finally we get to sit down face to face again, sis," Ebony says, "How are things with you?"

"Bad and getting worse," April says, "I wish I could divorce both sides of my family sometimes. Except my daddy and my uncles. They don't meddle."

"Oh April. This breaks my heart."

"I don't know how to get my family to stop all of the back and forth," she says, "And just learn to get along with each other."

"Are they still battling over who's best for you?"

"That's the lie they tell. Yes and more. First of all, I'm grown. But they argue over everything. Like who's the better role model when neither of them are. Then they hate Charles and I think he's the only one who really understands who *I am* and what *April* wants."

"They still refuse to accept that you love Charles?" Ebony asks.

"Yes," April says as she starts to cry.

"April it was like that for Anthony and I. Our mothers especially. They fought it for years," Ebony says, "That was one of the reasons I ended up moving to Houston and meeting you. Remember?"

"I do remember you saying that when we first got close," April says. Then she starts to mimic Ebony as she says, *'They just don't want us to be in love. Get your fast butt down to Houston before you end up pregnant. Baby Girl you're going to have to obey the rules of my house, young lady.'* You was mad and crying. I remember that. I do. But look at y'all now."

"That's my point. Don't give up on love. If it's real it *will* prevail. That's what big mama says all the time."

"I hope so. That move to Atlanta has helped some. But every time I talk to them. It's the same thing. It's like time stood still with them. But for us it's sailing on," April says, "They're just way to caught up in trying to run my life. I feel it's because they messed up theirs. Now they see a way to get theirs back through me. It's not fair. It's driving me insane."

"April I'm here for you *whenever* you need me and I love you."

"I know and I love you too. I am so glad we met," April says.

Then Ajay comes to the door holding the twins, who are now covered from head to toe in cake.

"Can I get a hand?" he asks as he laughs.

Ebony and April take the twins from him and go wash them up and change them into another set of matching outfits.

Later that night at the grown up celebration, Ajay who made 26 on the 11th had more than his share of Hennessy. He was very frisky with Ebony, as he usually is. They slow danced for nearly an hour straight and his hands and lips were busy, the whole time.

"Some things never change," Tank says as him and Nina join Ajay, Ebony and the other couples on the dance floor.

"Baby my birthdays get better and better," Ajay says, "For the last thirteen birthdays, I've been holding you."

"Uh huh but we wasn't going together until September seventh, nineteen eighty seven," she says and giggles.

"Maybe you wasn't," he says with a smile.

"We've been together for half of your life," she says.

"All of our lives," he corrects her as they kiss, again and again.

258

"Get a room!" Nina yells and they all laugh.

Jarvis and Gwen crack up laughing as Jarvis says, "They got a lot of rooms. And captain do that in all of them."

Everybody within the sound of his voice, laughs hard.

"Terrell, I love your family," Chrissy says, "It's wonderful how everyone has been together for so long."

"Yes indeed and most of these people in this room have been together since puberty," Terrell jokes as they all continue to dance.

"We have too," April yells, speaking of her and Charles.

Yolanda and David have dated for more than a decade as well.

"Oh we have too," Carolyn adds as Ron says, "Amen."

The event is wonderful. They call Rich and put him on speaker phone. Everyone has a chance to talk to him and they can hear that he's doing better. Everybody parties out and takes it in. All of the folk's from out of town, return home the next day.

2 days later, Ebony gets a call from Yolanda. April has turned deathly ill and had to be hospitalized in Atlanta. Ebony is so upset, she has to let Ajay talk to Yolanda *for* her. Ajay gets all of the details while consoling Ebony at the same time. After he hangs up with Yolanda, he holds Ebony next to his heart.

He says, "Baby you go on and go down there. I can handle the twins. I've got plenty of help here. You and the girls need to be there."

"I'll call big mama to come and help too, while I pack," she says.

"I'll call her," he says as he gives her a kiss, "You pack or I can have somebody to pack for you, if you need that too. I want you to be alright. Do you hear me?"

"Yes," she says, "I got it, Anthony. Thanks so much."

"You get that and anything else you need," he says, "Just calm down. *We* need for you to be okay."

"Okay," she says as she goes into her closet and starts to pack.

Her, Nina, Rebbie and T-baby fly to Atlanta on the night of July 28th. April's parents and extended family, the same ones she'd told Ebony about are there and they're already disagreeing. Just as April had always described them. Carolyn and her female crew are there too. April remains in the hospital on into August. But August 2nd is a day the foursome won't soon forget.

Ebony, Nina, and Yolanda take T-baby and Rebbie to breakfast for their 24th birthdays. The foursome are still in Atlanta visiting April, who is in critical condition. She had suffered a stroke, 2 days ago and has had

259

several seizures since then. Her diagnosis isn't good. The doctors haven't been able to find out the source of her seizures. Ebony and the girls return to the hospital after breakfast.

"Has there been any change?" Ebony asks April's mother, Felecia Lewis.

"No baby. She's had another seizure," Felecia says.

All of April's visitors feel helpless. No one can do anything for her but pray, sit and wait. Still the 2 sides of her family are divided. Even in the waiting room. Even as April's life hangs in the balance, her family members still can't get along. Charles sits with the foursome, for he's *truly* an outcast with her family. Her father sits with them too but he doesn't seem to connect with anybody. Not even his mother and sister. Ebony can feel April's presence in that waiting room. It's like she's hovering over them, trying to give her family a chance to come together and save her life. But they can't even give up their selfishness. Not even for her to have peace to heal in. Ebony remembers what April use to say back in Houston.

"I would rather be with God then be around a bunch of people who hate each other. They say they love me but not enough to love each other."

April was always strong in her faith. She remembers that too. She doesn't have any doubt that God is here too.

}In Cleveland{

Ajay is up early with his twins. After breakfast, he puts them in their swim suits and takes them to the outside pool.

"Y'all want to swim with daddy?" he asks playfully.

He puts all of their swim toys and floaters in the pool and brings them into the pool with him. Lannie and Lil Ajay loves to splash in the water. Along with their daddy, they are having a blast when the phone rings. Ajay brings the twins out of the pool. As he reaches the phone, it stops ringing. He checks the caller ID.

"That's mommy calling," he says as he dials Ebony back.

When she answers, she crying hysterically.

"Baby. Baby. What's wrong? Tell me what's wrong?" he asks.

"She died, Anthony! April *died*!"

Ajay tries to comfort her from his end. It isn't working.

"Baby what you want me to do?" he asks, "I can come today."

"My friend is dead, Anthony. Oh my God! She's gone!"

"Ebony listen to me," he starts, "I'll get big mama to take the twins and I'll get a flight out, okay?"

"No Anthony. I wanna come home," she cries.

TIME TO KNOW-RELOADED-Time Will Reveal- part 4

"Okay baby. Come on home then," he says, "I'll pick you up. Just let me know your flight info first."
With his help, she gets her flight updated to 6pm. He'll pick her up.

April's home going celebration is set for August 9th in Houston. The entire crew from Cleveland and Atlanta are going to attend. Big mama takes April's death just as hard as Ebony does.
"She was like a granddaughter to me, baby," big mama tells Ebony as they wait to enter the church for the funeral services.
Ebony hasn't stopped crying since she 1st learned that April had past. Felecia has asked Ebony to speak as a friend. Ebony said she would be honored to do it. But during the service she's shaking so much, Ajay has to hold her up. When it comes time for her to speak, he escorts her to the front. She starts to speak but she's so full she can't finish. Big mama comes up with her and Ajay to say her peace.
"Miss April was a beautiful young lady," she starts, "She was just like a sister to my granddaughter Ebony when Ebony came to Houston to live with me. That was over eleven years ago," she says "Them and Yolanda were inseparable. April and Yolanda spent every night at my house that they could. Until Felecia and Sara would come over and demand that they come home," she says with a smile. "Then Ebony would turn around and follow them home."
"She's my sister," Ebony adds, "She's my twins godmother. She just wanted everybody to get along and be happy-"
She breaks down again. This time Ajay takes her outside. Nina, T-baby and Rebbie speak next. Yolanda tries to speak but she's in worse shape than Ebony. Charles gives a tear jerking account of his life and love for April while her family members frown and whisper amongst themselves. Pearl, Rena and Jo sing a song for the Eulogy.
After the service they all go to the gravesite for the burial. Ebony puts 3 photos on top of April's casket. 1 of her, April and Yolanda, they had taken in 8th grade on a basketball trip. The 2nd one is of her, April, Yolanda, Nina, T-baby and Rebbie that they'd taken at The Crews House of Soul Food restaurant in April 1998. When April and Yolanda came to visit for spring break. The 3rd one is of April holding the twins on the day of their christening.
"April I won't ever forget you. I'll make sure the twins know you too," Ebony whispers to the close casket before they are all ushered away. "You and Yolanda helped me handle living in Houston without Anthony."
Everyone goes to Felecia's house to eat and reminisce. Terrell and Chrissy

are there and they help with the food service, along with the grandmother's from the crew and other friends of April's family from Houston.

Later all the crew get together at Ron and Carolyn's house, which is big mama and poppa's old house. It's 1 block from April's home.

"It's been awhile since we've been down here," Chill says to Ron.

"Too long, Cuz," Ron says, "I hate it had to be something like this, to get y'all back here."

"I know," Chill says, "It won't be, next time. I promise you that."

By Friday everyone returns home. Yolanda, David and Charles stay in Houston. Lynn and Jb tell them to stay as long as it takes to get back to normal.

"Your jobs will be there when you come back to Atlanta," Jb says.

****

By September, Ebony is back to work. She's still trying to deal with the lose of her good friend April. She keeps the picture of her, April and Yolanda on her desk. As she works on a stack of files she wants to get done by weeks end, T-baby comes over to her office and invites her to lunch.

"Alright Tee," Ebony says, "I was feeling kind of hungry anyway. Did you call Nina and Ree Ree?"

"Yes. They're gonna pick up the food and bring it by Nina's house. I turned in your order from Claudia," T-baby says, "We're all thinking about quitting for today. We really need to talk."

"Okay. Let's do it."

Ebony gets all the files she needs and leaves for the day as well. They meet for lunch at Nina and Tank's house. They talk about April's passing and how sad that had left them all and Yolanda too.

"It makes you realize just how much tomorrow *isn't* promised," Rebbie says.

Then they discuss their marital situations. Of course Ajay's bachelor party comes up a lot during the discussion about June and Rich's mistresses.

"Rich tried that defense on that same day he came to our house," Ebony says, "Big mama and I had just had lunch and he was all up in my face about me seeing them at the complex. I wouldn't come around y'all that day because I couldn't keep that a secret. Do y'all remember that? He thought I had told on him. June didn't pull that mess. June stayed away from me. That's why Anthony jumped Rich and not June, like I told y'all this spring. But still, they can't blame that on Anthony's bachelor party."

"Tank and Ajay was there too. All of our guys was there," Nina says, "But June and Rich took it outside of the bachelor party."

"Let's keep it real. They started with Regina and Diana, long before that *damn* bachelor party," Rebbie confesses, "June told me *everything*. There's *no way* they can blame it on Ajay's bachelor party. They was fucking around with those sluts in college."

"Anthony told me what he did at the party," Ebony adds, "I was mad at first. But he told me while we was on our honeymoon. He said he didn't want me to hear about it somewhere else."

"Jeremy told me about his involvement too," Nina says.

"And y'all husbands didn't carry it on," T-baby says, "Ours *did*."

"I feel guilty about that sometimes," Ebony admits, "I wanted all of our marriages to be happy and unshakeable. I mean, *damn*. We put up with the cheating shit before the marriage. And y'all know *I* did."

"Ajay was all up front with his too," T-baby says, "Maybe ours should've been."

"Maybe they would've gotten it out of their systems," Rebbie says.

"Me too Ebony," Nina adds, "I feel guilty too. And Jeremy was out there with his too. Maybe not *living* with a woman. But Alana was and still is around here as a reminder of when I first got my heart broken. Still I feel guilty because my husband is taking care of his vow to me."

T-baby and Rebbie tell them they should be happy their relationships have been affair free. And they shouldn't feel guilty because June and Rich had affairs.

"I just hope that Alana bitch disappear again," Nina says suddenly.

"The best part of it is that she's not an issue anymore, Nina," Ebony says, "Twin ain't interested in her at all."

"Tank's not gonna cheat, Nina," T-baby says, "He's over that bitch and over that shit. I can tell."

"So can I," Rebbie adds, "He's a hundred percent with you, Nina."

"He'd better be. Because he's all I want. I couldn't deal with an affair," Nina says, "Not as easy as y'all have. I know I can't."

"Anthony is trying to get to the Cavaliers," Ebony adds suddenly, "He don't even wanna be away from us, like that. He don't wanna be in that Condo anymore. Where the groupies get loose in the hallways."

"We've been with *only* them, all of our lives," Rebbie says, "Until death do us part is the vow we all took. I'm sticking with my word to God."

"We are too," the other 3 agree.

"I did tell Brian I would cheat, if he does again though," Rebbie admits, "And I will. I mean that."

TIME TO KNOW-RELOADED-Time Will Reveal- part 4

Tonya and Jr get results from Dr. Weston today. They have been successful in conceiving their 2nd child.

"Now that's a birthday gift, for sure," Tonya says as they prepare to leave the office.

"Our children will be nine years apart," Jr says with a smile. He's overjoyed to know they're having another child.

"And I will tell mama Walker, this time too. You just concentrate on having a healthy baby, sweetheart. I won't let anybody bring stress your way."

"Your Prince charming is still present," Weston says as she laughs.

"He's great," Tonya says.

"Are you hoping for a girl, this time?" Weston asks.

"Healthy is my only wish," Jr says, "I can work with two sons." They all laugh as Weston gives them a due date of May 22, 2001.

"Another May baby," Tonya smiles, "And I have my little sister here to help me out, this time around too. I'm so glad Venitia's here."

Her and Jr rush back o let the crew know they've conceived again. Chill predicts they'll have another boy. So does big mama. They listen to the new *OutKast* CD, *Stankonia* while at Jr and Tonya's home. Lil Brad is the most excited. He's already picking out the room in their house, for his new brother or sister. Tonya calls and tells her college roommate Terri Edwards, who is now a nurse at East General. She also asks Terri to be the Godmother. Terri says she would be delighted to Christian the new baby.

****

The crew go visit Rich in rehab for his 25th birthday. He's doing really well. He's started a weight training program. Jb had set it up for him to get him back conditioned and possibly back in the NFL. He hasn't given up on getting Rich back into the league. Ajay talks to Jb about his contract with Miami, which is up after next season.

"I wanna opt out of it, if I can," he tells Jb.

"I can look into it, Ajay," he says, "Where are you trying to go?"

"Cleveland. I wanna get to Cleveland," he says, "I'm tired of leaving Ebony and my babies. Plus I wanna make some more."

They laugh. Then Jb tells him he'll start negotiations right away. Ajay leaves for Miami's preseason camp, the next day. The night before, he tells Ebony he hopes this'll be the last season he'll have to leave them behind.

It's the last week of October when Mya gives birth to a baby boy. Greg Jr is there, along with his and her family when he sees some obvious

264

unlikeness's. Greg Jr has a dark complexion. Mya is biracial and the baby has Hispanic features. Greg Jr had suspected her of fooling around with a Hispanic guy name Juan, whom he'd had many fights with. But she'd convinced him there was no sex between them. Seeing her little boy, brings all of that back. Greg Sr suggests a paternity test and Sandy asks for it. It's granted the 1st day.

2 days later the results come in. Before Mya is released from the hospital, it is revealed that Greg isn't the father of her son. Greg is crushed and embarrassed as he tells Mya it's over before him and his family leave the hospital. By late evening, everyone in the crew knows Greg Jr and Mya are done for good.

By 7 pm, Mya's mother and her aunts come out to Shaker Heights. They're in front of Sandy's house with a lot of drama about Greg Jr. Simply because he isn't willing to be a sucker. Sandy has asks them to leave and they refused. There are 6 women outside who've shown up threatening her oldest son. Sandy isn't backing down as she recognizes 3 of them, right away. She remembers Mya's mother and 2 aunts from the fight at MLK, between their children. She tells them for the last time to leave her property or they will be dealt with. Debbie, who lives 2 doors down, hears the commotion. She comes outside and runs down to Sandy's house.

"What is this?" she asks Sandy, "What these bitches want?"

"These hood rats are pissed off because their relative got outed today about her whorish ways," Sandy tells her, "That baby Mya had ain't Greg juniors and they're mad about it."

"So!" Debbie shouts to the 6 females before turning her attention back to Sandy and saying, "Okay. Well the girls are on the way. We can get this handled sooner than later."

Within minutes, Rena and Brenda join them while Anna is running up the block towards them.

"Jo, Pearl and Belinda will be here in five minutes," Anna says as she reaches her friends who are huddled together in Sandy's yard.
She had noticed the females in front of Sandy's house and called Jo.

In another 5 minutes, the 8 mothers of the crew are here. Jo hops out of her van already in over drive. She has looked forward to the chance to kick off in Miss Dean's ass since Erica and Mya's last fight at MLK. Today she isn't going to be denied.

"Sandy go put on some jeans and let's get this mess cleaned up out of your yard," she says.
Sandy heads inside to change her clothes while her crew removes their jewelry and gets *Vaseline'd* up. They're wearing sneakers, blue jeans and

t-shirts. Just like they use to do it back in the day. Now the 6 females are acting as if the crew mothers are the forcers of this action. The disturbers of the peace. When in actuality, they're the ones who are trespassing. They had shown up and threatened Greg Jr and was attempting to damage his 2000 Durango. He ran out and foiled that plan but he hadn't been able to get the women to leave. They're using all types of vulgar references and profane language toward him, his mother and now the other 7 mothers who have come to assists.

"So you got all your crew out here to fight us?" Miss Dean says, "I thought you was bad. Thought you was gonna whoop us by yourself." Sandy doesn't even answer her because she knows none of that was ever said. The crew mothers don't argue with these women at all. They don't allow Greg Jr to, any longer either.

"I thought they was suppose to be big time *upscale* folks," 1 of Miss Dean sisters say.

"They're ghetto fabulous but not upscale," Miss Dean adds with laughter, "No where near big time."

"Never mind all this talking," Debbie says, "Y'all came to throw some. So lets get this shit off." The more ready the crew mothers are. The less ready Miss Dean and her posse seem to be. No longer able to contain herself, Jo grabs Miss Dean and begins beating her. Pearl grabs 1 sister. Sandy grabs the other. The 3 remaining women are pounced on by Rena, Brenda, Anna, Debbie and Belinda. The 8 mothers make quick work of these 6 trespassers.

By the time T-baby, Ebony and Nina show up. Their mothers are done. The 6 women had retreated to their vehicles and called the police. Only to be arrested when the cops do arrive. Nina calls Erica at Oklahoma University immediately. Rebbie, Renee and Tonya show up just as the police are hauling them away to jail. Pearl calls detective Hardin and asks for his assistance. He tells her, he's on the case and he'll make sure the 6 women are dealt with properly. Then the mothers and their daughters plus Greg Jr, get on with the rest of their day.

****

The crew's grandparents have always been poll workers. The 2000 general election is no exception. Big mama and poppa had gotten registered in Cleveland as soon as they moved back. They had signed up to work the polls along with their crew. They're working the precinct with Sally, Annabelle, Joshua, Charles and papa. Mrs. Ida Mae Graves and Mrs.

Green are working the poll station with them. All of the crew who are 18 are registered voters and they vote regularly. This election day is hectic. Not just at the precincts in Cleveland but nationwide. So hectic in fact that by the end of the night, no President has been declared. The votes haven't been tabulated and there is no apparent winner. Al Gore had been called the winner initially and he seems to be the victor. But then the national news changes it. They say they've made a mistake in the outcome and there is controversy in Florida. This controversy would go on for weeks.

By the end of November, there is still no new United States President declared.

"I say we go on and keep *Bill Clinton*," big mama says as they all agree that Clinton should've been allowed another term.

"We did so well during the Clinton administration," poppa says, "People was able to make a decent living and save some money."

"That's what the right wing nuts hate," grandpa Joshua says.

"And that's going to change if George Bush gets in there," papa says, "Only the top one percent are going to prosper."

"He's an oil man," Sally says, "We'll be at war, for sure."

****

Eric McNair has been adamant about dating Erica. He comes to Stoney's during the Christmas holiday season to talk to Al again. He impresses him with his determination. By now Al knows his daughter likes Eric as well. After having a talk with Ajay over the phone, Al gives Eric his blessing. Eric is allowed to ask Erica to be his girlfriend. He does so immediately and she happily accepts. She's in her sophomore year at Oklahoma where Eric had attended before the draft. And she has season tickets to his 1st NFL season with the Cleveland Browns. The Browns had gone 3-13 in only their 2nd season back home. Eric had a good year and so had Bruce. They're happy and look forward to next season.

June is having a wonderful year. His Ravens team has been having a great season too. Rebbie and Orian have made most of the games. The Ravens are playing the Denver Broncos at home in the AFC wild card playoff game on the last day of December. Which is Ajay and Ebony's 3rd anniversary. They meet up with all of their crew for the game in Baltimore.

June has another great game. Ravens win 21-3 and advance. The crew are super excited at the possibility of June going to the Super Bowl.

On a sadder note for the crew, the supreme court decides the 2000 vote for America. They give the White House to George W. Bush in

267

January, to the dismay of many Americans who knows that Al Gore won.
"He won the popular vote," Pearl says.
"That republican congress has too go," Belinda says, "They'll rob America blind."
"And we'll be in debt before long," Debbie says.
"And at war too," Sandy adds, "Watch what I tell you."
"Brian said that too," Brenda says, "Clinton left us a surplus."
"That'll be spent before Valentines day," Jo says as they all laugh, "And my babies will be in butt fuck Egypt, in no time."
"With a deficit too," Rena adds.
"A huge deficit at that," Anna says with a giggle.
None them think it's funny but as Jo's mother use to say,
"Sometimes you have to laugh to keep from crying."

****

The Ravens next game is against the Tennessee Titans on the 7th of January. Ravens defeat them 24-10 and advance to the AFC Championship against the Oakland Raiders. That game is January 14th. Rebbie made every post season game. The crew are back for the AFC Championship.

The Ravens are going to the Super bowl. They win the AFC Championship, 16-3 to advance. They'll play the New York Giants for the Championship. The entire crew are going to the Super Bowl in Tampa.

"Maybe we can help them with them *damn* votes, while we're down there," Chill says as he laughs.
They're all proud of June and the Baltimore Ravens for advancing to the Super Bowl game on January 28, 2001.

"Bush stole the shit anyway," Renee says, "We're fucked now!"
They all agree.

Bush is sworn in on January 20, 2001 and thus, the gradual tearing down of America begins.

"I'm going to keep my eyes on the surplus," Ebony says, "I have a feeling, with these tax and spend republicans. We'll be at a huge deficit before the end of his four years."

"Somebody needs to watch," T-baby says, "He looks like the devil."

}Tampa{
"Super Bowl time, my folks!" Brian Sr says.
Him and Brenda are very proud of June and his team and they surely show it.

TIME TO KNOW-RELOADED-Time Will Reveal- part 4

"We're going to win this thing," Brenda says, "There's a Super Bowl ring in our *near* future. I can feel it in my bones, crew!"

They're all dressed in Ravens jerseys and paraphernalia with big June's number. His fan section is over 200 people and the Ravens are victorious. They beat the Giants 34-7. June makes the *All-Madden team* which is a huge honor for him. He's already going to the pro bowl next week.

They have a party in Tampa, thrown by Ajay's team. The Heat host the party on Ajay's behalf. There are many sports and entertainment stars there. Jb, Cedric, Chill, Tank and Rob do a lot of networking. They manage to strum up some future business for the crew.

During Valentine's week, some of the crew go on vacation. Chill and Renee join Ron and Carolyn on a trip to Jamaica. Jr and Tonya go to Detroit to visit Tonya's family, so Jr can let them know about the new baby. Venitia stays in Cleveland. T-baby spends the week in Cincinnati with Rich at a halfway house. Tank and Nina go to the Pocono's while June and Rebbie go to Paris for lover's week. Ebony and the twins go to Miami and join Ajay as the Heat continue to have a promising season.

By Tank and Nina's 5 year anniversary, which they celebrate in Hawaii, they're talking about having another child. Tank wants a son and Nina wants to try again too.

The crew doesn't have anyone in the NFL draft this year. But 1 of Bruce and Eric's good friends from football camps and All-star games, *Michael Vick* of *Virginia Tech,* goes to the draft early and is drafted by the *Atlanta Falcons.*

Chaundra learns by her birthday that she has a full academic scholarship to Ohio State. Also her trust fund which was set up by Bre when her brother Stoney was killed, matured for her 18th birthday. Ebony handles the transfer of funds from Cleveland Bank and Trust into an interest bearing account which Chaundra can use at her leisure.

"She's the first person in the crew to receive a full *academic* scholarship," Renee says, "We've got to celebrate that, *big*!"

They have a huge party for Chaundra at the spot. Kenny gives her a promise ring. Chill and Renee are happy the 2 of them are in love.

But the next day, Renee is at her wits end about Farah Benson. That woman just doesn't know when to quit. Renee had received word from Chaundra at the party, that she believed Kenny had been intimate with Farah. Renee is livid and goes straight to Chill to find out what's going on.

"I think I'm gonna need to know what the ingredients are in that cake you're baking!" she yells, "And I wanna know just what my son's part is in it!"

"We can talk in my office or yours, baby," Chill says calmly.

Renee storms off to the elevator. She doesn't bother to wait for her husband. Chill takes his time so his wife will have a minute to breathe before he gets up there. He and Jr are talking about the auditions for The Juice Bar which they're holding in just a few minutes.

"You handle it," Chill says to Jr, "Get Kilo and Wayne up here with you. I need to talk to Renee."

"You did see that Alana is auditioning, right?" Jr asks.

"Yes I saw her application."

"So what? Hire? Not?"

"If you think she can bring in customers. Hire her. We're about our money, cousin. Ain't shit changed on that part."

He goes to the elevators and leaves Jr in charge of the stripper auditions.

Renee is in his office waiting for him when he gets up there. She has a very impatient look on her face.

"Baby we've got everything we need on Farah Benson," he says, "I need for you to arrange a meeting with her."

"Why the fuck would I do that? Did that bitch fuck my son? My *minor* son? That's what I need to know today."

"No."

"Kenny, I want the truth!" she demands.

"And I'm telling you the truth. She hasn't."

"What happened? I know something did. Tell me now."

"Sit down and I'll fill you in," he says.

He tells her that Jacobson security has caught and witnessed Farah performing oral sex on Kenny. He tells her, Bronson had seen her and reported it to him. They made sure security saw it and had film of her with Kenny in her car.

"I don't even wanna see that film," Renee says as her eyes well up with tears. "That's pedophilia. I don't give a damn if he *is* seventeen. He's *my* baby."

"That's not all," Chill says, "There's more."

He tells her that Farah has been sexual with Greg Jr, Jesse and Bruce as well. He suspects she's had Reaper too.

"But Sam refused her."

"How do you know all of this?"

"We got photo's and audio. She's admitting to the oral sex with Kenny and she wanted him to fuck her. But he wouldn't even try. He said

TIME TO KNOW-RELOADED-Time Will Reveal- part 4

he can't act *that* well. She told him she wanted him to do what his father was afraid to do," he says.

"I'm killing that bitch."

"Let the plan play out, Renee. She's either going to be extorted. Or she'll leave all of that bullshit alone," he says.

He tells her, he wants the meeting with her so she can see the photo's and video. Plus hear the audio and know that they want her to leave him and their son alone.

"You let him go this far? Why not let them break her ass?" Renee says, "If the school board finds out about this. That's her job. Try that on her first, with Kenny and Sam together. I don't want my baby around her alone *anymore*."

Chill agrees to release a plan to break Farah's bank.

"When Bruce, Jesse and Greg Jr come back home next month. I'm putting them on it," he says.

The subject is closed and the plan will be hatched when the college crew get home for summer break.

In May, Bruce gets his degree from Ohio State. Chaundra graduates high school as Valedictorian and signs her acceptance letter to attend Ohio State where Kim will be a senior. They both have aspirations of becoming attorneys. Steven and Ally graduate with Chaundra. But they're going to attend Cleveland State with Sam and Pam this year. They want to stay close to home with their 3½ year old daughter Ashanti. Kenny, who'll graduate next year is already committed to a football scholarship at Ohio State. His awesome play at Quarterback has him highly sought after.

"We're gonna have a son in the NFL," Chill brags proudly.

Everyone else agrees that Kenny should receive a great contract when he gets drafted in a few years.

****

Shannon-the-Reaper's record career has taken off. He has a video out and it premiered on the hottest video show on *B.E.T.* which aired this month. The show is called *106 & Park* with host *AJ* and *Free*. The show looks like it has promise to be the leading video show by years end. It's definitely immediate competition for *MTV's TRL* which is hosted by *Carson Daly*. The crew watches the 106 & Park show daily and casts their votes for Reaper's video. He stays on the charts for the entire month of May and most of June.

Bruce had graduated from Ohio State in May. Immediately he

271

Time To Know- RELOADED-Time Will Reveal 4   Black Coffee

TIME TO KNOW-RELOADED-Time Will Reveal- part 4

purchased land in Jackson Heights through Ebony's firm. His property is on Wilson's Way drive. This will be the future site of him and Kim's home. Jackson Heights has 8 residents now with many more to come.

By mid-June, Chill has the meeting with Farah in his office. The meeting was to make her aware that there are pictures and audio of her with Steven. Prior to this meeting, Bruce and Greg had confronted her about it and demanded cash to destroy the evidence. She didn't want to pay them. Bruce told Greg Jr they would tell Chill to keep the proof in the vault and they could use it when she did find something she gave a damn about. Bruce told his sister Bre about it. Bre was so disgusted, she called Renee the first free moment she got.

"She just really don't give a damn, does she?" Bre asks Renee via telephone on Father's day.

"She knows they got shit on her, Bre. She's still fucking with them. And now she's paying them money."

"Renee I'm surprised you haven't beat her dumb ass," Bre says.

"I can't just fight her, Bre. I want her dead. Kenny made me swear off of her and kill her through her pockets," Renee says.

"Bruce is game for it, I know," Bre says, "They got him hooked on doing that kind of shit before he was even crew."

"He got a whole generation of extortionist now," Renee says as they laugh.

She gets a call waiting beep and tells Bre to hold while she answers it.

"Hello?"

"I'm in labor, sis," Tonya says from the other end of the phone.

She's already at East General. Brad Jr is getting on her last nerve and she needs Renee and the crew to come rescue her.

"He's acting like we're brand new at this, out here," Tonya says as she holds the phone away from her ear.

Renee can hear Jr trying to coach Tonya. She laughs because he sounds hilarious. She clicks over and tells Bre that she has a new niece or nephew coming today. Bre asks her to tell Jr and Tonya that her, Cedric and CJ will be up in a few days. Renee says she will. Then her and Bre hang up and Renee clicks back over to Tonya.

"Can you bring Brad III down here for us?" Tonya asks.

"No problem. I'll bring him with us," Renee says, "In a minute."

"See ya," Tonya says and they hang up.

Tonya and Jr had decided to keep the sex of the new baby a secret. Her roommate Terri Edwards is on duty tonight in labor and delivery.

272

TIME TO KNOW-RELOADED-Time Will Reveal- part 4

"I'm ready to help deliver my Godchild," she says as she laughs. Jr and Tonya have another boy. They name him after Tonya's deceased father Donald. Bruce comes to see his new nephew. Brad III is there with his new little brother. After the crew have all seen the new addition, Jr runs them all out.

"My wife needs to sleep," he says and laughs, "And me and my junior need to go teach my new son how to eat. This is a happy Father's day to me."

DONOVAN DARNELL WILSON
BORN:JUNE 17, 2001 [Father's day]
TIME: 3PM
WEIGHT:7lbs 9ozs
LENGTH:19inches

Welcome to the world.......................Donovan Darnell Wilson!

By phone Alana learns that she's hired at *The Juice Bar*. The crew had all signed off on her employment and she is to begin dancing within the week. She's excited to be an employee. She goes by the CrewLand mall to tell Tameka and Michelle about her new employment. They're surprised and pessimistic. They both see it as trouble for Alana because they know she won't stay in pocket. Nina sees her employment as a sure fire way to let her hang herself with the crew, for good. She has no hang-ups about Tank. He's the only crew member besides Roo and Pam, who showed opposition to her being hired. Ebony and Ajay didn't care, either way. But they did make it a point to say, "We will never hire Angel. Just know that."
The whole crew agree on that point too.

For the next weeks, Nina, Justine and Matt run *Crews Cuts and Styles* while Tonya is on maternity leave. Matt has brought new flavor to the shop with his prim clients and their high strung manors. Which provide day-to-day excitement. Nina or Justine are always calling Tonya with the latest fiasco. This weekend Ebony goes in for her *do* and is a witness to the salon drama, *firsthand.*

"I'm coming in to get my hair done," she tells Nina from her office phone. "Instead of getting it done in my bathroom this week."

"I got you down, sis," Nina says, "Come on in."

273

TIME TO KNOW-RELOADED-Time Will Reveal- part 4

Ebony arrives at the shop in the midst of some controversy between Matt Johnson and his love interest, Ellen Barnes. Matt is no relation to big Jake but his choice of women will bring nearly as much drama and trouble, as big Jake's family had. When Ellen arrives, she has apparently found out about Matt's womanizing and wants to confront him.

"Who the hell was that white bitch you was at dinner with last night?!" Ellen yells, "I saw you coming out, so don't lie!"

"That was a friend of mine," Matt tries, "I'm still a single man."
But in fact, he's not actually single. Him and his wife Genia, the mother of his only child, a daughter named Kelly, are still legally married. But they haven't been active together for 15 years. Matt is a player. Ellen is a bit possessive and turning into a fatal attraction. Matt and Farah had gone to dinner the previous night to discuss another career day, in depth. He had also accompanied her back to her home in Parma Heights. He doesn't know it. But Ellen had followed them, sat outside of the house and knows Matt had stayed for hours. She doesn't tell Matt she followed them. Nor that she knows where his date lives.

"How are you gonna be fucking around with some bitch, on me?" Ellen asks.
She continues to yell to the top of her voice. Matt is noticeably embarrassed by this display. Nina steps in and demands that Ellen leave her place of business with this disturbance. Ellen isn't pleased about being ask to leave the premises. She argues with Matt, trying to get him to come outside. He tells her no and too leave at once. Ellen storms out of the swinging doors and into the parking lot. Instead of leaving, she goes to the trunk of her car, takes out a golf club which is part of a gift she had planned to give Matt for Fathers day. She runs directly toward his car. Before anyone can stop her. She smashes out the windshield of his suburban. Then she jumps into her car and speeds away before security can capture her. Matt files a police report and presses charges. But Ellen is long gone.

"That woman is psychotic," Justine says as she laughs.
Eventually her and the other workers manage to get all of their customers back inside the shop and back to getting their styles done.

"Matt it looks like you have yourself a fatal attraction, ha?" Ebony asks.

"She just don't understand that a pimp is gonna be a pimp," Matt says as he tries to mask his embarrassment.

"Well the pimp is gonna be buying a new windshield," Nina says as she laughs. "Ellen is a crazy bitch."

"We don't want her ass back around here, Matt," Justine adds,

Time To Know- RELOADED-Time Will Reveal 4   Black Coffee

TIME TO KNOW-RELOADED-Time Will Reveal- part 4

"She's just gonna have to deal with you *somewhere* else."
"I know that's right," Nina agrees.

Erica shows up as the commotion is ending. She's with Eric McNair. She formally introduces him to her crew, as her man. Nina is happy with her choice. Eric is a respectable guy and with his new Browns contract. He's also a very rich man.

Kim comes in shortly after Erica and Eric, with Bruce by her side. The 2 of them announce that they're getting married.

"August eleventh is our wedding date," Kim says.

"Why so soon, Kim?" Nina asks while smiling. "This ain't a shotgun wedding, is it," she laughs.

"No," Kim says as she laughs too. She adds, "We just wanna do it before Bruce leaves for training camp."

"But our baby will be soon after though," Bruce adds.

"Well we've got a lot to celebrate," Matt says, "I'll give the two guys a nice cut, on me."

"I'm with that," Eric and Bruce say simultaneously.

Then Erica goes with Kim to take *Crew Gear and Alterations* and the other crew businesses their list for the wedding. They begin preparations right away.

The heat lost in the playoffs and Ajay's season is over. Jb has worked his option. The heat releases him as a free agent and Jb gets him signed to the Cavaliers for the 2001-2002 season. Ajay is thrilled with the trade because he'll be able to be home with his family. While with the Heat, Ajay had racked up an impressive 281 wins to 127 lose record and a playoff birth in each of his 5 seasons.

"Anthony I'm so happy you'll be playing for Cleveland," Ebony says, "I know it's what you've always dreamed of doing."

"Yes baby," he says, "But I have to help Jarvis get the team into playoff shape though."

He's right. The Cavaliers haven't done anything significant during Ajay's 5 years in the league. The Cav's are looking at the next phenom from the state of Ohio named *Lebron James*. He's still in high school and already he has shattered records set by Ajay. He's the next best thing and many feel this kid can forgo college and come straight to the pros. The Cavaliers can sure use the help. Ajay and Jarvis alone isn't going to be enough. But Ajay has plans on changing their statistics in his 1st year.

JB has gotten June released from the Ravens and signed to the

TIME TO KNOW-RELOADED-Time Will Reveal- part 4

Cleveland Browns for the 2001 season. Him and Rebbie are pleased with his trade too. The crew are glad to have their star athletes on their home teams.

****

The Spot II is hosting a screening of the 1st annual *BET awards* show this year on June 28th. All of the crew families and friends gather to watch this historic event.

"This is gonna be an award show where we can relate to each and every one of the categories," Tank says, "And it's about damn time."

"Not since the *Soul Train Awards* and *The Source Awards*, has there been a show with the majority black nominees," Nina says.

"Yes and hopefully with less fights and shootings, afterwards," Kim says as she laughs.

"I know that's right," Erica adds.

The 1st BET awards show goes off without a hitch. *Kings of Comedy* staples and the *Steve Harvey show* stars, *Steve Harvey* and *Cedric the Entertainer* are the host. They're absolutely wonderful together.

The last Friday in June, as Ebony works in her office, she has a scheduled visit from Marvin Huntley. He had called her office a few weeks ago, after he found out her office is lien holder on The Chill Spot nightclub. Which in his mind, is what has taken Farah away from him. He finds out that *Jackson's Real Estate and Investment banking* holds the titles on the entire mall. So he scheduled an appointment and claimed he wanted to move to Cleveland. Saying that he's seeking a nice upscale area in which to build a home. This is Ebony's expertise, as she has become the go-to agency in the past 2 years. Her office led the state in land acquisitions and sales for 1999 and 2000. Marvin shows up for his meeting. Claudia brings him back to see Ebony at 10am sharp.

"Hello mister Huntley. Very nice to meet you. I'm Ebony Brown-Jackson. I've gone over your file and everything looks good so far. How may I help you?"

"I'm from neighboring Pittsburgh. I'm looking to expand my parents Insurance agency to Cleveland. I was hoping you could assist me with finding the office space or land, in which to build it," Marvin says.

"That shouldn't be a problem. What size acquisition are we talking about?"

Marvin says, "Thirty Five hundred square feet of office space. I would prefer a split entrance style. One such as this one your office is in, would be great. I will have my insurance store on one side. And our Textile's

276

manufacturing, perhaps a flooring store, on the other side."

"Give me a week. By next Friday, I'll have some sites for you to view. Or we can build it from scratch," she says, "We can decide then."

This is the conclusion of their meeting but Marvin Huntley takes it farther.

"That sounds perfect," he says before changing the subject to what his primary reason was for making the appointment.

Getting into the business of *CrewLand*.

He asks, "This is quite a nice business complex. Is there any availability space here?"

"No this is exclusive," she says, "This is private and family owned. All of the proprietors here are family. Including me."

"Oh swell. So you own The Chill Spot as well?" he asks.

"Yes I'm part owner. As I said, these are *all* shared businesses. Four generations of family share ownership, cost and all."

"Any possible avenue for investing?" he asks.

"Be born into, inducted by or marry into the family," she says as she smiles.

"Okay. Well who knows," he says, "Any chance I can talk you into a dinner date?"

"No chance. I'm happily married and very much in love with my husband."

"He's the NBA star, correct?"

Marvin has done his homework. He knows a lot about the crew, their accomplishments and their undying loyalty. He's merely trying to impress Ebony with his homework but he's up against a business mind and business woman.

"He's a devoted father and husband. Part CrewLand owner and my best friend," she says, "As well as an All-star NBA player. Yes."

Marvin takes the hint and lets up on the flirting. He picks up his briefcase.

"I think I've just been let down. Not sure if it was easy or not," he says and smiles.

"It was truthful. See you next Friday. Have your funding in place if you're looking for a fast forward on this," she says, "We can secure something and have the ground broken before the fall."

"Do you invest in such ventures that aren't say,.. uh family?"

"Only if it forecast lucrative," she says, "See you on Friday."

She leads him out to Claudia, who schedules his follow up and gives him a package for the CrewLand Mall. The package includes all cards, coupons and other discounts for the businesses. The same thing Farah had gotten that *he* saw, which ultimately *led* him here. He's led to the door. After he leaves, Claudia and Ebony chat before the next appointment.

"He seems strange," Claudia says.

"Pittsburgh, Claudia," Ebony says, "I have a sneaky suspicion that he's familiar with that Alana posse."

"Did he say something?"

"No he didn't," Ebony says.

"He seems way too classy to be mixed up with those jezebels," Claudia says and laughs.

"That's exactly why it fits so remarkably well," she says, "Send the next client on back as soon as they arrive."

She goes back into her office.

Alana will start her 1st shift at The Juice Bar tonight. This is 4th of July week. Heavy traffic is expected to patronize the CrewLand Mall. Alana is excited to have a job with the crew. She has high hopes of the new doors this could open for her and Farah. Darlene however, isn't as optimistic about her niece's new employment. She warns her of the possible drawbacks to the job.

"I told you when you first came back to visit. Don't come back here with that same shit. If Jeremy don't give you anything to go on. Don't push it," she says, "Don't get yourself into something that you can't shake loose from, Alana."

"I won't," Alana says, "I'm gonna cherish this job and hopefully, Jeremy will get to see me dance. Although he works at the kids club. I never got an answer on that application. I know his wife blocked my shit."

"Maybe *he* did," Darlene offers.

"I doubt it. He's not worried about me being here. *She* is." Alana says stubbornly.

Darlene lets the conversation go at that. But she knows this isn't the last time this new job or the discussion about Tank and his wife will come up.

Ajay celebrates his 27th birthday with his twins Lannie and Lil Ajay, who turn 2 this year.

"They're into everything, Anthony," Ebony says exhaustedly after dinner.

"They're in the terrible two's stage, baby," Ajay says as he laughs, "I'll get them ready for bed tonight. Okay? But first, I'm gonna run you a bubble bath so you can relax."

She takes him up on his offer. She goes into their master suite where he has set up champagne and strawberries. He has slow jams playing on their

TIME TO KNOW-RELOADED-Time Will Reveal- part 4

bedroom stereo and a very sexy sparkle in his eyes, that she recognizes.

"This is wonderful Anthony," she says as she stripes and steps into the Jacuzzi.

"Good. You relax here while I get the twins bathe and in bed," he says, "Then I'm gonna join you."

She relaxes as he goes back to their twins. He lets them play in the water for 15 minutes, so they can tire themselves out. After letting them splash water all over their bathroom. He finally gets them to settle down and take their baths. Within a half an hour, he has them sound asleep.

"That wasn't hard at all," he says as he kisses his sleeping daughter and tucks her in.

He goes into his sons room and does the same. Then he joins Ebony.

"Got my babies sleep," he says in a low voice, "Now it's your turn."

"Mmm. I missed this so much," she says, "It's gonna be really good having you at home, for a change."

She tells him how her meeting with Marvin had gone. They discuss his possible affiliations with Farah and what land, if any, he seems to be settling on.

"I've shown him some premium properties," she says, "But he's preoccupied with the mall and who frequents it. Like if our clubs are mixed crowds. That sort of thing."

"Why not ask him if he knows them?" Ajay suggest.

"Next week will be his third meeting," she says, "I'm waiting on him to ask me."

"Damn that. He's trying to take you to dinner and shit. Burst his bubble and let him know what you think he's about. He might go on and come clean," he says.

"I'll try that soon. But right now, I'm just happy to have you close. You can come in and protect me if you want too," she says with a smile, "Since you're on the home team now."

"Yes I am and I get to enjoy my pussy, before and after home games too," he says with a smile, "Come here baby."

He pulls her onto his lap and says, "I wanna taste you, baby girl."

He sits her on the edge and gives her some oral pleasure. He allows her to return the favor. Then they indulge in some heated sex in the whirlpool.

"Daddy still hitting this right, baby?" he asks in a whisper as he plunges inside of her.

"Yes daddy," she whispers, "You do. You do."

"Oh baby you feel so good. Henny and Penny still big as hell too."

He buries his face in her breast. She moans as he nibbles on her nipples.

279

"Oh yes daddy! Yes." She feels her climax approaching.

"Get it wet for daddy!" he demands.

"Yes daddy!" she yells as her body complies to his demands.

She's enjoying her orgasm and giving him plenty of action from the hips. All of a sudden,

"*Daddy! You hurt my mommy!*" the voice of Lil Ajay proclaims.

Ajay and Ebony stop immediately and submerge their bodies into the Jacuzzi.

"Son,.... What are you doing up?" Ajay asks as he's out of breathe and a bit embarrassed too.

"Mommy cry. Scared me," Lil Ajay says while wiping his eyes.

He had awakened and come downstairs to his parents bathroom after he heard what he thought was his mothers plea's for help. Ajay jumps out of the tub and grabs his terry wrap, throws it around him and goes to his son.

"Your mommy is alright, son," he says with a smile. "We're having fun in the tub. That's all."

"Come here, baby," Ebony says, calling her son to the edge of the Jacuzzi. "Give mommy a kiss goodnight. I'm not hurt."

Just as Lil Ajay gives her a kiss, Lannie walks into the bathroom crying.

"I wanna sleep with you and daddy," she cries.

"Ah man," Ajay says as he laughs, "You're up too?"

"I'm scared in my room, daddy," she cries.

She had awakened and started crying after discovering that her brother wasn't in his room, which is next to hers. She had come downstairs in a panic, looking for someone to comfort her.

"Can we sleep to your bed, mommy?" Lil Ajay asks.

Ebony looks at Ajay and smiles. She asks, "Well daddy. Can they?"

"I guess so," he says, "But that's the first thing I have to do is break them from sleeping in our bed."

He tucks the twins into their large bed, then rejoins Ebony in the bathroom to dry off and get ready for bed. They snicker to themselves about being caught making love by their son.

"I did that to mama and daddy when I was little," Ajay admits.

"Tank use to do that to mama and daddy, all the time," Ebony says as she laughs. "We have to be careful. We have toddlers in the house now."

Her and Ajay curl up in bed with the twins in between them.

"This is cool for right now. But y'all are going to sleep in your own rooms, tomorrow night. Understand?" he says to his twins.

"Yes sir, daddy," they both say.

Before long, they're sound asleep again. Ajay and Ebony take this quiet time as an opportunity to talk about anything that's on their minds.

"So baby girl. Now that I'm playing at home. Maybe you can try out for the Rockers," he says suddenly.

"The WNBA? I don't think so," she says.

"Why not? You don't miss playing?" he asks.

"Sometimes I do. But baby, I'm a mother, a wife and a Real Estate banker," she says, "My plate is full already."

"If you wanna play. We can work it out baby," he persists.

"I'll think about it, okay?" she says, just to assure him.

Ebony hasn't considered going back to basketball since leaving Cincinnati. She's happy in her role. Besides, with a set of 2 year old twins, a flourishing Real Estate firm, a professional basketball player for a husband and a huge estate to run. She doesn't have the time or energy to join the WNBA. Nor does she have the desire too.

A week before Bruce and Kim's wedding, Marvin Huntley settles on a piece of property in Brook Park. Just off of highway 71. It's just west of the Parma Heights community where Farah lives. In recent weeks, the crew had tied the 2 of them together. They used the information Marvin submitted for his initial appointment and Farah's background information, Ebony had gotten from Mr. Myers at MLK. She discovered they'd had the same addresses in common for the last 6 years. She shared those findings with Chill and Renee. They then suggested she settle him out near Farah, in hopes they'd run into each other again. Marvin had put Ebony's firm in charge of handling the potential investors for his new venture. He's also stressed to her, how much he wanted to expand his Pittsburgh roots. He said he preferred his partners be from the Pittsburgh area. But not limited too. Ebony was way ahead of him by now. She knew of him and Farah's link and thought they was a team trying to takeover the crew's lucrative market. For she knew Farah had been looking to invest in CrewLand since she first showed up. Ebony and her crew figured the 2 of them had underestimated their business savvy. If they had, they would have to pay the price. She told Chill to make Farah aware of the investment options her firm has available. If she bites. Then she can tie them back together from there. Whether they want to be or not. However clever the crew think they are against what they think is an undercover plot to overtake them. They're wrong on about half of it. Farah has no idea Marvin is even in the area. Nor that he *has* been. No way they're plotting together and Marvin isn't trying to take over the crew's businesses. He's just trying to use them to make gains toward Farah and find out where she lives, here in Cleveland.

281

And he's also interested in finding out which _nigger_ his former fiancée had bedded down with before she decided to dump him. His only lead is that he owns a nightclub. He has since found that nightclub. Only to find out through Ebony that it's owned by a whole family of _niggers_. With men of *all* ages. But now Marvin is determined to find out which one of them, his Farah has a thing for and it will only be a matter of time before he does.

Ajay had stressed to Ebony that he didn't like how Farah came on the scene, playing outstanding and bringing grief to his brother. He wants her caught up *however* she can be. Just to get her out of Chill and Renee's lives. Plus he wants whomever the smug ass white man is that's flirting with his wife and inviting her to dinners. Out of her office and business, right away. While the crew are aiding Marvin in finding his way back to his former house mate. Neither of them have a clue of how troublesome that reunion can be for them. Nor how deadly the whole scenario will become before it's finally over.

Kim and Bruce wed on August 11 with the junior crew as their wedding participants and Chill's crew as host and hostesses. All the crews children plus Terrell and Chrissy are in the wedding party. Aunt Jessica is 1 of the coordinators. She has become more of a fixture at the celebrations. The newlyweds honeymoon in Jamaica for 4 days and 3 nights.

Speaking of August trouble, Ebony had promised she would keep an eye on the economy for her crew of entrepreneurs. She pulls information from DC and finds out the White House has disclosed that the federal budget surplus is dwindling. The new figures by the administration's own economists predicted lower tax revenues would slash the projected surplus for 2001 from $281 billion predicted in April to $158 billion now. The Democrats are responding with attacks on the president's fiscal policies too. She figures the debates will dominate politics for some time to come. With very little actually be done to change it.

"And hopefully bring about some change," Claudia says.

"We won't get any change until we get those tax and spend republican's out," T-baby says.

"War mongers too," Wesley adds, "They love war. And me being military. I would've rather had Al Gore as president."

"We all would. It's gonna get worse before it gets better," Ebony says, "That's my prediction. My big mama and her crew will cosign that."

Eric McNair, who is passing by on his way to Stoney's, sees them in the lobby and comes in to speak. He joins in on the political discussion.

TIME TO KNOW-RELOADED-Time Will Reveal- part 4

"I don't trust this administration at all," he says, "People call our politics in Illinois, *corrupt*. But it's this Bush and Cheney white house that's gonna teach you the meaning of corruption."

"I agree with you Eric," Ebony says, "I didn't know you was so political."

"I wasn't until about four years ago," he admits, "We have a junior Senator named Barack Obama and he's the truth."

"What kind of a name is that?" T-baby asks.

"His father is from Kenya. His mother is white and from Kansas. And he was raised in Hawaii by his grandparents," Eric says.

"Wow. He sounds like a melting pot," Wesley says as he chuckles.

"He has one sister and she's half Indonesian," Eric says.

"Goodness. So what makes him the truth Eric? Because we are a political crew," Ebony says, "And we wanna know what's out there."

"He has organized so many things in the communities in Chicago. He helps the underprivileged get what they *otherwise* wouldn't get. I know this because he helped me get in touch with the right folks, who ended up helping me to get my college scholarship. Then they helped me get tutored whenever I would come home."

"He sounds amazing," Claudia says, "You sure he's a politician?"

"I'm telling y'all this guy is going places," Eric says, "You'll hear about him real soon. If you keep up with politics. Chicago won't hold him for too long."

"He sounds like a gem. We backed Al Gore, here at CrewLand. Is he a democrat?" Ebony asks.

"Yes he is. His wife Michelle was born and raised in Chicago. *Southside*. She's the daughter of a former hardworking Chitown father, like mine," he says, "Her brother is one of the assistant basketball coaches at Northwestern, where my best friend from high school goes."

"This Obama guy, he's black or white?" Claudia asks.

"He's both. But you know black is a dominate gene. So he looks like a light skinned brother and he's got hoop game too. I'm telling you this dude is a brother to his core. But he's gonna change the game of politics one day. And he's gonna change it, for the better."

"Keep us up on him, Eric. He sounds like a potential Presidential contender," Ebony says with a smile.

"Oh shit. They would steal it from him worse than they did Gore," T-baby says as they all laugh.

"Or try to kill him," Claudia adds and they all stop laughing.

"He does sound promising though," Wes says, "And he sounds like
283

someone I would not only vote for. But campaign for too. Has he said anything about moving up higher?"

"Not yet. He's running for Illinois seats right now. But we're trying to get him to run for the United States Senate," Eric says.

"Just keep us informed," Ebony reiterates.

Eric says he will as he leaves, heading to Stoney's to grab some lunch.

The crew are dealing with the new found Cleveland settlers and keeping an eye on the economy too. Their forecast on both has been on point, thus far. But they could never have predicted the most troubling thing about this August. The day after Bruce and Kim returned from Jamaica would bring devastation to the crew.

On August 16, the crew are dealt a terrible blow. Grandma Sally suffers a major stroke and dies within minutes, at the age of 63. Her death leaves the crew devastated.

"Both of my grannies are gone now," T-baby says as she cries.

Sally was the only grandmother Jan, Kim and Sam Jr had ever known. Belinda's mother was killed by police before Jan was born. She'd never known her father. Losing grandma Sally also brought back the sadness for Ebony, Ajay and all of the crew who had already lost loved ones.

Grandma Sally Logan's funeral is enormous. They have people lined up outside with no seats left in the church. The overspill has to march in to view the body and remain outside. Or along the wall to see the rest of the service. Grandpa Joshua is strong throughout it all but everyone still flocks to him as they had done with papa when granny Pearline died. Sally is being buried in Mississippi, which is where she was born. Sam and Sandy had been successful in recovering their land which held the burial plots for all of the Logan's and Greene's. There was an empty plot left for Sally and Joshua. Sally had always told her husband, kids and crew that when she died she wanted to go back home. They fulfill her wishes with a small ceremony on the land where she was raised, before they bury her. Then her children, Sam Sr and Sandy, put the deeds to the land in Ebony's hands to look out on and to help them keep up with. They want the graveyard marked and they're going to add tombstones for the other relatives whose graves had been desecrated. Ebony will also be in charge of having the rest of the land cultivated. Some for homes and apartments. The rest for farming, so grandpa Joshua can live off of the land that his family had been killed on while trying to save it for him. It's now back in his possession and he'll have renters on it, sooner than later. Ebony and Parkwood will have developers on the land by late fall and it will bring grandpa Joshua some

TIME TO KNOW-RELOADED-Time Will Reveal- part 4

steady and real property income from his 44 acres, by the middle of 2003.

SALLY "GRANDMA SALLY" GREENE LOGAN
APRIL 3, 1938..........AUGUST 16, 2001
YOU WILL LIVE ON THROUGH YOUR CREW.
WE LOVE YOU ETERNALLY AND WE WILL NEVER FORGET THE
SACRIFICES YOU MADE FOR US.
REST IN PEACE GRANDMA SALLY.
FROM YOUR CREW WITH LOVE!

The untimely death of grandma Sally Logan causes Bruce, June and Eric to sign into training camp late but excused for family emergency. They join the Browns for preseason camp after it was already underway. The Browns have a positive outlook for the 2001-2002 season. June is a welcomed addition to the team. He's a veteran player with playoff and Super Bowl experience and a Super Bowl ring. Eric and Bruce are returning standouts. The Browns team is expected to do well in just their 3rd season back in Cleveland. The crew have season tickets for the Browns and the Cavaliers.

They visit Rich in rehab and he looks great. He had been accompanied home to support T-baby when Grandma Sally died. Then returned. He has just over 6 months left to complete the program.

Just 9 days after loosing grandma Sally, the talented and beautiful *Aaliyah* is killed in a plane crash in the Bahamas. Aaliyah has 2 songs, *More than a Woman* and *Rock the boat*, the video she had just completed. Those videos are burning up the charts. Aaliyah is Nina's favorite R&B female artist of all time. Nina insists she attend the funeral. Tank takes her. Aaliyah was only 22 years old but she has been famous since age 14. The foursome feel like they'd grown up with her. Ebony, Ajay, Rebbie, Kim and T-baby attend the service in New York with Tank and Nina. Nina was a diehard fan of Aaliyah. She had *Age ain't nothing but a Number, One in a Million, Aaliyah* plus every single poster, interview and article on Aaliyah's 8 year career. The song, *I Care for you* stays in rotation in Nina's Navigator.

"That was so sad," Nina says during the flight back to Cleveland "That's why I hate flying."

"Aaliyah has been through so much in her young life," Rebbie says.

"And just as she was coming into her own, after the R. Kelly stuff," T-baby says, "Now she's gone."

"R Kelly is a pervert," Kim says, "He was married to her when she

285

was only like fourteen or fifteen years old. Mama couldn't stand him."

"She had finally found love with *Damon Dash* and they looked so happy together," Ebony says, "This is just not right."

"She deserved to have some happiness in a healthy relationship," T-baby says, "We all do."

"Aaliyah is an angel y'all," Nina adds, "She was given to us for a short time. I'm gonna miss her. But I will never stop playing her music and I'm gonna make sure Jerica knows who she was to me."

REST IN PEACE TO:
AALIYAH HAUGTON
AUGUST 25, 2001
WE PRAY FOR YOUR FAMILY IN THIS TIME OF GRIEF.
THE WHOLE HIP HOP NATION FEELS THIS TERRIBLE LOSE.
AALIYAH WILL LIVE ON WITH OUR CREW FOREVER AND
SHE WILL BE GREATLY MISSED.

CHAPTER   46

..............COMES AROUND

Mrs. Briar calls Rebbie on the day she returns from Aaliyah's funeral with news she's been waiting to hear.

"You're invited to the New York auditions," Mrs. Briar says, "Will you be able to make it?"

"Oh *yes* ma'am and thank you," Rebbie tells her. "I wouldn't miss this for the world. I've waited my whole life for this opportunity. Thank you *so* much."

"The wait is over. This is a remarkable opportunity," Mrs. Briar says, "So don't mention it. You're absolutely wonderful, darling. Make us proud."

"I will misses Briar and thank you again," Rebbie says before they hang up.

Rebbie has a professional dance audition in New York city. If she makes this cut. She will make pro status and go on a list to be added to major dance tours around the world. Not only that but she'll qualify for funding and the backing she needs to open her own dance studio at CrewLand. Her audition is scheduled for early September. June is totally supportive of this venture. He even promises to help make sure she has all the gear she *thinks* she needs. He also gives her a new credit card so she can really enjoy her time in the *Big Apple*. She'll leaves on September 10th. Her audition is scheduled for 10am, the following morning.

Matt and Farah have dinner at *Crew's house of Soul Food*. The 2001-02 school year started today. Farah is still teaching at MLK where Kenny is now a senior. Matt and Farah have become quite close but still she sees Chill as the ultimate prize. She had the ludicrous idea that dating Matt would make Chill jealous. But actually it has the opposite effect. Matt is looking to become more serious. But Farah isn't. She wants Matt as bait. A lure to dangle in front of Chill at the club. She wants Chill to see her being open to physical activities with a *Black* man. She thinks that'll convince him that she prefers melanin sufficient hues. Her and Matt watch Alana dance after they finish dinner.

"So that's your home girl up there?" Matt asks as they sits near the main stage in *The Juice bar*.

"Yes that's Alana. She's my best friend in the *world*."

"Is she as freaky as she dances?" he asks.

"Even more than *that*," Farah answers as she laughs.
Matt is envisioning a session with him and the 2 of them. He watches Farah as she watches Alana. He notices how turned on they both are. It's turning him on as well. Little do they know. They're both being watched by someone totally inconspicuous.

Ellen slid into the club for happy hour after she had spied on Matt and his white female friend laughing over dinner, at the restaurant. She followed them as they retired to the club for drinks. The more Matt and Farah giggle and lean into each other. The angrier Ellen becomes. She watches them the entire evening until they're ready to leave. She follows them to Farah's home where she sits outside in her car. She has done this for several weeks. On the nights that Matt is here. So is Ellen. Matt has been alternating his free time between Ellen and Farah. Still he hasn't let on to either that he's even seeing the other. This angers Ellen, even more.

On the previous weekend while Ellen waited outside the salon for Matt to finish his shift. A white male had approached her. He was asking questions about a white female whom he said frequented the establishments. He'd said he was looking for his fiancée and thought she might know her.

"I don't hang with white folks," Ellen had said to him. "Do I look like the type who would trust y'all?"
With that answer, the man had gone back to his Porsche 944, gotten in and drove away.

"I don't even know why they come around us when they know they're scared of black people," Ellen had said of the way he'd left so suddenly.

That inquisitor had been *Marvin*. He's getting closer. He just hasn't come through on the right day or time yet. As it was, he was already driving to Cleveland on his off days. Or during any free time he could get away from his father's company. He was spending all of his off time in Cleveland, looking for Farah. He had gone into *Que Psi Phi studio* that same weekend and purchased video equipment with motion sensor detection. He'd given Michelle a description of Farah and asked if she'd been in the store. Michelle knew exactly who she was and still she offered nothing. She has been with Arthur long enough to know better than to offer information to anyone, on anyone without knowing what the angle was. Marvin just saw that as a missed opportunity. He already knew Farah had been to the club. And since patronizing that club, she had completely crossed him out of her life. He's going to stake out the CrewLand mall. He hopes to get Farah on tape, doing something he can use as proof to her parents that she'd been dishonest. First he wants to get a building within the mall, so he can film

288

from his own place of business. And get evidence on Farah, *that* way. But after Ebony had assured him they were a self contained unit. Marvin had purchased office space, farther west. He knows the object of his affection is living here. So there's no question that he'll move here too. But he has to find his love or the move will be entirely empty.

Ajay started his preseason training camp with Jarvis and the Cavaliers, immediately after Labor Day. The Browns will play their 1st regular season game at home, this Sunday. Ebony and Ajay take the twins into preschool on the 10th before he reports to camp. The week before he started camp, Ajay managed to get the twins to sleep in their own bedrooms. Now him and Ebony have their daily schedules in order and they still have a flourishing sex life. He's going to keep it that way.

Nina and Tank have decided to have another baby. She stops her birth control for the month of September.
"Jerica is almost seven years old," Tank says, "She needs a little brother and I want a son."
Nina says, "We have no guarantees that we won't get another girl."
"Well we're gonna keep trying until we get my boy then," Tank says and laughs while Nina gives him a doubtful look.
"You'd better aim straight," she says as she laughs. "We're not gonna have ten girls while trying to get a boy."
"It won't take ten but it might take five," he jokes.
"Then you'll need to have two of them," she laughs.
They meet with Dr. Weston today and make her aware of their plans. She checks Nina out and gives them the go ahead. Everything is in order to get pregnant.

Tuesday September 11 starts off like any normal day for the crew. They had put Rebbie on a flight to New York yesterday and are eager to hear from her this afternoon, about her morning audition. Everyone gets ready for work and school as usual. June is on the phone with Rebbie before her 10am audition on *Park Row*.
"So are you ready to knock 'em dead, baby?" he asks.
"As ready as I'm ever gonna be, honey," she says as she smiles, "I feel confident."
"I'm glad everything worked out okay with Ced's brother and his family," June says.
Rebbie is staying at Bre's brother-in-law Darrell and his wife Charlise's

home with them and their 2 daughters, while she's in New York. Darrell Hamilton and Charlise are the parents of Valene and Aaliyah Hamilton. The 2 flower girls from the triple wedding in 1995 where their uncle Cedric married Breanna. Valene and Aaliyah are 12 and 8 years old now. Their parents work at The World Trade Center as advertisers for 2 very major companies.

"Yes Brian," Rebbie says, "And they're wonderful. They've been so great already. We have to do something for them and invite them down to Cleveland."

"That's a bet. So you've found out where you have to go for the audition and how to get there?" he asks, nervous about his wife moving around in New York city alone.

"Yes. It's on Park Row," she says, "Charlise showed me the route last night. And they took me on a little tour of New York. I rode the subway too. It was great. I went in the twin towers, Empire state building and on the Statue of Liberty ferry boat. I saw Ellis Island and went to Staten Island too," she says looking at her watch. "I have a car coming in five minutes."

"Alright baby. Good luck and call me when it's done. Let us know you got it. Because I know you will," he says, "I have to get to practice too."

"Alright Brian. I love you and kiss Orian for me again tonight. I'm flying home tomorrow."

They hang up and June goes into the bathroom to shower and get ready.

In Shaker Heights, his mother Brenda is watching *MSNBC Morning Joe* on the television before she has to leave for her job at CrewLand Mall. There will be breaking news this morning which will affect not only her life. But the lives of every human being in the world.

June comes out of the bathroom 40 minutes later and glances at the muted TV in their bedroom.
What movie is this?

He wonders aloud as he pulls on his t-shirt. His cell phone rings and he answers to his mother Brenda, who's frantic on the other end.

"June have you talk to Rebbie?" she asks in a panic.

"Yes ma'am. About an hour ago," he says, "Why?"

"Are you watching the TV? A plane crashed into one of the world trade centers!" she yells out of breath.

"What?! Is that what I'm watching?" he says, "I got the mute on and I thought this was a movie."

He releases the mute on the TV while his mother continues to speculate.

He becomes transfixed on the image of the tall tower with smoke pouring out of the top windows. There is a gaping hole in the tower which seems to go through to the other side. Then he notices people above that gaping hole, waving towels in an attempt to be seen by someone. *Anyone*!

The house phone is ringing. June answers it, never taking his eyes from this horrible image. It's Rena. She's in a state of panic as well. She's wondering if her daughter has called him.

"No mother-in-law," he says, "I talk to her like an hour ago. She was leaving for her audition."

"I've been calling her cell phone and getting her voice mail," Rena cries, "Oh my God! I need to know if she's okay. Isn't her audition near the Trade Center?"

"Park Row," he states in a low voice.

His mind has started to wonder away from the conversation his mother and mother-in-law are having. His mind goes in 500 hundred directions at once.

"That's right under the towers, isn't it June?" Rena asks tearfully and bringing his attention back to them.

"Yes but she'll have time to get out. *Damn*! What the-!" he yells as all 3 of them witness a 2nd plane hit the 2nd tower. He becomes anxious and yells, "We're under attack! I have to go get my wife!"

He hangs up with both of them without saying goodbye. His focus is only on Rebbie, at this point. He's wondering where she is and how frightened she must be. His phones continue to ring as he throws on his clothes and grabs his keys. He takes his cell phone and dials Rebbie repeatedly. There's no answer.

June heads to the airport while listening to reports on *WZAK FM 93.1* and hearing other Americans reacting to the events he'd just witnessed on his TV. His cell phone continues to ring. He looks at the caller ID. He isn't answering for anyone except Rebbie, at this point. He makes it to Cleveland-Hopkins International airport and tries to book a flight to New York. But he's told that due to the terrorist attacks in New York and Washington DC, all flights are cancelled for the remainder of the day.

"A strike in *DC* too?" he asks.

He'd missed that one. It happened as he was driving to the airport.

"A third plane has hit the pentagon," the ticket agent tells him.

He leaves the airport and heads back to Jackson heights, thinking Rebbie may try to call their home. But when he arrives back, he notice all of his crew are converging on his home. Hoping he's heard from Rebbie.

"A fourth plane just crashed in Pennsylvania, man," Ajay tells him, "That one was suppose to hit the White House or the Capitol Building."

TIME TO KNOW-RELOADED-Time Will Reveal- part 4

"We're under attack," Ebony adds, "I'm gonna bring the twins home."
Her, Nina and T-baby are already crying. They're worried for Rebbie's safety.
"I wanna know where my sister is," Nina cries.
"She's alright," June says, trying to reassure her and himself. He adds, "She'll call me soon."
He opens their front door and lets everyone come inside. They turn on all of the TV's to local news, MSNBC and CNN. That's when Bre calls him from Atlanta with horrible news.
"Cedric's brother Darrell and his wife Charlise work in the first tower, you guys," Bre says, "His office is on the ninety second floor and Charlise's is on the eighty second floor."
"Oh no," June says as he remembers where he'd seen that gaping hole in the 1st tower. "Oh no!" he repeats.
The others inquire about the news he's getting from Bre and he relays the information to them, just as Bre tells it to him.
"There is no way he made it out," Tank says sadly, "I think that's where the first plane hit or just below that."
"That hole trapped everybody that was above it," Chill says.
"That's a horrible way to die," Renee says.
She's in tears now and has to stop watching. Seeing folks waving towels from a mile high in the air with no viable means of rescue is more than any of them can take. Suddenly Ebony screams out and turns her eyes away from the TV.
"Oh God! Anthony they're jumping out of the windows," Ebony cries as Ajay grabs her and holds her tight. "Oh my God! Oh my God!"
The crew watch television in horror as person after desperate person, jumps to their certain death while escaping what has to be unbearable heat and flames. This sight is enough to bring all of them to tears. They watch in horror as things just continue to get worse.
"Oh my God! It's falling!" Nina screams as they watch the 1st tower collapse to rubble.
"Oh man. Oh man," June whispers to himself and feeling panic.
He's even more afraid and concerned as he wonders if his wife is trapped somewhere underneath that pile of rubble which was tower 1.
"Oh God please let them be alright," Tonya whispers.
"Baby, anybody that's in and around that building is gone," Jr offers, "If not from the fire and smoke. Then they got crushed to death."
He says that without thinking of June's agony. He's fixed on the television.

292

Much like the rest of the world. Then he remembers Rebbie's audition is near these burning towers and he looks at June. June's in pain. He's crying.

"I have to know if Ree Ree is okay," June says somberly.

He contacts every person of power that he knows. Hoping 1 of his colleagues can get him through to New York city. They all assure him they're going to do their very best to get him some answers. Meanwhile things are only getting worse.

"There goes the other one," Ajay says, just as June hangs up. "This is bad. *Real* bad," he says as he still cradles his wife.

"I wanna talk to my sister," Ebony cries, "Please God. Let her be alright!"

The crew leaves for work at the mall. They'll all still watch the continuing coverage of the attacks. June leaves with his crew, after he'd gotten excused from practice. They have TV's on throughout the mall as they watch the news and hope to hear something about the people in the buildings which still stand next to the where the towers stood. They stay on cell phones and communicate to each other, whatever new news they get.

"They just said there are other buildings on fire too," Chill offers as he, June and most of the crew gather at The Spot. "Where was Rebbie's audition? Park Row?"

"Yea man," June whispers as his voice is nearly nonexistent now.

"That's what they're showing right now," T-baby says, "Look at all the people running to safety. Do y'all see Rebbie?"

"I can't tell who's who. They're all covered in soot," June says with hope in his tone. "I hope she's in one of those crowds of people."

"Me too," Kim says.

Her and Chaundra had left their classes at Ohio State and come home to be with their crew. Bruce and Eric McNair come by after practice. Many of the Browns players come with them to show support for June. Ally and Steven have gone to mama Rena's house to wait for news from Rebbie.

Finally in the afternoon, the Mayor of New York gives a statement. There is no way they can estimate the casualties, at this time. He says many firefighters, policemen and emergency workers perished in the towers. Countless employees and employers of the many businesses which called The World Trade Centers home, have perished. Or may be trapped in the rubble. He also said the circuits are tied up and it's impossible to get phone lines in or out of the New York City area.

"Please God don't let my wife be dead or hurt and can't nobody find her," June prays.

"Do you think mister Parkwood can fly us out there?" Ajay asks.

293

TIME TO KNOW-RELOADED-Time Will Reveal- part 4

"He can't get no planes in the air either," June says somberly, "I tried him as soon as I left the airport. There was nothing flying but Air Force One and military personnel."

"They flew the Bin Laden family out earlier," Ebony says, "Why would they do that and not let us fly?"

No one has an answer. Though many of them guess that it had something to do with the attacks.

The crew and their families spent more than 10 hours watching the catastrophe of September 11, 2001. All day they were alternating calls on their phones. Calling Rebbie. Calling New York and anyone. Just trying not to feel so helpless. They spent the entire work day watching coverage and making phone calls. It's the close of the day for many of them. As they head home, still they haven't heard any news on Rebbie.

By nightfall, news reporters in New York are interviewing people on the streets. There are hundreds of families out there making pleas for lost loved ones. Ajay and Ebony are home with their twins. They're still transfixed on today's attacks. They sit in the 2nd story of their family room watching the projection size TV with Lil Ajay, Lannie, Ike and Tina. All of sudden Ebony screams.

"There's Rebbie! I see her! Oh my God! There's my sister!"

She breaks into joyous tears as Ajay dials June's phone immediately and finds out June had been watching a different network.

"Hey man. Rebbie is about to talk on *MSNBC*. Baby girl just saw her waiting to speak," he says, totally relieved, "She should be on right after the commercial break."

June immediately switches channels as Ebony alerts the others to switch to MSNBC. They all see Rebbie doing an interview and sending a message to her husband, daughter and all of her crew family.

"I'm Rebbie Shantell Wilson-James. I'm from Cleveland Ohio. I was here for an audition on Park Row when all of this happened. I wanna let my daughter Orian, my husband Brian James junior of the Cleveland Browns, my family and all my crew at The CrewLand mall know that I am alright," she says as she looks really exhausted but not hurt. She continues, "I'm still out here trying to find the family that I'm staying with here in New York City. Charlise and Darrell Hamilton."

She holds up their wedding photo that she had gone back and gotten from their house. She holds it up and continues, "They worked on the eighty second and ninety second floors of the South Tower. I'm still waiting to hear some news. I want my family to know that I'm alive and I'm not hurt."

Bre is calling June on the house phone. The crew down in Atlanta have seen

Rebbie on TV also. They are all relieved that she's alive and okay. But they have little hope that Cedric's brother and his sister-in-law survived.

"I've been trying to call home but I can't get a line out yet," Rebbie continues, "I've got to do something about their daughters and I'm not even sure of how to get to them."
June is relieved to see his wife in 1 piece. He has Bre on 1 phone and Ajay on the other one.

"My mother-in-law and father-in-law have already gotten the girls," Bre says, "They was at school, down there. They picked them up at a make shift emergency unit."

"I wish I could let Ree know so she could get from down there," June says, "I want my baby home *now*."

"Ebony's calling MSNBC. That's the network Rebbie is talking too," Ajay tells June, "She's gonna see if they can get a message to her, that way."

"Thank you cousin!!" June shouts loud enough for Ebony to hear him from Ajay's phone.

Later as Ebony puts the twins to bed, Ajay is still watching the news coverage. Hoping to hear that someone had been pulled from the debris alive. His hope fades after 3am.

In New York, Cedric's parents have come to Darrell's home with the girls. Rebbie has made her way back to Darrell's home also. They sit and wait for some news. As each hour passes, it brings to light the grim reality that their love ones had perished in the towers. Sedina Hamilton, Darrell and Cedric's mother, notices the message light blinking on the answering machine. She retrieves the messages. There are 2. 1 is from Charlise and 1 is from Darrell. They had called home from the burning towers. In each message they're saying what George, Darrell and Cedric's father had already concluded. They were *"trapped in the tower. It was on fire and the stairs were gone!"*
Sedina breaks down and so does Rebbie. It's chilling to listen too. Rebbie can hear mayhem in the background of both their voice messages. People are screaming and coughing and praying. And then more coughing and screaming and praying. It was the most horrible thing she's ever heard in her life. At this point, she just wants to go home to her family, hug her daughter and get out of New York city.

It is nearly dawn before Rebbie gets a line clear. She calls June, first thing. He has been up all night, waiting to hear from her.

"Hello baby!" he yells, elated when he sees her cell phone number on his caller ID.

She starts to cry, just hearing his voice and knowing how worried he must've been.

She finally says, "I'm alright Brian. But I can't get a flight out yet."

"Baby I love you. I love you. I love you. I love you so much. I want you to come home as soon as you can," he says, "I'm flying out there to meet you. So wait for me to get there. Okay?"

She agrees she'll wait so they can fly back home together. They only have 15 minutes to talk before the weak connection goes dead. She attempts the call again but can't get another line open. June calls the crew to tell them he's talk to Rebbie, she's fine and waiting for him to come and get her.

June flies out late night September 12th when the ticket agents open back up. George Hamilton and Rebbie meet him at the airport. He hugs Rebbie for more than 15 minutes. Then they decide, right then and there that instead of packing up her things. They want to help with the search and rescue.

All day on the September 13, Rebbie and June help out at *Ground Zero*, alongside Sedina, George plus Bre and Cedric who'd flown in the night before also. Bre and Ced flew in to help with the search. But they know Darrell and Charlise are dead. They have 2 daughters left behind to grow up without their parents.

It's September 17th before Rebbie and June return home. They had stayed and attended the service for Darrell and Charlise, before going home. Bre and Cedric stay in New York for 10 days and attend the memorial services for not only their lost loved ones but many others. Before she can even leave New York, Bre has already gotten word that she's on standby for possible U.S. military action against *Al-Quieda*.

Al Quieda is a terrorist organization *supposedly* headed by Osama Bin Laden. The same name of the family that was flown out on the day of the attacks. George Bush had blamed terrorist for this horrific act. Bre has to get back to her base. Her and Cedric fly home on the 23rd and take Valene and Aaliyah with them.

As if the terrorist attacks wasn't enough. Anthrax is now in the mail stream. The post office workers, magazine editors and Senator Daschle have been affected by it. Aunt Jessica's plant had a scare today too. Her and all of the employees at her installation had to be evacuated and was sent home for several days until the property could be deemed safe to work in again. A friend of Jessica's from the Brentwood Post Office lost her husband to anthrax.

TIME TO KNOW-RELOADED-Time Will Reveal- part 4

"The world can't go on much longer like this," Jessica tells Jo via a phone call from Boston.

"My gut tells me this is all happening because Bush stole the damn White House," Jo says, very agitated and Jessica agrees with her.

"Either that or just because he's in there and other countries know how crooked they are," Jessica says.

"Jessica I'm really worried about you," Jo says, "Please be careful. You're the only immediate family Allen has left."

"I know and it's times like these that makes me so happy that you helped us to overcome our differences," Jessica says, "You are alright with me, Jo. There was never anything wrong with you. It was me."
Jo thanks her for her sincere words. Jessica talks to Al for a long time before they hang up.

In Atlanta, Valene and Aaliyah stay with Bre and Cedric for 2 weeks before Cedric flies the 3 of them back to New York. The girls are going to live with his parents in Jamaica Queens. Ced returns to Atlanta in time to celebrate CJ's 10th birthday.

For Ajay's 1st preseason game, Ebony buys him a gift to officially welcome him home and to the home team, the *Cleveland Cavaliers*. Ajay's gift is a Black with cream leather interior, 2002 Mercedes Benz CL500 with 22 inch Sprewell rims. He loves his new car.

"I got my own little car lot up in here," he says and chuckles.
He still has the 1964 Classic Chevy ragtop. The 1978 Cadillac Seville and the Jaguar, all of which he keeps in the garages of the guest house. He only drives them on special occasions. He still enters them in Crew Details Car Show, yearly. He keeps the Grand Cherokee in their main garage next to Ebony's 2000 Escalade.

"We still got room for one more car, baby girl," he jokes.

"I see that but I'm okay with my caddy trunk, daddy," she laughs, "We can hold off for a while. We're doing it big enough."
They now have a boat, jet ski's and ATV's. They have 2 go-carts, 1 pink and 1 blue for their twins. Lil Ajay has driven his. Lannie hasn't yet.
The residence of Jackson Heights have added many upgrades to the community, including a park for the kids, another lake and a catfish pond.

"We got our community looking elegant," T-baby boasts, "Rich want even recognize this place when he comes home."
Her girls laugh as they finish their lunch at her and Rich's home.
"Madison-by-the-lake ain't got nothing on us, baby," she says with a smile.

TIME TO KNOW-RELOADED-Time Will Reveal- part 4

The war in Afghanistan starts in October. President George W Bush has declared war on terrorism, an inanimate object and targeted that country as a haven for terrorist training camps. He also claims that is where Osama Bin Laden is hiding out. The crew don't buy into this sale. They feel like Americans have been duped and are hanging on the Bush administrations every word. Bush is introducing bills and passing measures which will conceal his presidential actions. He creates the homeland security office in the crews opinion, to put another 1 of his personal colleagues in a powerful position. This further infuriates them and many more Americans. Furthermore anyone that speaks out against George W Bush and his administration's decisions are labeled unpatriotic by Bush, his administration and mainly, conservative talk radio. That won't last forever though.

As if that wasn't enough to aggravate the crew. Lynn's Squadron has been called to arms. Lynn is going to war. She'll leave the last week of October for Afghanistan.

"I swear I don't want my baby to go over there," Jo says, "This is not a *just* fight and I know it."

"I don't want her to go either Jo," Al says, "I didn't even want her to stay in *[the military]* but she wanted this career."

"It's a great career as long as there isn't a republican oil man in office," Jo snaps, "Just like his daddy when he was in office. We're gonna invade someone else's property."

Lynn, Jb and John III come home to visit before her departure date. The crew have a party for her at the club. Many of her high school, college and Olympic track teammates come to see her off. Julie Von Reese is 1 of the guest. There is still no sign of James "The Bulldog" Taylor. Julie doesn't mention him. Nor do the crew. It's like he was never there.

There is a happier announcement at the party. Nina is expecting a baby. Her and Tank have conceived their 2nd child.

"I had to get one in there, sis," Tank jokes with Lynn, "I'm trying to catch up with Ajay and Chill." *Their due date is May 25, 2002*.

"I'll be back to Christian this one," Lynn promises.

"You'd better come back," Nina says as her eyes well up with tears. She's scared for her sister but Lynn is ready to do her duty.

"I wish this was like that morning after Jb's sixteenth birthday party," she says, "When mama and daddy was looking for you. I was crying then too but you was closer."

"She was in our bedroom," Tank laughs, "Go hide in there Lynn." They have a good laugh and then Lynn puts their minds at ease. She's

298

ready to go. This is what she has trained for, for all of these years. She wants the combat situation in a foreign land. She'll be on the intelligence team in Afghanistan.

"Just know this. My squad is gonna get the truth for y'all!" she says during her speech at the celebration. "We're gonna keep it real for all of you guys and get some answers to this madness!"

Her Squadron leaves on the 29th of October headed to Kabul Afghanistan. The crew put up a huge map at the CrewLand mall and the Crew Complex in Atlanta, so they, their customers and their clients can keep up with Lynn's location.

Kenny is having another all-star football season. Him and Brandon's MLK team are a definite pick to win the high school state championship next month. Kenny has already signed a letter of intent with Ohio State. Chill, Renee and Destiny have made every game, along with Al and John.

"We've got another one going to the pro's," Al brags.

"I know that's right, man," John says as they watch MLK roll over Smith high school 35-0.

The Farah Benson affair has cooled off some. Only because Kenny has avoided her. But it isn't over by a long shot. It's about to heat up to record temperature's within the next few weeks. By the time MLK goes to the state tournament, there's a murder plot underway.

By the 1st week in November, Wesley has been placed on standby. His reserve unit may see action in Afghanistan. Bre's Platoon is still on Standby. She's been working detail at Hartsfield International airport. For now, Wesley has been ordered to do the same detail at Cleveland-Hopkins. Lynn has been in Afghanistan for a week. No one's heard a word from her.

****

"Ebony I'm on the way to pick up Lil Ant and Lannie," Jo says from her cell phone.

"Okay mama Jo. They're ready to go," she says.

Ebony has planned a romantic dinner for her and Ajay.

"Daddy and I are gonna have some private time tonight," she says to her twins. "And you two are going to see your grandmothers for the weekend." The twins are busy playing with their toys in their downstairs playroom.

299

Ebony is prepping items for dinner. Jo and Pearl arrive and Ebony lets them come in through the kitchen door.

"Hello mothers," she says with a smile.

"Hey baby girl," Pearl says, "You're in a great mood today."

"Yes. She is. *Isn't* she?" Jo adds.

"I'm looking forward to having my husband to myself tonight," she says with a big smile.

"It's a Saturday night. What are y'all gonna do? Go to the club?" Pearl ask as she smiles.

"We're not leaving this house," she says as she grins.

"Uh huh," Pearl smiles.

She's looking at Ebony with that suspicious look, mothers have. Then her and Jo head into the playroom to see the twins as Ebony follows them.

"How is mama Jo's babies?" Jo says to the twins as Lil Ajay and Lannie hurry to them.

"Hi sweethearts!" Pearl says as she grabs up Lannie and gives her a kiss.

Jo picks up Lil Ajay and kisses him. Then they kiss to the other twin.

"Are y'all ready to run away with us?" Jo asks Lannie.

"I wanna go," Lannie says clearly.

"She can speak so well," Jo says, "To be twenty seven months."

"I know," Ebony agrees, "Me and Anthony was talking about that the other night. She's already using full sentences."

"Mama said she's getting out the way for another baby," Pearl says with a smile.

"Not yet, she's not," Ebony says, "She's gonna be the youngest for a while."

"Lil Ajay is still acting like her bodyguard," Jo laughs, "Pushing the other kids away from her."

"Yes he is," Ebony says as she laughs. "He gets that from his daddy. Anthony drills that into him all the time."

"Ant gets that from Allen," Jo says as she smiles, "He drilled it into him too. He had to protect his sisters. Even though Lynora is older."

"He's still that way," Ebony says returning the smile, "But Lynn protects him too. She's very protective of her *only* brother. And I love that about her. Plus she's got my back too."

"They're close," Pearl adds, "Just like you and Tank."

Jo and Pearl are packing the twins things into the van. Ebony kisses her twins before fastening them into their car seats.

"Be good for your grannies," she says.

300

TIME TO KNOW-RELOADED-Time Will Reveal- part 4

"Okay mommy," Lannie says.

"Kay mommy," Lil Ajay repeats.

"We'll get them after church on Sunday," Ebony says.

"Are they going to the football game?" Pearl asks.

"Oh no. That's right," Ebony says as she recalls the big game.

"We'll keep them until they get ready to come home," Jo tries, "How about that?"

"We'll get them after the game," Ebony says with a smile, "Anthony's not gonna let them stay out. Not on a school night."

"They go to Granny's house," Pearl says, "We *can* take them, you know?"

"I know but Anthony isn't gonna let them stay on a Sunday night," Ebony reiterates.

She knows her mother and mother-in-law love to keep all of their grandkids. The only problem with that is. Once they get them to Shaker Heights. They never want them to leave.

"You ladies be careful with my babies," Ebony says as she laughs.

"They're our babies now," Pearl says as she laughs too.

She gets into the van with Jo. Jo starts up and they drive away while Ebony waves.

}CrewLand Mall{

Chill has a brief meeting with Farah in his office. Renee is in her office recording it. Chill wants to make Farah aware of the new investment offer from Jackson's Real Estate. It's the insurance agency and flooring store which is coming soon to Brook Park. Farah seems interested but wonders why the business is so far away from the CrewLand mall.

"We're expanding," Chill lies, "We wanna lock down the whole city eventually."

"Oh baby. You've got to let me get some of that action," Farah says, very provocatively.

"I'm offering it to you now," he says, "A chance to get in on the ground floor. Once investors find out that Jackson's is offering it. It'll go fast."

"I think I'm an investor of a different kind already," she says.

"Oh? How so?"

"With Kenny's crew. They've made me an investor of their goods," she says with a flirtatious smile.

"I'm not sure what you're talking about-"

"Sure you are," she interrupts, "I know you and your son talk."

301

"Whenever needed. Yes."

"And he hasn't told you how good I am?" she asks.

"Are you interested in the development or not?" he asks, sticking to the business at hand.

"I'm very interested. Can you show me the site?"

He pushes the plans around to her side of his desk. He also has virtual images of the layout on his office computer. It has simulations of how the property will look upon completion.

"Ah I was hoping we could drive out and look at it," she tries.

"Maybe after your bid is posted," he says, trying to lure her into this business with her ex.

"Okay I'm in. I'll talk with my funding source and get back with you," she finally says.

"Actually Ebony Jackson over at-"

"I would like for you to handle it please," she says in an insistent tone, "I'll do the investment. *Only* if I can do it with you on board."

"All of the businesses is my business, miss Benson. Even if I'm not hands on. Investments are not my expertise," he says, "That's Ebony Jackson's specialty."

"I need you to be hands on with my business though," she says, "Or I'm not gonna be comfortable taking part in it."

It takes every ounce of restraint Renee has not to rush into her husbands office and yank that jezebel up out of that leather wing back chair and whip her ass. But she remains in her office recording.

"We'll make sure it's taken care of properly. You can be sure of that," he says as he starts toward his door.

He opens it and stands just to the inside of it. He's letting her know that their meeting is done. She gets up from her chair, takes a business card from his desk and meets him at the door.

"I'm gonna go now. But I want you to know something," she says.

"What's that?"

"It's not just the business that I wanna do with you," she says, "I would really love to do pleasure with you too. I wanna suck your dick so bad it's like I can already taste you."

"I don't share women with my son," he says smugly.

"You wouldn't have too."

"I would rather keep *this, business.* If there's gonna be business," he says, "I never mix the two."

"Well perhaps after the business is done?"

"I'd rather not," he says, "Have a good day miss Benson."

He shows her to the elevator, then joins his wife in her office.

"You had better know that I love you and trust you," Renee says.

"I know baby and you can," he says, pulling her to him and kissing her tenderly on the lips. He says, "Be sure and file that tape with the rest of them."

Renee half smiles, pops the tape out and puts it in the safe. Then she quickly replaces it with a blank one. Her and Chill get on with their morning schedule of getting the club ready for the Saturday night crowds.

Farah leaves the Spot and goes directly to the Spot II. She sees Kenny, Archie Jr and Brandon going inside. She thinks they're going in for leisure activities. She soon finds out that they're there to work as usual. She propositions Kenny immediately.

"I would love it if you would come to my house with me. I've got some work for you out there," she says with a smile.

"Is that right?" Kenny Jr says.

"It certainly is," she purrs.

"I'm on the clock," he says.

"But you own the place, right?"

Officer Larry Davidson of Jacobson security is doing his opening walk through and notice her inside. He comes to her and asks her business.

"May I help you?"

"No thank you. I was talking to the gentleman," Farah says.

"We're not in hours of operation yet. Not until noon," Davidson says, "You'll have to come back then."

"I'm an investor with this family," she snaps, "I think that gives me the right to check out my investment. Don't you?"

"Yes it would. If that were so," he snaps back, "But I haven't been informed about any new people that are scheduled to drop by. The owners here, they do that."

"Sounds like you need to call your bosses then," she says smugly.

Even though Davidson knows this is a bogus claim. He gets on his radio and calls Renee. She tells him Farah has no special privileges at CrewLand mall.

"She needs to be escorted from the arcade," Renee says, "Do you need me to come over?"

"No misses Payne. I can handle it," he says and he does.

He escorts Farah to the door and explains the rules and procedures to her. She uses some foul language.

Then she tells Kenny, "Call me when you get a break."

He blows her off and goes on to work. Farah is heading to her car. Chaundra, who's home for the weekend, pulls up with Charlotte and Brina.

TIME TO KNOW-RELOADED-Time Will Reveal- part 4

"Crew we need to beat her ass," Chaundra says giving Farah the evil stare.

Farah wisely gets into her BMW and quickly pulls away, screeching her tires intentionally as she leaves the parking lot.

"We can get her whenever you want too, big sis," Charlotte says.

"Crew needs to get that handled quick," Brina says, "I know when I get to tenth grade next year. She's gonna be all up in my grill. And I'm punching her ass if she gets on my nerves."

"Dick riding the crew," Chaundra says in anger. "I'm a graduate of MLK now. Which means I can whoop her ass without consequence."

The 3 young ladies go into the Spot II and meet up with their guys. Charlotte dates June's baby brother Brandon. He's the twin of Brina, who dates Rebbie's youngest brother Archie Jr. They talk about the negative vibe Farah Benson brings when she surfaces, as they go about their duties.

}Jackson Heights{

Ebony is home alone. Except for Ike and Tina, who are playing ankle tag with her. She lets them out into the yard when she begins to cook.

"Now let me get this dinner going," she says to herself after going back into the house.

The house phone is ringing.

"Hello," she says, answering the phone in the kitchen.

"Hey sis! What's up?!"

"*Lynn*?!"

"Yes it's me! What's going on?" Lynn asks.

"What's going on with *you*?"

"We're doing okay over here, for now," Lynn says, "We're not really seeing any action yet. And no Bin Laden either. It's just a bunch of mountains and forest."

It's Friday November 10th and Lynn has been in Afghanistan for 11 days. She tells Ebony she'd called mama Jo's house first but didn't get an answer. She has already talk with Jb and the crew in Atlanta.

"Mama Jo left here fifteen minutes ago," Ebony tells her, "Her and mama came to get the twins for the weekend."

"So are you and Ajay trying to have a wild night of passionate fucking or what?" Lynn asks as she laughs.

"You already know what's up," Ebony replies with a grin.

"Yes I do. That's why I said it," Lynn confirms as she giggles.

Ajay comes in from practice while they're still on the phone. He gives Ebony a kiss, then takes the phone and talks to his oldest sister. He's happy

304

to hear her in such great spirits. He has a lot of questions for her about the war. Ebony goes back to her cooking duties while Ajay talks to Lynn. After about 20 minutes of thorough questioning, he turns his attention back to Ebony.

"Baby girl do you think mama has made it home yet?" he asks.

"They was stopping to buy ice cream first. But they should be home by now," she says, "You're gonna try to get her on the three way?"

"Yea."

They call mama Jo's house and Lynn gets a chance to talk to her mother, father, Pearl, John, Pam, Sam Jr plus the twins. She's happy to hear Lannie and lil Ajay talking.

"Oh my God. Lannie talks as well and Lil John does," she laughs.

"That's little Ebony, right there," Al says as they all laugh.

Before she has to hang up, she says, "Tell Nina I'll call her tomorrow night at seven, her time. Alright?"

Then they all say their goodbyes and Lynn goes back to her duties. Ajay goes to pick up a nice gift for his wife while she prepares dinner.

}CrewLand Mall{

Ajay stops in at Crew Cuts and Styles to give Nina the message from Lynn. The shop is bustling with clients like a typical late Saturday morning.

"I can't wait to hear from her," Nina says, "So she's doing okay over there?"

"Yea she's straight, so far," Ajay tells her.

Just as he's preparing to leave, Ellen blows through the door. Matt had blown off a date with her last night. Once again, she'd seen his car at Farah's house. She comes into the salon, very irate. Slinging accusations at him and insinuating that the crew are involved and covering for him.

"What happened to you last night!?" she yells to Matt while standing in front of his station.

"Something came up," he tries.

"You mean some white bitch came up-"

"-You will need to leave here with that drama, Ellen," Nina says immediately. "We have customers here who expect professional service."

"Oh so you think it's okay for him to run around on me with some white tramp too, ha? What part do y'all play in it? Y'all the ones who probably brought her scraggly haired ass around here," Ellen continues.

"You'd better check yourself," Tonya warns.

"So is your problem, him running around on you? Or is it more

305

because you think the woman is white that he's suppose to be running with?" Justine asks as she strains to hold in her giggle.

"What do you think? How would you like it if some white woman was taking over your relationship-"

"-Ellen that kind of bigoted talk is not allowed on these premises. Okay?" Tonya says, "We have white family members. Did you know that? Yes. Our aunt Rena and her entire family is white. So we really don't appreciate the negative talk about anyone. And definitely not based on their race."

"So white folks are the ones who got y'all in the position to open up a mall?" Ellen asks, "Is that why you're taking up for them?"

"No. Our families raised us to be entrepreneurs," Nina says, "We owned this mall before we was born. We grew up knowing that we had to do something with this place."

"Niggaz are only raised to be niggaz," Ellen retorts, intentionally sounding callous, "And niggaz should know better than to mix with devils."

"Ellen you need counseling," Tonya says as she smiles.

"Or Jesus," Justine adds.

"Both," Nina says as she laughs.

"So is the white bitch-. Excuse me. Is the bitch he's fucking around with related to you too?" Ellen asks.

"I don't know what you're talking about," Tonya tells her, "But you will need to keep your language pg and your personal life out of this shop from now on or you will be banned," Tonya says, "Do you understand me?"

"Ellen you're just as much of a bigot as the ones you're trying to complain about," Nina adds as Justine, Ajay and Tonya agree.
Matt says nothing while the ladies fight his battle for him. Actually he doesn't know what to say. He's caught up and Ellen has just made his personal business public. The ladies in Crew Cuts had no idea that he had been seeing Farah outside of the shop. But once they get Ellen off of the premises, they grill Matt about 2 things. 1. Ellen and her disruptive behavior. 2. About the way they had to find out he was seeing Farah. He's embarrassed as he gives up the details. Ajay takes this opportunity to leave. He doesn't want to hear about Matt's love triangle. There's way to much drama in the beauty salon for him.

"I'll have to keep my wife out of here," he says as he laughs, "Nina you'll have to do her hair at our house, *only*. If it's gonna be like this."
He heads out the door on his way to a jewelry store to find a nice piece of jewelry for Ebony. *Just because.*

TIME TO KNOW-RELOADED-Time Will Reveal- part 4

Over at The Chill Spot, the early afternoon visitors aren't getting any better then they had been this morning. Chill has another guest in to see him that he isn't enthusiastic about. No more than he was with Farah.

"Chill there's a Marvin Huntley here to see you," Kim calls over the radio, as she works her weekend job.

"Who?" Chill asks.

He knows the name but doesn't want to give that away. Kim repeats the name per his request. Chill is on the 2nd floor stocking the bar and buying time. He tells Kim he'll be down to greet Mr. Huntley momentarily. Then he leaves Jr and Wayne to do the bar backs and brings Kilo with him. They head to the main floor. Marvin Huntley decides to come on into the club after he had lightly questioned crew at all of the other businesses except the arcade. 1 by 1, he has managed to stop in at each of the businesses at CrewLand to inquire about Farah. Intentionally he saves the 2 clubs for last. No one gave him any leads at any of the other stops and they had all communicated his mission to the rest of the family, of course. Chill knew he would be stopping in, eventually. He knew Marvin would soon come to the source of whom *he thinks* is the *meat* of his problem. Which Marvin sees as the main reason why his college sweetheart has packed up her things and skipped states. He has to see what this nigger looks like whom he thinks he has lost his woman too. Chill and Kilo finally arrive on the main floor.

"Hello mister Huntley. How may I help you?" Chill asks as Kilo gives Marvin the once over.

"I was just wondering how could I get one of these?" Marvin asks as he holds up a frequent partygoer card.

Chill explains the procedures, even though he knows that isn't really the nature of Marvin's visit. Marvin had plans of asking about Farah. But after seeing Chill, he knew without a doubt that Farah had been here. And Chill was most likely the nigger who was the object of her defection from Pittsburgh. Marvin doesn't ask anymore questions. He decides he'll come back tonight and try to catch Farah in action.

}Parma to Jackson Heights{

Alana and Farah are at their house in Parma. Scheming as usual, on a way to garner some attention from Tank and Chill. Alana had found out where they lived from some students at CSU. She knows the directions to Jackson Heights and wants Farah to drive her out there to view it.

"It's not that far from their mall or from Shaker Heights. Where they all grew up," Alana says, "We can take Rockside road to Highway eighty seven. It's off of that highway somewhere."

307

TIME TO KNOW-RELOADED-Time Will Reveal- part 4

"It's not on a map?" Farah asks.

"No. It's a new suburb. They named it Jackson Heights. After Angel's man, Ajay.

"Do you mean *Ebony's* man?" Farah asks as she giggles.

"Whatever," Alana says, "They made their own neighborhood, girlfriend. It's all over campus that the crew is taking over Cleveland."

"My man just told me this morning, that they plan to spread out," Farah says, "Huh, let's go check it out and see if I can find Payne on a mailbox."

They hop into her car and head East. They ride out past Maple and Bedford Heights, then jump onto interstate 271. Go northeast to highway 87 and get off just south of Moreland Hills. They see a sign which reads; Jackson Heights next right. They take that right and drive a bit farther until they see the arrow pointing to the entrance. Farah doesn't turn in because she notices a guard gate and booth. She goes on up a bit farther and U-turns at the entrance to South Chagrin Reservation. Her and Alana head back toward 271 on Miles road. At 271, she heads north to 87 and on to CrewLand Mall.

"They got a guard on that shit," Alana says somberly and disappointed.

"You should've known that," Farah says, "They *are* prominent citizens, you know?"

They both laugh as they turn off of 87 onto Lee road and into the mall.

"I don't have to be at work for three more hours," Alana says, "Lets go back out there and see what the guard tells us."

"We need to think of what we can say to get in there," Farah suggests, "Like for instance, we're here to look at some property."

"Do you think that'll work? Maybe you should say we're meeting one of them out there," Alana suggests.

"They'll just call them," Farah says, "We'll just go back and see what the regulations are for buying out there."

They head back to Jackson Heights. Neither of them notice the navy blue Buick Regal rental car that pulls out behind them. Farah drives while her and Alana crack jokes and pretend to be heading home to their husbands. This time when they arrive at the *"turn here"* sign, Farah turns in. Only she stops just shy of the gate. The crew has a small parking lot, just outside of the gate which is extra parking for their security detail. Farah just happens to find the gate to that lot while it's opened. She pulls in and parks but doesn't kill the engine. The rental car had gone on past the entrance and down to South Chagrin to U-turn. In the rental car, Marvin waits down the

308

road. He's waiting to see if Farah pulls out again. Or if she goes in. After about 5 minutes, Farah pulls out of the parking lot and heads back to the mall. She wants to think of a better way to approach the gate. Perhaps after she invests, then she can get invited to a dinner party or something and gain passage. Then she would be *known* by the guards.

"Then I can go in and out at my leisure," she says.

"That might work," Alana says, "Let's go eat at Crew's House. Before I have to clock in. It's my treat."

"I'm with that one, girlfriend," Farah smiles.

They laugh and head back. After seeing the entrance to Jackson Heights, Marvin thinks for sure that it must be where his ex has moved too. A very nice upscale neighborhood with lakes, ponds, a bike trail, pool, a park and a covered cookout area. He feels sure this is where she must be living. He decides he'll approach the gate and say he's going to Farah Benson's house. He pulls forward and Jacobson leaves the arm down and the steel gate closed.

"May I help you?" Jacobson asks.

"I wanted to visit my close friend. She showed me the way out here. But she had to run an errand first. Can I wait at her home or should I wait here?"

"Who is the friend?" Jacobson asks.

"Farah Benson."

"What's your name?"

"Marvin. Marvin Huntley."

"Hang on here just a minute."

Jacobson closes his window and calls Ebony at home.

"There's a Caucasian man at the gate saying he wants to come in to visit that woman who's causing problems for Chill and Renee. His name is Marvin Huntley. The same guy who has been snooping around at the mall. We got his name on record."

"Let him know he's at the wrong place and send him packing," Ebony says, "He's the ex roommate and fiancée of Farah Benson. He's still trying to track her down. She must've been in the area, for him to be out here. Or maybe he's finally investigating us. We're gonna help him find her regardless. But not like this," Ebony says as she giggles.

She tells Jacobson to let him know that he's at the wrong place. Before they hang up, she says, "We'll be stocking your refrigerators tomorrow."

Jacobson thanks her and they hang up. Then he gets rid of Marvin Huntley.

"Sir. There's no one by that name who resides here," he tells Marvin, "This community is privately owned and operated by family."

309

"That seems to be the theme around Cleveland," he says, "May I ask by whom?"

"You can ask. But sir if that was for your knowledge. Then you'd already know," Jacobson tells him as officers McDaniel and Bronson approach the gate.

Marvin backs up and leaves the area. He heads back to CrewLand Mall.

}CrewLand Mall{

After they eat, Farah walks Alana to work. They go upstairs to The Juice bar. They haven't given up on gracing Jackson Heights. They just have to come up with a better angle. Alana has to go backstage to prepare for work. Then she'll come back out and talk to Farah until time for her to dance. Farah goes across the street to the Spot II to kill a few minutes until her girlfriend can come back out. She goes to the concession stand and talks to Kenny. He isn't too interested in talking to her. Especially not with Chaundra and the rest of his crew there. He plays her off.

Outside, Marvin arrives. He spots her car and drives on through the lot. He's looking into the windows to see which business she's in. At the Spot II, you can see in as far as concessions. He spots her talking to Kenny, so he parks his rental car away from her car. But he allows himself to have a good view inside. From there, he watches Farah as she makes nice with the young crew. Inside, Crew Y2K aren't thrilled to see her.

"You're stupid miss Benson," Archie Jr says, "We don't want your company but you keep coming around. Go hang with the grown folks." They laugh.

"I'm trying to hang on to my youth," she says and laughs to shield her embarrassment.

She soon realizes Kenny isn't going to acknowledge her. Not with Chaundra present. She buys a soda. After she's done with it, she goes back to The Spot to hook back up with Alana. After she has left, Marvin gets out of his car and walks into The Spot II and approaches the concession stand.

"May I help you sir?" Brina asks.

"That lady that was just in here. Does she work here?"

"Who are you?" Brandon asks.

"I'm a guy who thinks she's cute. I would like to know how I can speak with her."

Marvin's testing the young water since he hasn't been able to get any information out of the older folks. He tries his luck with the youth.

"I think you should've asked her," Charlotte says.

"I ain't no snitch, player," Archie Jr says, "You must be five oh.

310

Coming all up in here questioning us. You got the wrong spot, *Kojak*."

They all laugh as he prepares to exit. He feels as though he's been disrespected and these urban youth should feel honored that a prominent Caucasian business owner would be in their presence. But instead, they're whooping and hollering back and forth and cracking wise on him.

"I didn't think I was in the hood. But apparently I am," he says arrogantly.

"It can get *real* hood if you'd like," Kenny says, "Try something fool."

"You got an attitude about that tramp. Like she's high and mighty or something," Chaundra adds, "She's a slut and a teacher. And not that good of a teacher."

"I'll bet you could recognize a tramp and slut well. Couldn't you?" Marvin asks Chaundra and that pisses Kenny off.

"Hold up one muthafuckin minute. Don't disrespect my girl."

"Oh. Sorry. I thought y'all referred to them as bitches. I thought I was giving her a compliment," Marvin says, trying obnoxious this time.

"How about we bust your fucking skull," Archie Jr oozes, "Compliment *yo* ass real nice and *quiet* like?"

Tank comes down to check out the 1st floor, just as Marvin is getting his 2nd wind. Tank can now hear Marvin talking to his young crew.

"It's not your girl. It's your bitch, right? Am I right on that?" Marvin continues as his face bares an evil grin.

Tank intervenes just as Kenny, Archie Jr and Brandon are coming around the counter to whoop his ass.

"May I help you?" Tank asks.

"No sir. I was just chatting with the youth," Marvin says.

"This is a cash and carry establishment. For under twenty one year olds. That language you're using isn't permitted," Tank says.

"Wow. You should've heard the colorful words they said to me," Marvin tries.

"I did. In retaliation for what you said," Tank says, "Anyway we don't do referrals and we don't give out information on customers either. I think you've outstayed your welcome. So unless you're purchasing something or entering a tournament. I'll have to ask security to escort you away from the premises."

"There won't be any need too get security. And my intentions were not to offend anyone. I'll be leaving now."

He does. He heads out to his rental car while Davidson watches him and records the tag number. He gets in and drives off. When he passes the

guard booth and officer Teddy Joiner at the exit. He waves arrogantly.
"He's off the property," Joiner radios back to Davidson.
"Log that one too," Davidson says, "He had a minor altercation in the arcade. But mister Brown handled it. We still need to log it for the Lieutenant."
"Is he interviewing that beauty today?" Joiner asks.
"Miles? From Cleveland Police?"
"Yes. Deloris is what she told me her name was," Joiner says.
"He hired her already. She starts today. But she'll be at Jackson Heights with him until she learns the procedures."
"I look forward to talking to her again," Joiner says with a smile.

}Jackson Heights{

Ajay stops at the gate to speak with Jacobson. He meets officer Deloris Miles, the new hire for the security team. She's the same female officer who had stopped Ebony that day after she saw Rich and June cheating in the parking lot of the medical complex. She's the officer who had witnessed Ebony's near head on collision as she was trying to escape a confrontation with them. Ajay is feeling like his usual charming self. Until he learns more about Miles and her family.

"Finally somebody nice looking out here," Ajay says and smiles as Jacobson and Miles laugh.

"It's very nice to meet you, Ajay," Officer Miles says, "I was told to call you Ajay or mister Jackson."

"Ajay is fine. I hear you've already met my wife," he says.

"Yes I did. Lieutenant reminded me of that when I first came out here for my interview," Miles says, "How is she? Calmer I hope."

"Oh yes. There won't be any more of *that* stress for her," Ajay says confidently.

"I hear you. You guys had a beautiful wedding. I was there," she says, "And so was most of the state."
They all laugh.

"Cool and thanks. It was a big wedding and things have only gotten better since then," he says, "Wait until you meet our twins. We've got a boy and a girl."

"I look forward too it," she says, "And I actually found out that my niece played on the team with Ebony. Down at UC. Katrina Dobbs from Natty? They own the campus flower and gift shop. She came up for the wedding. So after she told me who was getting married. I went with her."
Ajay feels an attack of nausea as soon as he hears Katrina Dobbs' name.

312

TIME TO KNOW-RELOADED-Time Will Reveal- part 4

He's vulnerable on their history and had no clue she had attended their wedding. Most likely because she kept herself hidden from *his* view. He knew their teams, past and present was invited. He'd thought surely after his last conversation with her. She would've kept her distance. But it's apparent she hadn't. And now that her aunt is working security for him and his family. Katrina is bound to show her face eventually. She'll do it just to torment him, all over again. He doesn't particularly like this scenario but he tries to play it off.

"I remember Katrina. I haven't heard anything about her in the WNBA."

"She wants to try out for the Rockers. She ask me last week if she can stay with me while she try out. I told her to come on up," she says.

"Let us know when she's coming. Jarvis Rhodes told me she was going to try out for the league," he says, "Tell her there are other teams besides the Rockers."

"I will surely tell her. Thank you," Miles says and smiles.
Then Jacobson tells him about the traffic which had come through earlier. And that he had called Ebony about it.
Ajay says, "Good job. Stay on top of it. We'll talk on it later."
Then taking out the gift he's gotten for Ebony, he ask Deloris Miles for a female opinion. Really he wants to make sure she knows that he's dedicated to his wife. Maybe she can pass that on to her niece.

"That's gorgeous. Ebony is a *very* lucky woman," she says and smiles. "I see why she'd improve her driving."

"No not really. I'm the lucky one," he says, "Let me get on down here and see what she's cooked for me. Y'all have a good day."
They say goodbye and he drives down to his estate. As soon has he pulls into the garage, he hears Ike and Tina barking at the near distant kitchen door. They're waiting for him to enter.

"That means dinner's ready," he says to himself as he smiles.
He goes inside as Ebony is setting the table in the dining room.

"Hey baby," he says and gives her a kiss.

"Hey you. Go on and wash up," she says, "Your dinner's ready."
He heads to the sink to wash his hands, then they sit down for dinner.
He isn't going to let the knowledge of Katrina coming to town ruin this special dinner with his wife. He presents her with the diamond necklace he had just bought for her. She's all smiles as he puts it on her, then he plants a sweet kiss on the nape of her neck.

"It's beautiful, Anthony. Thank you. But you know you don't have to keep buying me stuff."

"I know that. But I like too," he says, "You bought me two sports cars. So I can keep my baby dripping with diamonds if I want too."
They laugh. She leaves that alone and goes to fix their plates.

They enjoy a wonderful dinner. After they finish, he's feeling his usual frisky self.

"That was so good, baby," he says, watching her every move as she clears the dishes away.

"You want some dessert?" she asks as she smiles.

"Is it you?"
She's still smiling as she says, "It can be but I made you a chocolate cake."

"I want your chocolate," he says as he follows her into the kitchen.
He moves up behind her at the sink and says, "I'll have the cake later."
He begins to kiss her on the back of her neck. She moans.

"What do you say we go work off this huge meal," he whispers.

"It's your night, daddy," she says, "Have it your way."
He begins to remove her clothing right there. Kissing each part of her body, he reveals. Ike and Tina escape to their bunks.

"I want it *right* here," he whispers, lifting her up onto the counter.

"It's been awhile since we could make love in the kitchen, baby."

"Too long," he whispers as he enters her, "You know how much your man loves this freaky shit. My pussy gets better and better everyday."

"Yes! Oh!" she moans as he grinds inside of her, "It feels so good."

"Uh huh," he whispers as he bites on her ear lobe.
He plunges into her with force and she yelps.
"You're gonna take it all for me. Right baby girl?" he asks in a heated whisper.

"Oh yes daddy," she oozes, knowing she'll never handle his full 14 inches. But she'll never say no to her man when it's about giving it to her.

After 5 minutes of pushing into her, he holds her next to his chest. He takes her head in both hands and raises her chin up. He kisses her and takes her tongue. She moans as he sucks on her tongue as if he's about to take it from her. Finally he releases it.
He looks into her eyes and whispers, "I wanna take you there, baby."
He's churning his dick into her. Hitting the spots he knows will give her ecstasy. She's feeling that familiar tinkle which proceeds her orgasm.
"Get it wet for daddy," he demands, knowing she's on her way.
She pushes herself against him with everything she's got. She wants hers.
"That's it, baby girl," he whispers, "That's it baby. Oh!"

"Oh daddy! Yes! Yes Anthony! Daddy it's sooooo good! Oh yes!" she screams as she climaxes.

"Yea baby. Get it wet for me," he demands, "Get this sweet pussy wet for me. Open it up. Open your legs up...., all the way."
He pumps into her very hard. Over and over, for several more minutes.
"Uh yes. Baby girl!" he says, his voice growing loud.
He's working for his climax. She's feeling the pain that usually comes when he gets to this point of excitement. But it's a bit more pain than usual. The kind of pain she feels when he's conflicted over something. He feels like her pussy can help him ease his mind and do all the forgetting he wants to do. He's still going.
"Give me my pussy," he demands, "Give it to daddy."
She screams as he stuffs his huge penis as far inside of her as he can get it. He's on his tiptoe's fucking her. Banging her as he ravishes her neck, face and lips.
"Oh! Oh! Yes! Here he comes baby!" he says, almost yelling as he throws his head back.
Then he lays his head on her shoulder. He's getting his. His body tightens up as he lets out a long sighing sound. She holds onto him as their bodies start to loosen. His knees give out and he slides down to the floor. His momentum, bringing her with him. They giggle at each other. To tired to laugh. They lay on the kitchen floor, panting for air.
"How was your day, baby?" he asks with a half smile and no air.

"Getting better," she says, breathless.

"Jacobson told me.., about Marvin being at the gate. And Farah's car, ..., being in the lot....., out by Jackson Rd," he says, "What the fuck are they doing out here? They stay prowling the mall enough. They ain't gonna be running up out here..., with that foolishness. I'll tell them both that shit......., soon as I see 'em."

"That was her and Alana," she says, "Huntley was probably following her. Jacobson said he was in a rental car. I'll bet Farah didn't even know he was following her."

"They're all gonna take that bullshit somewhere else," he says, "You know how I feel about those types of bitches around my family. I'm a father now. So they don't stand a chance."

"I didn't want you to get upset," she says, "Because I know your temper and I know this is the community and home you've made for us and our children. Alana doesn't realize how close she is to that bad memory of us losing our first child."

"Baby it's like *Dr Dre* say in *Forgot about Dre*. *'They gone keep fuckin around with me and turn me back into the old me.'* That's my word. We're gonna live in peace. One way or the other. I can't have peace with

the memory of that Angel bitch hovering over me. And no other bitch."
"I agree Anthony."
After regaining their strength, they move to the big couch in the great room for another session. It's dusk dark now.

}CrewLand Mall{
The entire crew are on alert tonight. They're expecting Marvin to show up on the property once the adult club is open. But he doesn't come back this evening. Farah, Darlene and their posse are at the club to support Alana while she dances. She makes excellent tips as a stripper. All of her talents of being provocative are finally paying off. All in all, there has been no drama for the crew. Other than the obvious females lusting after their guys. Or some jealous ex getting heated about her past boyfriend being with a woman he's met in the club.

June, Eric and Bruce have their Browns team outside of VIP doing autographs and meeting fans. They all leave by midnight because they have curfew. Tomorrow's home game is against the Pittsburgh Steelers. Perhaps Marvin is saving his clash with the home team for after their football game against his home team.

}Jackson Heights{
At 2am, Ajay and Ebony have just finished yet another session of hot sex. They finally make time to enjoy some of the chocolate cake she'd made for dessert. After cake, they lay back down on the sectional. He pulls her on top of him while he lays on his back. He grabs the remote, turns on the TV, then covers them with the comforter Ebony draped on the back of the couch for them.
"We can sleep right here baby. Naked," he whispers as he smiles.
"Good because I can't move," she whispers.
"I'm gonna hit it again," he says and smiles, "I'll wake you up."
They hold each other and watch *MSNBC* for war coverage. They sleep there all night, in each others arms.

}Before Church, in Shaker Heights{
The war in Afghanistan rages on. Now the surviving families of the victims from the September 11 attacks are demanding a full investigation. While most Americans have started to feel misinformed about everything from the attacks to the Anthrax to the bully posturing of George W Bush with foreign countries. Then the Bush administration deals another blow. President Bush accuses Saddam Hussein of having weapons of mass

316

destruction in Iraq. He says Saddam is aiding the terrorist organizations and cells and he's a definite threat to our country.

"Bush and Cheney are the threats to our country, Allen." Jo says angrily, "Bush is a crook." She's watching Bush as he address the Union. "He's retaliating against Saddam because Saddam threatened his father," she says in disgust, "Plain and simple."

"He needs to let the United Nations handle this though," Al says, "What he's rushing into is a UN responsibility. Not the United States." Big Al is angry too.

"He's going to get all of our babies killed with this shit," Jo snaps, "My oldest child is out there in those mountains of Afghanistan. For *nothing*. I'll bet you Bush don't even get Bin Laden."

"He wants to go into Iraq for oil, Joanna," Al says, "Saddam isn't a threat to us and I feel he knows that already."

"I don't care what he says," she says, "He's gonna go over there. No matter what the UN says."

Joanna couldn't have been more on point. Bush has even gone as far as to give the UN a deadline for finding the proof of the weapons of mass destruction. What's worse, the other countries in the UN aren't supporting his position. England is the only relevant country supporting Bush in this new conflict he's proposing. Americans continue to speak out against the present war and the new proposal. But Americans are attacked by the Bush supporters, Fox News and Rush Limbaugh and are deemed unpatriotic for not walking in lock step.

"They're covering up some massive shit, Joanna," Al says, "It's going to get way worse before it's all said and done."

They head to Church.

}Jackson Heights-after church{

The foursome stock the refrigerators for the security teams at CrewLand and at the entry gate to Jackson Heights. While doing so, the ladies discuss a lot of issues the crew have been dealing with lately. Farah, Alana, and Marvin's name come up a lot on the negative side of the issues. But Rich's name dominates their talks on the positive side, this time. He's being released next week. T-baby is so excited she can barely contain herself. Her girls are optimistic as well.

"He looks like the Richard I fell in love with," T-baby says, "His attitude is one hundred percent better."

"I'm just glad to hear it," Ebony says, "He's been gone for a long time."

"Almost *two* years," Rebbie adds.

"So much has happened since he went to rehab," Nina offers.

"Yes. Grandma Sally, Aaliyah, Darrell, Charlise and September eleventh victims all died," Ebony adds.

"Lynn is gone to war and we got asshole Alana and her buddies around here," T-baby says.

"Stirring up shit," Nina adds, "And about to get dealt wit."

"Brian told me something Bruce overheard last night from Alana," Rebbie says, "That crazy bitch Angel got a parole hearing. Farah hired her a *real* attorney."

"*What*? And those bitches are hanging around here like it's all good?!" Nina screams, "We needs to kick their asses on G P!"

"Ah excuse me? B*ig mama, keys in Tijuana!* But you ain't fighting *nobody*," Rebbie says and they all crack up laughing at the *Lil Kim* lyrical reference toward Nina, who's pregnant and talking gangster.

"Nah Nina," T-baby says, "You ain't swinging on nothing."

Ebony has no words. She isn't even going to get upset because there's no way Wheeler is going to allow Angel to get parole. She's going to call his wife Trina Yvette and put the nail in that coffin *today*.

She says, "She's only done five years y'all. She got twelve mandatory. There was nothing left open for appeal because she admitted her guilt after trial and signed a statement. She agreed to have her first parole hearing in two thousand and seven so she has at least six years to go before she sees any daylight."

"Maybe that's what the lawyer is for," T-baby offers, "To see to it that she gets out then."

"I give less than a damn," Ebony says, "If she comes around me. She's going in the ground. And all of you know I'm capable of getting rid of a fool for trying to harm me by *now*."

They all agree that Ebony is *very* capable of killing to protect herself. That said, they finish stocking the refrigerators. Then they head to the Cleveland Browns stadium for the home game. T-baby can't stop talking about her soon-to-be-released husband.

"He's going to tryout for the Browns," she says, "I know he'll make the team."

They enjoy the game, although the Browns lose 12-15 in overtime.

Thanksgiving is more than 2 weeks away. Tank and Nina will host this year. But the 2nd Monday of November is a big day as well.

Today T-baby, Rich III, Anna and Rich Sr go to Cincinnati to get

TIME TO KNOW-RELOADED-Time Will Reveal- part 4

Rich Jr from rehab. After 20 months, he's finally released on his on recognizance. He has gotten clean, healthy and he looks very good. When they arrive in Cleveland, they go directly to the mall where the whole crew has gathered as a show of support.

"You look good, Cuz," Jr says, "It feels good to have you home."
He thanks everyone for coming. Then he apologizes again for his behavior toward all of them over the years.

"Crew we're just glad you're clean and healthy," Chill says after hugging him again, "We're not sweating the past shit."
Ajay says, "Let's bring you home the right way. Get you back in football shape. You can train in my sports complex. I opened it while you was gone. Long as you stay clean. I can stay off your ass."
He smiles but Rich and everyone else knows he meant it. Rich Jr is moved by the overwhelming support from his huge family. He vows to do better and make them all proud. He also promises T-baby there'll be more lovemaking than she can handle. He starts fulfilling that promise as soon as they get to Jackson Heights.

He moves back home with T-baby and Rich III. He continues his vigorous training schedule. He had started it in the rehab program. So he's ready for the walk-on tryouts with the Browns which Jb had arranged, within a week. He makes the team with ease. June, Bruce and Eric are excited to have such an excellent and experienced wide receiver on their team. He passes all of his test and is eligible to play immediately. He dresses out for the game against the Bengals and catches a pass for a touchdown. The Browns win 18-0.

During Thanksgiving week, Ajay's 1st season with the Cavaliers gets under way. They play Saturday, Tuesday and Wednesday on the road and return with an unimpressive 0-3 record. Ajay remains optimistic. He's happy to be on his home team and he wants to have a great season too. He's determined to help Jarvis turn it around in Cleveland.

The Sunday after Thanksgiving, the Cav's have a home game at Gund Arena against the Pistons. The Browns are on the road in Nashville. *Crew cuts and styles* sponsors the Cavaliers home game. They had raffled off 4 tickets for the game with VIP access at *The Chill Spot,* after game party.

Kelly Johnson, Matt's daughter who attends Cleveland State with Sam and Pam, attends the game with Matt. They go along with the whole crew to watch Ajay play his 1st home game with the Cavaliers. Matt and Kelly sit next to Ebony, the twins, Gwen and Jarvis Jr. Who are flanked by the entire crew.

TIME TO KNOW-RELOADED-Time Will Reveal- part 4

"Your hair is still looking good Ebony," Matt says.
He had styled it that Wednesday evening before Thanksgiving.
"Thanks. You hooked me up," she says as she smiles, "Usually with Anthony at home, my styles wouldn't last this well. So you did good."
They both laugh, then they watch as the visiting team runs out onto the court. The Cavaliers run out next to a huge cheer. Then both line ups are introduced. Visitors first. Then the home team. Ajay receives a standing ovation when his name is called as the starting shooting guard. The twins cheer and yell, "*daddy!*" along with Ebony when he runs to center court. He feels loose and ready. He's glad to be home. The crew are all in attendance to enjoy the game.

Ajay is having an all-star performance again today. Cleveland seems to be headed for their 1st win of the season. Matt is so into the game, he hasn't noticed he has a stalker in the building. It's not Farah. Her and her crew aren't at the game but Ellen is. She had purchased a ticket to the game after she found out Matt was going. She has been stalking him about town since the windshield incident. She knows he's spent several nights with Farah. He's even stayed a few nights at another woman's home. She'll find out later that the other woman is his wife Genia. Ellen has watched him leave her house with the young lady who's seated next to him right now. She figures this girl is his daughter. He's spending quality time with his wife and daughter this weekend. He hasn't even made time to call her. This makes her even more angry. She has called him many times but he wouldn't answer his phone. Not when he saw her name on his caller ID. And not as long as he was at either of his other women's homes. Now she's at the basketball game with a good eye on him. He had extricated her from his life after she, not only did damage to his car. But she had also been to his home while he was out. She had broken a window and gone in, soaped up his kitchen floor and flung all of his flower pots around and broke them. She wrote her name in lipstick on his bed sheets and mirrors. She'd left his home in a mess. She'd also broken his flower pots outside and his hammock swing in his backyard. Matt had discovered this when he'd returned home with Farah, who was coming to spend the night. But when Matt saw the signs of Ellen, he quickly suggested to Farah that they go to her house. Farah thought it was a break in and suggested he call the cops. He declined because he didn't want to reveal to Farah that he knew who had done it. So they just went to Farah's house without any explanation. Since then he has relieved Ellen of any personal duties that she'd once had with him. Ellen is determined to speak with him today and get some of his time again. She watches him the entire game. Matt, Ebony and the crew cut up and cheer

320

loudly. They enjoy Ajay's 1st win. Being at home, makes it twice as nice.

Now that the game is over. Ebony, her girls and the twins go up the tunnel with Ajay to wait in the family area. While some of the crew, Matt and Kelly wait at the edge of the tunnel near the floor. They're waiting for him to get dressed and finish his post game interviews. That's when Ellen approaches Matt.

"Why couldn't you get me a good seat down here where you was sitting with all of your girlfriends," she snaps.

"I wasn't sitting with girlfriends," he says, "These are the people I work with. And *for*, for that matter. You know this already. As much as you be spying on the shop."

"You sure was up in that woman's face that had the twins," she says, "She don't work in that damn shop."

"No she sure don't. Ebony is Anthony Jackson's wife," he says as he grows impatient, "If you knew how loyal she was to her husband. You wouldn't even be in my face with this mess. He would cuss you out if he heard you saying it."

She changes the subject, "I wanna see you later."

"Hell no. Not after you fucked up my windshield and my house," he says, "You must be crazy. I told you to leave me alone."

"Shit if you can afford to drive a Suburban. Then you can afford a windshield for it," she says with an evil grin, "If you wish, I'll pay for whatever I did. Just spend some time with me and stop dogging me."

"Leave me alone, alright?" he says as he starts to walk away.

She grabs his arm and says, "I wanna see you *tonight*, Matt."

"It's not gonna happen Ellen," he says, "I want you to stay away from me, my job and my property."

She grabs his arm again and Kelly steps in.

"Leave my dad alone," she says, "He said he don't wanna be bothered with you. So leave him alone."

"Stay out of grown folks business," Ellen says aggressively.

"Don't speak to my daughter that way," Matt says, "She's grown too. You need to just go on about your business. Or I'm gonna get security on you."

With the threat of police, Ellen decides she'd better make her way to the exit. She still has a warrant out on her for the windshield incident. She doesn't want to be locked up. She lets it go for now. She leaves the Arena. She's stewed and even more upset at being shunned by Matt, once again.

"This shit ain't over by a long shot Matthew!" she says to herself as she makes her way out of the exit and to the parking garage.

321

TIME TO KNOW-RELOADED-Time Will Reveal- part 4

She gets into her car and makes her way out of the parking garage, hits Ontario drive and weaves through the slow moving post game traffic until she merges onto the interstate. She's soon out of sight. But not forever.

}CrewLand Mall{

Marvin shows up at the after game celebration at The Spot. He mingles with the other club goers and tries to stay as low key as possible. He came in very early. Long before Farah and her crew arrived. Alana is already on the 2nd floor dancing and entertaining, so he doesn't dare go up there until it's packed. He's planning to hang around until Farah leaves. Then follow her home. He wants to find out where she lives. Then he can keep account of her goings and comings. And also who visits her. He wants to know where she lives before letting her know that he's in town.

By 11pm the Cavaliers and the visiting Pistons inhibit the VIP. This brings out the gold-digger's and church girls alike. With much focus on the athletes, Marvin is freer to move about the club without drawing a lot of attention. He sees Farah, Darlene, Angie and others when they arrive. He sees the carrying on of his ex fiancée which bothers him a lot. He has plans of telling her this as soon as she has finished her night of partying. Unfortunately for him. Farah and her housemates accompany some of the Pistons to the Fillmore Hotel. He watches as they drive into the parking garage. He follows and parks just down the row from them, in his rental. He watches as they get out of the cars and get on the elevator to go to the rooms. He can't be sure of which floor they're on. Without a key, he can't visit the floors of this hotel. He needs a key to operate the elevators from the parking garage and all other outside entrances other than the front lobby. He had filmed Farah on the arm of a player. He hurries to the outside, hoping to park and set up his camera to film her when she leaves. There are "no parking zones" in every immediate area near the hotel. He isn't able to park and have unobstructed vision of the front door and lobby. Furthermore he has been asked to leave these premises by security, after reports come to them that a man is filming the guest as they come and go. He's bothered but he leaves when the concierge threatens to call the police.

Throughout December, Matt continues to have run-ins with Ellen. She comes to the shop and sits out front until she's seen by him. She escapes being apprehended because she leaves before security or the police show up, each time. After Matt tells Tonya about his stalker. She tells security to keep a tight lid on the parking area because Ellen has already damaged 1 employee's car. Ellen is annoyed with the crew for not helping her get

322

information on Matt. She might even try to damage their cars. She had avoided being caught until 1 evening, 2 weeks before Christmas. Joiner and Bronson had blocked her car in and she wasn't able to drive off. They retained her until the Cleveland police got there and arrested her. She went to jail and was bailed out the next day. That only annoyed her more. Matt had pressed stalking charges on her. He got a restraining order as well. In Ellen's mind, she just had to be more slick to avoid getting caught. She's obsessed with Matt and she isn't going to give up until she has him.

The crew have a big Christmas and birthday party planned. Nina and Ebony are turning 26. Roo turned 20 on the 8th. Kenny is turning 18. This is going to be a huge party. Chill and Renee's son will be old enough to vote. They had him to fill out his registration form a few days before Christmas. He had dated it for the day after. Renee will turn it in on the next business day. The crew do a lot of shopping this Christmas season. By Christmas eve, all of the decorating and shopping is done and they're ready for the big party.

Matt and Kelly come to the party as well as Genia Johnson, Matt's estranged wife. By now she has met and is familiar with all the members of the crew and their families. Lynn calls the club and Renee puts her on the intercom. It's bittersweet. Every person in the club is misty as they wish her a merry Christmas. Lynn still doesn't have any idea when she'll be home.

By 2am it's time to shut the party down and go home. Ajay and Ebony file out of the club with the rest of their crew. Matt, Genia and Kelly are close behind. Matt and his family head down to valet, along with Ebony, Ajay, Jarvis, Gwen and some of their Cavalier teammates. While Matt is waiting in valet for his Suburban. Ellen appears out of nowhere and runs straight up to him.

"I need to talk to you right now," she demands.

"Hey somebody get security-" Matt starts to say but he stops when he sees her pull a small pistol from her coat.

She doesn't hesitate nor does she request to speak with him again. She fires 3 shots toward him as she's running off. Matt dives onto Genia and Kelly, knocking them to the ground. Ajay, Ebony, the crew and others take cover. Ellen runs to her car, jumps in and speeds away. Jacobson security are in hot pursuit. Bronson radios the police. They move in and a chase ensues. Ellen isn't giving up or pulling over. She jumps onto bypass 271 and the chase continues. The police eventually ram her vehicle causing her to spin out. She hits a side rail and wrecks which brings the chase to an end. She only has minor cuts and bruises. She's arrested on the spot and charged with attempted manslaughter, resisting arrest and endangering the lives of others. The police inform her that she had shot 2 innocent party goers with 2 of the 3 shots she fired at Matthew. The 2 club goers have been treated at East General and released. A few others had been injured while they sought cover. None of the victims have life threatening wounds. However the incident is enough to lock Ellen up and hold her until she goes to court. Matt is bugging about the attempt on his life. He vows to end his relationship with Ellen forever.

Farah is at the club but she doesn't approach Matt. Nor does he approach her. He's with his wife. Marvin hadn't shown up tonight. Crew figure he's spending the Christmas holiday in Pittsburgh with his family. Instead of snooping around their businesses trying to get in *crew* business.

Christmas is wonderful and for the twins, it's a day of *first*. Ajay had gotten them a pink and a blue tricycle. He had also gotten them *Tickle Me Elmo's* and every other popular toy on the market for 2 year olds. He got them London fog coats with accessories and more clothes with matching shoes, then they'll *ever* wear. He gets Lannie her 1st jewelry and Lil Ajay gets his 1st tool set.

"Daddy will buy you all the jewelry you want," Ajay says to his daughter, "You don't need a man to buy you *anything*. You understand?"

"Yes sir my daddy," Lannie says as she kisses him on the cheek.
He smiles proudly as he helps his son identify his variety of tools.

"Papa John said that to me when I was little Lannie," Ebony says sarcastically, "But your daddy, *my man*, has bought nearly every piece of jewelry I own. And that's lifetime."

"That's right," Ajay says with a smile, "But papa was just saying what he thought was popular then. He knew you was mine, way back in seventy five."
Him and Ebony laugh and the twins join in. Even Ike and Tina get new doggy toys and beds this year.

Jerica gets her 1st 10-speed bike and she's very proud of it. She shows everybody in Jackson Heights that she can ride it. Her, Destiny and Jada, all got 10-speed bikes, clothes, shoes, toys and jewelry. All of the kids in the crew get bikes this year. Renee and Chill give Kenny the 1992 blazer. He wanted a brand new 2002 model but his parents tell him they're helping him to stay grounded.

After dinner, all of the kids take to the streets of Jackson Heights to ride their bicycles and tricycles.

"This reminds me of Christmas in nineteen ninety when all of our

324

little sisters and brothers got bikes at the same time," Nina says.
Her and the crew watch their own children ride their bikes around their private community.

"It's good they have a safe place to ride," Ebony says, "Not like us. We was almost to the highway on our bikes."

"If we had grown up out here," T-baby says, "We would've been climbing over the security fence." They all agree as they laugh.

"Look! *Tour de France!*" Rebbie says as they all laugh again.
It's another beautiful white Christmas and the entire crew family spend the day together at the homes in Jackson Heights.

"I'm glad we got this place out here," Ajay says, "There's plenty of space and room for everybody to visit at one time."

"I wish everybody lived here," Ebony says, "It would be perfect."

"Maybe everyone will," he says as he kisses her on the cheek.
Then him and Tank get busy pushing the twins around on their tricycles. They're helping them to keep up with the bigger kids. Steven pushes Ashanti on her tricycle, right next to them.

Ebony and the twins are on the road with Ajay for their 4th year anniversary and New Year's day 2002. When they return, she gets back into work at her office. She has to run the hot sheets from 2001. She's very concerned about interest rates. She has to set in motion the schedule for 2002. She goes over the yearly financial perspectives and forecast. Then compares the last 2 years. She notices the effects of the Bush administration on her interest rates from 2001. Though there had been reduction in regulations, all of their businesses had a slow down last year. This is the 1st time since any of them opened. She sets up a board meeting for later this week.

The new year is here and school is back in session. Farah is back from her parents and back to her usual routine. She is more determined than ever to get some of what Chill has to offer. Her, him and Ebony meet at Jackson's Real Estate. Farah puts up the funds for the new investment, out in Brook Park. She's excited that the business isn't far from her home. She's even inquired about how much Chill will work at the new business.

"A good manager spends the most time at the business with the most profit potential," he says.

"Make lots of money. We'll devote lots of time," Ebony translates.
Then they excuse Farah so they can get on with their CrewLand business meeting. Ebony sees where June has the opportunity to expand his business portfolio too. Chill leaves her and T-baby in charge and goes back to The

Spot. June, Tank, Renee and Wesley will join them shortly for the meeting.

"We have to get George Bush's ass out of the white house before we all go broke," she says to T-baby while they wait on the others.

"I know that's right, Cuz," T-baby agrees, "Some of my tax clients are getting antsy about their investments."

"I know they've all talked to me and they're good, so far. But with that Enron scandal, they have a right to be antsy," Ebony adds, "One crooked move after another one. Bush really needs to go before it gets worse. My feeling are, it'll get much worse for the middle class."

"For real. The class we came from. It's all of his people and friends who lose in these scandals when you get down to it," T-baby replies, "Him and Dick Cheney are both crooks."

A few minutes later, T-baby, Ebony, Renee, Tank, June and Wes convene their board meeting in the meeting room of *Williams Accounting and Finance and Jackson's Real Estate and Investment Banking*. They draw up a business plan to help them through a potential crisis.

"I think we should buy up the remainder of the land outside of Jackson Heights," Ebony says, "And build those luxury condominium suites that we talked about, June."

"I agree with you," he says, "We can rent them to the NFL and NBA players when they come in town. Instead of them staying in hotels. We're naming them, *CrewLand Luxury Suites and Condominiums*."

"Hell yes! And the entertainers that come to the clubs to perform. We can make *that* money too," Tank says, "And we can put them off Superior Avenue. We can afford that prime real estate now."

"I'll invest in them," Rich says as he sticks his head in the door. He had come by his wife's office to take her to lunch.

"We all will. June and Rebbie can manage them," T-baby says.

"Another business venture for the crew," Wesley says.

"Yes and you're crew now so you can invest too," Tank says, "We want you to be apart of it."

Renee says, "Ebony had an idea for a store. A tobacco and liquor store."

"I like that idea already," June says with a smile.

"Me too," Tank adds.

"Tell me more about it," T-baby says.

"One thing people are going to do no matter how hard times get, is party, get high and or drink to numb the situation," Ebony says, "And smokers are gonna smoke."

"I like it," Renee says, "Chill and I was all for that, from day one."

"We're gonna sell blunts in there?" Tank asks.

TIME TO KNOW-RELOADED-Time Will Reveal- part 4

"Of course," Ebony says and laughs, "And our family alone will keep that stock moving." They all laugh.

"How about we name it, *Crew Smokes and Drinks*?" Rich suggests.

"Yay!" they all agree.

"Wes, this will be your management opportunity," Tank says suddenly, "You and Eric will manage *this* business."

"And eventually Jarvis and Gwen," Ebony adds, "If everything works out with their addition to the crew."

Everyone agrees to Ebony's suggestion. Everyone except Tank. He doesn't say anything. From Ebony's observation, he looks guilty or distracted. Wes is excited to be included in the crew family investment opportunities. He quickly agrees.

"Alright cool," Wes says, "I like that too. I'm ready."

Ebony plans to talk with her brother, later on. She wants to find out why he zoned out at the mention of Jarvis and Gwen.

They draw up the contracts and Ebony contacts Mr. Parkwood to get the acquisition started. *Crew Smokes and Drinks* will be located next to *Stoney's* and will close at 11pm.

In just 2 weeks, they have enough to close on the new property for the condominiums. Ebony will handle the mortgage. Tank and June get the plans to Greg and Sam Sr. By Tank's 27th birthday, they're ready to close.

By mid-February the property is being cleared and soon after, construction begins. June and Rebbie take an office at Jackson's Real Estate. *CrewLand Luxury suites and Condominiums* is in the books as an official business by the end of February. June and Rebbie get busy getting all their crew colleagues, doctors and professional people on board. Their attorney Mr. Wheeler, his wife Trina Yvette and others in his firm reserve 4 units. Mr. Parkwood, Mrs. Briar, Dr. Weston, Mahoney and Stansfield, all reserve space as well. Nearly every professional they know from Browns and Cavaliers to Bengals and even Pistons and Lions have decided to invest. Some are looking for a getaway spot in Cleveland. Others want extra space for family to stay when they visit. Still others are looking for rendezvous spots. Rebbie and June turn no one away. In just a month's time, they have the 100 unit property, 50% reserved. Completion will be sometime in late April or early May at the latest.

"Just in time for the summer," June says, "We're gonna do well with this venture too."

Rebbie agrees and smiles but she doesn't offer a comment. Jarvis had already put in his bid for one and he purchased it directly from her.

TIME TO KNOW-RELOADED-Time Will Reveal- part 4

CHAPTER 47

STAYING POWER

Officer Deloris Miles is on the entry gate as Ebony leaves for her office. Ajay is still at home with the twins. He'll drop them at *Big Mama's House* on his way to his team meeting.

"Good Morning misses Jackson," Officer Miles says as she smiles sweetly. "You sure drive *much* safer these days." They both laugh.

"I did get it together, didn't I?" Ebony says and giggles.

"I wanted to let you know Katrina is here. She came to tryout for the Rockers," Miles says, "She'll be staying with me while she's here."

"Okay. Have her to give me a call. T-baby and I would love to see her. Maybe go to dinner or something. Tell her, she can drop by the office if she has time and we'll go to lunch."

"Okay, I'll be sure and tell her."

Ebony goes on to CrewLand mall. Later Katrina does drop by the office and her, T-baby and Ebony meet Nina and Rebbie at Crew's House for lunch. They laugh and talk about old times in Natty. T-baby is trying to be civil to Katrina but she's never liked her.

"I can't help but remember you two with y'all freaky butts up in our store for Valentine's," Katrina says and they all laugh.

"The edible panties? That was Ebony!" T-baby screams.

"You got some, Cuz," Ebony says, "And edible paint too."

"I told your brother that I apologize about the photo posters," Katrina says suddenly, "I was just trying to big up a fellow Natty athlete. I didn't mean to be illegal. I didn't think."

"Well y'all paid us *well*. So we'll let that one go," Ebony says with a slick grin. "Just don't ever do anything like that again. Or we'll be taking the *whole* store."

They laugh and have a great time. Katrina and T-baby talk a lot about the *WNBA*. Ebony isn't interested in the topic but T-baby surely is. She gets contact information from Katrina about the team's coaching and recruiting staffs.

By late February, T-baby has a yearning for the WNBA. She talks to Rich about it. But he isn't supportive of her idea at all.

"I always support you, Richard. No matter what," T-baby says.

"Yes but I'm playing football again and we have a son," he says.

"I know that, honey. But where there's a will. There's a way."

Rich is silent as she goes on giving him the points that makes it doable. "I wanna tryout for the Rockers," she says, "That's the home team, so I'll be here more than I'll be gone."

"I don't like it, Trisha," he says, "I don't think our marriage would survive it."

She looks at him in shock. It takes a few minutes before she can even speak.

"Our marriage can survive football in New York. Two years of you in rehab. An outside child and a mistress. But not the *WNBA*?" she snaps.

"You do what you want Trisha," he says bluntly, "But if you join that team. I'm out."

She's livid but keeps it inside. She has a feeling he's been up to his old ways since the new year. His habits are very familiar, though he *thinks* he's concealing it. She feels like he's back on his *"addiction"* again. She doesn't bother to mention it. She'd found her strength while he was away. Much like Ebony did when she'd moved to Houston. T-baby knows who she is now. She isn't insecure anymore. She loves Rich with all her heart. But she loves herself and her son more. Still she can't believe he has given her an ultimatum about *her* sport. When she supports him so much with his.

"So you're gonna divorce me if I play basketball?" she asks bluntly. "I just wanna be clear. Is that what you're saying?"

He doesn't respond. He leaves her sitting at their breakfast bar alone. He goes to take a shower and on to bed without another word. T-baby is so upset by his ignorance that she gets her girls on the phone, so she can tell them. Right away, all 3 of them are shocked at how selfish he's being. After all of the chances she's given him.

"T-baby if you wanna play," Ebony says, "You should play."

Nina and Rebbie agree with Ebony and encourage her to try out.

"I'm gonna *seriously* think about it," T-baby says, "If he wants to leave. He can but I'm not gonna let him hold me back anymore. No way!"

"Good for you," Her girls say.

And for the next month or so, T-baby agonizes over what she'll do. She trains at Ajay's sports complex. She has the blessings of her relatives and entire crew including Wes. *Everyone* except for her husband. As it turns out, this is just another thing for Rich to use as an excuse to mess up. He hasn't been able to hide his indiscretions. So he's been missing in action again and no one has to guess what he's doing. T-baby had long decided she wouldn't stay with him if he went back on the drugs.

Nina and Tank go to Atlanta for their 6th year anniversary in March.

"That baby is coming soon, ha?" Bre asks.

"Yes. Ten more weeks," Nina answers.

"Lynn says she might be back by May. But it's not certain yet," Jb tells them.

"I hope she can be back for John the thirds, fifth birthday," Cedric says, "He's really missing his mama."

"Have they gotten any answers for your family About the nine eleven tragedy?" Tank ask Cedric.

"They've put together a commission to investigate who dropped the ball first," he says, "They all dropped the ball, at some point. We all know it. They had info about this attack *way* ahead of time. That's what I believe. We're a country with the best intelligence *imaginable*. I'm suppose to believe they couldn't have seen this coming?"

He tells them all the survivors are steadfast about getting answers.

"We're not gonna be pushed aside," he says, "My big brother didn't die for nothing. I wanna know who's fault it was. I'm not buying this Bin Laden and Saddam shit either."

They all agree that there should be a thorough investigation. Then the subject changes to something more familiar but just as tragic.

"Jb, do you know Rich is most likely back on that shit?" Tank ask. To his amazement, Jb isn't surprised.

"Bruce told me he thought he was back out there, last month," Jb says, "If he fucks it up *this* time. He's through. There's nothing else I'll be able to do for him. Because there is no team who's gonna wanna fuck with him. Not after all that time he spent in rehab. He don't wanna do better. That's obvious to me."

"That's sad he got himself all fucked up, like this," Rob adds.

"He has to *wanna* do right," Jan says, "T-baby is gonna have to start thinking about making a decision to move on. Because he's gonna be beating on her again soon."

"He already don't want her to try out for the Rockers," Nina says.

"She already ask me to be her agent," Jb reveals, "Keep that on the low. But I'm working out something for her and it's looking good."

They spend that evening talking about situations going on with their crew.

"I really don't think T-baby is gonna stick around," Tank says all of a sudden.

"She shouldn't," Rob adds, "She's taken enough of his shit."

They all agree on that point.

It's the last part of April and Nina is less then 4 weeks away from her due date. Her and Tank are going to Dr. Weston every week. They had chosen to keep the baby's gender a secret until the birth. But Tank has already had a room in their home decorated for a boy. He feels positive this is his son. They finish up their appointment on the 25th and leave the medical complex. They hear some horrible news on the Navigator's radio. *Lisa "Left-Eye" Lopes* has been killed in a car accident in Honduras.

"Oh my God! No!" Nina screams, "What's going on in this world, Jeremy?"

She starts to cry immediately. Tank insist that she calm down. She has become very emotional over the lose of 1 of the foursomes favorite group members. *TLC* is T-baby's favorite group of all time. They know she'll be upset and they're right. When they get to her house, she's in tears.

"I'm going to her service," T-baby says, "I didn't need this to happen. Not now."

"We'll go with you," Ebony and Rebbie say.

Nina can't travel to Atlanta this late in her pregnancy.

"She's the spark in that group," Rebbie says.

"Her verse on *Waterfalls* is my favorite verse from *anyone* in Hip-Hop, too date," Ebony says, "Even *Tupac*."

"We're definitely going," T-baby says.

On the day T-baby, Rebbie and Ebony leave for Left Eye's service. Rich had been gone for 5 days straight. Arthur calls and tells T-baby, he'd seen him up in Mentor at a well known blow house.

"That use to be our private spot, back in the day," she reveals, "He use to be doing coke up in there, back then. I was to embarrassed and in love with him to tell y'all." Her girls are silent as she talks to Arthur.

"Maybe if I would've snitched on him back then. I wouldn't be in this hell with him *now*," she says as they ride the shuttle to the airport.

"Anthony said the same thing," Ebony offers.

****

The end of April sees *CrewLand Luxury Suites and Condominiums* completed and ready for occupancy. By the completion date, 80% of the units have already been sold. Jb, Cedric and Rob each bought a suite for their families for when they come home to visit. Ebony gets their deeds in order and mails them off as soon as their fund transfers clear. Then she hurries home to start dinner for her family. Ajay has something on his mind and wants to talk to her about it. They talk after dinner.

"Baby did you know Rich was back on that shit?" he asks Ebony, just as they're getting up from the dinner table.

"T-baby told me *she* was sure he was," she says, "And I think she's gonna leave him."

"She's got my vote," Ajay replies as he takes the twins out of their high chairs, after wiping them down.

"She's going to the tryouts for the Rockers next week," she says as she fills the dishwasher.

"I really think she should, baby," he says, "Do you miss playing?"

"I don't but I know she does," she answers, "I already told you. I don't wanna play anymore. I wanna teach our son and daughter to play though."

"That's automatic," he says with a chuckle. "But I know Rich told her, he would leave her if she tried out. But I think she should leave *him* and still try out."

"I agree with you Anthony," she says somberly, "She's taken enough of his mess already."

"I could hear him going off on her when I stopped by their house on the way in," he reveals, "When he saw it was me at the door. He tried to chill out. But I could tell T-baby was upset."

"Do you think he hit her?" Ebony asks.

"I don't know. But I hope she gets out of that marriage," he says, "I wished all of us could make it. But he's not right. He just won't do right. She deserves better than that and so does their son."

Meanwhile at Rich and T-baby's home, their argument has escalated into violence. He's heavily intoxicated on his crack cocaine and is no match for T-baby tonight. She has gotten the better of him.

"Rich I want you out of here now!" she demands, "Either you leave. Or I'm leaving and I'm not coming back!"

"Get the fuck on then!" he screams, "You don't do shit round here anyway!"

"I want a divorce this time, Richard," she says suddenly, "I'm done with this drug shit. It's time for me to move on with my life."

"Bitch get the fuck on!" he snaps, "I told you I wanted a divorce already. But *Yo* ass keep hanging around here!"

"Fine," she says calmly, "Thanks for doing me the favor. I didn't know you was ready to be over. I didn't hear that part. But I'm gone."
Without another word, she goes into their bedroom and gets her bags. Bags which she had packed weeks ago. She picks up the phone and calls Rebbie.

TIME TO KNOW-RELOADED-Time Will Reveal- part 4

"Hello?" Rebbie says, "What up T-baby?"

"Girl I need to get one of those condo's for me and Lil Rich," T-baby says, "Can you get me in there as soon as possible?"

"Yes I can. But T-baby what happened?" Rebbie asks, knowing full well her best friend has had enough.

"You know what happened. What *always* happens? I'm divorcing Richard," T-baby says clearly, "Lil Rich and I are going to a hotel until I can find a place for us to stay."

"Hold on a minute T-baby," Rebbie says, "Ebony is on the other line. Hold on."

Rebbie clicks over to Ebony and tells her what T-baby has just said. Ebony hangs up with Rebbie and tells Ajay what has transpired.

"I'll be right back," Ajay says as he heads out of their kitchen door. He jumps into his Benz and drives up to T-baby and Rich's house. He bangs hard on the door until T-baby opens it. He can see Rich sprawled out on the couch, looking an awful sight.

"Did he lay his hands on you?" Ajay asks.

"He tried too but I beat his ass *tonight*, Ajay. Look at him," she says, "I'm not taking his shit anymore."

"What are you about to do?" he asks.

She tells him that her and the baby are going to get a hotel for awhile. Until she can move into a new condo.

"No. That's not necessary," he says, "I'll get his ass out of here if you want him to leave. Just say the word."

"No. Leave him here," she says, "Then y'all will know where he is and he won't end up dead somewhere and we can't find him to bury him."

Ajay can hear it in her voice. She's over it completely. But he doesn't want her going to any hotel.

"Why don't y'all come stay with us," he says, "Until he makes another move. His ass is the one who needs to leave. But you have to enforce that."

T-baby tells him she doesn't want to be a burden on anyone but Ajay insist.

"I'm not taking no for an answer, alright?" he insists, "I got your bags and Lil Rich's bags, over by the door. So let's go," he demands.

She grabs her laptop and her purse. She takes Rich III by the hand and they follow Ajay to his car. She doesn't even say goodbye to Rich. He didn't say anything to her, Ajay nor his son. Ajay starts the car and backs out.

"We've been through this before, haven't we T-baby?" he asks.

"At the *U*, Arthur's apartment. The night of Tank's sixteenth birthday party," she answers, "That party is a bookmark for so much in

333

TIME TO KNOW-RELOADED-Time Will Reveal- part 4

our lives. Not to long after that is when I first found out he was doing powder. After the miscarriage, he admitted it. Before then I just knew he sold it. All of us did. But he took it too far, like always. It's been a rocky road every since then. But it's over now. I promise you that."
Ajay had used cocaine too. But he knew his wife was a keeper of his confessions to her. She had never shared that with her girls and he was never going to give her a reason to have too. He believes T-baby is sincere about leaving his 1st cousin. He pulls into his garage and parks. Then he speaks his peace.

"We'll take care of both of you, for as long as you need us too," he says, "Y'all are family and crew. There's nothing else to be said."
He grabs the bags as Ebony comes out to help.
"Come on in, T-baby," she says, "I've got your rooms ready. Right next to each other."
T-baby smiles and follows her 1st cousin upstairs to the room where she'll sleep. She puts Rich III's bags in the room where he'll sleep.
"This is where Lil Rich will sleep," Ebony says, "Between you and his little cousin Ant's room is on the other side of him."
"You're gonna help me unpack our things?" T-baby asks with another smile.
"You know it, cousin," Ebony answers with a bright smile.
They start with Rich III's suitcase. They stay upstairs unpacking and talking while Ajay entertains Rich III and the twins, downstairs with Ike and Tina.
"We want you to stay with us and save your cash," Ebony tells her, "You don't need to find a place. Anthony says Rich is the one who should leave because you've been paying that mortgage. Not him."
T-baby smiles, "I feel like I have everybody's support on this."
"You do, T-baby," Ebony assures her, "You do."

The 1st week in May, T-baby joins the Cleveland Rockers team. She'll play the 2002 season. Ironically Rich is released from the Cleveland Browns, the same week, after he fails another drug test. T-baby is so excited with her new team that she doesn't even allow herself to be down about him being cut.
"Our season starts in three weeks, daddy," she tells Greg Sr.
"I'm happy you're playing ball again Trisha," her father says, "I missed watching you play."
"We'll be there for every home game. With Rich the third by our side," Sandy adds, "I've got to get some jersey's for us, Greg."
334

He agrees with his wife. "We're gonna support you always, Trisha," he says, "You are our first born and we're proud of you. Always have been. Always will be."

Chill throws a party for the Rockers team at the club. The party is wonderful. T-baby and Katrina Dobbs play hostess. The crew meet the players, coaches, owners and other supporters. Ajay doesn't stay very long.

"Our family will support you. Just like we do the Cav's and the Browns," Chill announces over the speakers during his speech to the team. "The Chill Spot will be the official after party spot for all home games." Everyone cheers and applauds. The party continues.

Their opening game is May 18. The crew purchase season tickets.

Ajay and Jarvis' season had ended in mid April with a losing record of 29-53 and #7 in their division. Since the season ended, he's been working full time at his sports complex and getting the 2002 community summer football league ready to go. After getting his list of coaches ready, he pulls the applications for employment to see who he has to interview today. Darlene's youngest son Jamal Warren has applied for a job. His interview is set for today, within a few minutes. Ajay is shocked when he looks at Jamal's age. He can't believe he's 22 years old. He was 8 years old, back when he use to fuck his mother. But then, Ajay was only 12 or 13 when it started and it pretty much ended as soon as it started, for him. For Darlene, he doesn't think it *ever* ended. Still he holds no ill feelings toward her sons. They had never rubbed him the wrong way. Looking over Jamal's application, he sees where he's had some trouble as a juvenile and a sell charge or 2 as an adult. He doesn't discriminate against anyone, just because they've had criminal activity in their lives. None of their businesses do. However they do screen them. If a hire has a criminal history. They'll be subject to frequent personnel updates and hired on a 90-day grace period with monthly reviews, just to insure they're keeping their nose clean once the employment starts. He looks forward to seeing Jamal today and finding out what he's been up too. Ally is his secretary. His complex opens at noon. After Ally leaves her classes at CSU, she comes straight to work. He tells her to send Jamal on back to see him.

"You got it," Ally says as she brings Jamal back to Ajay's door and introduces him.

"I know him already. Except he's a man now," Ajay says with a smile.

"What's good, Ajay?" Jamal says as they shake hands and Ally goes back to her office.

"I've been okay, man. How have you been?" Ajay asks him.

"Dude you've been more than okay," Jamal says, "Your life is off the chain. Your crew is what it is, round here."

"We work hard to keep things tight, you know. I see you've had a few appointments with the Cleveland Justice system. Tell me where you're at with all that?"

"I've got some fines that I *really* need to pay," he says, "That's why I want a job. And then my girl is pregnant again. So I really just need to get a gig to take care of my family. I ain't trying to go to jail no more."

"You've got a baby on the way?" Ajay asks.

"I've got a daughter now and one on the way," he says, "We know it's a boy though."

"Wow. So Darlene is a grandmother?" he asks as he chuckles.

"She's *been* a grandmother," Jamal says, "Rodney got two sons and two baby mama's. He got a son that's six and one that's three. My daughter is three and I'm still with her mama."

"That's wild. I guess time stopped for me, as far as Darlene is concerned," he says, "Because I didn't even imagine y'all was grown now. But hell it's been like twelve years since I saw y'all."

"We use to come out here to the arcade, all the time. Then Rodney got locked up-"

"He's doing time?"

"He just got three years on a gun charge," Jamal says, "And he's got to do day-for-day. I would've went too but he didn't snitch on me. I put money on his books. I just wanna get up out of the game though, Ajay. I'm not trying to let my kids grow up without me, like my daddy did it."

"I feel you and I'm gonna give you a shot," he says, "You know I was heavy in the street game too. I did a little time, here and there. I just had basketball and folks who wanted me to make them some *real* money, one day. You're hired bro."

"Thank you, Ajay."

"Are you wanting to work fulltime?" Ajay asks.

"Yes indeed," Jamal says, "Forty hours, if you can spare it."

"You'll be working with Steven Brown. He's part time now because he's going to CSU. You'll be in charge of keeping the equipment inventory. You'll sign out equipment to coaches for their sports teams and for day-to-day guest of the complex who wanna play ball or badminton or ping pong or what have you. They'll have a membership card and a number too. Steven will get you trained during the first ninety days. After that man, I expect you to be able to handle it."

TIME TO KNOW-RELOADED-Time Will Reveal- part 4

"I won't let you down Ajay. I really do appreciate this, man," Jamal says, "I got my G.E.D. so I could get a job. I can't wait to tell Rodney I got it. He said if I see you, to tell you, *'what up and that he wanna write to you'*. I told him I would."

"Okay. He can write me," he says, "But he'll have to write to me *here*, though. Or send it by you."

"Okay."

Then Ajay tells him more about his new job.

"You've got to go through the probation period. Which is three months. You'll make Nine fifty an hour while on probation. Then after your ninety days, you will make twelve an hour."

"That's straight," Jamal says, "Thank you so much, man."

"Welcome to Allen Saul Williams All Sports Complex and Recreation Facility," Ajay says as they shake hands again.

Then Ajay sends him back to Ally. She finishes up his employee file, gets his name badge and gets him set up for his 1st day on the job.

In his office, Ajay hopes hiring Jamal won't give Darlene any ideas about hanging around his facility or coming here to see him. He calls Ebony and tells her of his new hire and how the interview had gone. She's proud of him for giving Jamal a chance to be a man for his family. She has no worries about Darlene. Even if she does show up. She knows her man will handle it the right way. This makes him feel even better about the whole situation.

T-baby goes to *Crew cuts and Styles* on Wednesday morning, May 15th to get her hair braided for her game on Saturday.

"Come on in here miss professional basketball player," Justine smiles.

"What's up, you guys?" T-baby ask, "Where's Nina?"

"She's not feeling good this morning so she stayed home," Justine says, "Don't worry. I'm gonna hook you up."

"Today is mama Jo and big Al's thirtieth anniversary," Tonya says, "And I think Nina is in labor."

"That'll be a good anniversary present for them," Matt says as he walks through to his station on the barber shop side.

"I know Lynn's gonna call today," Tonya says, "It's a shame she had to spend her twenty ninth birthday in Afghanistan."

"She's suppose to be home soon, don't she?" T-baby asks.

"Yes but they tell them that every other week," Tonya says in a doubtful tone.

TIME TO KNOW-RELOADED-Time Will Reveal- part 4

Justine starts on T-baby's braids at 8am sharp. 5 hours later, she's done. T-baby calls Nina again from her cell phone to check on her.

"I'm not doing to good, girl," Nina says, "I'm having contractions. But my water hasn't broken yet. Jeremy and I are gonna wait until the contractions get five minutes apart before we go to the hospital."

"We'll be there with y'all, alright?" T-baby assures her.

"I know our crew gonna hold us down," Nina says and laughs.

By 6pm Nina is in labor and delivery. Her water has broken and she has dilated to 8 centimeters.

"I guess we'll be spending our anniversary up here," Jo says to big mama, "She's having this baby before midnight."

"Another great grandson for me," big mama predicts.
She's been saying it's a boy, the entire pregnancy. There's only a few hours left to find out for sure.

Lynn calls Jo's cell phone to wish her and Al a happy anniversary. She's happy to hear that her future Godchild is on the way.

"I wish I was there with y'all, mama," she says, "But I'm coming home in three weeks."

"For sure, this time?" Jo asks doubtfully.

"For sure. June fifth. I'm leaving for the states," Lynn assures her.

"Now that's another great anniversary gift," Jo says, laughs and shares the news with all of the crew in the waiting area.

At 11:15pm Nina gives birth to a baby boy. Tank is so overcome that John and Al have to hold him up. He cries when he sees his son come into the world. Just as he'd done when Jerica was born.

"I got a son, daddy," he cries, "I finally got me a son."
He cuts the cord and helps the nurses clean him up, weigh and measure him. Jerica is in there to help too. Together they bring him over to Nina.

"He's gorgeous baby," she says, "You've got you a junior."

"Yes and you go on and hold him for the first and last time," he says, "Daddy got him from now on."
They laugh. Nina's ready to sleep. Tank has her moved to her private room. He stays with her, their new son and Jerica for the rest of the night.

JEREMY MARCUS BROWN JR
BORN:MAY 15, 2002
TIME:11:15PM
WEIGHT: 8LBS 3OZS
LENTH: 20 INCHES
338

TIME TO KNOW-RELOADED-Time Will Reveal- part 4

Kim graduates from Ohio State and Kenny graduates from MLK, on the last Friday and Saturday of May. Kenny will start at Ohio State in the fall, where his girlfriend Chaundra will be a sophomore. Chill and Renee are so proud of him for going on to college first. He has offers for the NFL already. Jb takes over as agent for his crew family. The league is already trying to entice Kenny to come out after 1 year.

As an MLK teacher, Farah is at the ceremony but she isn't about to cross paths with Renee. She hangs out with Matt, the entire time. The crew are having celebration parties at both clubs.

Kim isn't done with school by a long shot. In true crew fashion, she wants to get more education. She joins the foursome at Cleveland State University, where Ebony, Rebbie and Nina are 1 year off of a Masters Degree in their respective fields. However, Kim is going to law school. Mr. Wheeler is her inspiration. Not to mention; *Johnny Cochran*. Her older sister Jan is only 2 years off of her medical degree.

"We're gonna have a doctor and a lawyer in the family," she boasts at the celebration.

Kim starts her summer classes immediately. Her and Bruce have put off trying to have a baby until after she finishes law school. Belinda and Sam Sr are *so* proud of her.

"A few years back I didn't know which way you was gonna go, Kim," her mother Belinda says, "I just wanna say how proud we are of you and Janice. And all of the crew, for that matter. You have all done so well and we're all proud of you." Everyone agrees and applauds.

Mrs. Briar, Jerica's #1 fan and supporter, is coming to Cleveland on the 1st day of June. She has gotten backing through Mr. Parkwood and Jackson's Real Estate firm to open *The James' School of Dance and Performing Arts*. Rebbie's dream come true. She hadn't been able to do the audition in New York since the 9-11 tragedy happened. The building was destroyed. The auditions and the project had been shelved indefinitely. But Mrs. Briar didn't stop pulling strings. She was so impressed with Rebbie's skills and Jerica's potential. She wanted to see them have their school.

"I'm finally gonna open my dance school," Rebbie says to her girls as she cries. "The space is already there for it. It's right next to Ajay's facility. Now we can purchase the equipment and hire the instructors. Jerica and I are gonna light up the world."

"Finally," T-baby says, "We've all got our solo careers going the way we wanted them to go."

On the 5th, Lynn returns to the states. She goes to debriefing before she's allowed to return to Atlanta on the 12th. But by her, Bre and Jan's 7 year wedding anniversary's, them and their husbands fly to Cleveland for Tank Jr's christening. Of course there is a huge party at the clubs for Lynn. Rebbie and June celebrate 6 years of marriage. T-baby refuses to allow them to include her and Rich.

"He needs to sign those divorce papers and get out of my house," she says, "Then I'll celebrate."

Her and Wes have become closer. They've been on a few dinner and movie dates with other couples from the crew. Wes hasn't missed a Rockers game either. He has even traveled with them for their road games and brought Jada and Rich III along with him.

Lynn is hyped about the possibility of T-baby and Wes getting together. However, at the celebration party she notices 1 of the girls acting a little *too* friendly with her only brother. Katrina Dobbs is the girl. Ebony and T-baby's former teammate and present teammate with T-baby, on the Rockers team. Lynn is going to talk with Ajay about this before she leaves Cleveland.

John III has grown so much. He's 5 years old now. Him and Orian will both start Kindergarten this year. CJ will be 11 years old on her next birthday. They make plans for her to have her initiation to the crew party in 2 years, with her 1st cousin Brad III. He will be 11 this year too. Rob Jr made 2 on New Years day and he's already walking. The Cleveland crew are so happy to spend time with John III, CJ and Rob Jr. They don't get to see them all year, like they do with the other crew kids. They spoil them rotten, every chance they get.

This is Lynn's 2nd day in Cleveland. Her, Bre, Jan and their families are staying in their crew condo. She goes by *Crew Smokes and Drinks* and buys some blunts and 2 bottles of Hennessy for Jb, Rob and Cedric. That's for their relaxation time, prior to tonight's party. Next, she heads to Ajay's sports complex. Her and Ajay have always talked candidly about everything. She's never shy about telling him what or whom she doesn't approve of, for or around him. He always takes her opinions to heart and values them. She's his big sister, who has always been protective of him. Nothing will *ever* change that. Not living in a new city, marriage, motherhood nor war. Ajay and what's in his best interest is still a main priority for Lynn.

Lynn arrives at Ajay's facility and is greeted by Steven and Jamal. She stops in and talks to Ally.

"I can't believe how big Ashanti got while I was gone," Lynn says.

"She'll be four this year," Ally says with a smile.

"Who is that guy working with Steven?"

"Jamal. He works here. He knows you."

"From where?" Lynn asks.

"That's Darlene's youngest son," Ally says with a smile.

"Oh wow! Okay. I came to talk to Ajay. I'd better get in there." She smiles at Ally and winks her eye, then says, "See you later, crew."

"In a minute, crew."

They both giggle and Lynn goes on back to Ajay's office.

"What's up, big sis?" he says as he hugs her and smiles.

"*You're* what's up," she says, "You jetted so early last night, I didn't even get to have a drink with you. What are you doing with Darlene's son working up in here? What did Ebony say?"

"That she's proud of me for giving him a chance to be a man for his family," he says, "Like I am for mine. There's no drama, sis. I promise you that. He's a good kid. He just needs a chance, that's all. And no. I have no communication with Darlene and don't want any. The man has kids to take care of. And he's a good worker too. As far as last night goes. I was ready to get home."

"Oh okay. Then I'll let that go," she says and smiles. Then she says, "But tell me about that girl from the Rockers. And you know which one. I know she's the reason why you left the party."

"That's a different story," he says, "She's worsen as fuck, sis." he says as he frowns.

"Does Ebony know what she did last night?"

"No not yet. Lynn *please* let me be the one to tell her. Okay?"

"Okay. I won't say a word, *for now*. But brother don't let this linger. I saw that bitch rubbing on your ass last night at the spot."

"No. You saw her *trying* too. I don't allow that shit," he says.

"I'm talking about her rubbing up against you with her body. Before you turned around to see *who* it was," Lynn clarifies.

"Okay and I told her to stay the fuck away from me," he says.

"She's got to go before she finds out where you live," Lynn says, "And be out at y'all house, trying to spend the night with her *ex* teammate."

"Her aunt works security for us," he says somberly.

"Oh fuck! So she already knows?! Ajay you'd better fix this shit, *right now*," she demands, "I can tell something is really stressing you. Just mentioning her. Fix this shit. Whatever it is."

"I will Lynn. I know if I tell Ebony what she's been doing," he says, "She's gonna fire her aunt too."

"She may not. But she won't be allowing Katrina on the property though."

"She'll fire her," he says again.

"Why do you say that? What has she been doing? Has she been to your house already?"

"Yep."

"And?"

"She grabbed my dick, in my kitchen," he says, "She came there with T-baby. I didn't even know she was there. I got a *PowerAde* out of the fridge and turned it up. She came up on me...., she just walked up to me while I was downing it and *grabbed* me. I don't know if Deloris Miles knows about *that*, our history or if she knows the whole story. I feel like she knows more than you know. And she still keeps letting her *pass* the gate."

"Oh hell fuck no! I'm giving you twenty four hours to tell my girl. Or I will," Lynn says, "I mean that."

Ajay lets out an agonizing sigh. This is something he has struggled with for more than just a few months. It's more like *years*. Like since college. Katrina is a year younger than him. She had come to UC, the year after he did. The year *before* Ebony came. She'd been forward when it came to him, from day 1 and overly aggressive. He made her aware of Ebony and that he wasn't interested in being with her. She ignored his wishes. He always had to put her in her place. But she crossed a line totally, back when she did something which left him feeling as if he had been taken advantage of. *Assaulted*. He told her to never approach him again and she agreed to keep her distance. After Ebony joined the UC team, she had even begged him not to tell her what she had done. He promised he wouldn't as long as she kept her distance. For the rest of his tenure at UC, she'd left him alone. Only when she was intoxicated, did she seem to forget their agreement. He avoided being near her. They were both intoxicated on that night in Cincinnati when she'd done irreversible damage to their friendship.

Ebony was in her senior year of high school and already stressing over him fucking with Angel. He had made up his mind that he would not cheat on her or hurt her anymore. Katrina got drunk and fucked all over that option. As if she didn't get the memo that *his* girl was going to be her new teammate in a year. And that he was only interested in *his* girl. What Katrina did to him left him traumatized. Not to mention vulnerable. He abused cocaine a lot, just trying to deal with what had happened and to not let Ebony find it out. During that time he was already dealing with trying to make Ebony feel more secure about the Angel situation. That wasn't the time to tell her that a woman had taken advantage of him. He didn't think she would believe him. And with the player ways he had back then. He wouldn't have either. Ebony got pregnant the following spring and he didn't want to tell her *then* and ruin the moment. Then Angel killed their child which put him farther in a funk about confessing it. But this shit has worn on him long enough. It's been 8 and a half years that he's held this agony. But not *any* longer. He's told Lynn about what had happened here in the complex and in Jackson Heights. She saw what happened at the club last night. But that isn't all. He has more to tell her about Katrina.

"She comes in here to shoot ball all the time. When she's not at practice or playing a game, seems like she's in here. Sis it didn't just start. Something happened way before this."

"*Ajay*?! Like what?" Lynn digs and she's already pissed.

"In Natty," he finally says.

"What happened? Is this about the time you called me and said you felt like you had been sexually assaulted but was to embarrassed to talk about it to anybody?"

"Yep."

"Do you know you *never* told me what it was?"

"Yep."

"Well Ajay you're gonna tell me today. Because I can see that she has some kind of hold on you," Lynn says angrily, "It's like Ebony was about that Raymond nigga. Spill it Ajay. So we can get this shit over with."

"Okay," he says, as he's ready to purge his soul.

Lynn goes and locks the door to his office. She can tell this is something that's had him perplex for awhile. Having Katrina in the same town again has made him feel vulnerable. Lynn takes a chair and pulls it around next to her brother.

"Tell me what happened Ajay," she says, looking into his eyes.

"It was doing Tank's freshman year. We had a party after we first got the big house down there. All the athletes came. Cheerleaders and Greeks, popular students and all. We had a blast and we all got zooted. I mean *real* fucked up. I had to go lay down. I think she slipped something in my drink. I went to my bedroom and passed out. I was out cold all night. Well,...., at some point during the night, she had slipped in there and locked the door. Nobody knew she was in there. Tank, June, Rich, Jan. *None* of them knew and they still don't know to this day."

"She came in there unnoticed by anyone and what happened?"

"Sis I really don't know what all she did. I just know when I woke up before daylight, she was giving me head-"

"*Damn!*"

343

"I was groggy and shit. From the liquor, weed, blow,....it took me a few seconds to realize what was going on. Once I did. I grabbed her and slung her off of me. I told her to leave. She started giggling and laughing and shit. She was saying, *"Why you want me to leave now? We've been fucking all night and now you want me to go?"*
I told her I would never have fucked her. I never wanted too. And Lynn, I didn't. I've never been attracted to her type. She's built like a bull dagger. I didn't even think she liked dick. But she just kept laughing. Then she said we had done it three times. She showed me spent condoms in my trash can and everything. I started throwing up. I knew they had to be from that night. Because *you* know I wouldn't leave condoms in my trash. Besides, Ebony is the only girl I had ever had in that room. She's the only one I was gonna have in there. She was gonna live there, the next year. I wasn't gonna do that *Anita shit* to her again, you know. Me and Ebony used condoms, one time and that wasn't in the big house. I think she drugged me."

"She did take advantage of you," Lynn says, "Ajay you should've *been* told Ebony this! And that bitch got the balls to *show up* here? Hell no! You need to straighten this. Don't let her play Ebony like that. I'm beating her muthafuckin ass. Ebony's gonna know *then*. You better tell her before I see that bitch."

"I know. I was gonna tell her back then. But then Ebony got in the accident and she was always so emotional about me fuckin around. That wasn't something that I choose to do. I didn't cheat on her with Katrina."

"I agree with you. You *didn't*. That's not fuckin around. That's assault. Just like date rape and Ebony would've understood that. Now she may wonder why it took you so long to say something. Why you never told her. I mean Ebony considers this girl, a friend. She had your address in Miami after Valentines-"

"-And she sent me shit too. *All* the time. I threw it away or returned it. She had action photos of me and made posters. Jb wanted to sue them."

"I remember that."

"I didn't sue because I didn't want this to come out," he says, "I don't want the media to know I got sexually assaulted. What kind of shit is that?"

"Ajay you're my brother and I love you. I know you had some times in your life when you was fucking around. *Bad!*" she smiles, "But this isn't the same thing. Getting sexually assaulted by a woman to other men, won't even look bad. Listen brother. Tell your wife and tell her before it's time for me to leave. Or I will. I *mean* that."
He continues to confess, as he says, "I didn't wanna cause problems for

their team. You know the foursome would've beat her down. I didn't want my baby to lose her scholarship and get sent home. Because I would've left with her."

"She wouldn't have. Ebony was a star player. Her *and* T-baby. Not *Katrina*. Natty would've done whatever you wanted them too. Because you was *their* star. If you wasn't so worried about somebody talking about it. They would've sent that man looking bitch home. Hell Shantel has more game than Katrina does. She only started because her parents put money into the school and they are alumni."

"You're probably right. I didn't wanna lose Ebony though."

"You wouldn't have and you still won't. But she's gonna feel betrayed. You're way to protective of her and her heart, to let this linger on. Tell her and make her understand why you haven't said anything," she says, "I'll be here for support. Do this before I leave. Okay?"

"Alright."

"I've got some other business to handle, in the meantime. But it might help you speed up the process."

"Like what?"

"Being your big sister. Like always," she says with a smile. "Don't worry about it. It'll be alright. Talk to daddy first, if you want too. I'll be there with you all the way. Just don't let this sleeping dog lie anymore. You *got* me?"

"I got you," he says, smiling for the first time.

"I'll see you."

"In a minute, big sis. Thanks girl."

"You get that."

They smile and hug each other.

"Tell the United States Air Force I said, I still need you around here to help me out. You know?" he says, "No more parading around in mountains and shit. You got a little brother here who still needs you to put shit in perspective."

"Sir yes sir."

They laugh as he walks her to the door.

"We're coming to dinner tonight and bringing bad ass John the third, so he can get his crew ready for their reign."

She smiles.

He smiles back and says, "We look forward to it."

TIME TO KNOW-RELOADED-Time Will Reveal- part 4

REST IN PEACE:

LISA "LEFT-EYE" LOPES
APRIL 25, 2002
YOU WILL BE TRULY MISSED IN OUR LIVES AND HEARTS.
WE PRAY FOR YOUR FAMILY IN THIS TIME OF GRIEF.
YOU WILL LIVE ON WITH THE CREW, FOREVER!
WE KNOW YOU'RE IN THE RAINBOWS, THAT WE SEE AFTER
EACH RAINY DAY. YOUR VERSE FROM *"WATERFALLS"* WILL
CONTINUE TO BE A QUOTE TO LIVE BY, FOR US!!!!!!!

Come on
I seen a rainbow yesterday but too many storms have come and gone
Leavin' a trace of not, one God-given ray
Is it because my life is ten shades of gray, I pray all ten fade away
Seldom praise him, for the sunny days.

And like his promise is true, Only my faith can undo
The many chances I blew, To bring my life to anew
Clear blue and unconditional skies,
Have dried the tears from my eyes, No more lonely cries.
My only bleedin' hope, Is for the folk who can't cope
Wit such an endurin' pain, That it keeps 'em in the pourin' rain.
Who's to blame, For tootin' caine into your own vein
What a shame, You shoot and aim for someone else's brain
You claim to be insane.
And name this day in time, for fallin' prey to crime
I say the system got you victim to your own mind

Dreams are hopeless aspirations, in hopes of comin' true,
Believe in yourself, the rest is up to me and you.-
[This verse is the property of LaFace and/or Lisa "Left Eye" Lopes]

WE TRULY MISS YOU, LEFT EYE!

THE END OF PART FOUR!

346

TIME TO KNOW-RELOADED-Time Will Reveal- part 4

Get the Time Will Reveal short story series by Black Coffee

#1 MORE THAN 4 ADMIRERS-RELOADED- short story 1
#2 MR. WRONG AND THE RATS-RELOADED- short story 2
#3 Crew's 1st Priority-Crew Females-RELOADED- short story 3 [TBA]

BE SURE AND PICK UP THE FULL SERIES!
The Time Will Reveal, the series
Time To Learn-RELOADED-part 1
Time To Grow-RELOADED-part 2
Time To Love-RELOADED-part 3
Time To Know-RELOADED-part 4
Time To Feel-RELOADED-part 5
The Making of AJAY-RELOADED- Every Man- A Time Will Reveal novel
Time To Show-RELOADED-part 6
Ajay and Ebony-Time Will Reveal part 7-Time To Give [TBA]
Ajay and Ebony-Time Will Reveal part 8-Time To Live [TBA]

All works by Black Coffee at: www.blackdollone.com
www.truesrelatepublishing.com
Join us on Facebook:
Author Black Coffee & True's Relate publishing, LLC

Or the group on Facebook: Black Coffee's Crew Nation
Twitter: @AuthorBlkCoffee
Instagram: AuthorBlkCoffee
Tumblr: Lovely T. Brown
LinkedIn: Lovely T. Brown

WHAT'S NEXT? Click the "What's Next" button on the websites:
www.truesrelatepublishing.com or www.blackdollone.com
Or follow this link:
http://blackcoffee.homestead.com/WHATSNEXTFROMBLACKCOFFEE.html